'Compelling and absorbing'
Publishers Weekly

August: hottest month of the year, last phase of
the dry monsoon. Jill Bryant was due back on
the third; and still Hamilton had no lead on the
Chinese arms shipment.

Despite the nation's rush towards absolute
collapse, and the mounting violence in Jakarta,
he knew that his broadcasts on this theme would
not be enough to convince Biggins for long.
What he needed, he said, was evidence that the
PKI was truly poised for a takeover. And the
Chinese cargo was that evidence ...

The Year of Living Dangerously

C. J. KOCH

SPHERE BOOKS LIMITED
30–32 Gray's Inn Road, London WC1X 8JL

First published in Great Britain by
Michael Joseph Ltd 1978

Published by Sphere Books Ltd 1981
Reprinted 1983

The characters in this book are entirely fictitious.
Only the public figures are real.

Printed and bound in Great Britain by
Cox & Wyman Ltd, Reading

To my wife
and my brother
with love and gratitude

Author's Note

Billy Kwan's dossier on President Sukarno draws on two different sources for the dialogue with the farmer Marhaen. The first version is in Sukarno's speech 'Marhaen and Proletarian', made in Bandung in 1957 and published in the Cornell Modern Indonesia Project Translation Series. The second version occurs in Sukarno's *Autobiography as told to Cindy Adams* (Bobbs-Merrill, NY, 1965). I am also indebted to this book for details of Sukarno's years of struggle.

The poem 'To Li Chien' by Po Chü-I, is Arthur Waley's translation, from his *Chinese Poems*, published by Allen and Unwin Limited.

Some typographical and factual errors have been corrected in this edition.   C.J.K.

Contents

Part One
PATET NEM: HAMILTON'S DWARF   1

Part Two
PATET SANGA: WATER FROM THE MOON   121

Part Three
PATET MANJURA: AMOK   219

'Tartar prisoners in chains!
Of all the sorrows of all the prisoners mine is the
hardest to bear!
Never in the world has so great a wrong fallen to the
lot of man—
A Han heart and a Han tongue set in the body of a Turk.

—PO CHÜ-I, 'The Prisoner' (translated
by Arthur Waley)

God dwells in the heart of all beings, Arjuna: thy
God dwells in thy heart. And his power of wonder
moves all things—puppets in a play of shadows—
whirling them onwards on the stream of time.

—*The Bhagavad Gita* (translated by Juan Mascaró)

Part One
Patet Nem: Hamilton's Dwarf

1

There is no way, unless you have unusual self-control, of disguising the expression on your face when you first meet a dwarf. It brings out the curious child in us to encounter one of these little people. Since Billy Kwan added to his oddity by being half Chinese, it was just as well that we met in the darkness of the Wayang Bar. My attention was drawn to Kwan's arrival by Wally O'Sullivan, a correspondent for a Sydney daily.

'Hullo,' Wally said. 'Curtis is bringing in the black goblin.' We were sitting over our first gin-tonics at the big circular bar in the centre of the room, and Wally swivelled his twenty-two stone round to peer at two figures who had halted inside the entrance. The Hotel Indonesia in Jakarta was managed by an American airline, and the Wayang Bar followed the American practice and sealed itself against all natural light. Coming into this circular chamber, you stepped from the flat blaze of the equator into a permanent half-dark, to which air-conditioning added a Scandinavian cold; you would halt inside the doorway, the sweat drying on your back, and wait for your eyes to adjust so that you could see who was there. Pete Curtis, a red-haired Canadian working for the *Washington Post*, was a regular, but his companion was new to me. I didn't at first doubt that the man was a true dwarf; and I also took him for an Indonesian Chinese. He was squinting about him at the few sources of light: fat red candles that flickered on the black formica surface of the round bar, and a ring of electric lamps set high on the gold walls, across which were fixed Javanese shadow-puppets—the heroes and villains of the *wayang kulit*. He said something to Pete Curtis, who pointed to Wally and me. They began to move towards us.

'Jesus,' I said. 'Who's he?'

'Freelance cinecameraman called Kwan,' Wally said. 'He does a bit of television work for the ABS bloke, and for the Japanese. Been here about four months. I knew him in Sydney, years ago. He and Sydney didn't get on.' He had turned back to direct these remarks into his gin-tonic. Wally's throaty bass, always quiet, but so well produced it could cut through the Wayang's loudest babble, achieved many twin meanings, most of them wryly humorous, but not all of them intended for easy understanding. Underneath was the enormous sadness of the enormously fat: he was known to us all as Great Wally.

'He looks Chinese,' I said.

'That's his trouble. He's not sure whether he is or not.' Wally glanced at me as though suddenly regretting this offering. 'Chinese father, Australian mother,' he muttered, and swung ponderously on his stool to face Curtis.

The Canadian was already quite drunk; he carried both his work and his drinking to excess, and had the constitution to take the punishment. His freckled, muscular arm encircled the shoulders of his companion, who wore a lurid Hawaiian shirt of red and yellow.

'Cookie!' Pete called. 'Great Wally! Want you to meet my *mate*.' It amused Curtis to use Australian terms. He staggered slightly, coming to a halt.

Wally surveyed the pair with kingly calm. 'We've already met,' he said softly, and smiled at the dwarf.

'Hullo, Wally,' Kwan said. He moved free of the burden of Curtis's arm to reach up and shake our hands. 'Wally and I were at university together,' he explained to Curtis. 'We once debated against each other. You defended the monarchy, Wally.'

'And you were an anarchist. But what a long time ago that was, Billy. You're probably a conservative by now. Hm?'

Kwan laughed; it was a grating, eager laugh. His accent was

Australian, with British overtones. Examining him with cautious curiosity, I now saw that he was not really a dwarf in the extreme sense: that is, he was not a midget. His black, crew-cut head appeared large in relation to his body, and his legs were comically brief; but his chest and shoulders were powerful, and his hands square and capable-looking. Had he not had this physique, I reflected, he couldn't have managed the heavy sound camera on its brace, the cinecameraman's cross. I categorised him simply as a remarkably short man—wishing abnormality away.

'I figured it was high time Billy joined the Wayang Club,' Curtis was saying. 'He's been in Jakarta for months, working his tail off, but he goes home every night to this crazy little bungalow near the Indian Embassy.'

'Not a very safe place, surely?' Wally said. 'The Indians must be due for a demonstration soon—their Embassy hasn't been smashed up yet.'

The remark was not offered seriously, but Kwan appeared to take it that way. 'They won't sack *my* place,' he said quickly. 'No one takes me for a *Nekolim*—they think I'm Indonesian Chinese.'

He did look Chinese, except for one striking incongruity: his almond-shaped eyes were green. They went from one to the other of us now as though in search of a reaction to his remark. He had perched himself with some precariousness on a high bamboo stool and crossed one stumpy leg over the other. The disturbingly intelligent face above the comical body split into a grin, and I decided that I liked him.

'Hey Billy, I've got an Australian-Chinese joke for you,' Curtis said. Kwan glanced at him warily, and said nothing. 'It's about a Chinese market gardener in Sydney who brings his vegetables into the city markets every Friday. There's a really stupid Aussie pig running a stall—sorry chaps—who's a xenophobe, right? And every time the Chinese delivers the vegetables to him, the pig asks him when he'll deliver again. "Fliday," says the Chinese, and the pig always shouts at him, "*Friday*—can't y' say *Fri*day, y' Chinese bastard?"' Curtis gave a mangled imitation of an Australian accent.

I was beginning to be embarrassed for Kwan, and glanced at

him. He had now been given a Scotch and sat looking at it carefully, without expression.

'This happens every week,' Curtis said, 'and the Chinese gets very sick of it, so he spends a lot of time practising how to say "Friday". When he gets it perfect, and the pig asks him the question the next week, he's ready. "*Friday*," he says, "you flucking Austlalian plick!"' He went into a falsetto guffaw and wiped his mouth. 'Sorry, Billy,' he said happily. 'I thought you might enjoy that one.'

And Kwan, it seemed, wished to convey that he had done. Bent double on his high stool, his drink held out to one side as though in salute, he gave a flat, eager laugh. 'That's all right, sport,' he said. 'My old man owns a gift store in Dixon Street, not a market garden.'

Curtis clapped a hand on Kwan's brightly clad shoulder. 'Chinese plick,' he said.

Kwan, his face gone suddenly blank, was blinking rapidly, and leant slightly away from Curtis's hand. I began to be uncomfortable for him, and set out to change the subject. 'So you're working here freelance?' I said. 'That must have taken some nerve, in the present situation.'

He turned to me eagerly. 'Not really, old man. It's been dead easy, actually. There's not much competition; the local cameramen aren't exactly crash-hot, and I'm the only foreign cameraman permanently in town. Until now, I was working mostly for Potter, the ABS rep.—that is, when he got off his bum and did a television piece. Potter's been pulled out now—I suppose you chaps know that? I'm meeting his replacement in here tonight. He's arriving just in time, as far as ABS are concerned. To listen to Potter's radio reports, you'd never have known what Confrontation was.' He grinned with cheerful malice.

'Now now Billy,' Wally said. 'You're just annoyed that Potter didn't give you enough work.' He looked reproving; what he was saying was that he didn't care to hear a correspondent criticised in the Wayang by a stringer cameraman.

But Kwan, undismayed, became brasher. 'Potter was a

6

disaster,' he said. 'That's why he's been pulled out. I happen to know that, from friends of mine in the Sydney office. And do you know what he's done to finish up with? Pissed off to Hong Kong to have a holiday there with his wife, instead of staying here for the handover period, to give this new bloke his contacts and introductions. That's going to put Hamilton about a mile behind. Eh?'

This was true, and we all looked carefully into our drinks. ABS—the Australian Broadcasting Service—kept a permanent representative here with a well-staffed office. He could be a considerable competitor if he was good. Potter had not been good, and I awaited the appearance of his successor with some interest.

Kwan jerked round suddenly and squinted across to the doorway where a tall man in a well-cut tan suit had made the obligatory blind halt to adjust to the Wayang's night. 'This'll be Hamilton,' he said, and dropped like an acrobat from his stool to the floor. Fists lightly clenched, elbows out from his sides, he hurried off, with a ghost of that rocking motion peculiar to the large-headed dwarfs one sometimes passes in the street.

The newcomer's face, caught in the glow of a nearby candle, looked startled when he found himself confronted by Kwan. The cameraman extended his hand, tilting his head back and offering his broad Chinese grin. As he came with Kwan towards the round bar, Hamilton's tallness was fantastically exaggerated. The spiky head only just reached his elbow; it was as though the new man walked with a strange child.

We did our best to explain Indonesia to Hamilton, while trying, since we assumed he had done his homework, to avoid the obvious. I doubt if we succeeded; all of us were eager to convey the mad uniqueness of our situation, and he smiled at us with pleasantly quizzical amusement, like a sober man joining a drunken party.

It had been a busy day, and a busy week. Indonesia was once again the major story on the world file, as it so often was in that era before the Vietnam war swallowed everything. Five days ago, on New Year's Eve, formally menacing in his military uniform

7

and black *pitji* cap, President Sukarno had threatened that if the Federation of Malaysia were admitted to the United Nations Indonesia would withdraw. His audience had faithfully roared its approval; and this week he had confirmed the threat: the UN could 'go to hell'; Indonesia was resigning from the world.

We were all pretty much convinced, in the Wayang that evening, that what this signalled was Indonesia's total commitment to a 'Jakarta-Peking axis', and the long-threatened military invasion of Malaysia; and we were in that state of vicarious excitement over a possible international apocalypse which is a journalist's drug. I had managed to get an interview that morning with the Foreign Minister, Subandrio, but I had been unable to extract from him any firm statement about an invasion: only the usual generalities. From the wiliest of Javanese politicians, this was only to be expected, but I wasn't sure my agency would understand.

I was a wire-service man at the time, and my job had made me over-familiar with the bars of international hotels in a number of countries; I didn't generally develop any special feeling for them. But the Wayang was different; its red-and-gold cave was a refuge for the foreign press corps—all male and mostly unmarried—from what was outside. What was outside was *Konfrontasi*: Confrontation. Sukarno had popularised the term, hypnotising his crowds at the great rallies we covered almost every week at the Jakarta Sports Stadium he had built with Russian money.

He had made for himself and his people a sort of theatre there; a theatre of romantic-revolutionary euphoria in which they were spellbound. And he had created a strange propaganda world of paper and capital letters: a world divided between the NEFOS—New Emerging Forces—and the OLDEFOS—Old Established Forces—where we whites were called NEKOLIM: 'neo-colonial imperialists'. Bung Karno showed a genius for such coinings, as a substitute for economic management. Talismans, intended to change reality, they have all gone under glass now, with the other debased coinage of history: but in that year, *Konfrontasi* was a term to juggle with in most world capitals. Malaysia was confronted. Its protector Britain was confronted.

8

The United States was confronted. The whole western world and India as well were confronted, while the *Bung* warmed his ego at the blaze, striking dictatorial attitudes from Europe's nineteen thirties, his black *pitji* tilted in defiance: a baffling mixture of menace and playboy appeal. The people sometimes called him *Bapak*—father—but he was really the *Bung*, the daring elder brother, who carried out every outrageous scheme they had ever longed for, and shouted every imagined insult at the world's Establishment—and at shady colonial masters who might try to come back.

What *Konfrontasi* meant for us *Nekolim* in the Wayang Bar was life under a regime whose hatred for all Westerners had reached the dimension of insanity. We carried our white faces through the streets like ridiculous badges, ignoring insults and jeers and malevolent brown-eyed stares that had the intensity of religious fervour. Our stories were full of the stoning and smashing of embassies and Western businesses by mobs whose activities were approved by the government: and after we'd filed these stories we retreated gratefully to the Wayang, a foreigner's bar in a foreigner's hotel, out of reach of all but the most wealthy and powerful Indonesians. Off-stage, in these cool hours, we could be ourselves, no longer men in white masks.

The resident correspondents were drawn together— particularly the remaining English-speakers—in an artificially heightened good fellowship. Nearly all British and American journalists were now barred from the country: the media in Britain and America were served mostly by Australians, and by a remarkable goulash of other nationalities who spoke English, but did not carry the passports of the wicked OLDEFOS powers. And so we welcomed Hamilton with something a little warmer than our usual spurious *camaraderie*, and competed to explain what the rules were for survival in the country of *Konfrontasi*.

'You don't wear shorts—ever. The Dutch wore shorts.' This from Wally.

'See this bag?' Curtis pointed to a small airways bag beside his stool. 'It's full of rupiahs—my week's supply. No wallet could hold it. You can get 10,000 roops to the US dollar in any bazaar, and a packet of Lucky Strikes is as good as money.'

'All white faces are bad,' Billy Kwan told Hamilton. 'But you've got a big advantage being Australian. Australians aren't as bad as other *Nekolim* yet. We still get special credits for the time in the independence struggle when our wharfies wouldn't load Dutch ships.'

'It's a pity I'm not Australian, then,' Hamilton said.

We all stared at him; since he worked for ABS, we had assumed he was, but certainly his accent seemed to be English. His voice, resonant, pleasant, perhaps a little too bland, was almost a BBC news-reader's; but I wondered about some of his 'a' sounds.

'I was born in England,' he said. 'But I grew up in Singapore and Australia. And I travel on an Australian passport. So what the Indos don't know won't hurt them, will it?'

'So you're a hybrid,' Kwan said. From his vantage point on the high stool that raised him to normal level he was studying Hamilton with great intentness.

This personal remark caused Hamilton to look quickly at him. 'I suppose I am,' he said; and after a slight pause: 'They're not too keen on the Chinese in Indonesia either, are they? How do *you* get on?'

'Well, they find it hard to know what I am, exactly,' Kwan said cheerfully. 'Particularly since I don't speak Chinese.'

Hamilton was incredulous. 'No Chinese at all?'

'Not a bloody word,' Kwan said. 'So I must be Australian, mustn't I?'

Hamilton gave it up, shrugging and laughing good-humouredly. If Kwan had wanted to embarrass him, the attempt seemed to have failed.

Watching this exchange, I had been struck by the notion that there was some elusive physical likeness between this utterly unlike pair. At first I could not account for it, and was about to dismiss it as a pointless fancy. Then I saw that Hamilton's sleepy-lidded eyes were exactly the same pale pea-green as Kwan's. Moreover, since his eyebrows and lank hair were black, his appearance had the same dark-light contrast. But there the resemblance ended; and I very much doubted whether anyone else would have noticed it. He had that calm, unconscious certainty of being attended to which is common to men of unusual height, and he was only saved from a 'refined' handsomeness by a rather coarse nose, bulbous at the tip, which struck a discordant note: one thought vaguely of corner-boys.

He had said little, content to prompt us with brief questions. Now he turned to Wally O'Sullivan. 'I had to read some of your articles before I came, as part of my homework,' he said.

Wally's hand made a sideways motion of dismissal, but he blinked once with pleasure; his reputation as an analyst of the Indonesian scene was then at its height. 'There are not many news guys in here at the moment, I'm afraid,' he told Hamilton. 'But there'll be more later. There's a Crush Malaysia rally going on at the Sports Stadium. They're probably at that.' His voice trailed away on a note of sly irony, inviting questions.

Hamilton raised his heavy eyebrows. 'Are you all giving it a miss?'

'I've crushed Malaysia twice in the past week,' Wally said. 'And I attended a Young Student Demonstration against Big Corruptors this morning. Surely enough. Hm?'

But Hamilton smiled only perfunctorily, and began to question Wally about the likelihood of war with Malaysia. Under his easy manner, I could sense his hunger for Wally's ideas about this, and perhaps an attempt to get O'Sullivan's professional measure. Hamilton was going to be ambitious, I decided, and sighed inwardly.

Wally didn't answer at once, but reached for one of the bowls of peanuts that stood at intervals around the bar, alternating with the fat red candles. It was one of the jokes about Great Wally that he was costing the hotel a fortune in peanuts. He could demolish a bowl in about two minutes; the steward would patiently re-fill it, and Wally's thick, pale hand would reach out again. He munched, mouth moving between bulging, veinous cheeks.

'Do you know what the President called this year in his Independence Day speech last August? He gives each year a title, Guy, and I take the Sukarno year to run from one Merdeka Day to the next. The one we're in now is called the Year of Living

Dangerously. Hm?' He stared round-eyed at Hamilton; this little interrogative hum always invited the listener to join Wally in judgment. Two such hums signalled a good joke.

But Hamilton still wanted his answer. 'You think he'll actually invade, then?'

'I think the Big *Bapak* will live dangerously,' Wally said. 'He'll go on making trouble on the Sarawak border, and he'll go on dropping a few paratroops into Malaya. But he won't pull a full-scale invasion, no. The British would bomb Jakarta if he did. I have that on good authority.' He sighed, and reached for the peanuts again.

But Billy Kwan did not regard the subject as closed. 'You think Sukarno's entirely cynical then, do you, Wally?'

'I would never say such a thing of our President,' Wally said, with an actor's promptness. 'No one realises better than I do that the Bung is a god.'

'So he is, to the villagers,' Kwan said. 'Have you ever seen him arrive into a village in his white helicopter? To them he's Vishnu, coming down from heaven in his magic car.'

Wally made no comment on this, but continued speaking to Hamilton. 'Not only do I recognise his divinity,' he said, 'but I'm the only one here who can recite all the names of Sukarno.'

'Yeah! Say the names, Wally!' Curtis cried.

We were all somewhat drunk now, and Curtis and I urged Wally on. We had heard the performance before, and savoured in anticipation the way in which his well-oiled voice would taste each item.

Clearing his throat, Wally began, his rosebud mouth working solemnly, like an old lady's at prayer. 'Great Leader of the Revolution,' he pronounced. 'Mouthpiece of the Indonesian people; Main Bearer of the People's Suffering . . .'

But Billy Kwan's voice penetrated our laughter.

'Ah, yes. But he *is* the Main Bearer of the People's Suffering, isn't he?'

Wally stared gravely. 'Supreme Shepherd of the Women's Revolutionary Movement,' he continued. 'Father of the Farmers.' He munched.

'You think it's just words, don't you, old man?' Kwan said. His grin was challenging. 'But it's not just words. He *is* the father of the farmers. They're the people Sukarno called the Marhaen, you remember?'

'The who?' Curtis asked.

'Marhaenism—that's the Bung's answer to Marxism. It's a great concept for Indonesia—they're the people who matter here: the peasants who work their own few acres. They *are* Indonesia: that's why they love him; he's given them a voice. Say what you like about him, Sukarno's a genius.' Laughter redoubled, but Kwan pressed on. 'Look—when a great poet writes about his country, he actually gives it a soul it didn't have before, doesn't he, Wally? Well, Sukarno's done the same thing in his speeches. He's *created* this country.'

We made amazed noises at this dissertation. At a time when Indonesia's dictator seemed more of a bogy-man than a poet, and we had agreed among ourselves that he was half demented, it was an extraordinary claim for a member of the foreign press corps to have made in the Wayang; and the fact that most of us had never heard of Marhaenism probably added to our cheery derision.

'Sukarno the poet,' Pete Curtis jeered. 'Yeah, like Hitler was an artist.'

But Great Wally, who had continued to stare at Kwan with an air of wordless wonderment, now went on quietly with his recitation, as though the other had not spoken. 'Great Leader of the Workers,' he said throatily. 'Supreme Commander of the Mental Revolution.'

Kwan raised his glass to Wally amid the laughter, as though in a toast. '"Indonesia from Sabang to Merauke",' he said provocatively, quoting the famous slogan. 'Who else could make it come true, old man? Who else could hold this bloody country together?'

'No one but the Supreme Leader of the National Association of Football Clubs,' Wally said. 'The Supreme Boy Scout.'

Curtis shouted with laughter. 'I don't believe it, Wally—you made those two up!'

We were becoming quite noisy. A group of nearby Japanese

businessmen frowned at our din: juvenile, boorish Westerners, their faces said. And the *wayang* puppets up on the walls, their grotesque insect noses bent towards the floor, seemed to watch us, too, with pensive contempt.

A short time later, Hamilton took his leave. He had flown in from Singapore only two hours before, and wanted to stretch his legs, he said, before he turned in. He was booked in here on the Hotel's seventh floor; ABS did its people well.

'I'll come with you,' Kwan said promptly. 'I need some air myself.'

As the two of them retreated towards the door, the cameraman moving jerkily to keep up with Hamilton's long strides, Wally said to me softly, 'Billy's got himself a new hero.' It was a remark I would remember.

Emerging from the Wayang, Hamilton and Kwan entered the Hotel's wide, brightly lit arcade. The astounding heat of Java closed over them like a sack, permeated with a smell Hamilton could not identify: cloves, perhaps, or nutmeg.

'This is the most expensive shopping boulevard in Jakarta,' Kwan said, 'right here in the Hotel. The city's bankrupt. It's also the only place where the Indos won't call you names. Most of them can't afford to set foot here—and the beggars aren't allowed to. It's only for the generals and politicians.'

This was evidently true, Hamilton saw: other strollers who passed them were either European or Japanese. Some of these stared curiously as the big man and his dwarfish companion passed, Kwan's busy sandals clapping on the blue-figured tiles. Anywhere else, Hamilton might have been embarrassed, but his new acquaintance's oddity seemed a pre-ordained part of his first night in Indonesia.

The cameraman seemed eager to establish himself as guide, even as expert adviser; but Hamilton was only half listening to the rapid, nasal voice. His senses were open in that way which is peculiar to the first few hours of arrival in a strange country; but his only glimpses of Java so far had been from the car that had brought him from the airport. He had scarcely felt Jakarta's undulating ground under his feet yet, and he had a desire to get out of the arcade before he went up to bed. He halted not far from the main entrance; Kwan stopped too, and glanced up into his face. Hands in pockets, Hamilton stared out through the arches at the night.

Black limousines moved in an endless caravan around a semicircle of drive-way; a tall Indonesian doorman in a peaked cap swung open the car doors and ushered the mighty onto the steps of the arcade. He held an umbrella, this being the season of cloud-bursts: the north-west monsoon. Beyond the Hotel gates, in Friendship Square, the headlights of other cars revolved on a great circuit around an ornamental pool: a childhood wheel of magic lights, from the centre of which rose the twin pylons of one of Sukarno's many monuments. On the far side of the wheel, the forlorn grey hulk of the British Embassy could be made out; sacked, Kwan told Hamilton, over a year ago, and now abandoned. Beyond again was hot blackness, pricked with much fainter lights. They seemed to be gazing from the deck of a liner into a flat sea.

And in a sense, they were. The fourteen-storey Hotel Indonesia (always with a capital H) rode like a luxury ship in mid-ocean, being at this time the only one of its kind in the whole country. It stood in New Jakarta; and like Friendship Square, and Jalan Thamrin—the six-lane highway that carried the traffic here from the Old City—it had recently been ordered into being by President Sukarno, who considered an international hotel necessary to the nation's prestige. Paid for by the Japanese, managed by the Americans, it had its own power supply (since Jakarta's was fast failing); its own purified water (since Jakarta's now carried infections); its own frigid air, which no other hotel could offer. Food was flown in from San Francisco and Sydney, or grown on the Hotel's own farm. With its restaurants, night-clubs, bars, swimming-pool, and shops, it was a world complete. It was also majestically expensive; but heat or gastritis usually broke the resolve of those transients who tried the decaying colonial hotels of the Old City.

'You were lucky to get in here,' Kwan said. 'Air-conditioning's a bloody necessity, not a luxury, in this country. Will you take a bungalow later on?'

'I don't think so. ABS can subsidise me here in the Hotel.

Why not? I gather a bungalow would cost them just as much.'

'A bit artificial though, surely, Guy—living here long-term? In a bungalow you get to know the people.'

'I can take plenty of this sort of artificiality, as long as I can get on with the job,' Hamilton said. 'It'll be a nice change from bachelor flats.'

'Ah. You're not married then, Guy?'

Hamilton shook his head. Kwan used his first name frequently, as though to establish possession, and was now studying his face with the same concentrated interest he had shown all the evening. Hamilton had little doubt that what underlay this interest was Kwan's anxiety that he should continue to contract him for film work.

'It'll be a big day for you tomorrow,' Kwan said, 'picking up the threads. And Sukarno holds his press conference at ten. He won't say anything new, but you ought to go. I suppose you want to turn in now?'

'I thought I might take a stroll first.'

'You'd better let me come with you, old man. Not everywhere's safe to go on foot. Some Nervous Nellies won't go on foot here at all.'

Passing out of the Hotel's neutral compound into Jakarta, between the pillars of the gates, they arrived first onto a no-man's-land of broken, stony ground known as the Car Park, lying between the Hotel and Friendship Square. Here they came under the attention of scores of eyes. A permanent crowd of vagrants kept watch from the Car Park on the forbidden, glowing stage of the arcade, and on the foreigners who emerged from it; so did a row of gimcrack jeep-taxis, and a small squadron of the tricycle-rickshas called *betjaks*. As soon as they sighted Hamilton and Kwan, most of the *betjaks* creaked into motion like a flock of ponderous birds, wheeling towards them. Hamilton regarded them with some fascination, as everyone did for the first time; with their black canvas hoods, their sides painted in hurdy-gurdy colours with pictures of volcanoes and *wayang* heroes, and lettered with names such as *Tiger* and *Bima*, they belonged to another time. The riders, in ragged shorts and singlets, reared alertly on the pedals, muscular bodies like illustrations from anatomy texts. They rang what sounded like cow-bells, and made low-voiced cries that were oddly confidential.

'They can't believe we're going on foot,' Kwan said. 'They'd pedal you clear across the city for ten cents. They die young, of course.' He waved in dismissal, and most of them wheeled away. Some had never moved, the riders sleeping the sleep of exhaustion in the passenger seats, black-brown legs and arms dangling like charred branches from under hoods. But three of the *betjaks* continued to follow.

Shadowed by these hooded shapes, which kept to the kerb, Hamilton and Kwan began their walk beside Sukarno's new super-highway. It was still unfinished, Kwan announced; and Hamilton had the sense of entering one of those byways in a dream, which would soon dissolve into nothing. They had left the Hotel's blazing trains of windows behind, and dimness enclosed them; the narrow footpath, which ran beside bamboo fences, was crowded with Indonesians who seemed to be wandering without purpose. On this section, named Jalan Jenderal Sudirman, they were moving out towards Senayan, on the southern outskirts, where the President addressed his rallies. Hamilton, his jacket over his arm, walked quickly, his face already sweating, cleaving through air like moist cloth; Kwan was compelled to hurry to keep up, brief legs working in their wrinkled slacks. Blue lamps, receding on arrogant steel standards, appeared on the point of fading out; the showpiece highway was already cracked and pot-holed, and the humble food-stalls of the poor had begun to creep along its edges. Its traffic consisted mostly of converted jeeps, bicycles, and *betjaks*, which seemed to Hamilton to be moving through the pages of a frantic propaganda magazine. He had entered Sukarno's world of paper, and capital letters.

From bamboo fences, from the walls of new buildings, and from banners stretched across the highway rose a cacophony of cries, in Bahasa and English.

GANJANG MALAYSIA; U.N. GO TO HELL; CRUSH BRITISH AND U.S. IMPERIALISTS; HAIL BUNG KARNO, FATHER OF THE REVOLUTION; BOYCOTT U.S. FILMS; CRUSH MALAYSIA.

Kwan, who was apparently too accustomed to this silent

uproar to think it worth comment, was saying: 'It's safe enough to walk here—as long as you don't turn into a side road. And curfew's not for a couple of hours yet.' He was probably recalling warnings we had all offered Hamilton in the Wayang Bar: street hold-ups were increasing, even in daylight, and sometimes, when a *Nekolim* was the victim, the military police would look on, and later take a cut. 'You should really take your watch off, though, and put it in your pocket,' Kwan said. 'They've got a special hook for pulling it off your wrist.' Hamilton raised his eyebrows, but obeyed.

Glancing behind, he found that he and Kwan were the only foreign pedestrians to be seen. There were few buildings now as they walked beside the long bamboo fences. Moving towards the outskirts, they were entering a territory of deeper and deeper darkness; and in their wake came a small procession of giggling followers, male and female, who would not accept the legitimacy of this expedition by the white man and his presumably Chinese companion.

A small man in white trousers moved importantly alongside them. 'House of Joy, gentlemen?'

Kwan rounded on him with surprising anger. '*No*. Get lost.' The man fell back muttering, and Kwan glanced up quickly at Hamilton. 'There's quite a shortage of European girls in Jakarta,' he explained. 'They're all leaving, as the knives are sharpened for the white-faces. No respectable Indonesian girl will look at you, so that leaves you with Jakarta prostitutes. I hope your tastes don't lie in *that* direction, old man.'

Hamilton assured him, with truth, that they didn't, and Kwan nodded, as though something had been confirmed for him. Then, without any preamble, he said, 'Your work's your main interest, I can see that. I used to be a university history tutor, did they tell you?'

Without asking who 'they' were, Hamilton said they had not; and he glanced down at Kwan in surprise. 'That's an unusual background for a cameraman.'

'I was only temporary. Somehow they couldn't bring themselves to offer me anything permanent. It's difficult to break out of the restaurant and fruit-shop business if you're an Australian Chinese. Or it was when I was young.'

The dwarfish man's tone was not bitter: he used a light, elaborately careless voice. But now that the apparently unavoidable subject of Kwan's origins hung in the dark heat between them, Hamilton walked carefully.

'I wanted to be a secondary school teacher when I graduated,' Kwan said. 'I was young and innocent, then. Do you know what they said when they turned down my application? "Your appearance is against you." '

Hamilton murmured something sympathetic; but he could not help wondering which aspect of Kwan's appearance the authorities had been referring to.

'Yes,' Kwan said, '*that* was a step forward in the education of a young Chinaman.' The delicacy in his flat voice as he pronounced the word 'Chinaman' was extreme: it was as though he pulled back a flap of skin to show Hamilton a wound. But then he said cheerfully, 'History's still my first love, old man; history and ideas. I can't complain really—I'm recording history visually, and I enjoy it.' He offered his wide, frog-like smile.

The procession had melted away; and two of the *betjaks* had now wheeled off into the blue spaces of the highway, like baffled birds of prey. The third rider, a stern-faced man in a black shirt, black shorts, and a wide-brimmed straw hat, continued to follow steadily, without calling out. The side of his machine carried the yellow legend: *Tengah Malam*.

'He's persistent, that one,' Kwan said. 'Maybe he'd like to take us to a quiet spot for his friends to rob. Most *betjak* boys are decent enough, though.'

'What are those lights up ahead?'

'Just a *pasar*. It's not a bazaar for tourists; they don't come out here. A little *pasar* for the poor. Come and have a look. Or are you nervous?'

'I'm in your hands, matey.'

Flares, flares everywhere, in the flatland darkness, where gabled villas with orange-tiled roofs hid behind crumbling walls, and a

19

dark, drain-like canal moved with evil slowness. On an area of muddy ground beside the highway, the lights from the *pasar* burned uncertainly: kerosene and gas pressure-lamps set on the counters of many little stalls under tattered awnings. Above them, the final awning of the heat extended motionless.

Here the condition of the people was revealed. They lived on this waste place in huts made of packing cases and bamboo matting: one of those shanty settlements Jakarta called a kampong—using, with sad irony, the name for a rural village. Against the new highway's imaginary cold zone, they had spawned the warm, complex warrens of old Asia—setting up their stalls to sell one another sweetmeats grim as laboratory specimens, displayed in glass cases; lurid drinks; cheap cigarettes: nothing a European tourist would want to buy; knick-knacks the bazaars of prosperous Singapore would have despised. But Hamilton moved down the alleys smiling as though at a carnival, while Kwan, busily keeping pace with his stride, took note of this unconscious delight with upward glances.

Most of us, I suppose, become children again when we enter the slums of Asia. We re-discover there childhood's opposite intensities: the gimcrack and the queer mixed with the grim; laughter and misery; carnal nakedness and threadbare nakedness; fear and toys. This was now happening to Hamilton, who found that the puzzling clove-and-nutmeg scent, like the smell of the heat itself, had intensified; it suddenly became very important to know what it was. Questioning Kwan, he discovered that what he was scenting was Jakarta's most essential odour; that of clove-spiced *kreteks*—the cigarettes the poor smoked. It mingled with the spiced smell of *saté*, the city's favourite delicacy: little pieces of meat skewered on bamboo slivers, being grilled here over a charcoal brazier by a man in a baseball cap.

All the brown faces, floating in flatland dark, were theatrically lit from below, by the brazier, by the flares; and all seemed to smile. Young men in white shirts and sarongs walked by hand in hand. Doorless huts gave glimpses of public privacy, frozen in yellow frames: a table with a candle on it; a small, naked girl playing on a straw mat; a middle-aged woman in a sarong and incongruous brassière, heating water in a discarded can over a little fire. The rooms were so small they were little more than boxes, and could not be stood up in: children's playhouses. It was hard not to see the place as gay, and the poverty as a game.

'This amuses you, doesn't it?' Among the flares, Billy's broad cheek-bones cast the same deep shadows as those of the faces around them. Without waiting for a reply he demanded severely: 'But doesn't it make you want to do something for them?'

Hamilton was taken aback. 'Yes, I suppose it does,' he said. 'But what can you do? Give money away? What would that solve? It's up to Sukarno, don't you think? He could spread some of the money here, instead of spending it on women and monuments. I understand that's where the last of the country's reserves are going.'

'What then must we do?' Kwan murmured, in a tone of litany.

'Pardon?' Hamilton asked.

' "And the people asked him, saying, 'What shall we do then?' " Luke, chapter three, verse ten. The people were talking to John the Baptist—the ones he called a generation of vipers. They were asking him how they could flee the wrath to come. And he told them, if a man had two coats, he should give one to a man who had none. "What then must we do?" Tolstoy asked the same question. He wrote a book with that title. Have you read it? No? One cold night he went into the poorest section of Moscow— where the poor were hanging about the doss houses, starving. And of course, *they* had the Russian winter to put up with. So he bought them hot drinks, and then he began to give them money. He gave until he had nothing left, and still they came. You could do that now, old man. Think—five American dollars would be a fortune to one of these people; it would keep him for a month— more. Why don't you do it? You can afford it.'

Hamilton, who had decided to ignore this eccentric little man's over-familiar gambits, asked, 'What did Tolstoy do in the end?'

'Ah, he came to the same conclusion as you, of course—that it was a bottomless pit, and that even if he gave away his whole fortune he'd solve nothing. He decided that he was robbing them in the first place, since his class were parasites.'

Hamilton noticed now that the *betjak* called *Tengah Malam* had not gone away, but was lurking beside a stall: it had followed them into the *pasar*, and he wondered if he should find this sinister. His enjoyment of this small adventure was mixed with a nagging consciousness of his isolation from other Europeans. Remembering our warnings about the sudden hostility a *Nekolim* face could provoke, he reflected that only he would provoke it: Kwan, no doubt, could pass himself off as a local.

'Of course,' Kwan was saying, 'there's always the Christian point of view, to which I usually subscribe.' His voice had taken on its elaborately 'light' tone again. 'I mean the view that you don't think about the so-called big issues, or changing the system, but you deal with whatever misery is in front of you—and the little bit of good that you do adds its light to the sum of light. To most journalists, that'd mean nothing, but I think *you'll* know what I mean. Most journos have a standard set of phrases for dismissing pain, don't they? Put a label on it, and it somehow doesn't exist any more—it just becomes a problem.' Abruptly changing the subject, he said, 'This is your first overseas assignment, isn't it?'

'My first as a correspondent, yes. I worked on Reuters in London before I joined ABS.'

Kwan halted suddenly beside a stall selling Indonesian paperback books. 'Christ. You're in serious trouble, Guy,' he said abruptly. 'I suppose you realise that?' His green gaze had become steady, almost stern.

Hamilton stared back, and said nothing. He had a policy of refusing to be drawn by people who offered remarks like this.

'Potter's sabotaged you,' Kwan said, 'by not staying for the handover period. In my opinion he did it out of spite, because they pulled him out.'

Hamilton smiled. 'It's not as desperate as that, surely? I admit it's bloody annoying—he should have been here to give me the personal contacts and introductions. But we'll manage. He's left me some notes and names—the Indonesian assistant met me at the airport with them.'

'Ah, yes—Kumar,' Kwan said. His tone might have meant anything, and his gaze wandered off to the bookstall, whose

22

proprietor, a plump, avuncular man, was reading one of his books by the light of a candle. Kwan turned suddenly back to Hamilton. 'Look—I know why you're here,' he said. 'You were put in because Potter wasn't doing the job—and I've no doubt you're good. But I don't think you appreciate the situation. Without personal introductions here, you can't get off the ground.'

Refusing to show the uneasiness he began to feel, Hamilton said, 'Are you trying to make me feel glad before bed-time? Or is there some point to all this?'

'Well, you see, I may be able to help you.' Kwan was using his 'light' voice again. 'And you're going to need help.'

Hamilton strove to keep polite disbelief from his face. No stringer cameraman was going to give him the high-level personal contacts in government and diplomatic circles that Potter had failed to give; but he decided to humour Kwan. Potter's notes said Billy was good at his job, and cinecameramen were not plentiful in Jakarta. 'Thanks, I'll be glad of anything you've got,' he said.

'We'll make a good team, old man: you for the words, me for the pictures.' Kwan nodded with satisfaction. 'Are you a literary man? Do you like poetry?'

Hamilton's response to this new change of topic was to smile patiently. 'Literary man? I'm a news-man.'

'You never read poetry?'

'Not often, I'm afraid.'

'I'm rather fond of Chinese poetry,' Kwan said. 'Only in English translation, of course—I can't read it in the original.' He drew a much-creased piece of paper from his hip pocket and handed it to Hamilton; it was a poem in typescript. 'This is by a favourite poet of mine,' he said. 'Po Chü-I. He writes beautifully about friendship. Po was a provincial governor, and he had a friend called Li Chien—this poem's written to him when they were both old, and had been posted to different provinces.' Hamilton noticed that Kwan's pronunciation of the Chinese names sounded scrupulously correct, and wondered if it was true that Billy spoke no Chinese. 'Don't read it now,' Kwan said. 'Take it home with you. I've got another copy.'

Bemusedly, Hamilton took the piece of paper and put it in his pocket.

Kwan took out his wrist-watch and studied it. 'I won't be able to call on you in the office during the day tomorrow,' he said. 'I've got a job on for the Japanese. But maybe we can have dinner together. I'll look for you tomorrow evening, and we'll discuss this then. You'll have to move very carefully in Jakarta, Guy. The wrong steps are easy to take.' His tone became almost paternal. 'By tomorrow night I may have something for you. Go home and get some sleep: and don't forget Sukarno's press conference. I must leave you now, old man; I'd take a *betjak* home, if I were you. Good night.'

And while Hamilton stared after him in astonishment, Kwan rocked away over the threadbare ground towards the *betjak* called *Tengah Malam*, which was still waiting by the stall. Rain was beginning, loudly pattering on the awnings.

Without looking back, the cameraman threw himself jerkily into the passenger seat, and the black-clad driver began slowly and painfully to pedal the machine away. Soon it was wheeling in miniature under the highway's blue lights, with Kwan concealed by its antique hood.

2

President Sukarno pointed his swagger-stick at Hamilton. 'You,' he said. 'Who are you?'

In the palace reception room—whose chandeliers and gilt chairs made you half-expect Strauss waltzes—the usual big circle of correspondents stood around the President. There were knowing smiles. Most of us had been through this interrogation when we first attended the daily theatre of the palace press conference. Sukarno always spotted a new correspondent, and nearly always used the form of words the Caterpillar had used to Alice. He had done it to me, nearly two years before, and since then I had barely managed to have more than two or three sentences of personal conversation with him. He gave no private interviews, unless the journalist was female and pretty; and there were now no women correspondents in Jakarta.

When Hamilton had identified himself, Sukarno stared at him broodingly. The President's uniform today was dove-grey; on his head, as always, was the black velveteen *pitji* cap, the badge of nationalism. Wally O'Sullivan claimed the Bung did not remove it even during his celebrated love bouts: it was a magic potency cap. He was usually cordial to a new correspondent, even if the man represented the OLDEFOS news media; but this week he was generating an aura of controlled rage.

He rubbed his nose. 'Australian,' he said flatly. His voice was slightly hoarse, his English excellent. 'We welcomed your people here once. Now your government has shown itself to be a lackey of British imperialism. Your troops fight ours in Malaysia. A pity, that. We thought you more independent. What do *you* say, Mr Hamilton?'

Hamilton, standing a few paces from me in his perfect suit and the collar and tie we were all obliged to sweat in at these affairs, actually flushed; it was plain that he simply didn't know what to say. Towering speechlessly over the stocky little President, he looked like an overgrown schoolboy being dressed down by the headmaster; and he ended by standing on his dignity. 'I can't speak for my country's government, Mr President,' he said. 'I'm just here to report the news.'

I cringed for him; he sounded like Our Courageous Correspondent from a film of three decades ago. Sukarno stared him up and down without speaking. So did his two palace guards, Indonesians of unusual height, with smooth faces and body-hugging khaki uniforms. Then the President relented: his face broke into its celebrated smile. Despite his sixty-three years, the smile was an urchin's: part of the equipment that had made him so appealing to women, and could even win over people who detested him. He was said to be chronically ill; and in the two years I had been here the coarsely masculine good looks (likened by the American Ambassador to an Asian Clark Gable's) had grown coarser; the waist had thickened. But the smile and the cockily tilted *pitji* could suddenly tell you that he had not been serious after all, not about anything: all the threats he had issued to the world had been a game. This unpredictability was why he fascinated us, as he fascinated his people and the world, no matter what we might say in the Wayang. We never ceased to enjoy his outrageous behaviour, and to tell each other Sukarno stories: he had made the American Ambassador sing 'Home on the Range' at an official dinner; the Australian Ambassador had laboured through 'Waltzing Matilda'; when the Yugoslav Ambassador had annoyed him the Bung had rapped him smartly on the head with his swagger-stick.

'You understand diplomacy, I see,' he said to Hamilton. 'Tell me, then—how do you like my New Jakarta?'

'It's very impressive,' Hamilton said. 'But I'm told Bandung's more beautiful.' No doubt this reference to the city of Sukarno's youth was intended to please; it succeeded, since the President nodded, his smile becoming shrewd. But Hamilton had lost his chance to put a hard news question that day. As he opened his mouth to do so, Sukarno began to address us all.

'I cannot deny it,' he said. 'Bandung is more beautiful, and our capital still leaves much to be desired. But this is why I spend so much money on it. Oh, yes, I know what you say, gentlemen: that I spend too much on Jakarta—too many buildings, too many monuments. People come to me and they say, "Hey, Sukarno—"' He broke off, asking us to enjoy the cheekiness of his imaginary interrogator. He liked to address himself in this way, and we all laughed obsequiously. '"Hey, Sukarno,"' he repeated, '"why do you pour out all this money on Jakarta?" I will tell you the answer I give. My people cringed for a long time. They called us a coolie among nations. But now we are on our feet, and the world takes heed. And my people need a capital worthy of them—a capital to stiffen their spines: a world-capital.' He had begun to orate now; the public face was on, the urchin had gone, and he raised one finger. 'Do not yet judge my country by New Jakarta, which is not complete. Judge Indonesia by Borobudur, and the beautiful rice-bowl of West Java. Yet wait a little more, and you will see the New Jakarta I am creating. Already it is becoming a Paris, a city of light to inspire struggling humanity.'

'But you still escape from it to Bogor every week-end, Mr President.'

It was Wally O'Sullivan's throaty voice. Standing to attention, his vast belly straining the fawn suit protocol obliged him to wear, he smiled almost coyly at Sukarno, who did not smile back.

'That remark is impertinent,' the President said; and followed by the two palace guards he moved off around the circle to engage an AFP correspondent in a conversation in French.

The snub was probably calculated: because of the frankness of his recent articles about Indonesia's economic collapse, Wally was unpopular with Sukarno. And O'Sullivan's shaft had been accurate: the Bung escaped as often as possible to the exquisite palace at Bogor, in the hills behind Jakarta. He didn't enjoy the capital any more than we did.

It remained the capital through apathy: simply because in its earlier incarnation as Batavia it had been the chief trading port. In apathy it sprawled, on its flat, swampy plain where the heat was a changeless oven; and it barely seemed a city. This century's grids of glass and steel were rarities; it was still in spirit a Dutch-colonial town, a stretched-out frieze of squat commercial buildings in parchment-coloured stucco. Prim, dowdy villas with orange-tiled roofs and secretive, diamond-paned windows were reflected in a network of stone canals: mouldering memories of nineteenth-century Holland; scenes on painted tiles, upside-down below the equator. It had a curious, staid charm, this rejected colonial frieze; but now the mechanisms of the departed masters were ceasing to function. Public transport had almost stopped as fuel and spare parts ran out; the canals had become sewers; the roads were so pot-holed they pounded a car to pieces.

Meanwhile, huge loans were spent on armaments and new buildings, and the President had made his decree: Jakarta must be an instant world capital. Monuments rose, topped by ecstatically gesturing figures like ghosts from the Third Reich, or Stalin's Russia. Borrowed millions were spent to construct a mask, while old Batavia's arteries hardened and its vital organs ceased to function. Jalan Thamrin, speeding south from Merdeka Field and the Old City to the Hotel Indonesia in New Jakarta, carried a freight of new glass banks and offices and a vast, Western-style department store whose prices kept it empty. Engineer Sukarno flew over it all in his special white helicopter, supervising operations; and we in the Wayang Club watched as eagerly for the chopper's comings and goings as those villagers on whom the President would descend, as Billy Kwan had put it, like Vishnu in his magic car.

The world was convinced: fifty-five countries now had foreign missions here, and those of the US and USSR were lavish. The more Bung Karno insulted them all, the more they did to prop up his dream.

At six o'clock that evening, Hamilton sat in his deserted office in the Old City, tie and jacket off, once-immaculate shirt sweat-stained, staring at a cable on the desk in front of him.

REQUIRE MATCHER TO SYDNEY HERALD STORY ON STUDENT ATTACK ON GOVERNMENT CORRUPTION STOP ALSO GOVERNMENT INTENTIONS ON THREAT OF WITHDRAWAL FROM UN STOP WHERE ARE YOU — BIGGINS.

One fist clenched on the desk top, the big man remained motionless, his face set with worry. His Sydney news-editor's rebuke was deserved. He had spent two days in Singapore before coming here, and this had not been necessary, since one day had been sufficient for his briefing at ABS's Singapore office. He had not got away with it: too much had been happening in Jakarta.

To make matters worse, his first voice-piece, sent to Sydney by radio circuit this afternoon, had been quite inadequate. Sukarno, as Billy Kwan had predicted, had said little that was new at the press conference, adding no more threats to the ones he had already made. As for the big student demonstration the cable referred to, this was now two days old, and there had been little that Hamilton could say about it. He had made a very bad beginning.

But what worried him more than these things was his failure to get an interview this morning with Subandrio, the Foreign Minister—or rather, the manner of his failure. When Hamilton had presented himself at the Foreign Minister's office near Merdeka Square, the aide who had dealt with him had dismissed him with a cold indifference that gave him little hope of getting interviews in the future. This kept him pondering in the large, shabby room to which he had just come back: an office on the second floor of an old two-storeyed commercial building on Jalan Antara, overlooking one of the Dutch canals. An ancient electric ceiling fan swirled above his head like the wings of a carrion bird, and a chill gripped him, countering the warmth.

His staff had gone home. The official day ended at around two thirty, and it was now the Calling Hour, as we called it in Jakarta: a time when Javanese must traditionally receive with courtesy any unexpected visitor to their homes. Some of us took advantage of this, appearing on the doorsteps of officials and politicians we had acquaintance with, in the hope of getting stories. I liked the Calling Hour, which began at five, and was of flexible length: the official you called on, relaxing in his scented, overgrown garden, had usually hung up his official face with his uniform; now, lying in a rattan chair in his sarong and T-shirt, he would smile and offer you green tea. But for Hamilton this Calling Hour of his first day in Jakarta was one of some anguish: he had no contacts, no one to call on, and it began to appear that Billy Kwan had not exaggerated the seriousness of what Potter had done to him.

At twenty-nine, Hamilton had passed into that border country where middle age is still remote, but where failure (for the ambitious) can scarcely be afforded. As Billy Kwan had guessed, it had been made plain to him before he left Sydney that he was expected to make good where Potter had failed, in this first overseas posting. If not, he would be pulled back to the Sydney news-room—a place known to Hamilton and his ABS colleagues as 'the geriatrics' ward'—where he had just spent three unwilling years. This foreign posting was Hamilton's chance, as it had been for so many news-men; and he had been confident of succeeding. When I came to know him well, and he told me about this unfortunate start, I was puzzled. It was plain that his central focus was his work; he measured his life's worth by it, and he was a very good journalist. Why then had he put in jeopardy what mattered so much to him, by lingering in Singapore for that extra day? As he explained why, I began to see another side of him. Until then I had thought him unemotional, even cold.

He had been evacuated from Singapore to Australia when he was six years old, just before the island's fall to the Japanese. His mother had taken Hamilton and his brother to live in Sydney; his father, who had managed a Singapore insurance company, had stayed on, to be captured and to die in a Japanese prison camp. Hamilton had not been back until now; and it was his memory of that tropical childhood which had caused him to linger in Singapore: to walk, as he had once done with his hand in his father's, through the mazes of alleys and stalls around the Boat Quay, with their glazed ducks and sharks' fins hanging in the doorways, their special childhood smells of incense and frying. 'I wanted to see how much of it would come back,' he said awkwardly; and I saw that his nostalgia for this pre-war 'East' had an intensity known only to those for whom an entire world has been created in their early years and then snatched away. It lay outside his office tonight, in the Old City; and it was this which the cable threatened to take from him—not just his future as a correspondent.

Hamilton began to push papers into a brief-case. He had expected Billy Kwan to contact him about their dinner together, but there had been no sign of the cameraman. Unreliable as well as eccentric, Hamilton said; but he wondered whether Kwan's promises of help might have had some substance. He shrugged. That was really grasping at straws.

Two open louvered doors led onto a little balcony above the street, and, standing up to go, he saw Jakarta revealed, lying exhausted on its flat table, its weak lights coming on like messages he would never decipher. Across by the canal, a hawker was lighting a festive charcoal brazier, and Hamilton wondered what he cooked on it. As he stared, there was a shuffling noise on the balcony. Somebody was out there.

Hamilton stiffened, an icy prickling moving over the back of his neck. There was only one door to the office, and he had let himself in with his key; it had certainly been locked when he arrived. Whoever was on the balcony must have climbed up from the street, or from the next building. With stories of hold-ups coming back to him, he looked around for a weapon.

A stocky shape appeared in the doorway. At first he thought it was a child—then Billy Kwan stepped into the room, wearing the same Hawaiian shirt he had worn the night before.

'Ah—good evening, old man. Ready for our dinner? I thought a Chinese meal.'

Hamilton switched on a desk-lamp with a battered, green tin shade, and swung it round to give him a better sight of the cameraman.

'What the heck were you doing out there?'

Kwan smiled uneasily. 'Waiting for you. I was sitting there reading for a while and I didn't hear you come in. Sorry if I

31

startled you, Guy. When I saw you were busy, I decided not to interrupt.'

'But how did you get out there? The office door was locked.' There was an edge to Hamilton's voice; the frustrations of the day had stretched his nerves. He examined the small man as though Billy were Jakarta's familiar spirit.

Kwan held up a key. 'I have a key of the office. Sorry—you didn't realise. I know I'm not on the staff, but Potter gave me this because I keep some of my sound equipment here. It made things easier for me, and I used to do a lot of work for him.' He blinked rapidly. 'Do you want the key back?'

'No, no,' Hamilton waved at a bamboo reclining chair in front of the desk, and sat down again. 'Sorry I got edgy,' he said. 'I thought you were going to mug me. Let's talk before we go out. I damn well need to talk to someone.'

Without a word, Kwan threw himself into the chair and lay like a broken doll, hands resting on the bamboo arms, shoulders hunched to his ears. He blinked at Hamilton expressionlessly, utterly attentive: an obedient Chinese child. Hamilton, beginning to wonder if he were the victim of some private mockery, took out a small cigar and lit it. Outside, in Jakarta's gathering evening, horns and alien cries rose, and the ringing of bicycle bells.

'You have problems, old man?' Kwan asked.

'Well, it's early days yet,' Hamilton said carefully. 'But this isn't an easy town; you were right.' He drew on his cigar. 'You sounded last night as though you had something to offer me. What was it?'

Kwan was one of those people who rarely answer questions directly, and who start conversations in the middle. Glancing about the office, he asked vaguely, 'How do you feel about things?'

'Feel? I don't quite follow.'

'Do you think you're going to make it here?'

Hamilton was becoming tolerant of these demands for instant intimacy. Normally, they would have caused him to withdraw; but his disturbing day made him prepared to be frank. 'Make it? I don't know,' he said. 'If tomorrow's like today I wouldn't like to bet; but I'm damn well going to be trying.'

'It means a lot to you, then.'

'That's right—it means a lot.' The admission was uncharacteristic; but it was made natural by the half-dark of the office, the unknown city outside, and his sense of isolation.

'You can't have been happy, in Sydney,' Kwan prompted.

'Happy enough. But it was time to move. The news-room's a graveyard.' With an unusual display of feeling, Hamilton repeated softly, 'A bloody graveyard. And I'm not going back.'

'But a chap like you could have his choice of jobs,' Kwan said, and his tone was a question.

'Not really. I'll be thirty next year, matey. What's in front of an ageing journalist? And it's all I'm trained for. It's the subs' table for ever—unless you get a foreign posting.' Hamilton looked out at the weak, winking lights. 'Well, I got it. I've always wanted this, ever since I started flogging my way up from reading proofs.' He glanced at Kwan to see if he was mocked; reassured that he wasn't, he went on: 'But I have to get off the ground here. It's make or break—and they're not going to make allowances.' He was tense, his body unconsciously half-crouched like a runner's at the starting-line. Suddenly aware of this, he grinned. 'It'll probably be better tomorrow.'

'It won't, I'm afraid,' Kwan said. With an abrupt, almost spastic movement, he threw himself forward, crossing his stumpy brown arms on the table. 'Look—tomorrow there's probably going to be a US Embassy riot, and I'll shoot film for you if you like. You'll send it down to Sydney with a voice-over, and that'll keep them happy for a while. But not for long. Embassy riots are pretty routine here—the Yanks average one a week now. If you want real guts in your reports, if you really want to make a name here, you need the contacts in government and military circles: good ones. And that list of Potter's won't help you.'

'It can't all be bad, for God's sake.'

'It will be.' Kwan obviously savoured delivering these little jolts. 'Potter's contacts are no good, Guy—believe me, I know. He was hopeless. The sort of stuff he filed you could read in *Time* magazine—and *they* haven't got a man here.' He cackled with some enjoyment.

'What are you offering,' Hamilton cut in, 'apart from all this woe?' His voice had hardened.

Kwan stopped laughing, and his eyes retreated from Hamilton's in faint alarm; sea-pale, in this face which led you to expect other eyes of hard Mongolian brown, they had a curious vulnerability; they asked that care be taken. 'I suppose you tried to interview Subandrio today,' he said. 'Did you get an appointment?'

'You know damn well I didn't.'

'And you won't. I'm trying to make you realise the way it is in Jakarta, Guy. Most of the doors are shut, at top government level, as far as Western news-men are concerned. Just a few, like Wally O'Sullivan and Pete Curtis, who've got reputations that can't be ignored, get through now and then—and even they don't get through very often. Eastern-bloc journalists have been getting most, and its drying up even for them. Now that Sukarno's talking about this Jakarta-Peking axis, it's a very special situation here. For intrigues, this town's like West Berlin, old man. No one knows what anyone else is doing. The Yanks and the Brits watch the Russians; the West Germans watch the East Germans; and all of them watch the Chinese.' He gave a short bark of laughter. 'Only the Chinese are really on the inside now,' he said. 'The Russians are as much on the outer as our people are, now that Peking is the favourite. It's all *personal* here—personal favours. If Indonesian big-shots see you, it's for personal reasons, unless you're very well known. And you're not—not yet.'

'Can you come to the point?' Hamilton said.

Kwan elongated his wide mouth, and humorously spread one hand palm-down on the desk-top. His Australian accent had thickened, parodying itself. '*All* right, sport, *all* right,' he said. 'You want the guts of it straight away. Now suppose you could get any interview you wanted—short of a personal one with Sukarno—what are the questions you'd like answers to?'

'I'd like to know whether Sukarno's running his own foreign policy any more,' Hamilton said, 'or whether the Communists are calling the shots.'

Kwan smiled delightedly, as though something had been confirmed for him. 'Ah yes,' he said. 'So maybe you'd like to interview the head of the PKI.'

'Aidit? Who wouldn't? But I've gathered that's almost impossible lately.'

Kwan assumed a curious expression that seemed to resemble fondness: but it was difficult to tell. It wasn't, Hamilton thought, that a Chinese face was expressionless, but that the hard lids of the eyes made all expressions different: you needed a different set of keys.

'I can get you to Aidit,' Kwan said. 'Tomorrow.'

Hamilton stared at him for some seconds in silence. 'And how will you manage that?'

Using the elaborately careless 'light' voice which Hamilton began to realise accompanied statements of great importance to him, Kwan said, 'Well, you see, old man, Aidit's a friend of mine. I've already spoken to him about you. Don't ask me more than that. If you want it, it's on—and I mean a full sound-on-film interview: one that'll make quite a splash.'

Hamilton ashed his cigar, and studied the end of it for some moments without speaking. He began now to entertain a suspicion which was to be the subject of a number of discussions in the Wayang Bar: that Kwan was involved with the PKI, and was perhaps a Communist Party member. This might cause trouble in the future; but he decided not to question his good luck.

'If this works out,' he said finally, 'I'll make a deal with you. I'll give you all the film you can handle from now on; I'll use no one else, and you won't need to scratch for work again. There's just one condition. You check with me every day before you take any other assignments—and if you have any more contacts like this, you give them only to me. Okay?'

Kwan blinked twice, then broke into a broad grin. 'Fine,' he said. 'That's what I've always wanted—a real partnership. You're a hard bugger, but I think you and I will get on, Guy.' He jerked in his chair. 'You'll get an interview that'll make an international stir. It'll get things rattling on the diplomatic circuit here, I can tell you. An interview like this needs a good instrument to transmit it.' His chin lifted, and his face wore a new expression: one of almost fatuous pride. 'I've chosen a good instrument,' he said.

Hamilton's response to this piece of impudence was to laugh. Then he said, 'Another thing, Billy. There's no reason why you shouldn't go out and shoot film for me on your own initiative from now on—as long as you shot-list the stuff carefully.'

Kwan looked delighted; his eyes shone. 'That's great, old man —I've always wanted to do my own stuff. I take good pictures: you'll see. Bloody old Potter would never let me shoot an inch of film unless he was there. I have a motor scooter, and I can move around the city easily, with my old Bell and Howell on the back. The Indos don't take much notice of me—they think I'm a local. I could let you know everything that was going on.'

He was silent for a moment, staring into the desk-lamp. 'I can be your eyes,' he said softly.

The evening was to contain one more small surprise for Hamilton.

Coming into the hallway of his apartment in the Hotel after dinner with Kwan, he was gratefully inhaling the first chill wave of the air-conditioning when his eye was caught by something white on the carpet. It was a sealed white envelope: blank. Slitting it open, he pulled out a small square of paper on which had been typed a single line:

Your assistant Kumar is PKI.

There was no signature. Frowning, unbuttoning his shirt to let the cold air play on his wet torso, Hamilton crossed the room, switched on a standard lamp, and sank into an arm-chair, turning the note over in his hands. He wondered vaguely about Indonesian security agents, and glanced towards the line of sealed windows at the far end of the room, across which aqua curtains were drawn, concealing Jakarta. In the wall below these, next to the air-conditioning unit, was a radio receiver with a knob that selected two channels: one for radio and one for the Hotel's piped music system, which was now softly playing the Japanese hit tune 'Sukiyaki'. The Singapore office had informed Hamilton that this receiver would be bugged, and his conversations taped in the

Hotel basement, for the attention of Sukarno's security service. This hadn't disturbed him until now.

Pushing the note into the pocket of his shirt, he found another piece of paper there. He studied this second typed sheet for a moment in puzzlement, having forgotten what it was: the poem Kwan had handed to him the night before. He now read it slowly, his lips pursed, as though studying a dubious contract.

Hamilton, unlike most youthful journalists today, had not preceded his career with a university course. I learnt, when we came to know each other, that he had left school at sixteen to work his way painfully upwards to an A grading from the proof-reading room of a Sydney paper. And he had not developed any great taste for literature, although he had a sentimental attachment to certain authors from his childhood: I noticed Kipling's *Kim* in the shelf by the bed, when I first came up here to sit over a bottle of Scotch with him, as well as some Somerset Maugham novels and a number of James Bond thrillers. There was no poetry: he tended to 'go blank', he said, at the sight of verse. But occasionally, a scrap of poetry encountered accidentally will catch at such a man, stilling his spirit like a breeze from the hills. He will then pause uneasily in his ceaseless run to escape boredom, and tell himself that he ought to explore this stillness before the motor inside him begins to churn again.

This was what happened to Hamilton now. Being presented with a poem to read was a new experience for him, and he was eventually to speak about it with an air of indulgent wonderment. He came now to the final lines.

> *Suddenly I remembered the early levees at Court*
> *When you and I galloped to the Purple Yard.*
> *As we walked our horses up Dragon Tail Street*
> *We turned and gazed at the green of the Southern Hills.*
> *Since we parted, both of us have been growing old;*
> *And our minds have been vexed with many anxious cares;*
> *Yet even now I fancy that my ears are full*
> *Of the sound of jade tinkling on your bridle straps.*

There was no sly double meaning, as he had half-expected. He

37

heard only (as well as such a self-sufficient man could) the silent appeal for friendship rising from this sweat-stained sheet of paper like a cipher message. He turned the page over. Scribbled on the back in blue ball-point was a single sentence: *Stay away from the cemetery*. Was this addressed to him, and why had Kwan written it there?

He had decided that he liked Billy, he said, whatever the cameraman's secret affiliations were. A community without women such as this one would no doubt resemble the Army, Hamilton thought; you could come to value any man who could be entertaining—no matter how eccentric he was. So the poem's appeal would not be rejected—provided it didn't lead to any great embarrassments.

As he lay sinking towards sleep, he wondered again who had left the unpleasant message about his Indonesian assistant—whom he judged to be efficient. His last thoughts were practical ones; he fervently hoped that Kwan would produce the promised interview with Aidit, which might very well save him from 'the geriatrics' ward'. He wanted badly to stay here. *Betjak* bells floated up from the Car Park seven floors below, coming muted through the plate-glass windows into his head and lingering there, together with the curious directive on the back of Kwan's poem: *Stay away from the cemetery.*

Like most men who live alone, and have reached their maturity single, Hamilton had done so by numbing his feelings at crucial times, and turning to action for relief. Not selfish in a petty way, he nevertheless preferred the odourless, ethereal tensions of the world and his job to other people's emotions—with which, perhaps, he was mostly at a loss. And so he was often calmly unaware of their true natures, intensities, and needs, floating and dissolving around him.

All this made him the perfect vessel for Billy Kwan's purposes.

3

A middle-aged Indonesian technician in spectacles sat at the desk of the studio control room, watching Hamilton spitefully. In a glass recording-booth the size and shape of a confession-box, Hamilton sat hunched over the microphone. He guessed that the technician was one of the dedicated, who hated all *Nekolim*. There was no sound except for the hissing of an aged monitor just outside the open door of the booth. It was nearly 2 p.m. — time for his radio telephone circuit with Sydney.

The hissing told him that the circuit was open; but there was no contact yet, although by now there should have been. Hamilton fidgeted with his script, and lit one of his small daily ration of cigarettes. He reached out and flicked a key down behind the microphone.

'ABS Jakarta to ABS Sydney,' he said. The vast hissing continued from the monitor; minute sounds could be heard invading the line: shrunken voices; morse; ghostly musics. But there was no response from the safe, dry continent to the south. His jaw tight, Hamilton leant out of the stuffy booth. 'Are you sure we're hooked up properly?'

The technician nodded with malicious satisfaction. 'Two o'clock, now,' he said.

Half to himself, Hamilton said, 'Where are the bastards, then? The one bloody day I have to have them.'

It's not hard for me to picture how he felt; we all suffered here

39

eventually, in the cracked new telecommunications building off Merdeka Field which was our pipeline to the outside world: that world where all our frantic activity was justified. For a news-agency man like me, the big concern was to see that my cables and antiquated morsecasts (a relic from Dutch days) got past the Army censors, and that the bribes I had paid the half-starved operators had been enough to ensure they sent them. Hamilton used these channels too; but his chief worry was the state of the radio circuit link with Sydney—carried, in that year, by patched-up Dutch equipment on which the voice quality was invariably bad, and which he feared might fail altogether.

He had special reason to sweat over the connection today. Outside, on a portable tape threaded up and waiting on a machine at the severe technician's elbow, was the interview with D. N. Aidit, the head of the *Partai Kommunist Indonesia*; and it was the best story of Hamilton's life. As well, he had been granted a sound-on-film interview for television, already dispatched on a flight to Sydney via Singapore.

He didn't quite believe Billy Kwan's claim that the interview had been set up through Kwan's personal friendship with Aidit. Watching the two greet each other in Aidit's poky little office in PKI headquarters in Raya Kramat, Hamilton had detected little evidence of friendship; merely a casual cordiality. Aidit had announced to Hamilton that he had special goodwill towards Australians because of their remembered support for Indonesia's independence struggle. Possibly Kwan's being half Chinese made him a doubly acceptable curiosity; the PKI leader had clapped Billy on the back, calling him 'my Chinese-Australian friend'.

But there had been little conversation as Kwan had set up his big Arriflex camera and his glaring lights, watched by two stony-faced male aides. And when Hamilton, ready to record, had found himself face to face with his subject across a low table, he had decided that D. N. Aidit was unlikely to entertain feelings of personal warmth towards anybody: a judgment I entirely agreed with. A youthful, comfortably plump little man who chain-smoked cigarettes, Aidit had eyes like black glass, that told nothing. Together with a ritual glass of tea on a silver stand,

Hamilton had been given a clear message that he had been chosen over other news-men in Jakarta as a transmitter for the topic Aidit wanted to discuss, and that no comments would be made to other members of the press corps until later. He had a sense of triumph, but also of being used.

He was trembling now. For no one to be manning a circuit at two minutes past the hour was highly ominous: circuit time was too valuable for that. The filmed interview would not reach Sydney until tomorrow morning, to be processed during the day: so it was his radio piece, listened to this evening in Jakarta and other capitals on ABS short-wave, which must ensure that Hamilton got in first. He pressed the key down and made his call again. There was still no answer: only the hiss and tiny twitter on the monitor, like the sound of the whole world's tension, like a mockery of his own. He mashed his cigarette out in a battered tin ashtray. Extraordinary rage filled him; hatred of his own imagined failure mounted like bile; but he forced himself to sit still. Two minutes later he called Sydney again, without hope.

There was an instant crackle from the monitor, and a loud Australian voice came from it as clearly as though its owner had entered the room. 'ABS Sydney to ABS Jakarta. This is Les Butler. Yes, Guy, receiving you loud and clear. How are we doing, mate?'

Hamilton swung forward on his stool and began to shuffle the typescript in front of him. 'Jesus, where were you, Les, in the pub? Don't bother to answer that.' But his body had relaxed, like an athlete's after a race, and he grinned faintly in spite of himself: he felt a ridiculous gratitude to the voice on the other end.

He could picture the sub-editor clearly, in the booth off the humming news-room where Hamilton had spent so many hours and years, taking circuits from those fortunate ones who had achieved what he most desired, and who spoke to him from Beirut, New Delhi, Singapore, Jakarta . . . It would be five in the afternoon in Sydney now, and the home-going traffic would be building up outside in Pitt Street. Here in this dimly lit, alien city where the amalgam of hatred and danger was a constant odour, like that of its *kretek* cigarettes, it was difficult to believe that the

41

normal Sydney news-room, suddenly so falsely close, would ever claim him again.

With the Aidit story, and with a number of follow-ups to it on radio, Hamilton established his reputation in Jakarta, and began to build the name he has enjoyed internationally ever since. It was the perfect opportunity perfectly grasped. The blot of his late start was wiped out; he got a congratulatory telegram from Biggins, his news-editor (we called them 'herograms' in the Wayang), and the filmed interview with Aidit was syndicated widely on television networks in the United States, Britain, and a large number of West European countries.

D. N. Aidit had not been seen in an interview of this depth in the West before, and it became the subject of much newspaper comment, and of learned guessing by broadcasting academics specialising in South-East Asia. Aidit was now not only the head of the third largest Communist party in the world, but a member of Sukarno's inner Cabinet; and the swing to Peking was Aidit's triumph. This alone would have ensured the piece's interest: but as well, Aidit had chosen to use Hamilton's interview to put pressure on Sukarno for the formation of what he called a 'Fifth Force' in Indonesia.

We had heard of this Fifth Force before: a proposal to arm the peasants, to create what Aidit had also dubbed a 'People's Army', in addition to the three existing armed services and the police. And there was little doubt that it would be under Aidit's command. Sukarno, although he had given the idea his blessing in his 'Living Dangerously' speech last Merdeka Day, had so far skilfully avoided granting Aidit the Fifth Force; but in the interview with Hamilton Aidit now claimed that Sukarno had agreed to it. And this was what did most to cause a stir.

Billy Kwan's mysterious gift of Aidit was, of course, a sheer piece of luck for Hamilton. But I had to admit that the new man's follow-up analysis on radio showed penetration. The ABS's overseas service was widely listened to in Jakarta, and the piece caused much interest in diplomatic circles, as Kwan had predicted. I heard it myself, and ruefully concluded (while I smiled at his fugitive Australian vowels, and the romantically urgent pitch of his voice) that another keen young man like Curtis was in the field to keep me on my toes.

Hamilton had a hard, essentially simple cast of mind; he never lost sight of the notion that power in the state resides with the man who holds the gun. And all through the year he would simply keep asking who held it. Intellectuals and experts more subtle than he was failed to do so, and for that reason proved to be wrong.

It's always a nuisance when one of your colleagues mounts a story like this. It means that your editors at home demand matchers, and you have to start running to supply a variant of the same story yourself. There was much cursing in the Wayang Bar when we realised that Hamilton was going to be serious competition, and more when we found that Aidit would give us only very brief interviews. Pete Curtis was particularly incensed: I think he already saw his position as fastest runner threatened, and he began to be hostile to Hamilton.

'That goddamn, elegant bastard,' he said. 'So Aidit wants a Fifth Force. So what else is new? How does that rate all this international play?' And he began to sneer at Hamilton's dressiness: his Singapore-tailored safari suits, his Bally shoes and hand-made shirts. But Pete still had to supply a matcher; and we were to find ourselves supplying more and more matchers to Hamilton's stories as the weeks went by.

Because of the impact of the Aidit piece, many doors, such as Foreign Minister Subandrio's, now opened for Hamilton, as is always the way; and he was remorselessly active in pursuing his stories. He had no more need of Billy Kwan to provide contacts now; and Billy's part in getting him started was a secret I was to discover only months later.

But Hamilton remained grateful, and eventually he asked Kwan outright why he had done so much more for him than for his predecessor. The cameraman looked at him sternly; then he grinned. 'Let's just say I didn't fancy riding up Dragon Tail Street with old Potter.'

Hamilton was at a loss to understand for a few moments; then, with some embarrassment, he remembered the poem Billy had given him.

Their close partnership was now the source of many jokes. 'Hullo,' Wally O'Sullivan would say, as they came into the Wayang, 'here come Sir Guy and the Black Dwarf.' This amused us, and we would occasionally call Hamilton 'Sir Guy' to his face: I don't think he ever knew why.

4

A naked, deep-bosomed Javanese nymph, sculptured in green
bronze like the figures on Sukarno's monuments, sat among
flowers at the end of the Oasis swimming-pool behind the Hotel
Indonesia. Half-way down the edge of the pool, two of her living
counterparts, their perfect, teak-coloured bodies covered with
droplets from a recent swim, stood laughing with two rice-white
German businessmen On the bright green lawn, Hamilton
watched them from a reclining chair shaded by a rustic umbrella
of palm-thatching; and Billy Kwan, in the chair next to him,
followed his gaze.

'Yes, they're delicious, old man; but the future's bleak for
them.'

Hamilton looked sleepily inquiring.

'No respectable Indonesian girl will look at a *Nekolim*,' Kwan
went on, 'so they never set foot inside the Hotel. The Indo.
newspapers say this is a white man's den of iniquity. Those two
are finished with their own people for good.' He bit into one of the
enormously expensive hamburgers a white-jacketed waiter had
just set down on the wooden table beside them. Then, as though
this train of thought had reminded him, he said, 'By the way,
we're meeting my girl-friend here in a few moments. I said we'd
meet her at two o'clock.'

'Girl-friend? I didn't know you had a girl-friend, Billy.'
Hamilton was startled, and removed his sun-glasses.

Kwan did not look at him, and his flat voice took on its elaborately careless tone. 'She's a secretary at the British Embassy. Jill's a nice little thing—I'd like you to meet her.'

Revolving the ice in his Bacardi and Coke, Hamilton wondered what sort of girl, in a community where unattached European women were now so rare, would become involved with a man four feet six inches tall. He pictured her as the sort of plain and earnest young woman who took up lost causes, or became sentimental about the deprived. He was not cruel, but his habits of mind were realistic. Then he said: 'Jill? I think I may have met her. She was at a Brit. Embassy cocktail party I was at last week. Small fair girl. Is that the one?'

'That's the one. Probably the prettiest girl in the European community.'

Hamilton raised his eyebrows. The young woman he recalled, although not entirely unattractive, seemed to fit more with the private guess he had just made than with Billy's superlative: about twenty-five, slight, well groomed, with her hair in a chignon, and wearing glasses. He had spoken to her only briefly, and her face had given him an impression of severity—even plainness. The glasses had not helped, of course.

'She's a girl with problems,' Billy was saying. 'She had a bad marriage that lasted a couple of years; and in this situation, of course, she has a lot of chaps in the press corps and the embassies running after her: there are so few single white girls here, she has to beat men off. That's not what she wants at the moment—she prefers to be with me.' This statement was followed by a lift of the chin and an expression of complacency at which Hamilton smiled. Unlike some of us, he was amused even by Billy's vanity; the small man was now an endless source of puzzlement and fascination to him.

A few minutes later Kwan jumped up from his reclining chair with one of his alarmingly sudden movements and hurried to meet a couple advancing across the lawn. Hamilton recognised Colonel Henderson, the British Military Attaché, whose bald, tanned head gleamed in the sun; and he was surprised to find that the young woman at Henderson's side made Kwan's praises understandable after all.

The reasons for her transformation were simple enough. She had removed the glasses; and she wore a brief red bikini, exposing a pale yet athletic body quite unlike what he would have expected after meeting her at the cocktail party. Instead of being thin or angular, it was well rounded; and the frail waist and small bust would have given her a look of early adolescence, even of immaturity, had it not been for the fullness of her hips and thighs. Her shoulder-length mane of blond hair gave a top-heavy effect that was both faintly comical and charming.

As she saw Kwan, the girl raised her large blue beach towel and waved it hard, like a flag, with humorous exuberance. This simple action seemed to define her. Glancing round at the predominantly male groups under the other umbrellas on the lawn, Hamilton saw that nearly all of them, warily or openly, were following her progress. Billy had been right; the Oasis, for any unattached white girl, was an arena for male eyes.

As soon as Kwan reached the couple, he lunged, picked the young woman up by the waist, and with an ease which proved the power of his heavy shoulders, swung her above his head. The girl's little shriek, floating across the lawn, conveyed amusement rather than protest. This sort of horseplay was not common at the Oasis, and all the groups under the nearby umbrellas were now openly watching the dwarfish figure in the flapping Hawaiian shirt and inelegant black bathing trunks. There was faint laughter.

'Here's my little Jillie!' Kwan called to Hamilton. Clasping her waist, he advanced with her across the lawn, followed by the tolerantly smiling Henderson. Although his head came just level with her shoulder, Billy's conjunction with her was not as ludicrous as it might have been, Hamilton thought: she was small enough to look natural with him.

Under Kwan's and Hamilton's thatched umbrella, the wooden outdoor couches were now pushed into a pattern, of which Colonel Henderson's was the centre-piece. It was not merely Henderson's age and position that ensured this, but his voice, with its clipped, headmasterly tones of the pre-war imperial ruling caste: just a little louder and clearer than other voices, making nothing but pleasant and courteous remarks, yet containing a central ring of cold authority, and giving Hamilton, to his private annoyance, an impulse to straighten himself. The Colonel appeared to be in his early fifties, but might have been more. Despite his baldness, which left only a close-clipped fringe of sandy-grey hair above the ears, he seemed youthful for his age. A neat moustache completed him as the classic, almost cartoon type of British Army officer; but the wide-set, triangular grey eyes were shrewd.

'Delightful spot, this,' he was saying to Hamilton. 'Very lucky, you people based in the Hotel.'

This was true. The Oasis was an oasis indeed, an international Eden, where the town of *Konfrontasi* almost ceased to exist, in off-hours. But through cracks in the *chic* fence of rustic stakes, which screened the lawn from Sukarno's highway, occasional brown faces peered, watching not with resentment but with spellbound smiles, as though they knew that these pastures of bliss would some day be theirs.

'Mind you, *we're* rather lucky, too,' the Colonel said. 'After our Indonesian friends did the little job on our Embassy across the square, we were forced to move to the Ambassador's residence, which happens to have quite a good pool. Quite amusing, that day they smashed us up. We had a marvellous Scotsman there, and all the time they were looting and burning he insisted on marching up and down playing the bagpipes. Well, I don't think our friends are having such an enjoyable time with the Scots Guards in Sarawak.' He had a one-sided, tight smile that remained fixed in position.

'You're leaving out what *you* did that day, Ralph,' Jill said fondly.

It was plain, Hamilton thought, what bond linked them. Through an anachronism of history, Indonesia's campaign against Britain had flung them back into the days of the Empire; they were living through a sort of Indian Mutiny on a petty scale, and half enjoying it.

Henderson grunted dismissively and looked into his drink. 'I was being bloody ineffectual,' he said briefly.

But the young woman continued to smile at him, her chin resting on her hand, her gaze almost tender. Her dark-blue eyes

48

had none of the diminished appearance common to many people who have removed their glasses; but they obviously had an astigmatism, being slightly unfocused, and this gave them the dazed look that usually signals great affection or sexual excitement. At close quarters, Hamilton was able to see why he had originally found her face severe: whenever she ceased to smile, it had a sort of bareness, emphasised by her narrow, beaked nose. But it was lightened by flickering good humour, and certainly not plain. He found it difficult to keep his eyes from her near-nude body, stretched innocently on its wooden couch. Its childish navel was distracting, and he had no wish to be distracted by women at present; he had welcomed Jakarta's enforced celibacy.

The Colonel addressed himself to Hamilton. 'We listen quite often to your broadcasts on short-wave. I must say some of them have been very interesting. Your pigeon post is sometimes better than our pigeon post—especially where the PKI is concerned.'

'The one with Aidit was marvellous,' Jill put in.

Hamilton winked at Billy. 'I have an unusually valuable cameraman, with his ear to the ground.'

'I do my best, old man,' Kwan said. 'But you and the Colonel should do a deal. You both have good contacts.'

'Good idea,' Henderson said, a little too promptly. 'Perhaps you'd care to chat with me from time to time about the state of affairs among the Indonesian Army's top brass. I rather imagine our contacts there are better than yours.' He stood up. 'I'm for a swim in the pool. Anyone care to join me?'

He had taken off the green sports shirt he wore over his swimsuit, disclosing the powerful body of a man half his age, broad-chested and flat-bellied, the legs unmarred by veins. He held himself in a pose of self-conscious erectness, which reminded Hamilton of the models in physical-culture magazines. He looked down at the girl. 'What about you, Jillie? Just what you need.'

'I don't think so, Ralph.'

'Oh, come along, my dear.' He hesitated, his shrewd grey gaze affectionately pleading: a boy badly wanting a toy.

But Jill would not. 'I'll keep Billy company,' she said. She had one of those middle-class English accents that swallowed words;

her voice was low and rapid, and Hamilton had to strain to hear what she said. There was a caution in her, Hamilton saw now, which he had not been led to expect by her first extrovert waving of the towel: a well-controlled nervousness her humour would mostly hide. 'Billy *never* swims,' she said, and her slim, well-modelled arm shot out with electric suddenness to rub Kwan's spiky black head.

The Colonel turned away, and Hamilton stood up, taking off his beach coat. 'I'll join you, Colonel,' he said. He had sensed an essential coldness in the man, yet he also felt an unaccountable sympathy with him. He would not see him swim alone.

Colonel Henderson had proposed using the high board, which few people ever attempted; now Hamilton saw why. A strong swimmer, but no diver, he felt a pang of unease at going from such a height. There was no one but themselves on the top platform, from which the Colonel surveyed the pool's glittering, aquamarine oblong below. Small faces looked up at them. He glanced at Hamilton. 'Used the board before?' When Hamilton said he had not, Henderson said, 'Decent sort of height. Well, I'll go first, shall I?' The words were innocuous, but Hamilton felt he was being involved in some sort of childish competition.

The older man walked out to the end of the board, and then, to Hamilton's surprise, turned round, standing erect as a sentry, arms raised, perfectly motionless, his gaze fixed on a point just past Hamilton's head. From the top of his bald pate to his feet, the Colonel gleamed in the burning sun with that light amber tan peculiar to fair people; grey and sandy hair curled profusely on the broad chest. Surely, at his age, Hamilton thought, a backward dive from this height was dangerous.

Just before he flung himself backwards, Henderson's eyes flicked briefly to Hamilton's; his moustache twitched, his jaw jutted, and his mouth set. In that instant Hamilton realised that Henderson reminded him of his dead father.

The dive was perfect. The Colonel did not merely dive backwards, but performed a somersault, entering the water head-first. Hamilton walked out to the end of the board and looked down. The patrician face bobbing far below had a hint of boyish pleasure in it. 'I can't top that,' Hamilton called.

'Why not?' The sharp, military voice was challenging. 'You're young enough.'

Hamilton performed a simple pike, knowing with relief, half-way through the air, that the board was not as impossibly high as it looked, but that his legs were going over.

When he surfaced, Henderson, floating near by, called with unconcealed satisfaction: 'Lost your legs at the end there, I think.'

'I'm afraid I'm no great diver.'

'No? I thought all Australians were good at swimming.'

'Well, maybe that's what's wrong. I was born in England.'

'Really? But surely all British journalists are barred here now?'

'I'm on an Australian passport—I spent most of my life there.'

'Ah. Too late then—you're a colonial.'

'You mean you won't have me back?'

'Afraid not. You're a convict, aren't you?'

This silly banter had an odd poignancy for Hamilton, even an element of pain. They bobbed, facing each other, their faces made naked as those of boys by the water.

'We might try a little race to the end,' the Colonel said. 'Would you like me to give you a start?'

'I don't think so.' Hamilton grinned; he had known Henderson would want to race.

Hamilton began, with his smooth crawl, at a fairly relaxed pace. He had won races in his youth, and had no doubt at all that against a man in his fifties he was going to win, even though he was out of condition and had not yet succeeded in giving up cigarettes. But he had mixed feelings about winning, despite the Colonel's cockiness. He had a respect for age unusual in a man of his generation, and he suspected that the Colonel was going to be humiliated by losing.

But every time he rolled his head out for air, he found that Henderson was precisely beside him, swimming beautifully. The tepid water of the pool had an enervating, dreamlike effect, and Hamilton had to make an effort of will, half-way down, to increase speed. He drew ahead; but in a few moments the tanned bald head and moustached mouth sucking in air were beside him again. The Colonel was in astounding condition.

Hamilton now brought out all the speed he had, his legs beginning to ache, his chest pounding. They were nearly to the shallow end; he heard confused voices calling, and could dimly see, each time his head came up, the green bronze nymph in her flower-bed, and a coloured group of people. The tanned head was now just slightly behind his own, the O of the mouth and the grey moustache framed in spray. Effort gave the hard face a desperate expression as Hamilton began to pull away.

What happened then was something Hamilton was later to discuss with me in the Wayang Bar. He knew he had won, it seems; he had a little more in reserve, and was now head and shoulders in front. But instead of putting on the final spurt he relaxed his pace. As his hand hit the gutter, he saw that Henderson's had done so a moment before.

They stood knee-deep in the shallow water, unable to speak, panting, each leaning with one hand against the green tiles, looking at each other. Jill Bryant and Billy Kwan stood among a group of amused strangers, smiling down at them. Jill bent slightly, hands on her knees, directing her wide, infectious smile at Hamilton. 'Congratulations,' she called. 'That's the nearest anyone's come to beating him.'

And Kwan called to Henderson, 'Had you worried, Colonel.'

Grey chest heaving, blinking away water, Henderson was still looking speculatively at Hamilton. 'He certainly did,' he said. Then he smiled with genuine friendliness; and Hamilton felt absurd pleasure at this.

5

Swift evening spreads across Jakarta. The city lies inert in a hot brown twilight, which smells of petrol, frangipani, and fear. All energy burns low, like the failing street lights; but fear mounts like erotic excitement in these stormy nights of the north-west monsoon. Jakarta waits always for explosions.

Explosions: flames of overturned cars, satisfying smash of official glass: *Konfrontasi* in action. Fear: this February, certain highly placed officials and Cabinet Ministers take the precaution of sleeping away from their homes at night, as they fall from grace in the nightmare game devised by Bung Karno. There have been many imprisonments, and some enigmatic deaths among those whose thinking is out of line with the new orthodoxy charted by the PKI. All Ministers are summoned to week-end Cabinet meetings in the palace up at Bogor, where Sukarno makes them watch the *wayang*: the classical shadow-show, which he loves. But the classics are re-written to the President's orders, and in one of the darting silhouettes a Minister may suddenly recognise himself —his corruptions and deviations ruthlessly caricatured. Then he ceases to laugh and grows inwardly sick, for his fall has been signalled.

Sirens wail, their long fingers searching the nerves: night-time motorcades of the great, splashing by on mysterious missions, or bound for the night-club on the topmost floor of the Hotel Indonesia. The motorcade of Sukarno himself roars by—giant black Cadillac limousine, jeeps filled with armed police, motor cycle outriders with sirens in full cry: he too visits the night-club, or moves restlessly about the city to the houses he has built for his many wives. In the bazaars, where his prowess as a lover is the stuff of fable, they say his siren is the Bung's mating call. His appetite for women is admired: they are his due as a Javanese god-king. Out on Merdeka Field, in front of the palace, he has erected the highest of all his monuments, an obelisk topped with a flame of solid gold. And this is his *tugu*, his fertility object. We say in the Wayang, as they do in the bazaars, that Sukarno's member is tipped with gold; and no one enjoys these jokes better than Sukarno himself.

When the god-king's caravan has passed, the thrusting shafts of its headlights are replaced by the wan friendliness of flares on the portable food-stalls, and the sirens by the wistful croon and tinkle of Javanese popular music. *Betjaks*, with their straining riders, toil like giant cockroaches at the muddy edges of the roads, or shelter under trees from the sheets of rain.

Other siren calls of tense night: from the puddled Car Park outside the Hotel, the ululation of the *bantji*, the boy-girls from the Old City. Conveyed here in their own personal *betjaks*, their fantastically high-piled hair fixed with jewelled combs, they wear low-cut Western gowns to reveal their cleavages, and their faces are masks of Javanese beauty; but with troublingly heavy chins. Locked out, addicts of luxury, they wait night after night beneath the Hotel's glittering cliffs; and their coy banshee howls for attention, from which they get their name, haunt Wally O'Sullivan's dreams.

All the other watchers in the Car Park wear ever-hopeful smiles. Yet none of them will ever enter the arcade; none will ever cross that invisible frontier, at the edge of their stony tract of ground, to walk the pleasant tiles of the Hotel's promenade. Why, why do they wait?

The Wayang Club, evening. How the voices come back, from its candle-lit, permanent dusk!

'How did your Crush Malaysia go today, Pete?'

'Inspirational. The paper loves my crushing stories.'

'I got a herogram today. This round's on me.'

'Where's Condon tonight?'

'Driving the long way round the canals, looking at the boobs.'

Kevin Condon, a New Zealander who works for an American news-agency, is hopelessly addicted to glimpses of bare-breasted Javanese women—glimpses granted to him only among the very poor, the wives of the homeless tribe that lives along the old Dutch canals. These waterways, the city's sickly veins, are always snaking into our consciousness, presenting vignettes to which most of us grow hardened. Lines of bare-bottomed men crouch together in cheerful good fellowship on the stone sides, uncoiling their excrement into the water, while women stand waist-deep bathing themselves, a few yards downstream. The women are fully clothed; but occasionally, with a touchingly modest gesture and a confiding smile, one of them will loosen her sarong, baring herself to the waist.

Sallow Condon, who appears middle-aged but is not, and who has the look of an unhappy husband although he is single, makes leisurely tours of the canals in his battered Fiat, seeking such revelations of the jogging brown breasts of Java. An amateur photographer, he takes pictures when he can.

'Condon,' Billy Kwan says, 'reminds me of those lecherous Victorian gentlemen going about the East End at night, soliciting girls among the poor.'

'A bit solemn tonight, aren't we, Billy?' I say. I rather like poor Condon, who is always humbly amiable, his dog-quiet eyes searching naïvely for a legendary, erotic East Indies.

'Any news on Sukarno's kidney?'

'The stone hasn't shifted—and he's still bed-hopping. One doctor gave him two years if he kept away from women. The Bung asked him what point there'd be in the two years if he did that.'

Laughter: the Wayang, like the city's bazaars and embassies, is full of rumours of the little dictator's impending death which, if it comes, will change everything. One kidney is gone, and the other is said to be failing; if the stone shifts he will die. But he shows no sign of dying, indestructibly ranting at his rallies, and maintaining his sexual myth. He fears the surgeon's knife, because his *dukun*, his fortune teller, has said he will die by the knife. He's being given acupuncture treatment, it's said, by his new Chinese doctors.

'Sir Guy' Hamilton, drunk, holding an empty glass to his mouth as a microphone, commences a resonant, blaring parody of one of his own radio voice reports.

'One thing is certain. Sukarno's kidney will shift and he will die: or it will not shift and he will not die. Either way, the fate of Indonesia hangs by a kidney.' A blade of lank black hair falls on his forehead; drink makes his sudden green eyes more hooded than usual, his corner-boy's nose more bulbous. We sway in the glow of the fat red candles, laughing, saluting him with upraised glasses. Despite his constant successes, and our consequent chasing after matchers, Hamilton's professionalism and affability have made him popular.

'Good on you, Ham—keep it up!'

'I am reliably informed by the President's Viennese specialists,' Hamilton blares, 'that the kidney stone has commenced to move. Other reliable sources, however, say the stone is static. But one thing is certain ...'

'Ali's listening,' Kwan hisses warningly.

Ali the moon-faced bar-steward frowns severely, standing to attention in his Sukarno cap beneath an illuminated pagoda of bottles—the round bar's centre-piece. We change the subject; we fear that Ali is a government agent, and no one wants to be expelled from the country: it can happen all too easily.

Pete Curtis, drunker than Hamilton, lurches around the bar and slaps a cable down on the black lake of the counter. 'Looka this,' he says. It reads:

YOU UNSIGHTED ON LOMBOK FAMINE STOP REQUEST YOU MATCH REPORT FROM ABS'S GUY HAMILTON.

'You realise, you son of a bitch, that now I've got to go to that godforsaken island, too, just because CBS used your piece? If you can afford to be out of Jakarta now, I can't. I haven't got a goddamn staff covering for me. I'll tell you what—I don't believe there's a real famine there. You blew it up. When I file, I'm gonna piss all over that famine story. I'm gonna knock it down in print.'

Hamilton gives him a wide, false smile. 'Knock it down at your own risk, matey,' he says. 'And go and get grandly stuffed.' Drunk, he becomes more Australian, I notice: the vowel sounds have thickened.

A moment follows in which we wait for Curtis to swing a punch at Hamilton; he has been known to do this to others in public places.

'Gentlemen, gentlemen,' Wally O'Sullivan rumbles.

Then Billy Kwan breaks the tension by saying, 'Don't be silly, Pete. It's true—they're starving on Lombok. Not that any of you care, really.'

Curtis has obviously thought better of swinging on big Ham. 'And what does *he* care?' he says. 'It's just good copy to him.' He is inclined to parade his social conscience at times. Then, in sudden drunken irrelevance, 'Why do you always look so *dressed*, Hamilton? Do you ever wear the same safari suit twice?' But he grins loosely, to lessen the offensiveness; the moment's antagonism has passed. There is a pecking order among us, and in the Wayang Wally O'Sullivan's place is secure at the head of it; but Hamilton and Curtis, with their aggressive pursuit of stories, are neck-and-neck behind him. Each recognises this, and it makes a sort of unwanted link between them.

'What do you do for *women*, Ham?' Curtis asks next. 'There are plenty of outlets here, baby. If not, the banshees out in the Car Park will give you the blow-job of your life. Or you could come with me out to the cemetery.'

Hamilton raises his quizzical eyebrows at this, suddenly interested. 'The cemetery? I didn't know you went in for necrophilia, Curtis. What's at the cemetery?'

Curtis laughs. 'He's been here all this time, and he don't know yet where the Jakarta whores come out. You're really a square, aren't you, Ham?'

'I suppose I am, if it comes to paying for sex,' Hamilton says. 'Not for me, thanks.'

Curtis smiles. 'You'll go out there eventually, buddy. We all do.'

Billy Kwan, standing as usual at Hamilton's side, has been

frowning; now he bursts out suddenly at Curtis. 'Ah, *look*, Pete, we're all aware that you're prepared to exploit those wretched women for a few rupiahs, and keep on getting clap. And we're all aware that sex is just one of your routine physical functions. But it doesn't necessarily go for other people. I don't think Ham wants to join you at the graveyard.'

Curtis stares down at Billy in slow amazement: he can't take offence, because he likes to take the role of Kwan's defender. 'Hey, cool it, Billy,' he says. 'There are no nice girls around— *you're* going out with the only one, aren't you? A man's gotta do something for a piece of tail.'

Billy screws up his face in distaste; but Curtis leads him aside now, and they drink together on their own, a little way round the bar. Soon Kwan is laughing good-humouredly again. A little while later, I hear him say to Curtis: '. . . yes, *that* was a step forward in the education of a young Chinaman.'

Curtis is shaking his head. 'Disgusting,' he says loyally. 'Goddamn disgusting.'

I don't know quite why I became a father confessor to my friends in the Wayang Bar; but I did. I suppose a Catholic, even a lapsed one, is good at this, after years of observing the role in that coffin-shaped booth where all solutions to anguish seem possible—at least for a time. At thirty-seven, I was not quite ready to see myself as a father figure, but this is what I had become—even, ludicrously, to Great Wally, who was two years my senior.

I was separated from my wife, which also probably fitted me for my part. A separated or divorced man either becomes a bitter bard reciting his wrongs, or he becomes a good listener. I became a good listener. I don't mean to indicate that my friends were all bar-room weepers—none of them answers to that description, not even Condon. But their isolation from normal life and the day-to-day uncertainty of their position prompted them to occasional self-relevation. The Wayang, its changeless red candles flickering at intervals around the black mirror-surface of the bar, became my confession-box.

A foreign correspondent has a life without continuity, without a centre; he has few real relationships, either with the people of the country he happens to be in or with his colleagues. There isn't the time, there isn't the trust, nor, to be truthful, the inclination, journalists being what they are. 'Concern' is paraded as feeling, and in-jokes as a substitute for understanding. But in that year, I like to think, something more grew up between us in the Wayang.

Only one photograph exists to record us as a group. Taken by Kwan, it shows Hamilton and me pedalling tricycle-rickshas, which we have taken over from the *betjak* boys in Jalan Thamrin. My passenger is Great Wally, hands on monumental knees, chins held high, looking, in his straining tropical suit, like a figure from the remote Far-Eastern era of Hamilton's nostalgia: a Somerset Maugham character, perhaps. Just behind me, Hamilton pedals Kevin Condon, whose sheepish smile is that of a good schoolboy who knows he should not be here. Pedalling that creaking, ponderous machine with Wally's twenty-two stone in it through the humid heat proved unusually gruelling, and inside my laughter I felt a pang of pity for the lean, cheerful men who pushed these torturing toys all day for the price of an evening meal of rice and *saté*. When we winged creakily round the great circular pool in Friendship Square, to arrive finally at the gates of the Hotel, there were grim looks from both Indonesians and whites in the arcade: we had degraded the Hotel front, where the black limousines of the powerful made their ceremonious arrivals. As well as letting the European side down with this hackneyed charade, we had unthinkingly mocked the poverty of the *betjak* men, although we had paid them well and held the friendliest feelings towards them. We were not the most sensitive of creatures; but most men, as anyone who has done military service knows, revert to boyhood in a closed situation—and grow nostalgic about it later. I still smile fondly when I look at that silly photograph: it shows me not just our lost charade, but Indonesia's double face: its enormous hopelessness, its queer jauntiness.

I carried Great Wally's secret throughout the year. To record that he had a private predilection for Indonesian boys doesn't seem

59

shocking now; and it's a reminder to me of how much the world has changed since that year.

Then, young men like Curtis and Hamilton, although they enjoyed the Beatles, wore their hair behind the ears. They were able serenely to expect the women they became involved with to admire as well as desire them. They rejected any suggestion that society should be changed by violence; and so they were less than sympathetic to Sukarno's 'continuing revolution'. Recalling these simple things, as I look at that dog-eared photograph, has made me realise that 1965 is receding not just into the past but into the era of a different world society. You can't draw a clean line in time, I know; but I tend to draw mine there, as Billy Kwan does in his files. For Curtis and Hamilton, in that year, Wally's secret obsession would have been more than disconcerting. They would have pretended tolerance, of course, but they would have been uneasy with him. And being a product of the old society himself, Wally knew this.

Respect for Wally was one of the constants of the unofficial 'Wayang Club': just as Wally was himself. How he got stories was something of a mystery, since he seldom seemed to stir from the Wayang's cool night, being found there at all hours, monumental on his stool. But his feature articles were syndicated in major British and American newspapers, and academics pillaged them for their books. Even Pete Curtis, caustic towards most of us, was deferential towards Wally. O'Sullivan, Pete had once pronounced, with youthful solemnity, was a journalist: the rest of us were just reporters.

The club never suspected him. He had few effeminacies of manner, and his rumbling bass voice assured us that he was a heterosexual in good standing. Eating was the one passion to which he confessed, and even this was not laughed at very often: his dignity forbade it. Despite his thirty-nine years, he would still have looked youthful had it not been for the famous fatness: thick, wavy brown hair sat close to his head like a cap, and his snub-nosed Irish face with its round hazel eyes was a boy's, above the moon-vast jowl.

'You *understand*, Cookie,' he said to me, in one of our late confessional sessions at the round bar. 'You're so marvellously tolerant, dear boy. But, you know, I'm living on the edge of a volcano. The Indos would love to get something on me—I irritate them so often with my articles. It's all so bloody cloak-and-dagger here. I wish I were based in Singapore again. Singers was marvellous. I could send out from my room for the most beautiful boys—they deliver them there like *hamburgers*, Cookie. Hm?' I laughed and he allowed himself to do the same, perched on his stool, his flesh shaking steadily, his lips rounded protestingly at his own outrageousness. Then he went on: 'But in this bloody place, I'm frightened every time I bring them to my room. You never know who's watching in the Hotel—and the Indo. newspapers are always running articles on the white men's vice den here. God, if only there *was* one.'

'You take them to your *room*?' I began to be seriously concerned. 'Wally, that's got to stop. You know the rooms are bugged. If they want an excuse to throw you out of the country you're giving it to them on a plate. You ought at least to take a bungalow.'

He nodded his jowl mournfully. 'I know, I know. But I get nervous in a bungalow, with the military paying calls to shake you down—and the servant problems are such a bore. I've got used to having boys in South-East Asia, Cookie. The funny thing is, I never allowed myself at home. I only half admitted it to myself. You come here, and they're available, and they're almost like a new sex—so smooth and brown; like plastic.' He pursed his lips and gave a single snort of laughter at his own vulgarity. 'Somehow, with another race it doesn't seem so wrong. I felt like André Gide discovering the beautiful Arab boys—you've read the journals? South-East Asia—the Australian queer's Middle East. Hm? Hm?'

We both laughed; but I was worried about him. I urged him to give the boys up, and he mournfully agreed to try; but within two weeks he announced that he had broken out again, and was jovially defiant and obscene in defending himself. I assumed that his affairs were with discreet young men whom he felt he could trust; I didn't imagine that he was interested in the banshees in the

Car Park, although I had seen him peer at them from the arcade. Once I came on him standing by the gates watching the boys who swam naked in the Welcome Monument's ornamental pool. They dived and wrestled in the monsoonal showers, gleaming like frogs, slim brown penises jigging; they troubled his dreams, I suppose, as the women by the canals troubled Condon's.

By contrast, Condon's problems were simple. His inspection of the 'boobs' in the shanty-town *kampongs* had great importance for him. Like many such men, he was in love with his own frustration, and visual images of the unattainable were, I guessed, at least as important to him as physical consummation. Condon was looking for a sexual Eden in Java which could not be entered for money. I often wished that the green bronze nymph at the edge of the Oasis pool would come to life for him. He was much too fastidious and appalled by VD to go, as Curtis did, to the cemetery in affluent Kebayoran, where the teeming prostitutes of the city patrolled the walls at night, waiting to be picked up in prowling cars. He was truly appalled by the uncomplicated Curtis, who went there regularly—and just as regularly to his Chinese doctor for shots. Condon was a humourless, finicky man, essentially conformist in every way; and his humility made him aware that his own earnestness was amusing to us: he would play up to our mockery, caricaturing himself.

The dog-like eyes, under bushy brows that met across the nose, would watch me pleadingly as he spoke in the hushed voice of one for whom sex must always be illicit. 'I got the most marvellous photograph today, Cookie—the boobs were *immense*.' He sighed, patting down his dry brown hair. 'But there are people everywhere, all the *time*: you can never get to know one of the women. Would you like to see it when I develop it?'

'Please, Condon, it's hard enough here without women: spare me the picture gallery. Why don't you take a trip to the cemetery and get it out of your system?'

'I've got no desire for a dose like that madman Curtis.' He looked virtuous.

Though Hamilton came to make a confidant of me, there were no sexual revelations. He apparently had no erotic problems, nor was he the type to have discussed them if he had. I did wonder at a man of his looks remaining unmarried at nearly thirty, and I wondered whether he was perhaps over-fastidious where women were concerned—perhaps nurturing some wound, or in-grown, sterilising fantasy.

There was no way of knowing, in the early stages of our acquaintance; he didn't treat me as a father confessor. But he was able to relax with me, and we began in February to share stories, filing simultaneously—a practice that could make life easier for colleagues who trusted each other. As a news-agency man, I was not in direct competition with Hamilton; and I had long ceased to be interested in competition, unless it was necessary. When I passed some of my stories on to him, and he found I had sources he could trust, he began to pay me in kind—a thing he did with no one else. He had to be careful with many of the other members of the press corps, such as Curtis. But I enjoyed watching his greyhound run towards the success he craved; and he came to see that I was not a threat to him.

We talked (when Billy Kwan was not with him) more and more easily, in late-night sessions in the Wayang Bar, or drinking whisky in his room—there so often being nothing else to do after curfew. Reticent with men around his own age, he was prepared to open up a little with me. There's nothing so intriguing as the confessions of the reticent, and he sometimes let things drop that revealed more than he intended—as he'd done when he told me about his swimming race with Colonel Henderson.

He had a deference for Henderson I found odd at a time when the Colonel's type was becoming a subject for satire in the minds of Hamilton's generation. We all met regularly at the Oasis pool; and I found the Colonel rather dislikeable, with his coldly good-humoured politeness: a politeness that distinctly told you he was dealing with lesser mortals. I see him as a recurring image in those Oasis afternoons, frozen for long moments on the top board, arms outstretched, preparing for a dive, taking obvious pleasure in the remarkable physique he'd retained into late middle age. He would dive for hours, absorbed in his fetish, while we watched him from the lawn, flabby and unfit, heads cloudy with Bacardi rum. He could do six laps of the pool, and I doubted if I could do two: no wonder he annoyed me.

Hamilton showed him a careful respect, and at that stage of the year he and the Colonel became quite friendly. It seemed unlikely that such a relationship would have sprung up anywhere else; and I sensed that it had some private significance for Hamilton: perhaps because of Henderson's resemblance to his father, who had disappeared in this part of the world for ever. There was, too, a practical side to their relationship: they were trading political information. They met to do so in the Hotel's small sixth-floor cocktail bar; and it was when I joined them there one evening that I glimpsed the sentiment behind Hamilton's attitude to Henderson. It emerged after the Colonel had created an unpleasant little scene.

We had finished our drinks, and Henderson ordered a fresh round from the big white-clad Indonesian bar steward. He was a steward whom we all liked: plump-jowled, always smiling, he did not have the sullenness towards us which many of the others had. When he set our drinks in front of us, the Colonel picked up his glass and frowned at it with acute distaste.

'What's *this*?' His voice, always resonant, had now an extra incisiveness.

'Gin-tonic, sir,' the steward said. 'You order gin-tonic.'

'Yes—I ordered gin-tonic. Did I order *ice*?' It was the tone of a headmaster about to administer a dressing-down.

The glass was indeed crammed with ice. 'Gin-tonic always have ice, sir,' the steward said, and attempted to smile.

The Colonel's voice now rose to an intimidating level. 'Gin-tonic does *not* always have ice,' he said. '*Americans* always have ice—and I am not an American.'

I was acutely embarrassed, and glanced at the half-dozen or so other occupants of the bar, all of whom had now stopped talking and were looking at us through the darkness: at least one of them, I felt sure, was American. The steward stood staring, his smooth face bewildered under its black *pitji*; and I wondered, since the intensified hate-campaign against *Nekolim* was now affecting

64

even the Hotel staff, whether he would rebel. But he picked the glass up quietly when Henderson pushed it at him.

'Get me another,' Henderson said. 'And next time, *ask* me if I want ice.'

I sought Hamilton's eye; I expected him to disapprove as I did. But he was looking into his drink, his expression carefully neutral.

The Colonel glanced at us briefly. 'Ice in everything,' he said. 'Barbaric habit. Well, we don't *all* have to drink like barbarians.'

When he had gone, I expressed my disapproval, and Hamilton looked at me for a moment without replying. Then he said, 'Yes, I know, Cookie, he's a real *pukka sahib*. Jesus, those eternal suede shoes, when he's off duty! But they were tougher than us, those people, weren't they?'

'You're joking, Ham, surely?'

'Wait till they quit Singapore, Cookie. It'll all fall down. The Yanks won't save it. The British Empire was better—we're not supposed to say it, but it was. There'll be more tyranny without it, not less. Sometimes I feel I was born too late.'

He raised his glass in comic toast, to tell me not to take him seriously, and gave a rueful smile. But he had half meant it. It was then I saw that in some secret corner of his mind he was fascinated by an imagined British past in which men like the Colonel walked as heroes. There was in Hamilton an old-fashioned quality entirely out of kilter with the impression he gave of being an ambitious and pragmatic loner. He had certain sentimentalities; an almost Edwardian strain of romanticism, as it turned out. I found this touching: the secret vulnerability of the invulnerable.

Sitting over our bottle of Scotch in his room in the Hotel, I saw this even in his few personal effects, and in the way he dealt with them. He claimed to prefer living in hotel rooms, and to have no time for the clutter of a personal life. But, as well as the line of books, I noticed a framed Japanese print; a beer stein; a pair of ancient-looking silver-backed hair-brushes: the sort of objects which follow a bachelor from city to city or country to country, giving the lie to his claims of non-attachment like a collection of old love-letters. And he would sometimes touch and straighten these things, revealing an obsessive tidiness.

65

Generally relaxed yet guarded, Hamilton had a closed quality, and it was when apertures appeared that I found him likeable. As you approached him in the Wayang, he had a trick of sitting still and forbiddingly expressionless, watching you; then, at the last moment, he would run his fingers through his lank, dark hair, and greet you, and all was well. He seemed to wait for something. I could see why he fascinated Billy Kwan, who constantly shadowed him, even when they were not working. A certain type of large, good-looking man walks a stage, followed always by eyes: admiring or wistful or resentful eyes, as the case may be. It makes him self-conscious, and it also puts a sort of aura around him, which promises that things will constantly happen. This was heightened in Hamilton's case by the enviable reputation he was making, and because he *was* always waiting for something to happen. A born journalist, he was made permanently restless by the feeling that some rousing event was always about to explode not far away: something he might miss. He would look at his watch suddenly, and say, 'Got to go'—and Kwan would ask, 'Want me to come, Ham?' When Hamilton did not, Billy's face would become perfectly blank.

But I came to believe it was more than some ultimate news-event Hamilton waited for. He was one of those people who are secretly waiting for something more: that vast and glorious happening, delicious as speed, bathing everything in gold, which perhaps never comes at all.

Hamilton showed me the note about Kumar, his Indonesian assistant, and asked me what I made of it. Neither of us could see any sense in the Indonesian security service's having delivered it: we concluded that it might have been an act of spite by some unknown Indonesian who was an enemy of Kumar's. If so, Hamilton said, it had misfired. Since the evening it had been pushed under his door, he had come to value his assistant highly. Kumar had extremely good contacts in the Army, in government circles—and especially in the PKI. He had already given Hamilton many early tip-offs of PKI moves which had resulted in successful stories. If he was connected with the Communists, Hamilton said, it made the situation delicate; but it also made Kumár more valuable.

I asked him, with some diffidence, if he thought Billy Kwan might have left the note.

'I thought of that,' he said. 'But the little bloke isn't malicious, Cookie. And he doesn't seem antagonistic to Kumar. It doesn't really make sense.'

I was quick to agree. I knew that Hamilton would not hear Billy criticised; and I suspected that Billy's multiplicity of interests somewhat awed him.

All doors were opened for Billy because of the many influential people he seemed to know. Although only a stringer cameraman, he was invited to most embassy receptions. He was safe from rejection and snubs, and he knew it. No one wanted to dismiss a dwarfish half-caste Chinese in our age of conformist tolerance, and he would force his way in, with his brash, frog-like smile, and then tell stories in the Wayang later of just how far he had tested that tolerance with his eccentricities. Radical academics, conservative diplomats and liberal journalists were particularly good targets; they had to suffer a rude frankness from Billy they would never have put up with from anyone else. At first delighted with this intellectually brilliant human symbol with whom they could prove their hearts were in the right place (one who was not only racially but physically underprivileged), they must then watch the symbol dissolving before their eyes to become a sharp-tongued. iconoclast. To conservatives, he exhibited a worrying radicalism; while his way of tormenting unctuous radicals was to strike the attitudes of a racist!

Few of the members of the Wayang denied that he was entertaining; yet few wanted to take him on for the whole course. One West German journalist ended by refusing to speak to him. Hamilton tolerated with good humour Kwan's posturings, his exaggerations, and the occasional insults with which he would flick friend and foe alike. That this erratic behaviour sprang from a certain anguish over his identity all his friends took for granted.

But who did Billy truly wish to be? Perhaps, with his archaic slang and Public School accent, his 'old ma-an' drawled in mockery (of himself or of us?) he played an upper-middle-class Australian or Englishman of the pre-war era. Yet sometimes he played a special role as an Asian: he was to go through Confucian Chinese and Japanese Zen phases. It was as though, since his race was double and his status ambiguous, he had decided to multiply the ambiguity indefinitely. In the Middle Ages he might have found his true function as a *vagans*, a wandering scholar.

Hamilton had also been telling me about the poem Billy had given him, and the odd advice he had found written on the back: *Stay away from the cemetery.* 'I assumed he'd been doodling,' Hamilton said, 'or that he'd written it there for some other reason —not as a message to me. But something the other night made me wonder. When Curtis asked me to come out to the cemetery with him and pick up a pro., Billy got rather heated. Did you notice that?'

I said I had, but thought it merely showed Billy as something of a Puritan.

'I'd rather you didn't mention this to anyone,' Hamilton said. 'Billy's a terrific little bloke, and a marvellous cameraman. He's a bit sharp-tongued sometimes, but I'm really very fond of him, and he's carrying a double load with the problem of his physical size and his hang-up about being half Chinese. If it weren't for him, I'd never have got started here.'

He was telling me about the Aidit story when Wally O'Sullivan loomed up beside us, wiping his jowl with a crumpled white handkerchief. He settled himself gratefully onto his stool and signalled for Ali. 'Where's Billy tonight?' he inquired.

'Gone to a film evening at the Russian Embassy,' Hamilton explained. 'He has some strange interests.'

'He does, indeed,' Wally said. 'They change too fast to keep up with. So he's into a Russian culture phase.' Then, as though he had overheard our discussion: 'I'd watch that little bloke, Guy. He's good value, I know, but he's excitable, don't you think? I sometimes wonder if he's just looking around for something to commit himself to, or whether he's already committed—apart from his devotion to you. Hm?' His hum signified that the matter was one of some seriousness. When Hamilton asked him what he meant, he said, 'Well, dear boy, since I've known him—from our fervent student days—he's been a Buddhist, a Methodist, and then he entered the Church of Rome. He hasn't been a Communist yet. But who knows?' Wally's throaty voice grew lower. 'Have you ever considered that he might be an agent?'

Hamilton threw back his head and laughed resonantly. 'Oh, Wally, come *on*! An agent for whom—or what?'

Wally waited for the laugh to end with his fat man's gravity, his purse-mouth set. 'I don't know,' he said. 'Take your pick: the Chinese; the Australian security people; maybe even the PKI. I just think you should be aware. He's oddly enthusiastic about Sukarno, isn't he, for so intelligent a man? And I'm not sure that he's entirely open with us, Ham. For instance, did you know he speaks Indonesian?'

'Bahasa? I'm sure he doesn't,' Hamilton said. 'He's told me he only knows a few words.'

'He speaks it fluently,' Wally said. 'I happened to be in a restaurant in town one night and saw him with a group of Indonesians; he didn't see me, and he was speaking Bahasa with them. He denies speaking Chinese, too—but I wonder about that. He's secretive. It may mean nothing, dear boy, but I think you should be careful.'

It was the Calling Hour, and Hamilton left us a few minutes later to interview some general who lived out in Kebayoran.

'Really, Wally,' I said, 'you've got no evidence for sowing those seeds of suspicion. What are you trying to do? Break up the team?'

'The poor little bugger's in love with Hamilton, of course,' Wally said, swallowing peanuts. 'Understandable—Ham's a devastating bloke. Those dark Scots looks—like the man in the whisky advertisements.' He sighed.

'What nonsense, Wally! Kwan's not queer—you see fellow-spirits everywhere.'

The round hazel eyes warned me in silence to guard his

confidence; it could not be referred to when anyone was within earshot, and the Wayang was filling up. Wally had certainly been rather malicious; but his barbs had been unwittingly well-timed: the next day, as it happened, would bring Hamilton his first glimpse of Kwan's secret life, and of its curious repository: the files.

6

Billy sat cross-legged on top of an empty desk, drinking coffee. Although he had no allotted place in the office, not being officially a member of staff, he had adopted this desk for sitting on, for his film-cans and shot-lists, and for the books he seemed constantly to be reading on politics and theology. This morning a paperback by Teilhard de Chardin lay beside him, which he had been urging on Hamilton. 'You make the best coffee in Jakarta, Tiger Lily,' Billy called.

Hamilton's secretary Rosini, a pleasant, spectacled Javanese girl who always wore national dress to dissociate herself ideologically from this *Nekolim* company she worked for, giggled at the name Billy had invented for her, and fluttered like a bird over her desk in her multi-coloured, ankle-length *kain* and tight, long-sleeved *kebaya*. She was fond of Billy, and devotedly served him coffee as soon as he appeared, which he did each day at eight o'clock.

'I say, Ham,' Kwan said loudly, 'what did you think of de Chardin's idea of the Noosphere?'

Hamilton sheepishly grinned, sipping the delicious black Javanese coffee to which he had become addicted. 'Afraid I didn't get through that book,' he said. 'Thanks for lending it; but it was too heavy for me, matey.'

'But what a marvellous idea that we've reached a new stage in evolution: that thought is a *force*. That's what the Noosphere is, old man.'

Hamilton laughed and raised one hand. 'Please, Billy, it's too early in the day.'

He enjoyed this early morning routine in his office under the creaking fan, with the sun streaming through the brown louvered doors that opened onto the little balcony. It was a time of calm, before he went out into the hectic political day. The barking and gongs of the Old City's street-vendors floated upwards, and the new yet dusty smells of the first heat mingled with the aroma of Tiger Lily's coffee. The old commercial building by the canal was one of a line of such houses with crusty, orange-tiled roofs, crouched humbly by the Soviet-modern clock-tower of *Antara*, the Indonesian government news-agency. A hundred yards eastwards was a less official world: the corner of Pasar Baru, the city's biggest bazaar. Hamilton knew that if he stood up he would see the early pedlars hurrying along Jalan Antara, or across the little bridge over the canal from Jalan Pos, with their portable kitchens balanced on carrying-poles, their baskets and bundles of brooms. He liked all this, and liked especially to see Billy Kwan in his place on top of the desk: a dwarf Buddha in a Hawaiian shirt. The simmering of his cameraman's ceaseless mental life amused him, even though he found many of Billy's preoccupations eccentric. Each had a sense of humour which interlocked well with the other's, and they played roles, caricaturing themselves: Hamilton a callous journalist, Kwan a sensitive intellectual.

But his conversation with Wally now came back to disturb Hamilton. He had come to take Kwan's devotion to his interests for granted, and disliked the idea that he was not what he seemed, or was in some way deceiving him. In the optimism of morning, looking at the broad, tan face with its frog-like smile, he told himself that, whatever else was ambiguous about Kwan, his loyalty was hard to doubt.

Kwan was now what he had promised to be: Hamilton's eyes. It gave Hamilton a unique advantage. When he had been in the office writing his radio pieces, he had been dogged at first by that highly developed fear of his that something cataclysmic was for ever happening somewhere else, around some corner. But his deal with Kwan had solved that problem. By giving the stringer a blank cheque to shoot what film he saw fit of rallies and riots, Hamilton had an agent who kept him in touch with whatever was happening. On his little green Vespa motor scooter, carrying his silent camera ('Old Bell and Howell'), Kwan toured the troubled Jakarta streets for his master, unobtrusive in a way that was impossible for a European. His devotion to Hamilton's interests was remarkable; without any formal contract, he now worked for no one else. And, although Hamilton did not know this, Kwan would refer to him in the Wayang as 'the best news-man in Jakarta'—lifting his chin at us with a hint of challenge.

Kumar got up from his desk by the door, where he had been working on his translations from the day's Indonesian newspapers, and moved quietly across the room to seat himself opposite Hamilton. Erect, formal and Westernised in his neatly pressed white shirt and grey slacks, he began their daily discussion of the pieces he had selected.

'The PKI ask for immediate takeover of American oil companies and all other foreign interests, boss,' he said. 'It seems likely that Subandrio agrees. I think that is the big one today.'

'You think they'll really go ahead?'

'Yes, I think,' Kumar said. 'Also my friend in the PKI has told me there will be a demonstration this morning at the US Embassy: much bigger than usual. They demand a complete break with America.'

His wide-set, slightly slanting eyes had a peculiar watchfulness, which sometimes made Hamilton uncomfortable. Kumar was twenty-six, and one of those handsome Indonesians who are a puzzling mixture of strains: his thick, dry hair, brushed straight back, his short nose and square jaw, made him seem more Caucasian than Asian: he always put Hamilton in mind of the hero of some American television series for children. There seemed to be an extra watchfulness in Kumar's face today, as though he were interested in Hamilton's reactions; and Hamilton wondered again how close Kumar really was to the PKI. To draw him, he said, 'So this is the beginning of the end.'

73

'The end? I don't understand, boss.' Kumar sat, as always, very still, hands loosely crossed on his knee. Hamilton had once asked him to use his first name, but Kumar never did, preferring 'boss': which was nicely balanced, Hamilton sometimes thought, between respect and sly joke.

'Well, if the PKI get what they want, this cuts the last tie, doesn't it?' Hamilton said. 'The Yanks won't take this. They've gone on pouring their aid in until now, but not any more: they'll cut if off. Then it's either ruin or total commitment to Peking.'

'Would that be bad?' Kumar asked softly.

'You tell me.'

Kumar hesitated. 'Maybe my countrymen need discipline,' he said. 'There has been too little of it, lately.'

Kwan spoke suddenly from his desk-top. 'Who knows,' he said, 'you might even get a Stalin—and he wiped out ten million people. *There's* discipline for you. Do you want to pay that price, to fill the bellies that are left?'

Kumar turned to him. 'Do not misunderstand me,' he said quickly. 'I am not making propaganda for PKI. But PKI is an Indonesian party, which asks for planning and hard work—and it is hard to understand why we must come under China's or Russia's rule through them.'

'Oh, yes?' Kwan said loudly. 'If the PKI aren't tied to Peking, sport, maybe you can explain that network of Chinese agents working for them to infiltrate Malaysia.'

'I know nothing about that,' Kumar said quickly. 'But there are many things I do not know—except that the Chinese are not popular in this country.' He stared at Billy with an expression which Hamilton could only call meditative. Perhaps he visited on Kwan a hint of the hostility he would not show to Hamilton: and Billy seemed to sense this.

'Don't get ready to chop *my* head off, old chap,' Billy said. 'I'm an Australian.'

Kumar grinned, and turned to Hamilton. 'This country is in a lot of trouble, boss; that is all I know.' It was an attempt to defuse the conversation, and to present himself again as an uncommitted but concerned young man.

Hamilton decided it was best to accept this. 'Let's get to work,' he said. 'I don't want *Konfrontasi* in here.'

In the lane below the office, standing by the car, Hamilton and Kwan went through one of their comic routines before setting out for the PKI demonstration.

'Is all the sound equipment in the boot?'

'Yes—and no one helped me to put it there.'

'What about old Bell and Howell? Is he loaded?'

'On the front seat, old man. Of course he's loaded.'

'Any hairs on the lens?'

'You worry about the words, Hamilton.'

They roared out of the lane in the office Ford, scattering chickens and children, and wove across the bridge to Jalan Pos, on the other side of the canal, Kumar sitting beside old Hartono the driver, Kwan and Hamilton in the back. A few minutes later they were skirting Merdeka Field, the great domain of ragged, sun-dried grass on the north side of which stood the Presidential palace, and from whose centre rose Sukarno's gold-tipped *tugu*. Here, in Jalan Merdeka Selatan, the Ford was halted by a human river. Carrying a log-jam of coloured banners, chanting, singing 'Crush Malaysia' songs, the river flowed under the banyan-trees towards the closed iron gates of the U.S. Embassy, where impassive Marines stood guard as usual.

At first, while Kwan filmed through the open window, all went well; although the crowd pointed with loud jeers at the ABS press sticker on the car's windshield, it pleased them to be filmed. Most of them were toughs from the People's Youth—the *Pemuda Rakjat*—the PKI's most effective weapon in creating public disturbances for world publicity purposes. Dressed in pseudo-uniforms made up of a junk-shop array of discarded Army fatigues, scraps of combat gear, berets and sun-glasses, some of them carrying automatic rifles and knives, they surged about the car.

'Take my picture, man!'

Grinning, they capered for the benefit of Billy Kwan's camera, holding their weapons and their banners aloft—rightly confident that he would put them on television screens around the world.

But at such affairs, for all the burning cars by the roadside, and the gutted, windowless buildings, there was no killing—not here, not yet. The ceremonies of *Konfrontasi*, in that year, were a dream of violence without violent fulfilment; and news-men and 'student' rioters—many of whom had never been students—would salute each other in cheery recognition: after all, we were engaged in a partnership to our mutual advantage.

The People's Youth had a habit of commandeering old trucks, and one of these, loaded with youths carrying weapons, was behind the car. Finding itself blocked, it bumped the back of the Ford, reversed, and bumped again. Hartono leant out of the window and shouted shrilly in Jakartanese. He pointed to his *pitji* cap, perhaps affirming his nationalism, and his wrinkled face was plainly frightened.

Hamilton called to Kwan and Kumar: 'I think we get out. Maybe we can talk sense into them—and if not, they're good for some shots. Bring the camera.'

'Better not, boss,' Kumar said; but Kwan had already gone, and Hamilton followed, to find his cameraman surrounded by a group of youths in black berets, one of whom carried a placard saying: HANG IMPERIALIST TRAITORS.

Kwan had lowered his camera, his tea-coloured face blank with inquiry. As Hamilton came up, a youth swinging a bush-knife called, 'Get away, man! It is the Chinese we want. He is a traitor. He is a running-dog.'

'Australian!' Hamilton shouted. 'He's Australian!' But this time the formula didn't work. There was jeering laughter, and one of the group, a moustached man with sun-glasses, grabbed at Kwan's hand-held camera. Billy clung grimly to the hand-grip, and the man grasped the collar of his Hawaiian shirt.

Hamilton was surprised at the strength of his own reaction. He was later to describe to me the extraordinary outrage he felt at seeing his small squire's multi-coloured shirt wrenched, the big, spiky black head on the compressed body duck down, the pale eyes widening, not with fear, but with surprise. He shouldered two youths aside and chopped once, with the side of his hand, on the fore-arm of Billy's attacker; it fell away, and he put his hand in the man's chest and sent him sprawling into the crowd, sun-glasses falling askew. He found it ridiculously easy; the slight Javanese bodies he was dealing with were dwarfed by his own. A clumsy, foolish Gulliver, he looked around for fresh attackers; and when the youth with the bush-knife slashed at the calf of his leg, he was barely conscious of the pain. He looked down in irritation at his rent slacks, and the blood beginning to stain them.

It was Kumar who saved Sir Guy and his cameraman from the retaliation which would certainly have followed. Getting in front of Hamilton, shouting in Bahasa, he gained attention, and spoke at some length, in a voice which was no longer quiet, but pitched for oratory.

Hamilton was struck by Kumar's tone of authority: eyes rested on his assistant with a sobriety which made it plain that revenge was being passed up.

His slacks rolled above the knee of his wounded left leg, which was propped on a pile of newspapers, Hamilton lay back in a white rattan chair. Billy knelt at his feet with a bowl of warm water and antiseptic, dabbing at the still-oozing cut in Hamilton's calf with a wad of cotton-wool. It was very quiet here, and Hamilton could hear all the sounds inside the midday hush outside: the occasional scream of a bird; Javanese pop music wailing from a distant radio. He looked down on the pincushion of straight Chinese hair; seen at close quarters, it made Billy suddenly more alien. Then Billy looked up.

'It's not terribly deep,' he said, 'but you know the danger with any wound in this climate.'

'It's nothing—just a cut. What I mind about is the slacks.'

'You think too much about clothes. You'll have to watch this leg. I've got some penicillin tablets here—I'll give you one when I've finished this dressing.'

'You're set up like a pharmacy,' Hamilton said. 'Just as well for me you're such an old hypo.'

He glanced about the room curiously; it was the first time he had been in Billy's bungalow, whose location until now Kwan had been deliberately vague about. 'This isn't as primitive as I imagined,' Hamilton said. 'Living close to the people, eh? You're feeling no pain, with this air-conditioning. Very nice.'

Kwan, applying a bandage to the wound, looked faintly embarrassed. 'Ah, yes, I had that unit installed myself,' he said. 'I keep a lot of film and equipment here, and it's kinder to it.'

'Kinder to you, too.'

'Yes, okay. No one ever had any decent, consecutive thoughts in that climate outside. But everything else here is pretty much your basic Indonesia—I don't have running water: just the old Dutch *mandi*, through that door there.' He stood up. 'That should do,' he said. 'There's an old *amah* up at the house who'll make tea for us. Have a rest, old man, while I go and organise it.'

Hamilton lay savouring the room's peaceful silence, which was broken only by a loudly ticking alarm-clock. He felt somewhat weak and dizzy, but pleasantly so. He looked about him curiously.

Kwan had brought the wounded Hamilton to a little street off Jalan Kebon Sirih, close by the Indian Embassy, in New Jakarta. He rented a garden house here: a bungalow in the grounds of a wealthy Indonesian businessman.

The garden was overgrown, and Billy's little tile-roofed house was almost entirely hidden from the businessman's villa by red-belled hibiscus bushes and a spreading banyan-tree, whose immense trunk was a jungle of entwined creepers. From a hook in the bungalow's eaves, by the door, hung a square bamboo cage in which squatted a large black bird with a yellow bill. As they had come through the door, it had startled Hamilton by croaking, 'Gooday, sport', in a ghostly Australian accent. 'That's Beo,' Billy had said. 'It took bloody ages to teach him to say that.' 'Beo', he explained, was short for *membeo*, the name by which these pet birds were known in West Java: roughly translated, it meant 'following what the boss says'.

This one room was almost all the garden house seemed to consist of. Hamilton opened a door at one end to find a gloomy, stone-paved bathroom with its Dutch *mandi* in one corner: the deep stone tub of colonial Java, where water for washing was stored, to be poured over the body with a ladle. The place was also set up as a dark-room, with trestle tables holding developing baths, an enlarger, lamps, and many bottles of chemicals. Adjoining it was an Indonesian lavatory, consisting of a hole in the floor with foot-rests, and a can of water. Except for his air-conditioner, then, it was true that Billy lived Indonesian.

Hamilton continued to limp about the main room. He recalled again our conversation with Wally the previous evening. Was Kwan an agent? He wondered if the room might provide a clue.

Some rooms tell little; but this one was a teeming box of clues. Billy went in for photography it seemed, and a bewildering array of photographs covered almost every inch of wall-space. There were other pictures, too: drawings and prints that looked extremely odd. A narrow divan was covered by a purple *batik* spread. There were two rattan chairs, and a cheap varnished wardrobe, on top of which stood a remarkable number of bottles of pills and medicines. This was all: the room would have appeared featureless and almost ascetic had it not been for the pictures and the home-made shelves crammed with books, which ran half-way along one wall. It was a scholar's library: ancient and modern history; politics, economics, theology. There were a number of books on China.

Hamilton began to examine things more closely, being careful not to touch anything. A small teak desk, overflowing with books and papers, stood next to a metal filing cabinet in one corner; on the desk stood a framed, close-up photograph of Jill Bryant. Dangling from the wall just above the desk, in a space where there were no pictures, were five ornate Javanese shadow-puppets of the type Hamilton had seen fixed across the lamps in the Wayang Bar. Near them was a plain crucifix.

He examined the smiling photograph of Jill Bryant for a moment; then he turned his attention more fully to the pictures on the walls. Most of the photographs were black and white, and had been taken about the streets of Jakarta; Hamilton was struck by their use of stark contrasts and the quality of the compositions. He had had many reports from ABS on the excellence of Kwan's film, which he had never seen, since it was processed in

Sydney. This was the first time he had seen Billy's still work. Hamilton guessed most of the pictures to have been taken in Glodok, the Chinese section of Old Jakarta. They made a mosaic of Jakarta's poverty: powerful close-ups of the faces of the *kampong* people.

What interested Hamilton most were certain drawings that appeared to have been photo-copied from books, and enlarged. They were all of dwarfs. All of these dwarfs were of the large-headed variety, with snub noses. One was a reproduction of the painting by Velazquez of the dwarf Sebastian de Morra; Kwan had lettered this name underneath. Another showed a quite handsome young dwarf in a fur hat, carrying a stick: his sensitive face looked out at Hamilton in wistful inquiry; underneath, Kwan had lettered in Indian ink: *Aragonese Dwarf—Vincente Lopez, 1825.* Close by was a drawing whose sub-title attributed it to Möller the Elder, showing two wise men with a dwarf jester between them. Below, Kwan had translated the legend in the picture. *The wise men say: 'The secret of wisdom is open to me.' But the dwarf says: 'I cannot compete with fools who are eaten up with wisdom.'*

Finally, there was a print, in lurid colours, of an Indian goddess, blue-fleshed, hair dishevelled, dancing on the pale, prostrate form of a man.

Hamilton decided it was time to stop being diverted by these pictures, and to make a more serious investigation. He hovered. Should he open one of the drawers of the desk? He found he could not; prying went against his nature, he said; and he couldn't quite believe Kwan was involved in anything that could create serious trouble. His attention was caught next by the metal filing-cabinet.

It was unlocked, and the top drawer was slightly open. Hamilton crossed to it and, without touching it, stared into the drawer. It was stuffed with files: cardboard folders edged with metal strips, hanging on a runner, each of them carrying a bright orange tag. And these identification tags, of which he could read the first three without touching the drawer, interested Hamilton considerably. They read: *Aidit. D. N. (PKI); Bandung; British Embassy Military Attaché (Henderson, Col. R. B.).*

Hamilton had begun to reach for the drawer, when he heard

footsteps outside the bungalow, and the loud, throat-clearing noise Kwan often made, followed by spitting.

Billy appeared carrying a silver tea-pot and two Chinese cups on a tray. 'Tea,' he said. 'Admiring my pictures?'

Hamilton limped back to his chair with a smile he hoped was not embarrassed. 'They're very good,' he said. 'You should exhibit.'

'I have, old man. Won the odd prize in Sydney.' He set the tray down on the desk, and glanced at the drawer of the filing cabinet; without looking at Hamilton, he pushed it to.

As they sipped their green tea, Billy said, 'My pictures are a vehicle for my ideas, of course. I'm only a visual man in a very one-sided way. My environment means very little to me—furnishings, clothes, the things blokes like you are concerned with —I just don't notice them.' He lay almost at full length in his chair, propping his floral Chinese cup on his chest, watching Hamilton over the rim.

'So that's why you wear those terrible shirts,' Hamilton said.

'Ah, come on,' Kwan said, 'they're not that bad.' They both laughed.

'Those pictures up there tell a story about the people here that *you* don't tell in your reports—that no one's telling,' Kwan said. 'Who really cares about those people—bathing in sewage, scrounging for rice and a few pieces of vegetables and meat, for one meal a day?' He pointed to a photograph of a young Indonesian with a moustache who faced the camera with a tentative smile. 'He's a friend of mine; a government clerk. Lives down the road here,' Billy said. 'He's a good Muslim, that little bloke—he believes that without God men get crazy with pride, and go bad. He's quiet. He doesn't want to confront anyone. Most Indos are quiet people—they hate loud, aggressive bastards. They call them *kasar*—coarse. That's why we Westerners put them off, with our back-slapping. We're *kasar*.'

So Billy was in his Western aspect today, Hamilton noted.

Kwan pointed again. 'Did you see my *wayang* puppets? Beauties, aren't they? If you want to understand Java, Ham, you'll have to understand the *wayang*. Look at Bima, here—he's a bit crude and *kasar*, although he's a goodie. See the round, staring

81

eyes? Like a Westerner. But the more aristocratic heroes, like his brother Prince Arjuna—they're *alus* types. That means refined; courteous: the Javanese *priyayi* class. They look at the ground, because it's *kasar* to stare into people's faces. And they have almond eyes, see?'

Fixing Hamilton with his green, almond eyes, Billy had jumped up excitedly. He now began pointing to the *wayang* figures one by one. 'Here's King Kresna—Kresna the Black: he's obviously Krishna, who's one of the incarnations of the Hindu god Vishnu. Vishnu comes to earth as many things: as Krishna, who acts as charioteer to the hero Arjuna—and also as a dwarf, in Hindu myth.' He looked arch, as though he had passed on some titillating gossip, and then turned back to the puppets. 'Arjuna's a warrior; but he causes a turmoil in nature just by meditation: by building up his spirit-power—his *sakti*. But to build up that power, he first has to battle against his own weaknesses. Have you read the *Bhagavad Gita*? No? In the *Gita*, Krishna tells Arjuna how to master himself before he can master others. Nothing's black and white, you see. Arjuna's a hero, but he can also be fickle and selfish—that's his weakness. And when Arjuna asks Krishna what makes a man sin, Krishna says, "Greedy lust and anger: this is the enemy of the soul. All is clouded by desire, Arjuna: as fire by smoke, as a mirror by dust." Rather good, don't you think?' His 'light' tone had crept in. He turned to a female puppet. 'And this is Srikandi—the princess Arjuna's in love with.'

Hamilton stared blankly at the two-dimensional leather puppets. They evoked no response in him, neither pleasure nor dislike; they were too alien, and scarcely human. With their black and gold faces, elongated limbs and grotesquely long noses, they resembled insects rather than men. India's gods and heroes, so far south, had metamorphosed into weird cartoons.

He pointed idly to the bottom-most puppet, which Billy had not discussed, and whose unusual grotesqueness attracted his attention: a fat, hunch-backed, bald old man, whose pug face was painted gold. 'What about that one?' he asked. 'Is he *kasar* or *alus*?'

'Ah, now, he's special,' Billy said quickly. 'That's Semar. He's a dwarf who serves Arjuna. But he's also a god in disguise—the old Javanese god Ismaja.' He fingered the bald, gilded head. 'My patron,' he said lightly. 'The patron of all dwarfs.'

Hamilton grew embarrassed. The subject of dwarfism had not come up between them before; and he had long ago chosen to regard Billy's disability as minimal. 'Come on, don't talk like that, matey. You're no dwarf,' he said.

Kwan stared at him in silence for a moment. 'I get a quaint view of people from this height,' he said. 'You know, Ham, that's what I like about you—you really don't *care*, do you? Or maybe you just don't see. But you're honest. A true Capricornian. That's why we get on together; I'm Gemini—the same sign as Sukarno. He and I have two faces—the hard and the sentimental.'

'Lord, don't tell me you believe in astrology.'

Billy ignored this. 'You and I make a good team because we complement each other,' he said. 'I say—have you realised we even *look* alike?'

With all the goodwill in the world (as he put it to me later), Hamilton was not sure that he wanted to look like Billy Kwan. His face must have shown some hint of this, because Kwan smiled broadly. 'It's true, old man,' he said. 'It's been noticed.' (He didn't say by whom: and when Hamilton told me of this conversation, I was puzzled; the remote and absurd similarity between them was a fancy I thought only I had entertained.) Now Kwan repeated the remark he had made on the evening when they first met. 'You're a hybrid, old man, and so am I. It shows in our physical appearance. Scots ancestry makes you a mixture of Anglo-Saxon and Celt. I'm a mixture of Anglo-Saxon and Chinese. But I think it runs a little deeper than that. I'm unable to be Australian because of my Chineseness. You're unable to be Australian because of your Englishness. Or is it the other way round?' He smiled with what looked to Hamilton like sudden spitefulness.

Hamilton found it difficult to conceal the quick irritation he felt. He disliked this probing, and told himself that Kwan was growing altogether too personal—and perhaps taking advantage of today's adventure. 'Look,' he said, with an attempt at good humour, 'I don't think you have it clear. I *am* English—there's no confusion about it. I'm sorry—I'd like to share your problem, but I don't.'

Billy now wore that expression the other found most Chinese in him. Whether he was offended or not was impossible to tell, and Hamilton was suddenly ashamed of his rejection of Billy's attempt to link them. The silent little room seemed to demand intimacies, and he said, 'There's something I can never quite understand. Granted it can't always have been easy being an Australian-Chinese—but why do you reject your Chinese side? A great people—a great culture: why turn your back on it?' Having said this, he half regretted it, feeling he had broken some rule in the game Billy played. Allusions to his Chinese origins were permitted, but not a frontal assault on the subject.

Kwan wriggled his shoulders and avoided Hamilton's eyes. When he spoke, it was in the unnaturally flat, hectoring voice he used for bar-room arguments. 'Ah, *look*, old man, you're being a bit superficial, aren't you? Only my father speaks Chinese, and he came out to Australia as a boy. I don't speak it at all. How do I manage to belong to a culture I never grew up in?'

Hamilton was surprised and stung by the note of scorn in Kwan's voice. He was not the most sensitive of men, but he felt almost humiliated at having his sympathy rejected. Yet he was aware that this sympathy was complacent and sentimental, and that his annoyance sprang partly from having been found out. These were novel feelings for him, and he said abruptly, 'Sorry if I annoyed you—I meant well.'

Kwan softened, his face and voice becoming a shade less hard. 'Yes, I realise that, old man; but I don't think you understand. My heritage isn't China—my heritage is Europe, just as yours is. Tell me, what books did you read, Ham, when you were twelve years old? Sherlock Holmes? The Saint? The William books?'

'All of those. Used to love them. Why?'

'So did I. Do you see? I used to want to be William. I suppose you did too. But I couldn't be—my face wouldn't let me. Sooner or later, you see, at a party or in a bar, there's a character who's always waiting for me. He says, "Kwan: now what sort of a name's that?"' He was imitating a crass Australian. '"Half

Chinese aren't you?" he says. I can never get rid of that bastard.'
He was speaking as quickly as usual, in the flat, almost flippant
voice which made its wounded or wounding remarks, and then
hurried on as though nothing had happened. 'It's rather a bore to
be *half* something, you see, old man. There's no great problem
belonging to any *one* race—but a man needs to be able to choose.
Well, I chose. William was part of *my* family past, like
Christianity, and the Renaissance, and Parliamentary de-
mocracy.' He crossed to the window by the bookshelves, where he
stood with his back to Hamilton, hands in pockets, looking
through the glass at the green of the garden, which throbbed
under the other climate outside. The *membeo* screeched once.

When Billy spoke again, his voice was if anything more flat
than before. 'It wasn't an Asian heritage, but it was mine,' he said.
'Except that they wouldn't let it be. They wouldn't bloody let it
be.'

Hamilton was now touched by feelings quite new to him, by
something more than sentimental concern. He stood up and
limped over to drop one hand lightly on Billy's shoulder. He was
searching for words to tell Kwan that he had understood him. But
the other moved instantly aside, so that Hamilton's hand fell
away from the green-and-yellow material of the Hawaiian shirt.
Kwan's face in profile was unmarked by any anguish; it was as
dry-eyed and smoothly blank as ever, and Hamilton saw that
Billy would never be able to show the emotion he half wished him
to show; saw also that he had touched a being to whom he could
not get closer. He shrugged inwardly, and accepted this revelation
of his own mental limits.

Billy turned now and made a breathy noise, imitating a
Japanese karate fighter. 'Hoh!' It was both a nervous tic and an
expression of fooling which, Hamilton had learnt, signalled the
end of a mood.

'You'd better get going soon, if you're going to take that two
o'clock circuit,' Kwan said. 'How's the leg?'

When Hamilton assured him it was better, and stood up to go,
Billy made an unexpected, cheery swoop back on the subject
Hamilton had thought dismissed. 'I was happier when I lived in

England,' he said. 'In England they accept you for what you are. Jill Bryant accepts me for what I am—that's why I'm so fond of her, the little Jillie.' As he made this last statement his voice took on an exaggerated, sentimental tone. Standing by the door, about to show Hamilton out, he said, 'How did you like my little Jillie, old man? I've never really asked you.'

'She seems a nice little thing. Very pretty. I envy you.'

'No need to envy me, old man. She's refused to marry me.'

Hamilton was at pains to keep his face neutral. 'I'm sorry to hear that.'

'Yes, it's happened since I last spoke to you,' Kwan said. Holding the door-knob, wearing his broadest smile, he blinked rapidly. 'But I haven't entirely given up hope,' he said. 'She's promised to think about it—and she could change her mind. She and Colonel Henderson are very close, you know. He's a widower —he's pretty sentimental about her, and Jillie's fond of him. I like the Colonel, but he's much too old for her. If she's going to marry unsuitably, I think I'd be a better choice.'

'You mean they're having an affair?'

Kwan's cheek twitched once. 'No, I wouldn't go that far. Jillie did have an affair here last year with another diplomatic type—a young French ponce with a pretty face. It ended badly, and she doesn't want any more affairs—she feels better on a friendship basis with me and the Colonel. Well, you'd better get to your two o'clock circuit.'

He opened the door, and Hamilton limped out gratefully into the heat. He had had enough of revelations, and his leg hurt. As he started up the narrow path between the long grass and hibiscus bushes, Kwan called after him, 'Ham, are you going to that house-warming Wally O'Sullivan's holding on Saturday night? Yes? Jillie will be there—I hope you'll talk to her.' In his most casual, businesslike voice, he said quickly, 'You're the best friend I have—so I want you two to know each other better. And I thought perhaps you might talk to her on my behalf. About the possibility of marriage, I mean.'

Hamilton stood still. Kwan, he saw, for all his dwarfishness, had qualities a woman might find interesting; but he caught

86

himself regretting the possibility of such a union—for the girl's sake, he said, and then felt ashamed: he had found her very attractive himself. Aloud, he said, 'Speak for you? Jesus, matey, that's a bit old-fashioned isn't it?'

'I am old-fashioned. You see, Ham, if she does decide to accept me after all, I don't want it to be for the wrong reasons.' And with a disconcerting flash of vanity, he said, 'Actually, Jill's pretty devoted to me—I just want her to make sure, if she does take me on, that she's taking on a real person, and not her image of him. Of course, she may not accept me at all—but you could sound her out. She's very interested in you—wants to know you better. She asks after you, and listens to your broadcasts, and so on. I'm sure she'd take notice of you, old man.' His voice remained at its most rapidly casual as it dropped these extraordinary directions.

When Hamilton murmured in some embarrassment that he would carry them out if the chance arose, Kwan nodded quickly with satisfaction, waved once, and disappeared inside the bungalow, slamming the door. The *membeo* hopped about in its cramped cage, fiercely seeking an exit.

7

We are all in Billy Kwan's files: Hamilton, Jill, Great Wally, President Sukarno, myself—together with earlier acquaintances of Kwan's whom none of us knew. His little tower of dossiers and notebooks—giving off already the tragic perfume of age—rises in front of me now in the light from my kerosene pressure-lamp.

My cousin's hilltop farm here was long ago connected with electric power, and the lamp is a relic: but when I told Jim I preferred its softer glow, he dug it up for my work-table. Its flicker and smell bring back the farm when we were boys; they also bring back the kampongs of Java. I come south almost every year, from one or other of the cities of Asia, to spend my bachelor's leave on this hill with Jim and his family. The cool, dry spaces of south-eastern Australia are sanity; they are home; and I tell myself each time that I won't go back. But I always do.

This time at the farm, I've finally decided to work on Kwan's papers. Over the decade that has gone since the last year of *Konfrontasi*, I've often considered editing them for publication; they seemed remarkable enough to demand it. But I found them too disjointed to stand alone, and I've begun instead, with their help, to tell Billy's story myself—a story which has turned out to be Hamilton's as well.

There are gale warnings on the radio tonight; a strong wind is racing through the pines and eucalypts above the top paddock. The lamp hisses like thought; I adjust its position. Billy, Billy: what passion and industry went into these presumptuous dossiers! Sorting through them, I whisper the invocation of the Javanese *dalang*, the master of the shadow-show: '*May silence prevail: may the strength of wind and storm be mine.*'

How we all came to the café with the Mickey Mouse murals I no longer remember clearly. We had been to a cocktail party given by the West German Embassy, and after the affair expired we had climbed into our cars, full of the earnest desire to continue drinking which a cocktail party always creates, and had gone into the centre of Jakarta looking for a restaurant where we could buy beer.

We had with us a sharp-faced London journalist called Harold Sloane, whose paper had just sent him here; he was one of the last English news-men to get a visa before the ban on British and Americans came down entirely. He was young, nondescript, full of brandy and the elation of being back in Asia, and kept shouting, 'Take me to a colourful Jakarta café—not one of your dreary bars, something filthy and *colourful*, damn you!'—a phrase we all took up as a chant, using Hindu accents: 'Yes, yes, filthy and colourful.' It was that sort of evening, and that sort of silly drunkenness. Sloane was a friend of Pete Curtis's; the two had been based in Hong Kong together at one stage, and reunion made them particularly loud and schoolboyish.

There is a blurred period, after which I find us all in the café with Mickey Mouse murals. It must have been in Glodok, the Chinese quarter in the Old City, north of Merdeka Square. Here, among the mazes of low, gabled buildings reflected in the canals, we ate to oblige Sloane, and drank warm Indonesian Bintang beer. Hamilton and Kwan were with us, and Wally O'Sullivan. The food was suitably bad—the inevitable dried shrimp crisps and vegetables swam in peanut butter sauce—and I ate with the resigned certainty that I would go home to a bout of 'the dreaded Jakarta trots', as Wally called them. The heat was intense under the asthmatic ceiling fans, and the flies clustered around the rims of our beer glasses. It was all very well for Sloane, who was just passing through; but I had lasted eighteen months here by avoiding cafés like this.

It was a cave-like, dimly lit, open-fronted place, set right on the street, almost empty, with bare wooden tables and iron chairs. I doubted whether Europeans had eaten here since the Dutch days; but it must have once been Dutch-owned; only this, we decided, could explain the archaic Mickey Mouse murals, painted in black and white on the dim walls. There was such noisy amusement about them; and, being something of a comic-strip buff, I pointed out that on the evidence of their style they had certainly been there since the twenties. 'You will note, gentlemen, that Mickey is in his very primitive period here—he is little more than a hieroglyph. Note the early gloves and trousers, the fixed eyes. He is also accompanied by the now-defunct Horace Horsecollar and Clarabella Cow. . . .'

Wally O'Sullivan, who would eat anything, gulped down the last vestiges of his curry, sat back, and belched. In a soft, almost expiring voice, he said, 'Sloane, dear boy, you'll of course come to my bungalow-warming tomorrow night? Hm? I've taken a bungalow—I may live to regret it, but I've taken a bungalow.'

We toasted Wally's new bungalow with our fly-patrolled glasses. Pete Curtis turned to Billy Kwan and said suddenly, 'Are you bringing Jillie Bryant, Billy?'

'Yes, old chap, she's agreed to come.'

Addressing himself to Sloane, Curtis said, 'While the rest of us are all sex-starved, Harold, this little guy is squiring the most beautiful chick in town.' He shook his head and I perceived suddenly that he yearned after Jill; and at this stage of his drinking his yearning was in conflict with his usual loyal enthusiasm for Kwan. Billy blinked rapidly and went on eating without answering.

'And here's his buddy,' Curtis went on, waving at Hamilton, 'always dressed to kill, and not a doll to be had. It's unjust. It don't seem right.'

'Belt up, Curtis,' Hamilton said.

'Won't even come to the cemetery,' Curtis went on. 'Goddam it, Hamilton, I'm *concerned* for you—it'll wither away, if you don't give it exercise.'

The evening flowed on—carried for me on a rising tide of

biliousness. Spectators on the footpath outside—Chinese children, Indonesian youths with nowhere to go—stood and watched the drunken white men eating and drinking on their iron chairs. Then the beggars began to creep in.

First came a man with no legs, who propelled himself across the floor to us with wooden blocks tied to his hands, blocks which hissed and shuffled slyly on the tiles at our feet, as we fumbled for our money. Next came a woman dressed in a hood-like head-scarf and a crazy assortment of coloured rags and tatters, who carried what appeared to be a baby wrapped in a filthy shawl. It was an old trick; there was nothing inside the shawl but rags, and we all knew it. But as she whined and gestured at the bundle and then at one limp, exposed brown breast with its fantastically elongated nipple we all gave her money anyway, in a hiatus of painful quiet: all of us, that is, except Kwan, who waved her away with a frozen stare.

It was a little after this that I noticed Curtis and Sloane whispering together. When they disappeared from the café, I was talking to Wally, and was too drunk to wonder seriously what they were doing or whether they would be back. But a few moments later they reappeared, surging in off the street with fixed grins and a startling companion.

He was a hunch-backed Indonesian dwarf: a genuine midget, with close-cropped hair like a black cat's fur, and wide-set, clever dark eyes. He had a tin cup around his neck for money, and was dressed in a brown shirt and a sarong, from beneath which peeped his fantastically abbreviated brown legs and stubby bare feet. He could not have been more than three feet high: his extended arms were like flippers—ending, I noticed, in tiny infant hands whose fingers were strangely splayed. Compared to him, Billy Kwan (at whom I dared not look), was a normal man.

'Hamilton!' Curtis called. 'We've brought you a present!'

The midget rocked instantly up to Hamilton's chair and smiled broadly and trustingly at him, like a dog attending his master. Behind, Curtis and Sloane staggered clutching each other, red-faced, while the café's lean proprietor watched uneasily from his cash-desk in the shadows.

'He's *yours*, me boy,' Sloane said. 'Ask him to dance.'

'What?' Hamilton said. Big and stupefied, upright in his chair, his black-haired arms folded on the table, he stared at the dwarf. Kwan, beside him, sat with an absolutely blank face. But Wally O'Sullivan's shoulders and belly had begun to shake, although his mouth remained dubiously pursed. Sloane, wheezing with laughter, his sharp-nosed, anonymous face seeming to me now to have a malicious slyness, gathered enough breath to repeat, 'Ask him to dance. He'll do anything for you.'

'He's our present, Ham,' Curtis explained. 'Don't you like him?' And he bent and spoke in Bahasa in the dwarf's ear.

The dwarf smiled and nodded, and began instantly to dance on his little legs, breaking at the same time into a droning song. Great Wally released deep chuckles which had in them a protesting, appalled sound, as though he were being forcibly tickled. 'Oh, really,' he said. 'Really.' I believe I laughed too, although the memory of Billy Kwan's face makes me ashamed to confess it: he watched with no expression I could read; but this in itself, as the laughter from the others became wilder, was ominous enough.

The dwarf ended his dance, and stood panting. In the little silence, Hamilton looked up at Curtis and Sloane. 'What the hell are you bastards playing at?'

'He's *your dwarf*, Hamilton,' Sloane said. 'Don't you see? We've bought him for you. He's yours for ever—he understands that, and he's happy about it. Where you go, *he* goes.'

With a loud screech of his iron chair on the tiles, Hamilton stood up, towering and swaying, his smile crooked. He seemed to be distressed: 'For God's sake,' he said. 'You bloody idiots. This isn't very funny.' He glanced at Kwan, who still said nothing.

'Hey, don't *go*, Ham,' Curtis said. 'He'll only go with you. You can't give him *back*, buddy.'

The dwarf looked up with sprightly interest at the three swaying men above him, as though trying to comprehend his fate.

Curtis had now noticed Kwan's withdrawal, and called, 'Hey, Billy, what do you think of him? Isn't he terrific?' In his freckled face, I seemed to detect some sort of doubt. He wanted perhaps to be reassured; but Kwan did not answer.

And Hamilton, I saw, was in a cleft stick. If he did not show amusement, he was a poor sport; but if he did, he encouraged the joke on Kwan—if this was what it was. His solution was retreat.

'You'll have to play your games without me,' he said. 'I've got a heavy day. Are you coming, Billy?' When Kwan shook his head, Hamilton moved quickly across to the cash-desk, threw down a handful of rupiahs in front of the proprietor, and made for the door. Even allowing for his natural embarrassment, I was struck by the ill-concealed urgency of his movements. Beneath his discomfiture, I saw, there was a more profound alarm: it was as though Sloane and Curtis had tapped some childish fear, and Hamilton believed that the joke would come true, that he would be saddled with the Indonesian dwarf for ever.

As he stepped into the street, they set up a cry and followed, the dwarf rocking busily after them. They reeled on the footpath outside, with the little man between them, and I heard Sloane call after Hamilton, 'Wait! he's all paid for, Ham—we won't let you *discard* him like this.' Their laughter rose and receded.

Wally got painfully to his feet, giving small grunts of laughter, and looking at Kwan and me inquiringly. 'Better be off,' he said. 'See those silly buggers don't do anything worse. Hm?'

Kwan now spoke for the first time. 'I'll stay here,' he said.

'I'll stay, too,' I said. 'I've had enough boarding-school jokes for one night.'

I stayed with Kwan because I felt for him. There was little doubt in my mind that the joke had been aimed mainly at Hamilton; but that Curtis had been prepared to risk humiliating Billy shocked me. Probably Curtis and Sloane wouldn't have carried the thing through had they been sober; but I saw by Kwan's blank face that the damage was done. Perhaps my sympathy wasn't entirely disinterested: I wanted to know him better, and I saw this as an opportunity. My curiosity had been whetted by Hamilton's mentioning the files in Billy's bungalow.

I ordered coffee, and we sat sipping for some time without speaking. Billy's liveliness had vanished. He coughed, and said suddenly, 'Clever of them to find an achondroplastic.' When I looked puzzled, he said, 'The dwarf. He was an achondroplastic.'

I decided that the subject was better explored than avoided. 'You mean there's more than one sort of dwarf?'

'A number,' he said coldly. 'But there are two major categories which most people get confused: achondroplastics and ateliotics. An ateliotic is your true midget—a perfectly formed miniature. He's the one you see in side-shows. Unfortunately he's usually rather sickly, and not very bright. But the achondroplastic is a normal man whose arms and legs are stunted. So he's in something of a predicament.' He shot a glance at me. 'A normal man, of normal intelligence, capable of having normal children, but whose body is a joke.' He smiled blandly, lifting his head. 'You probably thought that one's head was rather large.'

I agreed that I had.

'If you'd looked again,' Kwan said, 'you'd have found it was of normal size—it just looked big in relation to the arms and legs. I've made something of a study of achondroplastics, Cookie, since I'm one myself.'

I began half-heartedly to protest, but he held up an irritable hand. 'Let's skip the bullshit, Cookie. I know what you're going to say—that I'm much bigger than he is, that I look more normal. Well the lower limit of normal height in a man is placed at four feet eleven. I'm four feet six. Okay? But there are lots of variations —from the extreme type to people like me—who've just missed normality.' He laughed, on a single note: it was more a bark. 'There are some achondroplastics on the border-line passing as normal people,' he said, 'like part-negroes passing for white. And we all share the achondroplastic features to some extent: the pug nose, the shortened legs and arms. But some of the other features I've been lucky enough to miss: the sticking-out bum, the dwarf hands with splayed fingers: what's known as the *main-en-trident.*' His voice grew brutal. 'But I'm still a member of the great race of dwarf fools.'

'You're being a bit hard on yourself, aren't you, Billy?'

'I'm using the word in the medieval sense: surely you realise nearly all the great jesters at the courts of the Middle Ages were achondroplastics? We have a long history. Kings were especially

94

fond of us: they liked to have their dwarf fools around; and we were the only ones allowed to tell them the truth. Women liked us. Some of the ladies at Renaissance courts were quite indecent with us.' He chuckled. 'There's one great advantage in being a wise dwarf, you see—you can be wiser than other people, but no one will envy you.'

Although I was distressed by the cheerful self-torment of his 'us', I no longer attempted to dissuade him from claiming membership of this dwarf race. I was frankly fascinated. I understood now that the pictures in the bungalow which Hamilton had described to me had not merely been put up in some sort of self-mockery. This talk of ours made me more capable of appreciating, when I came to read it, Kwan's massive file on dwarfs, and his many references to the achondroplastic 'race', as he called it, in other files and journal entries.

When I asked him about the causes of the condition, he said sardonically, 'Ah, yes—well. Western medical science is delightfully vague. For some reason it can't explain, the long bones of the limbs in achondroplastics are stunted in the womb. The condition tends to run in families, with two short parents producing an achondroplastic. But I believe an older theory, Cookie—that there was once a dwarf race, to which we're throwbacks. You can still see vestiges of it in Europe, running in a belt from Bavaria to Wales and Ireland. Muscular little men who mined precious metals—you remember your fairy tales? The Celts said we lived underground. Brownies—little people—who were there before the Celts and Saxons came, and who put the dark strain in the Celts. They're my true ancestors, Cookie. I didn't get my dwarfism from my Chinese father—I pretty certainly inherited it from my Irish-descended mother. She's just five feet; and I take after her. But Attila the Hun was achondroplastic. So the Mongols had a dwarf sub-race too.' Billy began to use a toothpick, and fell silent.

'I'm pretty disgusted with Curtis and Sloane,' I said. 'That wasn't funny.' I sounded prim, but it was the best I could do.

Kwan moved impatiently, pushing his cup aside, and his flat voice was harsh. 'Ah, don't worry about it, old man. The dwarf would be used to it. That's why dwarfs play the fool—they must. He took their money and played their game—he knew exactly what he was doing. But I'm afraid I didn't find it funny either; nothing about the poor in Jakarta is funny.'

'You're very concerned about them, aren't you?' I said.

'I'm concerned about them, yes,' Kwan said. 'As a Christian, I have to be concerned about them—they're my brothers.' It was the sort of thing he seemed able to say without self-consciousness; and he glanced at me, as he often did in such conversations, to check my reaction. Polishing my glasses to avoid looking at him, I said, 'We belong to the same faith, I believe.'

'You're a Catholic, Cookie?' He was interested.

'Not a very good one, I'm afraid. But you stay a Catholic even if you sometimes wonder if God's there—it's a cast of mind, don't you think?'

'I wouldn't know, old man—I'm a convert. The Jesuits didn't have *me* as a child. But I don't think the Faith is much good unless it's passionate. Lately I have a feeling the Church has spent its passion. If it has, it's no place for me. There's something rather fine about Islam, don't you think? The passion's still there. I'm attracted to it.'

I began to see what Wally O'Sullivan had meant about Kwan's bewildering changes of allegiance: they happened as you watched.

'Religion's no good without passion,' he said. 'That's why I left the Methodists. Yeah, I even tried *them* at one stage.' He laughed for the first time that evening. 'The Methos in Sydney used to invite me to little suburban gatherings to show how broadminded they were with their tame Chinese—but then they'd get uncomfortable. They only like multi-racialism in theory, poor darlings.'

I smiled, picturing the discomfort Billy would have created.

'The Catholic Church is the only Western institution that doesn't get uncomfortable with anybody,' he said. 'It inherited that talent from Imperial Rome. But it's possible I may leave Rome for Islam all the same—that's even purer. No priest caste. Equality for all believers under God. And they have *force*. That's what the Communists in this country underestimate—the fury of the Muslims at being told there's no God.'

We talked for some time about religion, and I asked him if he was certain of the existence of the supernatural.

'Absolutely, old man,' he said. 'The unseen is all around us— particularly here in Java. There are a lot of spirits about—the Indos believe they're everywhere.' He shot a quick glance at me. 'There's one near my bungalow,' he said. 'I hear it moving about in the garden. It came in one night, and knocked some bottles of developer off the shelf.'

'Really? Was it a good spirit or a bad?'

'Mischievous. Just about all spirits are bad. Where animistic religion is still strong, you're obviously going to have a lot of them hanging about. Demons can't come without invitation, can they? It's the same in India, I noticed—Hinduism encourages them.'

'I suppose you're thinking of the Left Hand Way.'

'That's right,' he said flatly, as though we were discussing business. 'The worship of the Mother—that brings them out. Here, she's called Dewi Sri—the Goddess of Rice.' He yawned. 'But one's not so conscious of anything intensely, here. Do you know why? Spiritually, this place is still a colony—not of Holland; of Hindustan. It's the óld Hindu kingdoms that are most real here. And it's like all colonies—like Australia: because Java's one remove from the cultural source, there's a slackening— something missing. Even the air goes slack. A country of second-hand.'

I was struck by this. Like everything he said, it was exaggerated, but there was a core of truth. Java seemed always to promise some weird revelation; but it was never quite seen. It was round a corner; in the next kampong; out in Central Java, perhaps; but never found. And the Hindu and Muslim cultures here seemed superimposed: even the mosques were like flats on a stage; it was all two-dimensional. Underneath, something much older grunted or moaned: a thing that lived in thickets or in drains; something like the spirit that lurked near Billy's bungalow.

At this point, I thought I saw my opportunity to probe his allegiances. 'It's interesting to hear that you're not a materialist. I'd rather thought you were a Marxist,' I said. 'Some of the news blokes have the impression you're sympathetic to the PKI.' Having so crudely played this card, I watched him carefully.

He blinked once, shot a glance at me, and betrayed no particular emotion. But he answered loudly. 'Do they? Do they? Yes, some of them would. I won't ask you to name names. They'd think so because I take the plight of the people here seriously, and because I support Sukarno. Well, when I see these people living like stray dogs I get angry. I think a Christian should get angry. I'm a Christian radical, if you like. I don't expect those yobs to understand that—but I think *you* will, Cookie.' His voice had a deceptive casualness as he threw out this compliment. 'As to Sukarno,' he said, 'I just don't believe he's a stooge for the PKI. He has to co-operate with them, just as he does with the Muslims —he has no choice. But he'll make stooges of *them* in the end. Sukarno's a romantic, not a materialist. The trouble is, most of you don't bother to read his speeches. Remember what he said about revolution? "I'm crazed, I'm obsessed, by the romanticism of revolution." He really is. And when he talks to his crowds, it's a mystical communion. No wonder they love him. He's got this passion for the people—and it's a *poetic* passion. He understands that after years of being humiliated, of being nobodies, they have their self-respect back when Bung Karno thumbs his nose at the world. When he tells the Yanks "to hell with your aid", he does it for *them*. Do you know what he said in one of his speeches? That when he spoke to the people, he was *possessed*.' Kwan's flat voice took on a tone of liturgy, and he quoted: ' "Then for me, fire isn't hot enough, ocean isn't deep enough, the stars not high enough!" ' He sat back, visibly controlling his emotion, one hand clenching and unclenching.

'You really admire him,' I said.

In answer, he quoted again, half-closing his eyes. ' "*Betjak* boys, you are my brothers—we were born together in the flames of revolution!" ' He smiled almost tenderly. 'That's not a Marxist talking, it's a mystic,' he said. 'And a good Muslim, at heart. I believe in the man who spoke those words. He moves me. I've never had a personal meeting with him, but I feel a lot in common.' His rapid, rattling voice stopped. He picked up his empty coffee cup and looked at it. Then, in a lower tone, he repeated what he had said to Hamilton. 'Sukarno and I are the same astrological sign, you know. Sometimes I almost feel we share the same identity.' He lifted his chin proudly, and half closed his eyes; his face suddenly had an expression of extraordinary, grandiose arrogance. 'I could have been him,' he said quietly.

Despite Billy's eccentricity, I had not considered him until that moment to be anything but troubled in a way natural to a man with his disadvantages. This last remark, spoken as though to himself, had half opened a door: I felt that I was being warned. But I put the feeling aside, as we nearly always do such warnings.

And I was none the wiser, as I realised when I was driving home shortly afterwards to my bungalow in Kebayoran. He had told me that he was not a Marxist; he had made it plain that he was opposed to the PKI; but how did this tally with his supposed friendship with Aidit, and the existence of the files? If he was not collecting information for the PKI, or for the Russians, then whom was he doing it for? Possibly, just possibly, for the CIA or for Australian Security. But why then should he have a file on Henderson, the British Military Attaché? Back to square one. Well, he had told us that he wore two faces.

We spoke together often after that; he even invited me to the bungalow to drink tea; but to say we became friends would be an exaggeration. Though he liked me well enough, it was to Hamilton he gave his special devotion.

And yet how often Billy used the word 'friend'! 'Ah, yes,' he would say lightly, of some prominent public figure in Indonesia, Britain, or Australia, with whom he had slight acquaintance, 'he's a friend of mine.' Perhaps simply because I wasn't important to him, our relationship never broke down.

'Cook?' I hear him say. 'Yes—Cook's a friend of mine.'

8

Hamilton and I stood shouting at each other in a corner of the crowded living-room, next to a set of bookshelves newly jammed with Wally O'Sullivan's library. Conversation was difficult above the babble of voices_and the sound of the Beatles (banned as decadent by the Government) singing 'Can't Buy Me Love' at considerable volume. Wally had elevated the Beatles into his special pantheon alongside Puccini, Verdi and Gilbert and Sullivan, and had a kingly expectation that we would share his enthusiasm.

His newly acquired *amah* and houseboy padded with trays of drinks and bowls of curry among the throng of news-men, junior attachés from various embassies, and the few female clerks and secretaries they had brought with them. Wally had rented this bungalow near mine in the fashionable southern suburb of Kebayoran; and I earnestly hoped that his assignations would be safer here.

Seated on a bamboo couch, bulging in a vast white bush-shirt, he was drinking red wine out of a tall glass vase from which he had removed the flowers. He was obviously beginning here as he meant to continue: seated on either side of him on the couch were his only Indonesian guests, two slim, handsome young men with long, blue-black hair, formally dressed in immaculate tropical suits, their narrow brown hands moving like those of Balinese dancers.

There was a commotion and cheering at the other end of the

room. Billy Kwan had arrived, riding on the shoulders of Harold Sloane and Pete Curtis. As they set him down, he was laughing wildly, like a child being tickled: he seemed to bear them no grudge for the night before; and they, perhaps, were making amends. Jill Bryant had followed them in.

As the shouts over his entrance subsided, Billy cried loudly, 'What a marvellous lot you are! I've changed my mind: Anglo-Saxons are better in the tropics.'

At this pronouncement there was a wave of laughter from those members of the Wayang Club familiar with Kwan's climate theories of civilisation: he had been lecturing us lately on the ideas of the American geographer, Huntingdon. 'Anglo-Saxons are better in the tropics' became a drunken catch-cry, and would linger in the Wayang for some weeks; and Billy was to ride through Wally's party, as he had ridden through the door, on our sudden tide of affection for him and for one another: a mood triggered by alcohol, by party euphoria, by an element of guilt, and also perhaps by the mysterious telepathy through which a group dimly perceives its own fleeting uniqueness; group self-love, if you like.

'Anglo-Saxons are better in the tropics!'

Some were singing it, some were dancing to it. While we swayed about him, Kwan struggled out of the cheap cotton jacket he wore and flung it in a corner. 'Off, you lendings. Yes, Great Wally, I will have a beer.' Catching sight of a black *pitji* cap Wally had hung over a wood-carving of a Balinese dancer on a nearby table, he put it on at the same jaunty angle as Sukarno, and thrust out his chin; and he did somewhat resemble the Bung. 'Who do I look like?' he demanded.

'An Australian-Chinese wearing a *pitji*,' Wally rumbled promptly, and fresh laughter broke out. The puzzled expressions of Wally's other guests—many of whom had not encountered Billy before—increased our possessive amusement.

'Hey Billy, hey Billy'—Curtis was red-faced, drunk, and proprietary. 'What happens to that cold-climate vigour you've been telling us about, when we come here? Anglo-Saxons go *bad* in the tropics, they go seedy.'

'No no, old man, they bring their vigour with them—

Huntingdon proved that. But the heat modifies their coldness—helps them to unwind and be more generous.'

Our laughter increased; his absurdity delighted us.

'And what does all this mean for Indonesia?' Kevin Condon wanted to know. 'Don't tropical peoples have a future?'

'Of course, old man,' Kwan said. 'But they'll never be efficient. We're not efficient in Queensland, after a few generations. It's too hot to be efficient. That doesn't matter—why be efficient? The Indonesians are a nation of artists: *artistenvolk*.'

But now, laughing and roaring, Curtis put an arm about his neck and pulled him backwards, and the Sukarno cap fell off. 'Enough!' Curtis yelled, 'Enough horse-shit for one night!'

And Kwan, his dignity cast off like a shirt, laughed with abandon, lying against Curtis like a big doll. 'Only the Chinese and·Japanese,' he gasped, 'have the climate in Asia for efficiency.'

'Enough!' Curtis set the *pitji* back on Billy's head and dragged him away across the room towards the table where the beer was.

Towards eleven thirty—curfew time—when most of the crowd had gone home, Wally O'Sullivan moved over to where Hamilton and I were sprawled in rattan chairs near the double doors leading onto the veranda. He rocked ponderously, holding his empty vase. 'Gentlemen,' he said seriously, 'have you seen my study?'

When we said we hadn't, he insisted on taking us there. He had bought a large and expensive teak desk, which we duly admired. A green-shaded lamp standing on it provided the only light in the room. We were about to leave, when Wally said, 'Don't go. I want you to see me sitting at my desk.'

Puzzled by this odd request, we stared down at him: he was unusually drunk. Mountainous in his rumpled and wine-stained white bush-shirt, with the light from the lamp striking upwards to illuminate his jowl and put deep shadows in his eye-sockets, he posed at his handsome desk as though for a photograph. 'It's a nice desk,' he said. 'Hm? I just wanted you to see me sitting at it. Do you like my bungalow? Cookie? Ham?' He looked up at us with a sort of mute appeal. And we laughed, and answered these childlike questions patiently: yes, we liked his study and his bungalow.

But he had more to communicate, it seemed, from inside his drunkenness. Folding his hands over the great white orb of his belly, nodding, he said, 'I'm happy in this bloody mad country, you know. They might be on the wrong track at the moment, but the Javanese have everything, really: intelligence, subtlety, sense of humour, and sen-sensitivity.' He hiccuped. 'I love them. I think I may never leave,' he said. 'This is my home, now. I may apply for citizenship.'

At this, we laughed in disbelief; but he raised a stilling hand; even in drunkenness his dignity was paramount. 'I'm quite serious —really, I have something to *give* them; they have something to give me. There are young men here who are hungry for education, for guidance that they can't find in the present breakdown. You met my young friends tonight—Hadji and Abdul? Fine young men. I teach them English—supervise their reading—guide them in their political thinking. They'll be leaders, some day, and they'll set this country on a civilised course. And I can be *myself* with them. Can you see that? I can't be myself in Australia. Hm? Why should I go back?' And the round eyes look up at us almost pleadingly.

Hamilton and I were embarrassed into silence; and I saw now that Great Wally had posed at his desk to gain our blessing for his dream of a new Javanese life. I recalled his library outside: Plato's *Republic*; Aristotle's *Politics*; Gibbon; Thackeray; Proust; E. M. Forster; Angus Wilson; and an expensive volume dealing lavishly with Art Nouveau. Art Nouveau: here! Outside, the immense heat squatted like a malignant force, making these fragments of an alien civilisation seem infinitely fragile; doomed. The books would gather mildew fast in the equatorial humidity; and very soon the military, as well as thugs disguised as military, would be knocking with their gun-butts at the door, demanding donations of money. And after that . . .

If this was Wally's imagined home, he had no home in this world.

Seeking coolness, Wally and I moved out onto the veranda, where we found Billy Kwan and Kevin Condon. Curfew was not far off;

the only other guest remaining now was Jill Bryant, who sat on the couch in the deserted living-room, turning over a pile of records.

Hamilton didn't follow us to the veranda, but joined Jill; and seen through the double doors they seemed to inhabit a picture-frame stage, its straw matting littered with used curry bowls and empty glasses. The forbidden Beatles were singing 'Ticket to Ride', but at low volume now, so that the cold Liverpool voices mingled almost wistfully with Java's thick heat, and with various cricketings from the garden. Wally had rolled onto a bamboo reclining-chair and appeared to sleep, pouting like a monstrous baby. Billy was still wearing Wally's Sukarno cap. He and I and Condon leant our backs against the stucco balustrade, talking in snatches, slow with liquor. And our eyes were constantly drawn back to Jill and Hamilton, who sat half turned towards each other, on the couch.

There was no sexual interest to be read in their faces; and they did not smile. Yet I had never seen a couple who seemed more inevitably intended for sexual linking. They looked cooler than the rest of us: she in a pale blue dress of some sort of linen; the big man in one of his innumerable safari suits. Dark and fair in their lit frame, they had ceased for a moment to be themselves, and resembled the human shadows of universal wish. Jill picked up a cushion and began to fidget with it, head bent, no longer looking at Hamilton. I couldn't bring myself to glance at Billy Kwan, and feared that Condon would make some obvious remark.

A few moments later, Hamilton stood abruptly and came across to the double doors, stooping to peer at me. 'I'll give you a lift, Cookie,' he said. 'Time to go, if we don't want to get shot at. You're seeing Jill home, Billy?' His long jaw was set, his heavy-lidded eyes somewhat cold. Behind him, still seated on the couch, Jill examined the cushion. I wondered why their conversation had ended so abruptly; and I was to find out the following evening. Hamilton told me about it, as he did so many other incidents connected with Billy Kwan, because he was puzzled.

We left without waking Wally; and it was that night, I'm certain, that Billy stole Wally's Sukarno cap. He simply took it home with him; and when Wally taxed him with this, he refused to admit it, or give the cap up.

'I suppose you *realise*, Mr Hamilton,' Jill said, 'that you're practically required listening at the British Embassy now? I'm getting tired of hearing your name.' Her low voice was pitched a little louder than it had been at the Oasis—perhaps in competition with the Beatles—but she spoke very rapidly, so that he still had to listen carefully to catch her words. 'Ralph's a bit cheesed off that you didn't let him know about that Siliwangi story,' she said. 'He thought you and he were going to keep in touch on things like that.' She was referring to a recent piece of Hamilton's which had exposed a secret government plan (discovered by Kumar) to put commandos from the crack Siliwangi division into Sarawak. This had been taken in Kuala Lumpur and London as a portent of outright war, and the story had done as much to make Hamilton's name as the Aidit interview.

He told her politely that he had not been able to reveal his sources. Her top teeth rested on a recessed lower lip; when she ceased to smile, the lip was consciously and rather comically set firm again. She was not wearing her glasses, and he noticed again the slightly unfocused crookedness of her gaze, which seemed to look just past him rather than at him.

'I see. Well, I'm glad you and Ralph *do* help each other,' she said. 'We should all do that in this bloody mad-house, don't you think?'

'You've really got your boss's interests at heart, haven't you?'

'Ralph's a marvellous man,' she said. 'Of course I want to help him, in every way I can.' And she added defensively, 'I'm sure you're glad of loyalty from your own staff, aren't you? You're very lucky to have someone who's devoted to you, as Billy Kwan is. I suppose you realise he practically hero-worships you?' She dropped her eyes, picked up a small batik-covered cushion, and began to fidget with it.

'I'm sure that's an exaggeration.'

'It's not an exaggeration at all.' Her speech grew even more rapid. 'He calls you the best journalist in Indonesia. He idolises you. You should appreciate it.' She looked up quickly. 'It worries me sometimes. I hope you don't mind my speaking like this; but Billy and I are close friends. When one person makes another the centre of his life he can sometimes be left out on a limb, can't he? I mean, you'll get transferred eventually, won't you?'

It was now that Hamilton took what he thought was his opportunity to carry out his absurd, delegated task. He cleared his throat. 'I'll be around for a while,' he said. 'But I'm glad this came up, because I'd like to talk to you about Billy. I think you're wrong about him. He's a very independent little bloke essentially. He's not likely to depend on anyone—except you.' She looked up again, and he smiled. 'Here we are both saying the same thing.'

But Jill's hands had become absolutely still, on the cushion. 'What is it you're trying to tell me?'

He saw that something had gone wrong; but there was nothing to do except blunder on with his mission. 'I know you haven't settled anything, but I understand you've been thinking about marriage.'

She began to laugh, staring at him with resentful incredulity. Her speech became pitched even lower: a passionate mutter. 'Marriage! Are you joking? If so, it isn't very funny, Guy. Or is it what those bloody idiots in the Wayang Bar are saying?' The crookedness of her gaze seemed to have increased; he saw she was genuinely upset, despite her attempt to smile.

'I'm sorry,' he said. 'I seem to have got it wrong.'

'Yes, you *have*. I'm very fond of Billy; he's a marvellous little guy—but one marriage has been enough for me.' She looked at her watch. 'It's nearly curfew, isn't it? Time we were all gone. I'm *so* glad we talked.'

Why on earth, Hamilton asked me at the round bar, had Kwan sent him on a fool's errand? When he told Billy what Jill had said, Billy seemed unconcerned. 'Ah. Yes. Well she *would* say that, wouldn't she?' he said; and that was all. He had a knack of closing up, which baffled Hamilton.

9

I can see now that Billy Kwan's popularity with the members of
the Wayang Club reached a sort of peak on the night of Wally's
party, when he wore the *pitji* cap. He would never bathe in quite
the same universal benevolence again; and his behaviour began to
grow more and more strange, and to most of us, more and more
unacceptable.

This was a slow and erratic process, and I didn't then pinpoint
its beginning. But I'm able now, through Kwan's files, to trace it
back to that night when the affair between Hamilton and Jill
Bryant began—or rather, was seen to have begun by the watchers
on Wally's veranda.

How I came by Billy's papers must wait its turn in this account.
I only acquired them on the eve of leaving Indonesia; but it's now
becoming necessary to refer to them more directly. It's doubtful
whether Kwan was ever employed as an agent by any intelligence
service. There was never any real evidence—although that doesn't
rule out the possibility: where Billy was concerned, anything was
possible, and he may have destroyed the evidence. Perhaps, at one
stage, he had undertaken work for Australian Security. But I'm
now certain that he kept the bulk of the dossiers for his own
amusement. Nothing so eccentric as most of them are could
possibly have been of use for any intelligence purposes; and this I
find more fascinating than any revelation that he worked for the
CIA or the KGB or ASIO.

Since Hamilton, on the day of his injury in the US Embassy riot, had glimpsed only the files on Aidit and Colonel Henderson, he and I decided that Billy was keeping records on figures of purely political interest—either for his own information, as a journalist might, or else because he was using his television work as a cover for spying. What we did not suspect then was that he might be keeping files on us.

Now I find we are all there; and the file on myself—certain forthright parts of which still make me wince—could have had no possible political purpose. Nor could those on Hamilton, Wally O'Sullivan, or Jill Bryant. Others—on such figures as Sukarno and his top ministers—are highly political: but even these are kept in a way that would not have been satisfactory for espionage purposes.

As well as files on us all, the cameraman had files on every subject under the sun, from ethnology to cities, from abnormal psychology to Zen. Is there a word for an obsession for filing? Indexomania, perhaps? It was Billy's chief obsession—as though he wanted to file the world. Most of us, at one time and another, have been tempted to play the Peeping Tom on other people's souls. Kwan was 'a Peeping Tom on life'. I am quoting from a dossier labelled *Dwarfs*, where he discusses what he sees as his own nature.

Much that is in the files is cryptic, and some of it is intimate and even perverse. To spare my friends who are their subjects, I must limit direct quotation.

The dossiers on individuals are divided into two sections. The first section has a photograph (presumably taken by Billy, under some pretext or other), and biographical details in a quasi-official style. Some of the details, such as the subject's Zodiacal sign, would hardly appear on any official dossier. The second section is much less orthodox: it consists of an appendix containing a series of dated entries which make up a sort of diary of the subject's progress. In many cases, these peter out as he lost interest.

All this, I think, justifies my decision to reconstruct and explain rather than to quote from the papers verbatim. Billy kept these records, after all, for no other eyes than his own—and it's only because I was involved with the people concerned, or present at the events referred to, or because I compared notes with Hamilton, that I have been able to make my deductions.

For Kwan to have compiled such dossiers seems cold-blooded —and many people will see it as distasteful and childish. The people in his files are transfixed like butterflies, and the diary entries are analytical, and so appear cruel. But I believe these papers chiefly chart the shoals of Kwan's own torment. And although thinly masked pain, bitter humour, and vicious dismissal—the compensations of an outraged ego—all come through, there is no self-pity. My heart goes out to him for that.

It was only when I examined the file entitled *Dwarfs* that I fully understood how Kwan saw himself. In addition to a voluminous study of the history, mythology, and psychopathology of dwarfs (with special attention to achondroplastics), there is an essay dealing with what he sees as his own destined role in life. In it (at his most fancy and literary), Kwan addresses an entity he calls 'the Unmet Friend'.

DOSSIER D 2: DWARFS

In Celtic mythology, the kingdom of the dwarfs below the earth, filled with precious metals, is called the Antipodes. Joke: I'm a dwarf from the Antipodes: and my files are my underground work— my secret mine of paper.*

It's to you, my Unmet Friend, that all these atlases of other lives are addressed: to you, whom we all idiotically wait for. You will read every word with sympathy; forgive all my secret foulnesses; smile on all my hopes!

Here, on the quiet page, I'm master—just as I'm master in the dark-room, stirring my prints in the magic developing-bath. And here, among my files, I can shuffle like cards the lives I deal with.

---

*Kwan makes cross-reference here to his notes in the Mythology section of the *Dwarf* file. One of his sources is Gervase of Tilbury's *Otia Imperialia*, in which the Antipodes is said to have been ruled by a high-minded dwarf king called Bilis. Kwan's notes trace Bilis's transformation into Beli, who apparently became the prototype of nearly all mythological dwarfs, and of Pelles, in the Grail legend.—R.J.C.

Their faces stare out at me from these little pieces of glazed card:
people who will become other people: people who will become old,
betray their dreams, become ghosts. But they wait, in my files, to see
what I'll do with them. Charting their blind course on paper, I own
them, in a way! They can lock me out of their hearts, dear Friend,
but not out of their lives. They are tenants of my secret system,
whether they like it or not . . . .

Hamilton and Jill Bryant, whose dossiers are extensive, are
important tenants of Kwan's secret system: for my knowledge of
what it was that Billy wanted from both of them, I am heavily
dependent on the files. Hamilton's affair with Jill was dogged
from the beginning by the puzzle of Kwan. Thus, in giving an
account of that affair, I am in possession of two halves of a map,
as it were: Hamilton's half, and the half in Kwan's dossiers. The
resulting map may have certain distortions, since the flaw of
Billy's peculiar viewpoint runs through it.

Hamilton, although he confided in me, and spoke of his feeling
for Jill, didn't go in for sexual confessions. But the privacy of
these two was invaded by Kwan; and glimpses of those paper
invasions of his must be part of this account. I keep recalling
something he said to Hamilton: 'I get a quaint view of people,
from this height.' So he did; he had a child's cold wistfulness; and
this should be borne in mind when you view with me these lovers
whom he loved.

Hamilton sat at his desk, hammering out a radio piece on his
typewriter. He was tired; he had covered at midday a vicious
smash-up of the US Information Service library: a favourite
target. The Jakarta working day was over. It was late afternoon,
his staff had gone home, and he was alone in the big, pleasantly
shabby office above Jalan Antara, under the slowly turning
ceiling-fan. That day—the second following Wally's party—
Kwan had not checked in for work, nor had he appeared the day
before; and Hamilton was growing concerned. When there was a
knock on the door, he jumped up instantly, hoping to find Billy.
But, instead, he found Jill Bryant.

She gave him the wide smile we were all so fond of in the Wayang, as though nothing unpleasant had taken place between them. 'Hullo, Guy,' she said. 'I'm looking for Billy. Is he here?'

Hamilton was considerably surprised. Jill had never called looking for Kwan before, and now that anti-Western feeling had reached the pitch it had, European women did not move about the city alone. 'He hasn't been here all day,' he said. 'I'm looking for him myself.'

'Really?' She frowned. 'That's a bit worrying. He was supposed to call at our flat last night, and didn't come—and he's not at his bungalow. I *thought* something was wrong.'

'I wouldn't worry too much,' Hamilton said. 'He'll turn up. He'd better, or I'll have no cameraman. He's irreplaceable.'

There was a pause in which the awkward recollection of their last meeting hung over them; but she did not turn to go. Small on the hot, dim landing with its dirty walls, she seemed to glimmer. From under a wide-brimmed straw hat, two bright wings of hair fell to her shoulders; she wore a white sun-dress with a full skirt, and she was twirling a pair of sun-glasses in her fingers with the electric restlessness he remembered. She looked as though the weight of heat on the landing did not press down on her; as though she did not perspire, moving in her own temperate zone.

Hamilton stepped back and invited her in, apologising for his slowness to do so. In the middle of the empty room, she swung around to face him. 'I don't know whether there's any point in my waiting for Billy, is there? But if you don't mind, I'll stop a few minutes before I face the town again. It's a steam-bath since the rain stopped.'

'Of course. How did you get across here?'

'One of our chaps was coming over to the Old City, and I got a lift,' she said. 'Generally, I have the use of Moira's car—Moira's my flat-mate. But she's gone up to Bogor for a week—so it's bloody hell getting about. I'll get a taxi back.'

'No, you won't—I'll drive you. It's not safe in town for white ladies going solo.'

'That's nice of you. But you're working.'

'I'm glad of the excuse to stop.'

'I wanted to see you,' she said, 'to apologise for my rudeness at Wally's.'

'No need. I should have minded my own business.'

'Maybe it *is* your business.' She spoke rapidly, and was barely audible.

A silence fell, in which they stood and looked at each other, as though trying to decide something. A panel of sun lay between them on the glazed ochre tiles of the floor; the dusty quiet took on an illusion of tenderness as the blades of the aged fan gestured above their heads. A set of fan-shaped wrinkles, white in the sun-tan at the corners of her eyes, made Hamilton guess her to be older than he had first thought: perhaps twenty-seven.

After they became lovers, they would look back on this brink, and admit that each had guessed the other's awareness. Despite past affairs, they were both still young enough for the excitement which springs from sensing that a story has begun whose end can't be foreseen; and they were both old enough to know that life could offer them few if any more such beginnings. Youth was giving them each a last chance, since each had reached youth's outer suburbs.

It was Jill who broke the silence, sandals clicking on the tiles as she turned away to pace about the office, examining the battered desks and filing cabinets, the grimy yellow walls whose bareness was relieved only by a sentimental Indonesian water-colour of a *prahu*, sailing into a sentimental sunset above Kumar's desk. A copy of *Merdeka*, the Indonesian national newspaper, had fallen to the floor. On the desk Billy had commandeered stood an empty soft-drink bottle and a copy of St Augustine's *Confessions*.

She picked up *Merdeka*, replaced it on the desk, and smiled. 'You certainly don't go in for comforts, do you?'

'I don't think the landlord's interested in improvements,' Hamilton said. 'He's a heavy Javanese in permanent sun-glasses with two heavy sons—he owns property all over the town. He has a Swiss bank account I pay the rent into. The roof of the balcony leaks, but he won't fix it. He never smiles. All three of them drive Chryslers.'

'Black, of course.'

'Black.'

They laughed, with a mirth that was disproportionate: a signal of the shared sense of humour that can make affection outlast desire.

'I'd offer you coffee,' Hamilton said, 'but my girl's gone, and what I made would be terrible. How about a long gin-tonic on the way home?'

'As long as it's not the Wayang. I'm sick of the Wayang—do you mind?' She turned quickly to the door, her expression hidden under the wide straw hat.

Instead of heading for New Jakarta, Hamilton edged the Ford in the other direction through the canal-side traffic of Jalan Antara, and out onto the highway which runs north towards Kemayoran and the coast.

'Hey,' Jill said. 'Where are you taking me?'

He grinned. 'I thought we might go out to Priok, and get a breath of sea air—if there is any. I know a nice little bar out there.'

'Great,' she said. And then: 'I wish it were the Norfolk coast. God, I miss cold air, don't you? You can *have* the glamorous tropics. Thank you for taking me for a drive, Guy, when I was so bloody the other night.'

He was still adjusting to her quick darts from subject to subject, and her low, rapid speech. But the nervous good humour in her face flooded him with hope. 'I'm glad you came,' he said.

They both sat carefully; his hands did not move on the wheel, nor hers where they rested in her lap. Suddenly she called, 'Billy! There's Billy!' She craned to look through the back window. Hamilton could see little in the driving mirror except a jeep-taxi crowding close and the usual black bicycles, like tall insects.

'He's gone. I can't see him any more,' Jill said. 'I'm sure it was him, though, on that mad little motor scooter.'

In the port district of Priok, in sight of the flat, grey lid of the Java Sea, they wandered for a time under the awnings of a *pasar*. The heavy heat was very little different from that of the city, but it seemed to them that it was. The eternal cheap silver-ware and Balinese wood-carvings in the peeling gift-shops became remarkably interesting. They had forgotten about going for a drink.

Sunset advanced, and huge storm clouds stood above the sea. The north-west monsoon, soon to end, was bringing more rain-squalls: drops began to patter on the canvas awnings, and they hurried back to the car. Its humid intimacy made them constrained again; her bare arm brushed his, and they drew slightly away from each other. She did perspire after all; little tendrils of blond hair stuck to her damp temples.

They began to speculate about Billy's disappearance. 'Was that really him you saw?' Hamilton asked.

'Positive. Maybe he was following us.'

They laughed, and Hamilton said, 'Look—I'd like to explain about the other night. It was bloody stupid of me, opening up the question of your marrying Billy.'

She listened to him with her eyes fixed in her lap. After he had made his explanation, she sighed. 'Christ,' she said. She had a habit of saying 'Christ' with harmless vehemence; it somehow made life and all its disasters seem like a game. 'I was afraid something like this would happen,' she said, 'but I never thought he'd be so silly.'

She turned to Hamilton quickly; and he saw that although she smiled easily her eyes were always troubled, holding a constant, sea-dark sadness under her gaiety. 'Of course it's not *true*,' she said—'that I ever gave him any reason to hope, I mean. But I suppose it really is my fault. It's so hard to have any sort of male friend in this crazy situation; you must see that. Every man I meet wants to race me into bed in five minutes. And when I go out with someone, everyone in the Embassy decides I'm hopping into bed with him. I'm sure they talk the same way in the Wayang Bar. You may think it's flattering to be in my position, but it isn't. The wives hate me—and the men make this crude play. I used to feel I was on display all the time—in a shop window. It was so bloody *tedious*. So Billy and I made a deal.'

'He took you out of the shop window.'

'That's right. He was a friend, an escort—we agreed not to be emotionally involved. He's stuck to the agreement until now, but I suppose it was stupid of me to expect it to go on. We've seen less of each other lately, because Ralph Henderson and I have been going out together. I thought Billy understood about that too.'

Hamilton digested this last statement, and the pang of

114

disappointment it gave him. Then he said, 'Well, I suppose it's understandable. You wanted him for a mascot. His size makes a lot of people want that.'

Her lips tightened. 'That's not *fair*, Guy.' Her voice, being raised, had achieved normal pitch. 'I really do care about Billy, although that may surprise you.' She picked savagely at the clasp of her handbag; and this display of feeling from so quiet a girl mildly alarmed Hamilton.

'I'm sorry,' he said. 'I've got a lot of time for Billy myself.'

'It's all right. It's just that I get so tired of things being taken the wrong way. Jakarta's beginning to get me down, I suppose.' She stared through the rain-spattered wind-screen at the grey harbour, visible between two wharf-sheds at the end of the road. Lines of fish-traps made it a ghostly chess-board, and far out lay freighters from the northern hemisphere: that longed-for zone beyond the sea's rim. The freighters could berth no closer; Priok, for want of dredging, was slowly silting up.

'I wish we were leaving on one of those ships,' she said. And then, with a nervous jauntiness, 'How about it? Let's go!'

'Let's,' he said. 'I'll buy the tickets.'

'If only we could. This hot mad-house.' Her arm touched his, and did not draw away. They had reached each other, it seemed, in a common longing for escape—not just from Java, perhaps, but from reality.

'I'm glad you're fond of Billy,' she said. 'You've got so much, Guy—everything falls at your feet. You're everything he wants to be.'

'Nonsense.'

'It's not nonsense. You're terribly unaware, aren't you? You're the one everybody envies, in that journalist crowd—you're not really aware of that, and you take it for granted that Billy should be your Man Friday. But he's frightfully intense about you.'

'Billy's intense about everything,' Hamilton said. 'You shouldn't be too embarrassed about what's happened. For anyone who knows Billy embarrassment has to be a permanent condition.'

She laughed, but still looked troubled. 'It doesn't make sense.

He didn't need *you* to chat me up about how he felt. Why did he do it? And there's something else.' She fidgeted again with the clasp of the handbag. 'He several times suggested I should go out with you. He said he'd rather I did that than see so much of Ralph Henderson.'

'Maybe he's right,' Hamilton suggested.

'Let's change the subject, shall we?'

The rain had become heavier; twilight had brought rolls of thunder, and the full downpour arrived now, drumming like threat on the roof of the car. Hamilton wound the window up. Within moments, the sea, the suspended wharf-sheds, the ships, all distances, had disappeared under pewter sheets of water; they were enclosed in a roaring cubicle where normal speech was impossible.

'I'll take you home,' Hamilton shouted.

She stared into his face without answering, her mouth open, top teeth resting on the slightly receding lower lip, her expression curiously dazed. He assumed that the monsoonal storm frightened her, and grinned at her reassuringly. Outside, dim and uncertain as memory, a pedlar jogged by, shouldering a carrying-pole with baskets of vegetables. *Pasar* awnings waved and shook.

'When it eases, we'll start,' Hamilton called. He had been longing for some time to touch the round, naked shoulder beside him; it now seemed natural to do so, and his hand enclosed it. If he had meant to soothe her, it had the opposite effect: her head jerked further back as though in alarm, and she searched his face almost imploringly. The rain filled their heads and increased in violence. It was no longer possible to speak; and the downpour's excess had released a spring in them to kiss as they were now doing, stopping only to examine each other's faces in surprise: but each had known this would happen. She held to him with the hunger of the desperate, and he wondered why. Then, her hands against his chest, she pushed him away, and shook back the thick, straight mane of hair. Her mouth set again, with its faintly comic discipline, so that her lower lip covered her teeth. 'Please let's go,' she said.

Until they were on the highway back to the city they both remained silent. Then Jill said, 'Let's forget that, shall we? I'm sorry. I'm pretty involved with Ralph. I realise how bloody silly that sounds.'

Billy Kwan, on his little green chariot, had not only shadowed Hamilton's car through the traffic of Jalan Gunung Sahari, but had followed all the way to Priok. This is made plain in an entry in the diary-appendix to Jill Bryant's dossier—'*Dossier B 26, BRYANT, Gillian Edith*'. Dated 2 March, it addresses her in the second person: *You go alone with my giant brother to Priok. In the pasar, he dares to kiss you. So it begins.**

Billy must have watched Hamilton and Jill from one of the bazaar alleyways across the road. He revealed himself only when they reached Jalan Diponogoro—the fashionable diplomatic thoroughfare in New Jakarta not far from the Hotel Indonesia, where the British Residency stood. Jill had her apartment a few doors down, on the top floor of a big, Dutch-built villa leased by the British mission.

When Hamilton drew up there, a motor scooter appeared beside the car, its engine revving with two loud snarls. It had stopped raining, but dark had fallen and Hamilton did not at first recognise the scooter's rider, who thrust his head into the window-frame and exclaimed in a comic Japanese accent, 'Hoh! So!' He was dressed in a black shirt and black slacks, and grinned at them cheerfully.

'Where the hell have you been?' Hamilton asked. 'And why are you dressed as an undertaker?'

'I decided to take a little holiday, old man. Things were pretty quiet; you said so yourself.' Under Billy's airy manner there was

---

*Kwan often refers to Hamilton, in the files, as his 'giant brother'—a fancy he does not explain; but I believe I have traced it in the mythology section of his *Dwarf* dossier. In a long thesis on the origins of the Arthurian dwarf, Kwan notes that the ancient dwarf-figure Pelles was 'split into two men—a knight and his dwarf squire'. And this, he says, can be traced to the fact that his ancestor Bilis, in Celtic legend, had a giant brother called Brian, or Bran.—R.J.C.

something new and frantic, an unnatural quickness. He leant sideways to peer past Hamilton at Jill. 'There's my little Jillie,' he said. 'How are *you*, sweetie?'

'Fine, sweetie,' she said. 'We decided to run down to Priok and get some air.'

'Plenty of air at Priok,' Billy said. 'Now why don't you ask us both to dinner, since old Moira's away? I'd love to taste your amah's cooking again.'

'For heaven's sake, Billy!' Hamilton said. Embarrassed at this proposal, he felt a stirring of anger.

'I'm sorry, Billy,' Jill said. 'I just don't feel up to it tonight. Today's been rather hectic.'

Unabashed, bestraddling his machine jauntily, Kwan studied them both. 'Ah, I see,' he said. 'Then why don't you just ask us in for a drink? Or if you don't want *me* today, why don't you ask Ham in for a drink?'

'You're obviously drunk already,' Hamilton said.

Leaning forward, Jill was now staring at Kwan angrily. 'Really Billy, would you stop this bloody silly behaviour? And do stop pushing me at Guy—it's ridiculous.'

Kwan's voice became louder and flatter. 'Why not, sweetie? You're going to fall for him, anyway.'

Before Hamilton could speak, Jill had opened the door on her side. In a mutter that was just audible, she said, 'No, this is too much. Good night, Guy.' Within seconds she had hurried across the footpath and into the driveway of the villa.

Hamilton turned angrily to Kwan; but the cameraman had started the motor of his Vespa again and was buzzing away without looking back, down the tree-lined street of embassies.

Near midnight, Hamilton lay in bed in the Hotel, the muted, hollow clinking of the *betjak* bells floating up to him from the Car Park through the sealed windows. Just as he was sinking towards sleep, the phone beside his bed began to ring.

'Guy? It's me.' He recognised her voice instantly. 'I had to ring,' she said. She hurried as though afraid she would regret her words, unless they were said quickly. 'I shouldn't have rushed away like that; it was stupid. But Billy was being so ridiculous. I'm sorry. Here I am apologising again.'

'No need,' Hamilton said. 'Billy was acting like a maniac. I'll wrap his camera around his neck tomorrow.'

'Please don't,' she said. 'I get upset with him, but he's been very sweet to me. And besides—' She broke off for a moment, and then said something else in a rapid mutter.

'I didn't catch that.'

'I said maybe he was right.'

Hamilton smiled in the darkness. 'That's what I was hoping,' he said.

'It's the last thing *I* was hoping. I'm afraid my life's been rather a mess. I was married for two years and then divorced; then I had a bloody terrible affair with a guy from the French Embassy— everyone knew about it, of course—and that ended badly, too. I'm not very satisfactory, I'm afraid. And that's why I've thought of marrying Ralph Henderson. He's an old friend of my family's; we've got a lot in common; and he's so terribly kind. He's just a marvellous man, under that *pukka* manner. I never think about his age. Are you there?'

'I'm listening.'

'Guy—why did you have to appear?' She was whispering.

'I'm glad *you* appeared. When can I see you?' he asked.

There was a silence; then a sigh. 'Tomorrow night. Moira will still be up at Bogor.'

They spoke for another quarter-hour. 'I don't want to hang up,' he said.

'Nor do I.'

When they finally did break off, he got out of bed, crossed to the windows in the darkness, and stood staring out at the people on the Welcome Monument. Its twin pylons rose level with his window, supporting a floodlit platform on which a handsome, greenish couple, arms up-flung, struck dated attitudes of zest, arching themselves into a figurative wind. In the cold of this room it was possible to believe in that wind; but the furnace outside, he knew, was unmoved by so much as a breeze.

Trying to summon up Jill's face, he found it had a quality that

119

eluded him. It was like an old drawing, he said; and when I asked him to be more exact, it turned out to be a picture by Arthur Rackham: some waif or nymph or other in a childhood book of legends.

As he stared at the couple on the monument, Hamilton felt guilty. He hadn't meant to do this to Billy. The *betjak* bells floated up from below like hopeless, patient requests, in a language he could not understand: *bink; bonk; bink.*

Part Two
Patet Sanga: Water from the Moon

10

We have come to the end of June.

At this time of the year, the rain-bearing north-west monsoon is long past, and the south-east monsoon rules in Java. As the months go by, the dry, steady heat it carries from the deserts of Australia, moving across Timor and the Java Sea, will mount in intensity; and it is in these nights of the dry monsoon that the screens of the *wayang kulit*, the shadow-shows, light up all through the countryside.

Whole villages stay awake until dawn, watching the capering, beloved silhouettes, lost in the ancient dreams of the Ramayana and the Mahabharata. They applaud the victories of the hero Arjuna; they laugh in joyful recognition at the entrance of Dwarf Semar and his capering clown sons. And underneath it all, the cascading bells and gongs of the *gamelan* music hurry and run and pause and run on again, like Java's mountain streams, while the deep, reassuring voice of the *dalang* explains everything that happens, in these lost kingdoms of the Javanese heart.

He is more than a puppet-master, and these are more than puppets: their shadows are souls. Squatting beneath a lamp which fills the screen with deathless light, the *dalang* is God, and the screen is Heaven. The gilded, richly dressed puppets of both Left and Right are all in his hands: and who can doubt that the *Wayang* of the Right will triumph? On the other side of the lighted screen, they are seen as filigreed shadows, silhouettes; and this is the side to sit on, if you are a true lover of *wayang*.

123

Many sit on the *dalang*'s side, and watch him work; but who except the earth-bound would want to view the machinery of the gods? Such people merely see a puppet show. No, the side of the shadows is the magic side, where ancestral spirits with nervous, insect profiles, elaborate as lace, bow and fight and make love, or grow to giant-size, or vanish. There, one is truly transported to the Kingdom of Dwarawati, the land of all good things, through the long dream of the *wayang* night; a night divided into three stages: foolish youth, middle life (when a man seeks the right path), and old age's serenity—after which the sumptuous salmon dawn of the equator brings it all to an end for the blinking villagers.

Billy Kwan, like the watchers at the *wayang* shows, often stayed awake through these nights of the dry monsoon. He suffered from insomnia, and it was his habit to move around Jakarta until dawn, either on his motor scooter or on foot, defying the curfew. None of us knew this at the time, but there is a record of these nocturnal wanderings in the files. Diary entries for 30 June appear in the dossiers of President Sukarno and an Indonesian woman Kwan simply calls 'Ibu'.

DOSSIER: I 22 : IBU

Age approximately 28. Sundanese, native of the village of Krawang, in West Java. Husband deserted. One girl, aged eight; one infant boy, Udin.

30 June

Encountered subject tonight in Pasar Baru: she no longer frequents front of Hotel Indonesia.

Several times the subject tried to beg from me as usual, but I would have none of that. Neither gave to her, nor would I stop following. Followed her for an hour, despite her distress and shows of anger. Knew in the end she must retreat to her kampong, and I was determined to penetrate her home . . .

Here he comes, riding in a *betjak* through the breathless dark of the Old City in June: a large-headed Australian-Chinese in a gaudy Hawaiian shirt, a camera in a battered leather case slung round his neck. He wears on his head Indonesia's national symbol; Wally's stolen Sukarno cap! Horns blare; he is carried through swarms of bicycles along Jalan Antara, past Hamilton's office to the entrance of Pasar Baru, where the grinning *betjak* boy comes to a halt.

Kwan pays him off, and moves into the crowded *pasar*, which is the biggest in the city, where the chief rumours are born, and where President Sukarno is said to wander at night *incognito*, bathing in the crowd that jams the long alleyway between leaning old Dutch and Chinese business buildings, with their steeply gabled roofs and walls of dingy stucco. The big head in the black *pitji* bobs along under dun-coloured awnings like sails; under swarms of weak electric bulbs. Billy stares from side to side, as though searching for someone.

In front of a stall displaying cheap sun-glasses and combs stands a tall Javanese matron holding a small girl by the hand. She smiles at Billy, and winks.

Her hair is done in the traditional bun, secured by a comb. Her figure, in its tight-fitting, ankle-length *kain* and long-sleeved *kebaya*, is statuesque, but her face is distinctly plain, equine, with long front teeth. She has a respectable air, as most traditionally clad Javanese women do, which makes the roguish Western-style wink peculiarly incongruous. As Kwan looks at her, she winks again, and jerks her head, indicating that he should follow.

He follows.

Behind the outward face of Old Jakarta there is a second, secret city. It consists of warrens of earth-floored houses of cane and thatch, and of crazy shanties made from flattened oil-cans and cardboard, spreading like a bacterial growth along the canals. This is the hidden system of the kampongs, where it is possible for a man to walk all day out of sight of the official town.

Devoid of clean water, drainage, or electricity, these intricate slums, which bear the old name for a village, have their own simple government, their own minute shops, even their own elementary schools. It is generally regarded as madness for a European to venture into a kampong at night—although it has been done by people such as Curtis, ferreting for prostitutes. Prostitutes and petty criminals do nest in the kampongs; but most of those who live here are the respectable poor—*betjak* men, small traders, clerks—who are one step above those homeless ones who sleep along the canal banks.

It is into a section of this secret city that Billy Kwan follows the winking woman, crossing into the kampong's lake of darkness by a swaying suspension bridge over a canal. She has given up her purpose of soliciting or begging from him, and has ceased to wink and smile. Instead, gesturing him away with angry, furtive signs, she hurries faster, dragging the little girl, along a plank walkway through a no-man's-land of mud. I know the place. The roofs of thatch and tin are low, and the constructions bewilderingly interconnected: it is like a tenement district for dwarfs.

And dwarf Billy follows along the walkway. Men squat over cards by the light of a candle outside one of the huts; they eye his camera, but do not molest him. One, in a battered straw hat, singlet and shorts, calls mockingly, '*Mau main, bung?*'—and the rest laugh. *Gamelan* music from a radio jangles somewhere underneath the laughter of invisible women. There is a smell of something frying in coconut oil. The men's shadows, cast against the palm-mat wall of the hut by the candlelight, are huge, distinct and fantastic: they lean and sway like children's bogies as Kwan passes.

The woman stops at one of a series of huts and, without looking at Kwan again, stoops and enters. Billy follows, removing the black *pitji*.

The hut, which consists of one room, is lit by a coconut-oil lamp, and has no other occupants, although there are signs of them. Billy's dossier describes it minutely: a man's straw hat on a box, with a crumpled shirt under it; two of the bamboo beds called *balai-balai*; a low wooden table on which stand old butter cans used for cooking, and some dipper-scoops made from coconut shells. The little girl sits on her *balai-balai* watching Billy fixedly. The woman, ignoring him, kneels on pandanus matting spread on the earth floor, reaches into a packing case filled with dirty wrappings, and draws a sleeping infant from it. She holds it in her lap. It makes no sound.

Billy, kneeling down, now draws out a thick wad of rupiahs and holds them out to her. At first, she takes no notice. The sheer amount is no doubt puzzling rather than exciting to her: the equivalent of some twenty American dollars—a fortune. Then she whispers a question in the Jakartanese vernacular, seeking the only explanation she can imagine for this miracle: it is the same question the man outside addressed to him. I translate as best I can, since Kwan's record doesn't.

'*Mau main?*'—You want to play?

Billy shakes his head and answers in the same rough Jakartanese. '*Tidak. Tidak mau main.*'—No. I don't want to play.

He continues to hold the money out, at arm's length. Then he says, '*Buat Ibu, dan buat bayi.*'—For you, mother. For the baby.

Carefully, she takes the money and pushes it into the neck of her *kebaya*. The baby begins to cry feebly, and she croons to it. Billy says, '*Apakah dia anak laki-laki?*'—Is it a boy?

'*Enya–laki-laki.*' She nods and smiles.

'*Bayi sakit?*'—Is the baby sick?

'*Ya, sakit,*' she says. Then she speaks too rapidly for him to comprehend, and he shakes his head. He reaches out and touches the infant's smooth brown cheek with one finger, and the woman smiles.

Then Billy says, '*Pakailah uang itu untuk beli obat.*'—Use the money for medicine. He points to the little girl on the bed. '*Beli pakaian.*'—Buy her some clothes.

The woman nods. '*Tuan baik sekali. Betul 'nggak mau main?*'—Master is very kind. You really don't want to play?

He shakes his head, and continues to kneel in front of her. They talk further; he questions her about her life. Her husband deserted her soon after they arrived in Jakarta; she lives how she can, and shares this hut with a street trader and his woman, who are away at present.

The infant begins to cry again, and the crying feebly persists. The woman begins to unfasten her faded violet *kebaya*. Billy stands up, and says, '*Kasih obat, ya!*'—You get him medicine, understand?

She smiles and nods, freeing a swollen brown breast which the infant blindly devours. Billy waves abruptly, and disappears into the foul, secret toy-town: travesty of a decent village of the Javanese countryside. The *gamelan* music runs on in the steady heat, and the shadows of the card-players on the plank walkway loom to giant size, sway alarmingly, or flatten into nothing.

It has taken no great detective work on my part to identify 'Ibu'. Her photographs, of which Kwan took many, are in her dossier, and I recognised her immediately. I had often noticed her, with her small girl, hanging about the gates of the Hotel, as I made my way to the Wayang Bar; she was one of those who kept vigil on us there, like the *betjak* men and the banshees; she hovered always on the edges of one's consciousness.

She had winked and jerked her head at me once, and she had roused my curiosity. I assumed she was a prostitute, but the national costume and the presence of the child didn't fit: she looked, as Kwan puts it, 'respectable', and her roguish expression and prominent teeth put me in mind of some forgotten film comedienne of the thirties. She was odd.

It was Kevin Condon who discovered the nature of her little confidence trick, and gave me a long, aggrieved account of it. One night, out on Jalan Thamrin, just beyond the Hotel gates, she had winked at him and given the conspiratorial jerk of the head. She still had the little girl with her. Condon, putting aside his reservations about Jakarta prostitutes, and his nervousness about being on foot at night, had followed: in her traditional dress, she must have seemed the answer to his dreams, the incarnation of all his canal-side nymphs, summoning him to an assignation at last.

She led him up a dark, muddy side road, he said. ('I was bloody nervous, I tell you, Cookie. She seemed such a nice woman; but it began to look as if I was being lured off to be mugged.') But when she stopped by a fence and turned to him, she pointed to the little girl, and then made the mouth-to-belly sign of hunger, ending with graceful palm extended: the universal gesture of the Asiatic beggar.

When Condon bemusedly put money into her hand, she hurried away, without looking back. And when he followed her again she angrily waved him off. Poor Condon, it was like a practical joke arranged by someone who knew his weakness!

I noticed her on a few other occasions, early in that year, and saw that she was pregnant; then she ceased to come to the Car Park. It was only when the files came into my hands that I discovered Kwan's relationship with her: no one, I think, ever knew it. If he knew her name, he does not use it. He refers to her only as '*Ibu*': that Indonesian term reserved for maternal figures to whom great respect must be shown.

Two photographs are particularly striking. In the first, she is holding her little girl by the hand. Behind her, tier on tier, rises the Hotel Indonesia, its metal awnings glittering in the sun. She appears puzzled, and looks what she is: one of thousands of such peasant women from West Java, trapped and reduced by this shabby capital, which the country people believe is literally full of gold. But the only gold was up on Sukarno's monument, and so Ibù must have turned at times to prostitution, although there was little of the prostitute about her appearance. She has that closed and decent air common to all Javanese women, except for the lowest Westernised whores of the cemetery and the bazaars, in their cheap cotton frocks. It is an air which can only be put off with the national dress. One can see, despite her plainness, why Billy in one passage talks of her 'bodily majesty'.

In the second picture she is seated, nursing the infant. It is one of the best Billy ever took: touching and strangely awe-inspiring, shot against the hut's dark interior, and lit from below, perhaps by the coconut-oil lamp. Her face is entirely solemn now, deeply shadowed under the high cheek-bones. She no longer has the look of a winking Western comedienne, but is entirely Asian, more Northern Indian than Indonesian, uncannily like a piece of Hindu temple sculpture: a stone female divinity. This, from certain passages in her dossier, was no doubt an intentional effect: her offered breast looks ponderous enough for stone, and the sickly infant, its eyes closed, appears to be swooning away from the black fruit of the nipple as though from an abundance it cannot bear. Under this picture in the dossier is the following sentence:

Ibu is Durga incarnate: she is life.

The dossier is a thick one. After this first visit of 30 June, many more visits are recorded, with more gifts of money. I am not able to say whether Kwan ever became sexually intimate with her: the diary entries never hint at this, and I'm inclined to think he did not.

What Ibu's dossier does reveal is his obsessive concern for the Jakarta poor—of whom Ibu appears to have become a personification. That she also personified something else, something more complex, seen through those thickets in which Kwan was compelled to wander waist-high, also emerges from the dossier.

Billy was as ambivalent about women as he was about religion. On the whole, he was idealistic about the opposite sex: and this attitude, I think, was paramount. He worshipped, he said, 'the mystery in women'—and I am quoting from a dossier on the mythological history of the Divine Female entitled *Durga*. But in another more clinical dossier, simply entitled *Women*—in which nude photographs appear of orphaned-looking Sydney delinquents—he appears to aim at nothing less than a complete atlas of the female body, classifying women physiologically into twenty-five 'body-types', with separate classifications for parts of the body: his own private geography of the female anatomy! Here, he is less attractive, and the texts show the sterile curiosity of a child looking up a woman's skirts. It is the vision of a man imprisoned in a child's body, a man who is still a man, but whose gaze is often level not with women's faces, but with their torsos. To me, the dossier has a certain innocence about it: in none of his photographic charting of these strange shoals does that butcher's crudity and viciousness towards the body appear which I would call pornography. Nevertheless, I suppose this file has to be seen as Billy's dark side, the outcome of his lonely deprivation. It is also the outcome of the devouring curiosity which made him compile dossiers on whole cities: Sydney, Melbourne, London, Jakarta. I think he might eventually have destroyed the *Women* dossier. He genuinely and passionately hated lewdness, and the abuse of the body and neglect of the spirit he saw as our current folly. This, too, was an obsession with him; and I don't see him as a hypocrite.

Some readers may. They may see his visits to Ibu, and even his charity, as nothing more than a variant of Condon's furtive voyeurism. But I don't see compassion or idealism as automatically cancelled when some subterranean stream can be identified beneath. In our current cartoon philosophy, opposites, and even two sides of the same coin, cannot co-exist. I prefer the medieval wisdom, which said that lust thwarted could become love, that barriers to the body could lift the spirit. Civilisation is based on what's called hypocrisy, whether we like it or not. And so I tend Billy's memory, and mock neither his passion nor his compassion.

A final passage in the entry in Ibu's dossier for 30 June needs quoting in full, if you are to see Billy's activity as he saw it himself. He begins by posing that question put by the people to John the Baptist, the question he had once put to Hamilton: 'What then must we do?'

'What then must we do?' We must give and give, wherever we can. I have decided that Tolstoy was wrong, and that political solutions are for those with no hearts, only consciences—and consciences go rotten: hence tyrannies. The task may be hopeless, but we must still attempt it. We must give with love to whomever God has placed in our path. So I give to Ibu. I can't take her out of that hut—but I will transform it. If money is all I can give, then I'll give it on the spot, and change her life where she sits: a bed, chairs, medicine for little Udin, clothes.

Ibu has great cheerfulness, and bodily majesty. Entirely illiterate: can only just converse with me. Does not understand where Australia is, and thinks I'm Indonesian-Chinese. Can't make her understand that the canal which she and the child bathe in and drink from carries disease. She laughs. In another country she would be a decent woman. Here, she begs, and perhaps sells herself. She is a nullity—a vacuum. But with what dignity she holds herself together around that vacuum, as her shabby national dress holds her body! Her tragedy is repeated a million times in this city.

No other dossier provides such a clear graph as Ibu's does of the obsessions that would come to dominate Kwan's mind as the Year of Living Dangerously drew on. And it is possible to see, at this point in the year, that his prowlings are not caused just by the heat or insomnia.

He went to Pasar Baru to seek not only Ibu, but President

Sukarno. His main dossier on Sukarno is worth reproducing fairly fully.

DOSSIER S 9: SUKARNO, Doctor Engineer Raden (Kusno Susro), President, Republic of Indonesia

The title 'Raden' is that of a member of Java's aristocratic priyayi *class. Names 'Kusno Susro' were dropped in childhood, because he was sickly, and his father re-named him Karna, to bring him better health.*

BORN: 6 June 1901, in the opening year of this terrible century, under the sign of Gemini. Says this is his good fortune: he has twin personalities, hard as steel, or poetic and sentimental. He was born at dawn, and a volcano erupted—both portents of future glory, of his role as a Javanese god-king! (The 6th of June: the double six! Dread possibility: is this the mark of the Beast? Is this the source of his charismatic power?)*

NATIVE PLACE: East Java

RELIGION: Muslim. But his mother, a Balinese, was high-caste Hindu. His father a Muslim of the priyayi *class. Thus he unites in himself the two great religions of Java. A double man, a man of dualities!*

To the people of the outer islands, he is the incarnation of the god Vishnu, who sometimes comes to earth as a dwarf! Are you a secret member of my race, Bung Karno? Are you, in some aspects, Dwarf Semar? You who love the Wayang must sometimes think about Semar—who is the old Javanese god Ismaja, transformed into a dwarf and a clown. Your people say Ismaja could still rule the world, if he wanted. The Javanese dream of glory! A god in disguise—and when he throws it off, the gods of the north, who colonised you, will all bow down!

You tell that in the days of your youthful struggle against the Dutch, as you prepared to lead your people to freedom, you were pedalling through the southern suburbs of Bandung on your bicycle.

* *Revelation*, xiii, 18: 'Let him that hath understanding count the number of the beast: for it is the number of a man; and his number is six hundred threescore and six.'—R.J.C.

*You were going nowhere, thinking. (O Bung Karno, how often have
I done the same in my own sub-tropical city to the south, alone on
Sydney Sundays, walking past the crazy orators on the Domain, or
through the moist Pacific breeze on South Head, thinking my
thoughts!) And you tell how you found yourself watching a ragged
peasant hoeing a tiny field there: a property of less than one-third of
a hectare.*

*You spoke to him, and asked him who owned the lot he worked on.
When the farmer told you he owned it himself, you asked who owned
the tools he worked with. 'I do,' said the farmer. You then asked if
his crop was sufficient for his needs. 'There's just barely enough to
keep us alive,' the peasant said.*

*'But brother, you live in poverty,' you said. And you tell how you
realised that although a landowner, although not a member of the
proletariat who sell their labour, this typical Javanese farmer was in
fact a pauper. You asked his name, and he told you 'Marhaen'. And
you used this name for the poor landowning peasants of Indonesia,
on whom the nation's well-being depended, and whose voice you
would be.*

Remain their voice, Bung Karno—never forget little Marhaen!

Billy was fascinated by the story of the Bung going to Pasar
Baru at night, disguised in shabby civilian clothes, to 'bathe in the
crowds', to rub against the masses who intoxicated him. Kwan
often spoke of this to me. I didn't repeat the bazaar rumour that
the President also hunted nubile girls; nor did I pass on my belief
that those night rovings of Sukarno's no longer took place,
belonging as they did to an earlier and happier period, when the
nation and Sukarno were less sick. Billy maintained an almost
wistful belief that the visits continued; and the entries in
Sukarno's file show that Kwan wandered in Pasar Baru on the
off-chance of seeing his hero.

By the night of 30 June, his hope had begun to die, it appears;
and so had other hopes. For the first time, in a diary entry in
Sukarno's file bearing that same date, real unease appears about
the wisdom of the course on which Sukarno has set his country.

30 June

I looked for you tonight in Pasar Baru, Bung Karno, remembering your words: 'I'm a man of the people. I must see them, listen to them, rub against them. They're the bread of life to me.'

But you were not there, and I wonder if you will ever come again.

You are still the great dalang. The Wayang of the Left and the Right are still in your hands. But what predominance you now give to the godless Wayang of the Left! Does expediency really demand so much? And is it true, as some of the press are saying, that the dalang could end in the hands of one of his own creatures? Can't believe this: but the shadow of Aidit grows and grows. It's said he now dominates the Cabinet meetings at Bogor.

Bung Karno, what path are you taking? In Comrade Aidit's heart there is no romanticism about revolution, no true love of the soil of Indonesia, no belief in the five principles of Pantja Sila! He and his cadres would stamp out the ancient dreams which are the spiritual life-blood of the country. The myths would be perverted into propaganda, the life of the spirit stilled in the name of the full belly, and love of God made an offence. Islam would be extinguished, and so would joy.

Only Nasution, of the Muslim Army leaders, could check the PKI if you were removed, Sukarno. But Nasution is no Bung Karno. Why, Sukarno, if you are a true son of God, can you no longer see the danger you are courting? Unless we love God and reverence life, we are bound for extinction, I believe you know that; why do you seem to forget it? If the puppets fall from the dalang's hands, what then?

A kilo of rice now costs a worker's daily wage. Your people suffer, Sukarno! Marhaen suffers! How can you bear his suffering? When will you come again to Pasar Baru?

It's possible to see that Kwan begins to be gripped at the end of June by two parallel obsessions. The first is his doubt over Sukarno's policies for Indonesia (and this is constantly linked with his concern for the well-being of Ibu and her children). The second is his strange, proprietary interest in the affair between Guy Hamilton and Jill Bryant. Step by step, these preoccupations begin to lead him to a wild disappointment.

11

When Hamilton began to take Jill out, he had been afraid that Kwan would be extravagantly upset—would quite reasonably regard it as a betrayal. But Billy had been strangely affable; and he was shortly to make an offer whose motives Hamilton found difficult to fathom.

The cameraman had made brief, delicate references to the affair, in his lightest voice; remarks showing that he knew and approved of it.

'You make her very happy you know, old man. She's a changed girl.'

'You sound very fatherly, Billy. She's no girl, you know. She's nearly my age.'

'Ah, Jilly needs looking after, just the same. And I wouldn't really have been good at it, even though I love her. You two are made for each other.'

This pronouncement, made in Kwan's driest and most matter-of-fact tone, had caused Hamilton to become silent with embarrassment. They were seated side by side in the back of the office car; Hartono was driving them to the Foreign Office, to film an interview with Subandrio.

'Jakarta's a hard place to be alone in,' Kwan said blandly. 'And I suppose you and Jill hardly ever *are* alone, really. Look—if you want to get away from everyone, there's always my bungalow. I'm often out, and I'll lend you the key. All you have to do is tell me when you want it.'

Hamilton found it difficult to know what expression to wear at this, and studied the relay-race of Jakarta's traffic. But he took the key, with muttered thanks.

'Right, that's settled then,' Kwan said. Neither of them looked at each other again, throughout the drive.

As Kwan had said, privacy was very difficult to find in Jakarta; and the curfew made love affairs even more difficult. Moreover, Hamilton and Jill were extremely noticeable, not just to the European community, but to the Indonesians. Their relationship had quickly become guessed at. They were even mentioned in the gossip column of the English-language Jakarta newspaper—a penalty of Hamilton's prominence here. It was obvious to me that she hoped to marry him: she would watch him, at the official and unofficial dinner parties we all attended, as though the future hung on his decisions.

And Billy's bungalow was a boon to them. Hamilton could rarely visit Jill's apartment, since Moira, a middle-aged cipher clerk in the Embassy, objected to men being brought there at night; and Jill refused to come to Hamilton's room in the Hotel. She had a great fear of gossip in the Wayang Bar: a fear which seems very dated now, but which then had some foundation. She had already been involved with at least one newsman—now transferred—and there had been a time, before the breakdown of that particular affair, when she had joined us regularly in the Wayang, the only woman in our group. Her lively friendliness and her looks made her very popular with the Wayang Club (we were all a little in love with Jillie, I suppose); but she inhabited a region where she was regarded with genuine affection by some of us, and seen as 'easy' by others. Since, in that year, supposed sexual fickleness in a woman was still often held in contempt, a particular smile appeared on some faces at the mention of Jill's name: it could have expressed pleasure at her liveliness, or else a sly irony. For some time, Hamilton remained ignorant of the reasons for this smile; and early in July, it was to cause him distress.

Jill was late.

Sitting at a table in the darkness of the Wayang Bar, Hamilton tore a beer mat into pieces. She had never been so late before. They had arranged to meet here at seven o'clock, to go to dinner in the Hotel's top-floor restaurant, and it was now nearly eight. He found himself urgently resenting each lost minute of their evening, which crept steadily towards curfew, since tomorrow was the beginning of a three-week separation: Jill was going on leave to Singapore.

Pete Curtis moved over from the bar. Swaying above Hamilton's table, he seemed drunker than usual. 'It's come, buddy, it's come,' he said.

Hamilton tried to look interested.

'My transfer to Saigon,' Curtis explained. 'In ten days, I love and leave you.'

'We'll miss you, Pete.'

'No, you won't, you bastard, and I won't miss you. But maybe I'll see you over there. That's where the action is now, baby—with those B52s bombing the north, I figure it's only a matter of time before the Chinese come in, boots and all. If your outfit have any sense, they'll move you there. But maybe they have a better man to send.' He gave a loose, offensive grin.

To Hamilton, whose gaze kept searching for the door through which Jill should come, Curtis's rivalry and trade jargon were wearisome; and he was determined not to ask him to sit down. He raised his glass with a dismissive gesture. 'Lots of joy in Saigon,' he said. 'But I'd rather be here. The big scene's still to come, and I want to see it.'

With the ponderous sensitivity some men have in drunkenness, Curtis stood taking in Hamilton's mood. Then he said: 'Yeah, well of course, you're real cosy here with little Jillie, right?'

Hamilton stared up at him impassively, and said nothing.

Curtis swayed, in the half-dark. 'Can't blame you, old buddy. They say she's a very good lay.'

'Is that what they say, Pete?' Hamilton stood up quickly, put the heel of his hand under Curtis's chin, and heaved. Curtis staggered backwards with crab-like motions, colliding with the round bar; and Hamilton walked quickly from the Wayang. According to Kevin Condon, who was watching from his stool, darkness prevented the incident from attracting the attention it might have done elsewhere; and Pete merely stood shaking his head, without attempting to follow.

Hurrying furiously along the arcade outside, Hamilton swore under his breath. He was already ashamed of his juvenile action, and almost as angry with himself as he was with Curtis. This was what Jakarta had brought him to, he said: this adolescent anguish over Jill. He was stopped by one of the bell-boys from the lobby: a late, falsely smiling bearer of good tidings in plum-coloured jacket and *pitji* cap. 'Letter to you, Mr Hamilton.'

He read as he walked: it was from Jill.

Darling, I have to work late with Ralph Henderson. Meet me at Billy's bungalow at 7.30. It'll be too late to have dinner and still have much time together. So who wants dinner?

He drove with vicious recklessness down Jalan Thamrin towards Jalan Kebon Sirih and their trysting place; and his anger continued. She often sent such notes by messenger to the Hotel. Sometimes, when they had not seen each other for some days, she would send him a letter simply to make contact. *Just to say hullo . . . know it's stupid but I miss you terribly . . . you'll get sick of my persistence, I suppose . . . Love you . . .* And Hamilton had smiled indulgently over these blue scraps of paper; evidence of an urgency he enjoyed, but thought he didn't feel himself.

Now he was not so complacent. Those who are devoted to us are supposed to stay that way; it's very disconcerting to find they may withdraw, or put on another mask; and Pete Curtis's remark had disclosed an entirely different Jill to him.

I found this naïvety extraordinary in a man of Hamilton's age. When I tackled him light-heartedly about the Curtis incident, I was forced to discuss Jill with him, and I defended her; and in doing so I discovered the extent of his anachronistic romanticism. He simply found it difficult to believe that an English girl of Jill's type could ever be sexually undiscriminating: it was a painful paradox to him.

For over four months they had seen each other constantly. Their situation had been unnatural, of course: under the yelling visage of *Konfrontasi*, they had drawn together with a special closeness; and he was happy with her, he said, in a way that made him feel he had never really liked a woman before. They were linked by the usual shared enthusiasms to which lovers give exaggerated importance: a fondness for Vivaldi and the Beatles; for similar jokes; and they had enjoyed the same childhood books, at their opposite ends of the globe, in particular the 'Alice' books.

They shared, as well, a curious common homesickness. Jill longed for a cool, actual Norfolk; but Hamilton, through her, looked for an England that had never been his and had never, in fact, existed. But this made for a friendship as important as their physical need of each other. As they wandered hand in hand through the burning alleys of Old Jakarta, surrounded by odours of drains and human flesh, she had pictured for him the house in Great Yarmouth where she had grown up, and an England of winter concert-going, of yachting in summer on the Norfolk Broads: a past not his, but one that a wistful corner of his mind said should have been. Her father was a solicitor, whose firm was not doing well; she had a brother and sister. He never grew tired of reconstructing the details of her background: it was a story which dissolved Jakarta's insane uncertainties.

'Poor old England,' she said. 'You might not like it, now. Daddy's firm's been in awful trouble over the past few years. The bloody taxation's just about wiped him out. But he never stops being cheerful—he's a darling.'

She was oddly unsure of her own attractiveness. 'My breasts are too small,' she would say. 'Admit it.' She complained also about the beaked, high-bridged nose, which Kwan calls 'Danish' in his file. ('What a beak!') Hamilton thought her face delicate; but it had good and bad days, appearing sometimes bare ('Gothic', as Kwan says), with a hint of the plainness that might overtake her in middle age, but at other times having a quality Hamilton found haunting—presumably recalling that melancholy Edwardian nymph of his, whose eyes held the same sadness as Jill's.

I could see all this, being susceptible to Jillie myself; but I found Hamilton's sentimentality disastrous. It made him simply unable to put the two halves of her together. How could this Arthur Rackham nymph, his English Alice, be Pete Curtis's 'very good lay'?

They lay on Billy's divan bed, Hamilton on his back, Jill curled at his side. A handsome blue 'Suzy Wong' dress, worn in honour of their abandoned dinner, hung over a chair on top of Hamilton's tan safari suit. Billy's big cheap alarm-clock ticked loudly in the darkness; a shaft of light through the window picked out the desk, the puppet Arjuna on the wall, and a small section of the photograph gallery. The filing cabinet was locked as usual. So too, rather oddly and inconveniently, was the door to the dark-room-bathroom, just to the right of the bed. Billy never left this room open; Hamilton assumed it was to give his equipment added protection against burglars.

He sprawled a little apart from Jill: a difficult feat on so narrow a bed. Suddenly, she twisted herself and knelt over him, supporting herself on both outstretched hands, peering through the darkness. Pale, twin sheaves of hair dangled just above his face; the small breasts she worried about pointed tragically to accuse him. 'You didn't believe me, did you?' she demanded.

She was harking back to her lateness. Hamilton had not complained of it; nor had he told her of the incident with Curtis. But he was abstracted and over-polite in a way he had never been before, and this was maddening to Jill. All her security and all her hopes, although he had made her no promises, now rested on their intimacy; and she watched him, with an almost childish anxiety, for clues to what had gone wrong.

'Something terribly important broke tonight,' she said. 'The biggest thing for years. I can't tell you more—it's classified information. But Ralph really needed me urgently.'

He grinned. 'Tonight and every night,' he said. 'The Colonel's needs must be answered.'

Jill grew angry. 'What a rotten thing to say. It's not like that any more. And what do *you* care, anyway?'

This was check and mate, and Hamilton kept silent. Her oblique references to a serious commitment had always been

140

made in a joking tone until now; and the convention between them had been that she was free to make these wry little gambits, but that he was not obliged to take them seriously. At the same time, he knew very well how serious for her they were becoming. But he ignored them, since marriage would mean the death of the career he had successfully begun. No foreign correspondent, the wisdom ran, could successfully combine the job with domesticity. This logic suited Hamilton, who equated marriage with suffocation; with aeons of boredom in some terrible Australian suburb; with Sydney and 'the geriatrics' ward'. All the trapped sub-editors around that table in the news-room, wearing out like old chairs, had wives and children and mortgages, he said.

He and Jill had not seriously exchanged a hostile word until now. They had been at that stage of an affair which he found most delightful: showing only their 'good' selves; exploring unknown country. The stage in which we hear our own voices repeating complaints and accusations from other love struggles was one he had always walked away from; he remained single at twenty-nine largely for this reason. Sensing the approach of this phase in him seems to have changed Jill's defensive indignation into a sort of alarm.

'I suppose I should have come straight to the Hotel afterwards,' she said. 'It's closer than here. But then we'd have gone to your room, and I hate those rooms. All that plastic teak-wood.'

'I thought you'd never been in one.'

'Christ, you *are* suspicious tonight All right, I've been in one, a long time ago. I didn't want the gossip starting I had to put up with then.' There was a silence; she knelt upright, her dimly furious face peering at his in bafflement, her pallid nakedness suddenly sad: a child's. 'There's something wrong,' she said. 'Isn't there?' She sighed, and seemed to come to a decision. 'Would you perhaps think the possibility of a civil war here was important enough for Ralph to call me back?'

'What are you talking about?'

'Look—if you use this information, I'm finished with the service—do you realise that?'

'So don't tell me. There's no need.'

But she continued to kneel, and went on, clasping her hands in the deep shadow between her thighs. 'We've been getting off coded cables to Whitehall,' she said. 'Our Hong Kong people have passed on some information about a ship that's just left Shanghai.'

'A ship?'

'Apparently it's on its way here with some secret consignment of arms, courtesy of the Chinese Government. You *do* see the point, I suppose.' Her tone was bitter. 'I've only told you for one reason; to make you see. Ralph works very hard, and he needed me tonight more than he's ever done before. He's been around often enough when I needed him. I want you to *understand* that. Do you?'

'Jesus,' Hamilton said. 'Arms. A gift for the PKI. So Peking really are backing a takeover. You say the ship's already at sea. Do they have a date of arrival?'

'I don't *know*,' she whispered miserably. 'Look—if you ever use this, I'll never forgive you.'

He lay back and began to laugh. 'The greatest story I could ever want,' he said, 'and I can't use it.' He pulled her down against him, and she came with pathetic quickness. 'Don't worry,' he said. 'But we'll all know, soon enough. It means the PKI have got the hardware for their Fifth Force—they're on their way. And having a white face will be very bad news. Are your people making plans about that?'

'We'll be airlifted out if things get bad enough,' she said. 'Guy—what about you?'

'I'll hang on till the last second, and then it's rabbit run to the Australian Embassy,' he said. 'We live from day to day.'

'Don't stay here. Come to England.'

'You stay. You're my England.'

'I love you. Please believe that, Guy. I need you to believe it.' She lay with her head on his chest. 'You're so big,' she said. She often repeated this, like some sort of charm. They lay quiet for a time in their darkness; then she muttered, 'You're terribly suspicious of women, aren't you?'

When he asked her the reason for this question, she countered by asking him why he had never married.

'There was a girl in England I was going to marry once,' Hamilton said, 'when I was working on a London paper.' He began a story punctuated by long pauses: a story he said he had told to no one else. He had been going to marry the girl, and then had changed his mind. But he had been very sorry for her, and had not known how to break it off. It was his first time in England. She had been loyal to him, and was very much in love with him. She worked as a clerk in a bank. Young and poor, they had gone to cinemas and theatres in the cheap seats, or spent the freezing nights huddled in front of the gas-fire in his bed-sitting-room in Earl's Court. She had suffered from deep depressions, which distressed him more and more: it was this which had made him decide to break with her. As his job—the first one he had held on a major paper—had grown more demanding, he had made this an excuse to see less of her.

One evening, she had phoned him, asking him to come over to her room in Bayswater and talk to her. But Hamilton had an assignment: in an hour, he had to be at London airport to interview an important American senator. He told her he couldn't come, but would phone her the next day.

'I did phone her the next day,' he said, 'but I couldn't talk to her.' He groped for a cigarette, lit it, and lay back again. 'She was dead. She'd gassed herself, with one of those bloody dreary gas-fires they have in London.'

'You weren't to blame,' Jill said quickly.

'It was a good interview with the senator,' Hamilton said. 'I got up-graded because of it.' He passed her the cigarette. 'Of course I was to blame. You know I was to blame: and I'll know it all my life.'

She drew once on the cigarette, then put it in the ashtray on the bedside table and laid her head on his chest, her arms about him. 'Don't you ever leave *me*,' she said.

He was silent. Marriage, the notion underlying everything they said, hummed monotonously in the dark like Billy's air-conditioning unit: but not to be given voice by Hamilton. Jill raised herself on one elbow, and tried to read his expression. After a time, she said, 'You *will* leave me eventually, though, won't you? You'd already decided that before you came here tonight.' Then, with a transition to inappropriate cheerfulness, she said, 'Don't worry, sweetie, you don't have to answer. It's just that I rather needed to know, tonight. There's a reason.'

'What reason?'

'Nothing that really matters. I don't cling, Guy; don't worry. We might all be dead soon, anyway, no? Just a lot of dead *Nekolims*.'

They both laughed; she had a way of intoning '*Nekolims*' he always found funny.

They lay quiet for a long time; softly, on Billy's transistor, Indonesian pop music crooned and cried. Outside the bungalow were teeming, difficult lives: stern brown faces that expected little; plump faces that were prepared to look coldly on appalling pain; all of dark, threadbare Java, moving towards its holocaust.

There are moments when we live in a larger story, or think we do. Hamilton saw now in his mind's eye the gleam of the South China Sea under the moon; and somewhere on that expanse, which was like a space in the mind, the cargo ship from Shanghai, approaching through the womb-fug of the tropics, bearing down on this gimcrack country for which he was developing an unreal attachment, but where horrors were now certain to be unleashed. What she had said was true: they could be spun apart like fragments, then, as though they had never met. They could be killed, in some wholesale PKI purge of Europeans. It made their relationship take on in the present the poignancy of the past; and he held her more closely against him. He was profoundly happy. Yes, perhaps it was still possible to love her.

In Billy Kwan's file on Jill Bryant there are certain passages concerning her relationship with Hamilton that are both 'literary' and highly intimate. The floweriness of these passages leads me to believe that they are most likely the product of inference, and of Kwan's imagination. But I wonder sometimes about that locked door in Billy's garden house, leading to the bathroom he used as a darkroom. Hamilton and Jill had no suspicions about it, apparently, and I wish that I didn't either: I'd prefer to believe

that passages like the following are the product of an extraordinary insight. Kwan addresses Jill directly.

6 July

*He holds you, my giant brother. His big body masters yours: you
arch to meet him. Is it you, this white animal? That grotto of golden
weed: is that, after all, your core?*

*No. He masters what he thinks is you, but he can't hold you,
though you beg him to! You are abandoned: your eyes dance, are
gay: and yet, like a naked wraith, you dance down the tunnel ahead
of him—smiling, beckoning, yet not to be held.*

'Come on.' *Teeth clenched like an athlete's.* 'Come on, oh, come
on!' *But the grotto has a secret door—which is locked, always
locked.*

12

Two days later, at the Calling Hour, Hamilton's peace of mind was to be disturbed again.

He had just interviewed a Foreign Ministry official whose house was in the little street off Jalan Kebon Sirih; and he decided to call on Billy, whom he had not seen since the day before. He wanted to make sure that Kwan was coming in to the office next morning. The cameraman was getting less reliable about these calls lately, and Hamilton needed some filming done.

He made his way through the motionless heat into the overgrown garden behind the big villa, and knocked on the door of the bungalow. There was no response. The *membeo*, in its bamboo cage, looked sharply at him, but made no sound. Hamilton did not like to use his key when Billy was not expecting him, but he opened the door and looked in. Finding the room empty, he sat down in one of the rattan chairs to wait.

He enjoyed, as always, the absolute quiet of the little garden house after the buzz and jangle of the city; he stretched his legs, and yawned, and looked at the array of pictures on the wall. When fifteen minutes had passed, and Billy did not appear, Hamilton did what most of us do in such circumstances: he got up and began to move about the room, looking at whatever attracted his curiosity. In his account of this to me, he said defensively that he had no intention of prying.

A file was lying on top of the grey steel cabinet: it was the first time Billy had left one out. Hamilton was startled to see the name on the bright orange tag: *BRYANT, Gillian Edith*. He opened it.

DOSSIER B 26: BRYANT, Gillian Edith
NATIONALITY: British. Born: 1938, under the sign of Pisces.
NATIVE PLACE: Great Yarmouth, Norfolk
RELIGION: lax C. of E.
OCCUPATION: Secretary, British Embassy, Jakarta
FORMER POSTINGS: Brussels, Singapore. Divorced: no children
BODY TYPE: 4C*
REMARKS:

  Subject is of athletic-pyknic physique, and is hyper-active. Physiognomy of a type common to the east of England: Gothic. One of the people of the Danelaw. High-prowed Danish nose.

  In temperament, effervescent and optimistic: tends to be extroverted, but is given to cyclic bouts of melancholy, and shows a strain of hysteria, for reasons which are not fully established. Neurosis of guilt suspected: unusual attachment to father may be a clue. While subject cannot be described as entirely promiscuous, sexual history is disturbed.

  Reasons for failed marriage unclear, but subject has intense need for affection, and wishes to idealise man of her choice. Tendency to narcissism, and enjoys company of older men. Again, query relationship with father. Some sort of sexual search is going on. Need for protection intense.

  Subject is at same time highly organised, intelligent and efficient at her job. No security risk, unless through vulnerability to men. Values, those of the present British upper-middle-class: i.e. collapsing. Little religious feeling, yet has a reverence for life. This is a spirit like a wavering flame, which only needs care to burn high. If this does not happen, subject could lapse into the promiscuity and bitterness of the failed romantic.

  Essentially devoted to order and stability, but sometimes pays lip-service to current anarchic values, etc.

* This is a reference to Kwan's anatomical types, in the file *Women.*—R.J.C.

147

In this dossier, there are three pictures of Jill. The first is a duplicate of the portrait Billy had in his room. The other two are nude studies.

The first, well-composed and softly lit, is a frontal view. Taken in a seated position, she smiles off to the right, her eyes alight with that dazed tenderness which had its source mainly in astigmatism. Her hands are behind her head, her arms raised to expose smooth hollows like those of pre-puberty. The second study is a full-length back view, so that we don't see her face: but the top-heavy mane of blond hair, the delicately marked shoulder-blades and slight back, above the sudden widening of the hips and buttocks, are all unmistakable.

I can only conjecture why Jill permitted these photographs. Her motive may have been charity, or she may have consented out of natural female vanity: he was, after all, a brilliant photographer, and she may not have been able to resist having her youth immortalised on his 'glazed cards'. But she got more than she bargained for: she can hardly have anticipated entering the 'secret system' of the files.

Hamilton stood reading the dossier with frequent swift glances at the door. In his first bemusement, he was inclined to guess that its main purpose was political. The nude photographs caused him to recall stories of agents having obtained such material for purposes of blackmail; and this seemed all the more likely in the light of his new knowledge of the sensitive information Jill was handling.

But as he read on he began to dismiss this idea; the private and eccentric nature of the file became apparent to him. He began to flick through the 'diary' section, the entries in which had begun nearly a year before. The final entry bore the previous day's date —Billy must have made it last night, and then left the file lying on the cabinet. The entry made Hamilton stiffen, and stare for a long time.

7 July

So you are pregnant. Is the child Hamilton's? And if so, what will you do? Of course it's his; it must be.

The entry stopped there, perhaps unfinished. From the portrait

148

that began the dossier, in which she wore the modest dress with the Peter Pan collar, Jill smiled up at Hamilton with frank, treacherous friendliness. But he felt he no longer knew her. The other pictures made public a body he had never really possessed: something from one of Condon's onanistic fantasies, or Curtis's jokes; the darling of the Wayang Bar.

Hearing a noise he took to be approaching footsteps, he hastily closed the file. But the noise came no nearer, and finally disappeared.

Hamilton opened the door; the grass-grown path under the huge banyan-tree was empty. He closed the door quietly and moved away up the path.

That night, as we sat over our bottle of Scotch in his room, he told me what he had found.

'Good lord, Cookie,' he said, 'if he's got a file like that on Jill, who else has he got them on? You? Me? The rest of the press corps? And what for? He could be bloody dangerous.'

His tone made it obvious that he had become both angry and contemptuous towards his devoted cameraman—and less inclined to take Jill seriously. But he didn't tell me, that night, about the entry claiming she was pregnant. I think he hoped this was a fantasy of Billy's, or something that would just go away.

He had by no means decided to give her up; but the groundwork had been laid, and this disturbed me: I had reached the age to be sentimental about a couple as well matched as they were. I was disturbed also about Kwan, knowing what Hamilton's regard meant to him; and I was less repelled by his private file-keeping than Hamilton was, and said so. I also suggested that Hamilton tell no one else in the Wayang what he had found, to which he agreed.

'I don't think Billy's an agent,' I said. 'We'd be silly to dismiss the possibility, but I doubt whether the Chinese or the KGB or the CIA would be crazy enough to employ him. He's too unstable.'

'Which means he's keeping them for his own purposes,' Hamilton said. He swirled the Scotch in his glass, his usually humorous lower lip angrily out-thrust. 'That's bloody creepy,' he said. 'The idea of dossiers being kept on people gives me the creeps, anyway; but when a private person does it—' He searched for words. 'The little bastard's playing God,' he said. Even the bulbous nose that marred his handsome face had an appearance of outrage: I had to check a smile.

'Yes, I suppose he is,' I said. 'But he might be a benevolent little god, mightn't he?'

He didn't laugh, but drank off his Scotch contemptuously. Then he said with studied casualness, 'I wonder how many other people in the Wayang have seen those pictures?'

That he actually suspected Kwan of showing them around surprised me. I did my best to convey my own certainty that Billy would have shown them to no one. But Hamilton, smiling dubiously, seemed unconvinced. It was the photographs that had pained him most; he really was quite Victorian about women.

'I hope this won't change things between you and Jill,' I said. 'I've no doubt she posed for Kwan before you came along. And it's no crime to have had affairs, is it?'

But he smiled without amusement, lying in the Hotel's aqua arm-chair, his beer-stein and Japanese print standing behind him; and he made a remark in which easy cynicism and some sort of genuine bitterness were oddly mixed. 'Little blonde girls,' he said softly, staring into the standard lamp. 'Why can't we trust them?'

He was not as adolescent as he sounds. He cared about Jill more than he wished to know; and he now had that touching puzzlement of the man of action for whom the complexities of other people have suddenly become too much. Not to take action —not to simply smash something, or begin something new—is unbearable to such a man at such a point. The next day he was to be given his opportunity; or perhaps his excuse.

13

Rosini handed him the air-letter from his news-editor as soon as he came into the office. He sat reading and re-reading it in a sort of horror. He had known it would come, he said, but he hadn't believed it would be now.

ABS Sydney, July 2nd

Dear Guy,

Your recent coverage has been impressive, but we may have to move you shortly to Saigon. Burgess has taken shrapnel in the leg in an ambush incident (not serious), but we've moved him to Singapore for 'rest and recuperation'. As you'll realise, now that President Johnson has stepped up the bombing of the North, and our own combat troops are in, Vietnam is increasingly becoming the major story. Meanwhile, the Indonesian-Malaysian situation, although it's tense, seems to be at something of a stalemate.

I'd like your personal assessment of the situation, to help me decide whether to keep you there. Perhaps Kumar could keep us covered for a month or so. If anything big broke, we could recall you, or send someone from the Singapore office to take over.

Maybe Saigon will give you a fresh eye!

Regards,

BILL BIGGINS

He looked about the room: at 'Tiger Lily' Rosini, in her bright national costume, spectacled and demure, tapping away at her typewriter by the door; at Kumar, his white-shirted back bowed intently over his analysis of the Indonesian newspapers, under his picture of the *prahu* in the sunset; at Billy Kwan, cross-legged on his desk-top, reading a book called *The Expansion of Islam* while he waited for Hamilton to take him out on a film assignment. He had never really come to know these people: now, it seemed, he never would, and it became to him a matter of tragic importance. And his resentment of Billy had become petty and absurd, he found; it was to Billy that he needed to speak in this crisis.

He stood abruptly, jerked his head to Kwan and, carrying the letter, went out through the louvered doors onto the little balcony above the street: the bridge on which they had so often happily charted their course in these past months. Billy was accustomed to this signal, which meant that Hamilton wished to have a discussion the others should not overhear. Kumar cautiously watched them go; as Hamilton caught his eye, he lowered his head again.

Kwan read the letter carefully; then he burst into rattling speech. 'For Christ's sake, they can't do this—they're mad. That bloody Vietnam thing could drag on for years—and everything's coming to a head here. You've got to convince that idiot Biggins.'

'Right—that's what I want to talk to you about,' Hamilton said. 'I don't want to leave Indonesia. I'm involved here.'

Billy broke into a broad smile. 'Of course you are, old man,' he said. 'How could I work with anyone else? They'd send me another Potter. Besides—there's Jillie, isn't there? I know she'd follow you eventually, if you decided to marry her—but that could take time. And it would give Colonel Henderson too much of a chance to influence her again.' He looked across the canal to the distant traffic running along Jalan Pos. 'You're going to have to do something about Henderson, old man. I don't like the fact that he's gone on this trip to Singapore with her.'

Leaning against the balcony, squinting in the sun, Hamilton stared down at him in what at first was absolute surprise. Then he threw his head back and gave one of the full-throated laughs with which he always expressed enjoyment of a joke. Kwan blinked rapidly, with no answering amusement on his face. 'No, *really*!' Hamilton said. 'Is that true?'

'Don't misunderstand me, Guy,' Billy said quickly. 'He's not on holiday with her—he went on business. I don't think it's anything more than that.'

But Hamilton was no longer listening; he was welcoming back the full flow of indifference that was his natural state. He was free again.

'Don't jump to any conclusions about this,' Kwan was saying. 'Jillie needs you badly just now.'

But Hamilton, who had been looking over the balcony, swung around sharply and cut him short. 'About this question of hanging on here,' he said. 'I can advise Biggins that I should; but that doesn't mean he'll take the advice. It's going to be very tough to convince him. The only thing that might do that is the possibility of a complete takeover by the PKI inside the country. And the one way I can persuade Biggins is to back up what I say with a hell of a story. I think I've got one.'

'That's good, old man. But about Jillie—'

But Hamilton cut him off brutally. 'You'd better listen carefully,' he said. 'I'll want you to follow this up. I'm not telling you my source, and you tell no one about it; especially not Kumar. Right? If the PKI know we're after this information, we could both come to nasty ends.'

Kwan began to speak, but again Hamilton interrupted. 'Just *listen*. You want me to stay in Jakarta, don't you?'

Kwan stared down at the bicycles swarming over the bridge on the canal, his expression uneasy and baffled. 'Yes, old man—I want you to stay.'

Hamilton completed his report to Biggins the following afternoon.

'You are thinking very hard, boss?'

He started, and looked up to find Kumar directly in front of his desk, smiling down at him. The soft-voiced question seemed to hold some note of sympathy; and Hamilton had the irrational

153

feeling, as his assistant's watchful eyes rested on the report to Biggins, that Kumar knew what was in it.

'You should relax more,' Kumar said. He continued to stand respectfully in front of the desk, neat in his well-pressed shirt and slacks, applying for conversation. This was unusual; the office day was almost over, and Kumar usually approached Hamilton only on work matters.

Hamilton swung his feet up on the desk and leant back in his chair. 'That's a good idea,' he said. 'Although relaxing's not one of my talents, I'm afraid.'

Kumar sat down in the chair opposite. This, too, was unusual, when no work was to be discussed. Hamilton drew from his shirt pocket a packet of the American cigarettes that fetched an unreal price in Jakarta, and Kumar's eyes went to it immediately, as Hamilton had known they would.

'Still you cannot quite give them up, boss,' he said.

This was the opening of a ritual dialogue between them, and referred to Hamilton's efforts to cut down his smoking by changing to cigars; it was also a request for a cigarette.

'Cigars aren't enough,' Hamilton said. He lit up, and tossed the packet across the desk. 'Here: it's one less that I'll smoke.'

Kumar smiled with pleasure, but without warmth. Most Javanese smiles light the whole face; but Kumar's did not touch his eyes. 'Thank you,' he said, and took a cigarette with the expression of a man receiving a rare gift. He cadged nothing else from Hamilton; but his love of the precious Lucky Strikes overcame his Javanese dignity. At first, Hamilton had been embarrassed by this; now he had grown used to it. Kumar was paid an enviable salary by Indonesian standards, and was unmarried; he should have been able to afford the Lucky Strikes himself. Hamilton suspected that most of his salary was being siphoned off in some way: perhaps to the PKI; perhaps to relatives.

Holding the cigarette in an odd way between his third and middle fingers, Kumar now blew out smoke luxuriously; and the two looked at each other in good-humoured silence. It was one of those odd moments in which a new familiarity seems imminent;

yet this was almost certainly an illusion. Despite their similar ages and their common profession, they eyed each other from separate thickets, forced by the symbolism of race to be more and less than themselves. They had never pretended to any sort of familiarity: they recognised in each other a common quality of hardness, and a distaste for those almost girlish gestures of sympathy with which so many Europeans and Indonesians tried to bridge the gap. Finally, Kumar said, 'No luck today at the Foreign Office?'

'No—I tried to get to Subandrio, but I got fobbed off.'

'I think you are worried at the moment.' It was not a direct question; but it did, with Javanese delicacy, ask for a comment of some sort, if Hamilton felt inclined to make one.

Hamilton did not.

'You should take a rest—a break from Jakarta. If you want to get out of the heat this week-end, boss, I can take you to a bungalow at Tugu, up in the hills. The air is very cool up there— just like home for you, I think.' Kumar ashed his cigarette with care.

This was a surprising proposal; Kumar and he had never spent any leisure time together. But it was unusually attractive to Hamilton just now. On this Friday afternoon, the week-end stretched in front of him like desolation: he had no invitations, and there was no escape from the grilling heat of July except to the Oasis or the Wayang Bar; no escape, above all, from thoughts of Jill, on her Singapore holiday with Henderson—thoughts he was determined to quell. 'You will be missing Miss Bryant, now that she is away,' Kumar said. 'Nothing to do in Jakarta, I think.'

Hamilton stared. Kumar's conventionally handsome, watchful face hid mysteries. Had he some Javanese technique for reading thoughts? His assistant continued to speak with soft eagerness. The bungalow was an official holiday house belonging to one of the Ministries; at present it was standing empty except for the servants, and Kumar's cousin (highly placed in the Ministry) could make it unofficially available to them. A small sum of money for the cousin might be of help in cementing the matter.

Hamilton accepted. He would forget both Jill and his work; he would have a simple week-end in the hills, with Kumar as a guide, and explore the Javanese countryside. He knew that Kumar's motives were not entirely disinterested: Hamilton would pay all costs of the holiday, which would be Kumar's holiday too; and he would provide the office car, at a time when a functioning vehicle was a rare treasure. He thanked Kumar with polite warmth.

'No need to thank me, boss. Without you, such a holiday would be impossible for me. I could not afford it.' Kumar smiled, apparently quite un-embarrassed, watching Hamilton with steady curiosity.

14

No kingdom on earth can equal this one, which is the Gate of the World. Its countless islands, from the Moluccas to northern Sumatra, balanced in an arc between Asia and Australia, shield it from the storms of the Indian Ocean and the South China Sea. Active volcanoes form its spine, and Vishnu, its guardian god (who sometimes takes the guise of a dwarf), protects it from all harm. Its children are more numerous, its women more beautiful, its soil more fertile: foreigners covet it. And most favoured of all is Java.

As you fly into Java from Sumatra, over the Sunda Straits, the most crowded island on earth appears mysteriously devoid of human settlement. Indigo cones of volcanoes rise into the clouds from jade territories which seem as empty as those of the world's dawn. But these are the paddy fields and terraces the people cultivate to the very rims of the craters. President Sukarno, Vishnu's incarnation, tells us in his speeches that Java's spirit is the terrible volcano Merapi, which seems to sleep, but is always ready to explode in violence.

In flat, grey Jakarta, it is difficult to recall that this countryside exists. But it begins only half an hour's drive away, where the bright green hills rise from the coastal flatland. Dotted about these hills are a number of small resorts—if the term can be used for what are simply complexes of smart bungalows and occasional swimming-pools—providing, for those who can afford it, an escape from the stupefying heat and confusion of the flatland capital below, which drones like a sick brain.

To small, cool Bogor, capital of thunderstorms, where his white, fairy-tale palace stands among pines, and legendary deer roam, Bung Karno himself continues to escape this July, and to watch his rewritten *wayang* shows, while his Ministers laugh and tremble. Like the hill-stations of India, such former playgrounds of the colonial masters have now become those of the new nation's élite: generals wealthy from rake-offs; Chinese merchants; favoured officials; and foreign envoys who enjoy the pleasures of colonialism without colonialism. Tugu is one of these resorts.

Hamilton walked along the Hotel Indonesia's arcade, squinting with pleasure at the mid-morning sun, and at the rhyming pattern of light and shadow the arches laid down on the yellow and blue mosaic tiles, which a boy was slowly washing. He was looking forward to his holiday in a Java without politics. Outside the glass doors of the foyer, among the potted plants and groups of foreign businessmen, he put down his overnight bag and stood waiting for Kumar. He had lent his assistant the office car overnight, to save Kumar the journey across the city to meet him from his unknown home in the suburbs—perhaps in an expensive taxi, more likely in a slow *betjak*.

After five minutes, Kumar appeared in the arcade, smiling broadly, carrying a small suitcase, and dressed for the holiday in the casual attire many Indonesians of modest means wore: faded green sports shirt, cheap chocolate-brown slacks, and the sort of black leather lace-up shoes that belonged with a suit. It looked, Hamilton thought, like the holiday garb of an Australian factory worker of ten years earlier: yet Kumar did not look pathetic; his hard-faced good looks and wiry, athletic build made clothes unimportant.

'*Merdeka*,' Hamilton said. Kumar had taught him that this word for freedom could also be used as a greeting.

Kumar smiled, pleased. '*Merdeka*,' he said.

They crossed the Hotel's asphalt driveway to the gates leading to the Car Park. Out here, beyond the gentle Mediterranean warmth of the arcade, the full force of the equatorial sun struck down on their heads like iron, and as Hamilton, half-blinded, fumbled for his sun-glasses, Kumar reached for his overnight bag. 'Let me take that, boss.'

'No, no.' Hamilton waved him back, embarrassed at Kumar's assumption that he should act as a servant out of office hours.

Kumar glanced back at the glittering front of the Hotel, and said, 'You enjoy living here, boss?'

'It's got all I need.'

'It costs a lot, I think.'

'ABS can afford it.'

'Most Indonesians have never seen inside it,' Kumar pursued softly. 'Neither have I.'

Kumar lost no time in harping on the topic of economic inequalities, Hamilton thought; it was difficult to avoid the conclusion that he made points about it purposely to embarrass. He had once invited Kumar for a drink in the Wayang Bar, but his assistant had refused, with a transparent excuse.

As they entered the area of the Car Park, Kumar said suddenly, 'We have a passenger in the car, boss, I hope you don't mind. Her name is Vera Chostiakov. She is attached to the Soviet Embassy.'

Hamilton stopped short, removed his sun-glasses, and squinted at Kumar in surprise.

'Don't be alarmed,' Kumar said. 'She is just a lady I met at a film evening given by the Embassy. She needs a lift to the hills.'

'What's her position at the Embassy?' Hamilton asked.

Kumar appeared uneasy for the first time: he put down his suitcase and spoke rapidly. 'She is a cultural attaché, that is all—not a political person, boss. She has asked if we will take her to the Russian bungalow near Puntjak. She is spending the week-end there with friends, and has no transport: her car has broken down.'

'"Not a political person"—really? I thought they were all political people at the Russian compound.'

Kumar picked up his suitcase; he was obviously anxious to move on, so that the discussion would end. 'Oh, they are quite friendly, really,' he said.

Hamilton, moving towards the car again, considered the

almost insolent absurdity of this last remark. He knew that the people from the Russian mission never fraternised except at official gatherings; and for a Soviet Embassy female to spend off-duty time alone with foreign journalists or Indonesian nationals, and to travel about the countryside with them, was unheard of. Even Kumar's possible membership of the Indonesian Communist Party could not fully explain this, since the PKI was estranged from the Russians.

As they approached the car, he could see a woman in a pale green dress sitting in the back seat; she had smooth, copper-coloured hair drawn back into a bun. She did not look out at them, but sat erect, staring ahead of her, waiting calmly as though in a taxi.

Kumar passed Hamilton the keys. 'You drive, boss. I will keep Vera company in the back.' And so Hamilton found himself 'playing chauffeur', as he put it, to Kumar and his Russian lady.

Within twenty minutes, the stream of air through the side window cooling his face, he had the Ford out of Jakarta and on the road to Bogor, climbing steadily into the hills. The straggling capital, in which the slums of east and west had mated in hot bewilderment, was left behind, and they were surrounded by Java.

The jade green of Java is like hallucination. As he drove, Hamilton blinked at it as though for the first time, savouring his freedom from the tension of an assignment. As the road wound higher, the blazing air became more tepid; the slow breeze of the south-east monsoon moved in the coconut-palms beside the road, and a sweet-sour mixture of smells reached him: scents of frangipani and jasmine; reek of copra and moist earth. The humid land was like a huge creature stirring to life. Beyond the wet rice paddies and the tea estates rose the deep green cones of terraced hills, and finally the silk-blue cones of the great volcano chain that is Java's spine.

All colours were more intense here, in this land of cones; all smells more insistent. He swerved his way through squadrons of bicycles. Dignified West-Javanese peasant women pedalled grace-fully, comical yet gravely charming, their Junoesque figures outlined in tight, multi-coloured *kains* and *kebayas*, their hair in gleaming, antique buns; goddesses on wheels. Except for whirring military trucks filled with soldiers, and occasional armoured cars of the Siliwangi Division, motorised traffic was sparse. Occasionally they passed disintegrating old American cars, held together with wire and patched with beer cans, pulled over in mortal illness at the roadside, with crowds of men anxiously inspecting their engines.

Out here, if you wanted to pretend so, there was no real poverty: he drove, it seemed, through the pastures of a fortunate elect. Kampongs flashed by among groves of palms and papaya-trees; neat white palm-mat huts at whose doors women stood suckling babies, smiling as the car passed. That the great green tracts of the paddies were deceptive, being divided invisibly into hopelessly small holdings; that the rice they produced was never enough to feed Jakarta; and that the peasants were constantly being harried by middlemen, government officials, and PKI activists—these were things from which Hamilton deliberately turned his mind today. It was his holiday, and he savoured deliberately the unrolling rich images of his secret, pre-war 'East'.

All the ceaseless throngs by the roadside smiled: those brilliant Javanese smiles that always seemed to signal a childish happiness —the happiness that co-exists with misery everywhere in Asia. Other regions of Indonesia might be facing starvation, but these people along the Bogor road were surviving. It was easy to forget, out here, the swollen bellies he had seen on the island of Lombok, to forget that Sukarno had recently suggested in a speech that the people add rats to their diets.

But, despite his enjoyment, Hamilton could not entirely relax: he was too conscious of Kumar and the woman from the Soviet Embassy, seated behind him. Soon after they had started, he had been presented with a second surprise: Kumar spoke Russian.

When Hamilton asked him where he had learnt the language, Kumar told him he had studied some years ago at the University of Leningrad. This, too, was news to Hamilton. Kumar's office file showed no university degree, no Russian experience, only a background in journalism in Indonesia. As Hamilton had stared in surprise, it seemed to him that both his assistant and the Russian woman wore expressions of sardonic amusement. She spoke little English, it seemed; so she and Kumar now conversed steadily in Russian.

Hamilton straightened himself a little in his seat, and glanced at the woman's reflection in the rear-vision mirror. He was disconcerted to find bright, slanting grey eyes looking back at him. She smiled, and he caught once again a glint of amusement. She was about twenty-four or -five; that she was attractive is something I knew myself, since I had met her at a number of functions put on by the Soviet Cultural Mission. Well-groomed, as Soviet women abroad often are, she put out a sort of coolly balanced and correct sex-appeal which had an anti-aphrodisiac effect on me, but which was to have more positive results with Hamilton. But at this stage he had formed no clear impression of her.

He was both curious and suspicious about Kumar's connection with her; but he wished to dismiss these feelings, and to enjoy the serenity of his holiday. In an hour or so, he said, they would have delivered her to the Russian bungalow at Puntjak.

Not far from Bogor, Hamilton sighted a restaurant-swimming-pool complex with high walls of pink stucco roofed with tiles, like those of a Chinese palace. He pulled the car over and proposed having drinks and something to eat.

They sat at a table near the swimming-pool. There was a sprinkling of Indonesian officials at the tables about the lawn and in the arcade, but the crowd was mainly Chinese: that uneasy caste which still carried on the businesses for which most Indonesians had neither the interest nor the expertise.

Kumar drank his imported Heineken beer with relish; he made a joke about being a bad Muslim. The Russian girl sipped carefully, and avoided Hamilton's eyes; her silence made them all constrained, now that they faced each other around the table. She was by no means the heavy, broad-faced Slav Hamilton had half-expected. True, her round cheek-bones were emphatic; but her tilted nose was narrow, her chin pointed and delicate; she had an unusually thin neck. The green sleeveless dress, buttoned down the front, was simple, almost severe.

As they ate, Hamilton noticed Kumar's intense and almost awed enjoyment of the place.

'This is a very nice place, boss. It is like Europe.'

There was such a hushed yearning in his voice that Hamilton repressed a smile. He found the place neither very European nor very lavish; prices were moderate by Western standards, and the chipped, blue-painted wooden table at which they sat recalled certain seedy beach-side cafés in Sydney. But Kumar had become like a small boy taken on a treat. The cutlery, which he toyed with, intrigued him; the *saté*, which he ate slowly and carefully, was obviously a very special *saté*; and he turned the bottle of Heineken in his fingers, examining the label with great intentness. All this, in a man of twenty-six who was in many ways sophisticated, was suddenly touching to Hamilton.

Kumar made him uncomfortable; and he also had a knack of making him feel he *ought* to be uncomfortable. Kumar knew how much money Hamilton made in black-market money deals with a certain Mr Lal, a nervous Indian money-changer in the suburbs who maintained a Swiss bank account; he also knew the size of Hamilton's salary, which was beyond the wildest dreams of almost any Indonesian. If Kumar was a Communist, then far from being indifferent to worldly gain it occupied most of his waking thoughts. The things of this world were not despised; they were simply in the wrong hands; and the soft remarks pointing out contrasts were meant to indicate this. As he sat there, in his well-pressed, faded sports shirt, his cheap slacks and unsuitable dress shoes, there was a poignancy in his strength and ambition. He could almost, with his jutting boxer's jaw, have been Irish or Welsh, Hamilton thought, had it not been for his wood-brown skin; there was far more of the aggressive European in him than of the gentle Javanese: a bottled hunger, always working its way upwards, seeking an outlet.

'So you like it here, Kumar?' he said lightly.

The slanting black eyes looked back into his without answering amusement. 'This?' Kumar said. As though searching for words, he stared for a moment at the Russian girl, who was looking abstractedly at the artificial blue of the swimming-pool where plump, privileged Chinese and Javanese children splashed and shouted; Kumar also looked at the pool, then at the hurrying waiters and bright lawns. 'I have not been in a place like this before,' he said.

'Not in Leningrad?'

'No. I was a student. We did not go to expensive places. I have not been anywhere like this.' He smiled. 'This is water from the moon.'

'Water from the moon?'

Kumar drank off his beer and set down the empty glass. 'We use that saying often, in Java,' he said. 'It means: anything impossible.'

Hamilton asked Kumar to drive now, since his assistant knew where to find the Russian bungalow at Puntjak.

The Puntjak Pass, nearly five thousand feet above sea level, lies a little beyond Tugu, at the summit of the road's climb onto the Java Plateau. Hamilton assumed that they would go up to Puntjak first, deliver the Russian girl, and then return to Tugu. As they drove through Bogor, huge clouds which had been building up on the mountains released the first of the afternoon showers—the regular cloudbursts strung like glass beads through every sunlit day up in the hills. Lightning flashed over the remote, pale dome of the President's palace, and the parklands of pine and mimosa; and Kumar and the Russian girl, in the front seat, were isolated from Hamilton by the noise of the rain.

He watched the girl lean to say something in Kumar's ear, laying her pale hand on the brown fore-arm on the steering-wheel; Kumar turned to her with the indulgent smile some men reserve especially for women, and they laughed quietly. The moment instantly declared them lovers; and Hamilton felt ridiculous for not having guessed this before. That his assistant should be having an affair with a member of the Soviet mission startled him considerably.

The rain stopped; the sun blazed again on the landscape's primary colours; the road steamed. Kumar suddenly swung left off the highway down a road of chocolate mud, through the jade, papery leaves of a banana plantation. They crossed a little bridge over one of the streams that hurried down every slope here, and began to climb towards a yellow bungalow set on a rise. Hamilton waited for Kumar to explain where they were; he was accustomed to Kumar explaining things promptly. But his assistant said nothing: the two in the front remained silent.

They drew up on a patch of neatly gravelled drive in front of the Ministry bungalow: a long, tile-roofed, L-shaped building with many shuttered windows. At one end was an empty terrace set with tables, overlooking the hills; below it, sloping into a gully, was a garden, thick with flowering trees and shrubs. As the engine cut, Kumar said, 'We all get out now. Here is Tugu.'

'Tugu? But I thought the lady wanted to go to Puntjak?'

Kumar turned to look at Hamilton, and the woman turned too, with an expression of faint curiosity. 'But we are here now, boss, at Tugu,' Kumar said. 'Vera can join her friends later. You do not mind?' His object appeared to be to create a sort of Javanese screen of confusion, which would prevent any questioning of his mistress's being introduced into their holiday.

As they took their bags from the boot, a gnomish old man in a starched white jacket, checked sarong, and *pitji* cap shuffled across the gravel from the entrance, bowing and smiling. There was no other sign of life: the place was intensely quiet, except for the loud, harsh cries of birds down in the garden, and the calling of children somewhere at a distance. The many rooms behind the closed brown shutters were obviously empty, waiting for nothing, and unrolling behind this little rise, where the bungalow stood, the near, green, tea-covered hills and towering violet volcanoes generated a weird tension: the landscape appeared to wait for some vast event. On the peaks, cumulo-nimbus clouds rose terrace on terrace and dome on dome, storing their storms.

A swimming-pool was hidden in the gully below the terrace. Hamilton, Kumar, and Vera, clad in swim-suits and carrying towels, descended through the heavily-scented garden by a flight of ancient-looking, grey-green stone steps.

The pool proved to be made of the same rough-hewn stone.

Hamilton almost expected to see lotuses on the water: it suggested some tank in an old palace garden in India. Surrounded by a border of lawn, long untended, it was walled in on all sides by the hillside garden: giant ferns, frangipani, red-belled hibiscus, and the surprise of roses. The property had once belonged to a Dutch planter, and the gully smelled seriously of the past; it was like an old room suddenly opened, and the three stood in awkward quiet on the pool's rim.

After their swim, the two men sat side by side on the stone ledge, dangling their feet in the water. The Russian girl, although she had put on a white, two-piece swim-suit, had refused to swim, giving no reason. She had lapsed into total silence, and wandered alone on the grass on the far side of the pool, examining the flowering shrubs. She had picked a frangipani flower, and twirled its white star in her fingers, holding herself with a military erectness that went oddly with her semi-nudity. Hamilton had gained the impression, perhaps from her thin neck and general compactness, that the severe green dress clothed a generally slight figure; but she proved to have low-set breasts of an almost matronly roundness, contrasting with narrow hips. Against the greenery, her unsunned flesh had the secret whiteness of a peeled fruit. The sun picked out copper lights in the smooth hair, whose bun, at this distance, gave her a vague resemblance to one of the local women: he wondered if she did it in the Javanese style to please Kumar. The posturing with the flower was no doubt done for their benefit, he said; but the setting made it effective. From time to time, he or Kumar would glance across the pool at her, but she never looked at them. Her silence seemed to imply contempt.

'What a marvellous spot,' Hamilton said. 'The President should move Jakarta up here. Maybe Billy Kwan's right: he says the capital should be at Bogor or Bandung. He's got a theory that civilisation's only possible in temperate regions.'

'You think everyone is equally affected by the heat?' Kumar asked. 'But surely Europeans feel it more.'

'I wonder,' Hamilton said. 'We expect it to be cool, and you don't. But we're not really physically different, are we?'

Kumar glanced at him quickly. 'You think not? We are very

166

different, I think.' Something in his face made Hamilton feel they were on delicate ground; it was the first time the subject of race had come up between them.

The Russian girl, walking without any sound on the grass, had meanwhile appeared a few feet away, having circled the pool. She behaved as though she were alone, and to Hamilton's surprise now began to do a series of slow-motion callisthenics. Her face was severe; she was entirely absorbed, as though in the practice of a religious ritual. Standing on one foot, she extended the other leg behind her, arms outstretched, her narrow back deeply arched. She froze in this position, presented to them in profile; a pallid garden statue. In her exposed armpit an innocent nest of copper hair oddly disturbed Hamilton; he mentioned it to me with distaste, being accustomed, as most of us were then, to young women with shaven armpits.

'Perhaps you think,' Kumar was saying carefully, 'that there is little hope for Indonesia—not just Jakarta. After all, most of it is tropical. You agree, I think, with Mr Billy Kwan's theories.'

Hamilton laughed. 'Good Lord, Kumar, I never take any of Billy's theories seriously. I can't keep up with them.' He saw he was being drawn in deeper than he wished; Kumar's face had an almost bitter seriousness.

With unusual vehemence, although his voice was still quiet, Kumar said, 'I have listened to Mr Kwan. He believes that geographical position has made my people lazy—and that the two races which have been favourably located for energy are the Mongols and the whites. This doesn't surprise me—we are accustomed to an attitude of superiority from both. We remember the Japanese.' He gave, briefly, his polite Javanese smile; but Hamilton, not usually sensitive to such things, became aware of some unusual agitation. Kumar kicked with sudden viciousness at the water; his eyes kept wandering to Vera, who continued her decorative exercises.

'Look,' Hamilton said, 'I never listen to Billy's mad theories too carefully. Don't think they're *my* theories.'

The Russian girl, facing them, was now bending sideways, feet apart, arms reaching upwards like a diver's. Then she swayed with infinite slowness in the other direction to repeat the action, her pale face cocked between her upraised arms as though attentive to a distant music. Hamilton tried, unsuccessfully, not to glance at her.

Kumar, digesting Hamilton's last remark, seemed to have relaxed a little. 'Of course,' he said softly, 'I know you do not think as Mr Kwan does.' But his eyes remained wary, watching his feet stir the green water. 'We Indonesians do not seem to be running things very well,' he said. 'Everywhere there is corruption. I will tell you something. My father is dead, and I live with my uncle and aunt. My uncle runs a small shop—he sells *batik* cloth. But he can never get ahead, because every week he must pay money to the military. This is not right, is it, boss?'

'No, it's certainly not.'

'He and my aunt are now in great trouble—the payments have increased and they cannot afford them. They have many bills and may lose the shop.'

'That's bloody terrible.' Hamilton grew indignant. 'Look, I'd like to help. Maybe I could make your uncle a loan. I make plenty out of Mr Lal. I'd be glad to do it.'

Kumar stared at him. 'That is very good of you, boss. But I did not tell you in order to get money. This is not the way we should manage—by handouts.' He looked distressed. 'I tell you this to show you our problems.'

Hamilton decided philosophically that no more could be done to mollify Kumar; but he resolved to renew his offer when they got back to Jakarta. He found himself staring abstractedly at his own and Kumar's legs, mottled by leaf-shadows, side by side on the grey-green stone: his own pallid, and filmed with dark hair; Kumar's teak-brown and almost hairless. As though reading his thoughts, Kumar said suddenly, 'Brown.'

'I beg your pardon.'

'Brown,' Kumar repeated, pointed to his own legs. 'A bad colour.' There was a naked disgust in his voice.

'Nonsense—it's not a bad colour at all,' Hamilton said lamely. But then he realised the uselessness of apologising for their contrasting skins, which apparently woke such exquisite bitterness in Kumar. He lit a small cigar and smoked in silence.

'Time for a siesta, I think, boss,' Kumar said. 'Siesta is good for you, in our bad climate.'

'Siesta's a habit I can't get into,' Hamilton said. 'I'll have another swim soon, I think. What about Vera? Shouldn't we be getting her up to Puntjak?'

Kumar said softly, without looking at him, 'I thought Vera might have dinner with us here.'

'I see. She's certainly in no hurry to join her friends, is she?'

Kumar did not reply; instead he turned to the girl, who was now sitting on the grass a little distance away, and spoke to her in Russian. Hamilton guessed that he was suggesting they go up from the pool to the bungalow; but she answered briefly in obvious refusal, and continued to sit, serenely clasping her knees, staring across the pool at the wall of bushes and shrubs.

Kumar spoke again, but she shook her head, said, '*Nyet*', and followed it with two or three dismissive sentences. She lay back gracefully on the grass. Hamilton smoked, privately amused by this little conflict.

It was that mid-way point in the afternoon when there is a hiatus, a blank spot in time. Hamilton and Kumar sat on, side by side, and the Russian girl continued to lie a little apart from them, apparently meditating. The sun beat down through the foliage, and the flower-scents grew heavier. Finally Kumar shifted a little, cleared his throat, and turned to look sideways at Hamilton. 'You are going swimming again?' he asked. He watched slyly, as though the answer to this would decide something.

'Yes, in a moment,' Hamilton said.

Kumar picked at a broken nail. 'I will go for a siesta now,' he said, apparently choosing his words with some difficulty. 'Vera says, may she join you for a swim?'

'She's very welcome, tell her,' Hamilton said. He hid his amusement.

As soon as Kumar had disappeared up the steps, the girl got to her feet and walked to the edge of the pool, tucking her hair into a plain white rubber bathing-cap. She had not looked at Hamilton. She raised her arms formally above her head and dived into the water, with uncanny smoothness.

But she did not surface. For a time, Hamilton was unperturbed; she was giving, he supposed, another exhibition of Soviet athleticism, and he waited lazily for the white cap to reappear. But a good minute went by, and no cap. The water had little transparency; its dim, dark green reflected the trees and the weed-grown sides, and he could see no sign of her. There was no sound except for the chuckle of water entering the pool through a rusty pipe at the far end. It seemed to him now that another minute had passed.

He dived in at the spot where she had disappeared, and went down deep, swimming through the green film close to the bottom. Rays of sun were striking down from the surface. His head was beginning to pulse when he saw her, a white, discarded vegetable, hanging limply in the green. Deciding that she had hit her head, he swam up and reached for the swaying arm nearest him.

But her face rolled over towards him like a thing in a dream; her eyes were open, and she smiled widely. Then, uncoiling her white length, she kicked once and shot upwards.

Hamilton followed her. But when he neared the surface her hand clasped the top of his head and pushed him under again. No matter how he struggled, the hand, gripping his hair, held him under; and in a swift panic he knew to be ridiculous he fought against the notion that she was no longer joking, that she was attempting to drown him. He struggled, glimpsing her white legs above him, and his thoughts became melodramatic. Under water, the Cold War stereotypes of his James Bond thrillers became real, as bizarre figures do under the surface of sleep; the fact that she was a member of the Soviet mission became absurdly sinister. He now badly needed air, and he seized the wrist above his head with all his force. The hand let go.

When he surfaced, she was swimming away up the pool, towards the other end. He followed.

She hung facing him, laughing, her arms extended backwards to cling to the ledge above, in the posture of a victim on the rack, shamelessly exposing their nests of copper hair. Laughter distorted her face so that she became almost ugly: her short upper lip almost disappeared under her nose, and the unsexing, skull-like cap emphasised the pixy mask of malicious amusement; the oblique grey eyes were as blank as glass.

'Don't look so fierce. Just a joke,' she said. She had little accent; her voice was light and rather high; it sounded more tentative and feminine than when she had spoken Russian.

'Your English is quite good,' he said.

'Of course.' In a single, fluid movement she hauled herself onto the ledge, and Hamilton did the same.

She was rubbing her wrist, and Hamilton, surveying the red mark there, the thinness of her neck, and the long, vulnerable valley of her breasts, began to feel foolish about his violence. But he reminded himself again that her mere presence here was suspect.

'You have hurt my wrist,' she said mildly.

'Sorry about that—you scared the life out of me. Why did you pretend to speak so little English?'

'Kumar is very—sensitive.'

He was not sure that she had found the right word, but made no comment. She pulled off the bathing-cap, sitting companionably close. He noticed now that her ears projected slightly: an incongruous schoolgirl touch. Long copper switches escaped from the bun to fall on her neck and shoulders: a disarray in striking contrast to her recent careful grooming.

'I hope you don't mind my joining you on your vacation,' she said.

'I wasn't aware you had.'

She chose to ignore this. 'I do not meet British journalists very often,' she said. 'And you are a very good one. I have admired your broadcasts. I should like to see you again when we get back to Jakarta. That would be nice, would it not?'

Hamilton who knew that this was entirely outside the range of normal possibilities, agreed guardedly that it would be nice.

Her next proposal was more prosaic. 'You might care to come to one of our film evenings at the Cultural Mission,' she said. 'Perhaps, when we are back in Jakarta, you will phone me.'

She stood up and walked sedately away down the edge of the pool, to a spot where her outsize white handbag lay with her towel in the grass. Picking both up, she marched back, and took from the bag a small card. He got to his feet.

'Here is where you can always contact me,' she said. Then her right arm stretched upwards and she cupped the back of his neck in her palm. Her eyes held his, as though her extraordinary action had a purpose they both understood.

'See you later,' she said, bringing out the colloquial phrase with care. She bent, picked up her handbag and towel, and ran at surprising speed, as though in a mock-race, up the stone steps leading out of the garden.

Hamilton wandered through the long, musty-smelling corridors of the Ministry bungalow, which were utterly silent. All the low wooden doors were closed: like Alice's rabbit hole, he said.

The old servant, in his white, starched jacket and *pitji* cap, suddenly appeared round a bend ahead of him, and Hamilton tried to ask him where Kumar's room was. But the old man spoke no English, and could not understand Hamilton's feeble attempts at Bahasa; he bowed and smiled eagerly, saying something about '*makan*'. Hamilton said that he wanted no food, and gave it up. He began to feel that his position was ridiculous.

It was now five o'clock, and Kumar's 'siesta'—which Hamilton assumed Vera was now sharing—appeared to be continuing indefinitely. To go knocking on all the doors would make him appear foolish; but to continue much longer in his isolation seemed just as foolish. He had tried walking about in the vicinity of the bungalow outside, but there was little to divert him. It was peculiarly isolated, on its rise above the plantations. There appeared to be no kampong near by, and in fact no signs of life at all, which was unusual in Java. The silence of the place, broken only by the drilling of cicadas, began to work on his nerves.

There seemed nothing to do now but to retreat to his room and attempt a siesta of his own. He didn't mind his own company as a rule, he said, but not on such terms as these. Since he had pictured an active holiday, he had brought no reading matter; and he was not in a mood for his own thoughts, which would simply return to Jill. He did have a transistor radio—a necessity, since if anything

172

of importance broke in Jakarta, he would need to return immediately—but he was no longer diverted by listening to newscasts and music. The tedium was complete. There was nothing to do.

Naked on the narrow bed, Hamilton sweated and tossed, for what he told me sardonically were the longest hours in his life. The old ceiling-fan did little to cool the stifling, cell-like room, which was crudely functional. It put him in mind of a Salvation Army hostel: yellow walls, cheap wooden cupboard and one bamboo chair, and a single glassless window with brown shutters, overlooking the front drive. What was he doing here?

On the bed beside him lay a long, tubular, bolster-like object— unique to Java and the subject of many jokes: a *guling*, made especially for hugging during the night. The prosaic Dutch had claimed to use the *guling* to absorb the sweat from the backs of their legs. No one believed this, and the object was generally referred to as a Dutch Wife. Hamilton punched it savagely to relieve his feelings.

He would see the humour of the situation when he got back to Jakarta—but not now. The Russian girl had aroused both his curiosity and his lust, and he could not sleep. He looked at his watch for perhaps the hundredth time, waiting for sunset and the dinner hour, when she and Kumar must surely reappear. His mind revolved tediously around a question he had now decided was basic: whether she was using Kumar to get to him—for some reason he could not yet fathom—or whether he was merely being used so that she could spend time with Kumar.

A loud creaking noise sounded in the room, as though the door had opened. Hamilton started up, but the door was shut. The noise came from a purple and green lizard some six inches long, clinging to the wall above his bed. He grimaced and cursed, feeling an unreasonable loathing of the creature. He sank back, and finally dozed.

The road they had driven on to get here this morning unwound in his mind like a film, and the film kept winding back to one persistent image: the Javanese mothers nursing their babies at the doorways of the roadside kampongs, and then blending together

173

to become one mother with one baby. Green-framed by the palm-grove's liquid green, she smiled in great friendliness—her gleaming, oiled hair in its traditional bun secured by bright combs, her bared, yellow-brown breast resembling one of the fruits piled in baskets by the road: as though human and vegetable flesh were nurtured alike by the hill-country's deep red soil and myriad streams. In shallow dreams such as these, we are still half-consciously thinking; and Hamilton said: *But that's the picture in Billy Kwan's room.*

He did not know why he said this. The pleasant Javanese matron did not really resemble that wildly dancing figure with snake-like hair in Billy's picture of the Hindu goddess; and yet it seemed to him in his dream that her hair had now come loose from its combs, and fell in snake-like coils and switches on her shoulders: that she had become someone else.

He woke to find it was nearly dark; the room was hotter than ever, and darkness made the air seem suffocating. Alarm gripped him. He had not understood his dream, but it had given him a feeling of dismal isolation. He squinted at his luminous Swiss watch. Seven fifteen. He sprang from the bed and threw open the shutters.

The gravel outside was alive with small, heaving bodies: hundreds of brown frogs, hopping in a panel of light coming from the front entrance. He dressed quickly, and hurried from his prison.

The low corridors were still empty and silent, and he wondered if Kumar and Vera had simply left. He discovered a deserted dining-room, with heavy furniture, starched tablecloths and solid silver cutlery belonging to the Dutch-colonial thirties, and passed through multi-paned glass doors to find himself on the terrace outside. Here he sat down to wait, at a battered iron table.

The old man in the starched jacket materialised beside him like a ghost from the dining-room's past, to set an ashtray for Hamilton's cigar; then he stood at attention by the doors, where he was joined by a boy in a sarong. The two of them watched Hamilton, and whispered; there was nothing at all for them to do, if the *tuan* would not eat dinner. He sat on, above a darkening landscape which had transformed itself into a Chinese painting:

high, indigo peaks suspended in cloud; gigantic white masks of mist coming down into the banana plantation below, swirling and changing with eerie speed. The sparks of fireflies moved in the garden.

Ten minutes later Kumar appeared on the terrace, dressed, his hair freshly combed. 'You are hungry for dinner, boss?' He sat down at the table, smiling as though they had both enjoyed a hugely entertaining afternoon.

Hamilton, striving to conceal his annoyance, asked whether Vera was joining them.

'No—I have already taken her up to Puntjak—while you were having your siesta.' He smiled.

'Not before time,' Hamilton said. 'I should think her people were worried. That's if they knew she was running around the country with members of the capitalist press.'

Kumar gave a small, deprecating laugh, which meant that he did not wish to comment. 'You are enjoying your holiday?' he asked.

'Beautiful. Water from the moon, Kumar.'

'Yes, boss. Water from the moon.'

'But a little quiet.'

'You must relax, boss—this is why you came. You are too restless, like all Westerners.'

'Have you known Vera long?'

'No—as I told you, I only met her last evening. She is very pretty, isn't she, boss? And she likes you, I think. She commented how tall you were. But perhaps you are not allowed to like Soviet people.'

There could be no mistaking the hostility behind Kumar's smile: a hostility not personal, Hamilton saw, but of the type directed at symbols. He understood now, he thought, what Kumar's watchfulness had always meant: it had been directed at what Hamilton represented. The thought was wearisome; he had always liked Kumar, and had thought him somehow mentally free of the crude stereotypes of *Konfrontasi*.

'We're not allowed or disallowed to like anybody,' Hamilton said. 'I think it's the Russkis who have that problem.'

'You are told by your leaders you must be anti-Communist,'

175

Kumar said. 'I understand. But—forgive me for saying this—you people do not care about us, you only pretend to. The Communists do care about us—and they know that real freedom for us can only come through struggle.'

Hamilton was surprised. The job Kumar held was one of the most highly prized a young Indonesian could obtain, at a time when few earned real wages at all. If Hamilton got rid of him, hundreds would be waiting to take his place. For this reason, Hamilton had always taken for granted the veil of absolute courtesy and neutrality Kumar wore. But now his assistant had allowed the veil to slip a little: his smile was frankly a sneer.

'What do you really know of Communism?' Kumar asked softly.

Hamilton decided to keep his temper; but he had also decided to return to Jakarta the next day. 'Not much,' he said. 'But I'd imagine the hardest thing to bear about a dictatorship would be reading the same propaganda in the papers every day—wouldn't you?'

'There are worse things to bear.' Kumar stood up, his face hard, but carefully masked again. 'Shall we go in to dinner—boss?'

They went into the dining-room, followed by the delightedly smiling spirit of the house in his starched jacket, and sat at one of the ghostly tables, where they ate in silence. Rain began again, whirling and hissing on the empty terrace, lashing at the glass doors.

15

In the Wayang the following night Hamilton gave us a rueful account of his holiday. He had regained his sense of humour.

'Held me by the hair like a doll,' he said, picturing himself in the swimming-pool, the petite Vera's plaything. Long chin firm and serious, 'he shook his head, while our laughter and ribald speculation gathered momentum.

We were all a good deal intrigued by Vera, of course. Some of us had met her briefly at official functions; none of us knew her well. There was a general agreement with Hamilton that no one from the Soviet compound, especially a woman, could possibly have been allowed to place herself in such a situation normally; the Russians were simply not permitted to fraternise with foreigners under any circumstances—and this ban included Indonesians.

Henri Bouchard, the French AFP correspondent, was emphatic about this, I recall.

'But she is certainly spying for her embassy,' he said. 'A member of the Cultural Mission—that makes an excellent cover. Culture is always a useful prostitute, no?' His heavy-lidded grey eyes surveyed us all with weary irony: he was a thin, elegant man whose blond hair appeared to be dyed: a *philosophe*, for whom the world held no more surprises. He addressed himself to Hamilton. 'You have said that this assistant of yours is likely to be a member of the PKI. *Bon*. But the PKI is no longer making love to

Moscow, it is making love to Peking. So how do you explain his connection with the lady?'

'I don't,' Hamilton said. 'Do you?'

Henri squinted through the pungent smoke of his Gauloise. 'Our Soviet friends are being driven crazy because the Chinese have won the day here. All that aid given to Sukarno, all that beautiful military hardware—and yet our poor Russkis find themselves snubbed. They do not know what is going on, the Indonesian Government does not speak to them, and worse—it makes love to Peking, as the PKI does. You agree?' He waited theatrically, well-marked eyebrows raised. 'So let us assume your young man is high enough in the PKI to know something of secret policy. If so, not only will the gentlemen at the Soviet compound allow the lady her games with him—they will also provide the bed.'

Wally O'Sullivan's deep rumble, more serious than usual, cut through our laughter. 'If what you're saying's really true, Henri, she's quite a big fish. In fact she has to be KGB.'

Henri gestured with his cigarette. 'But of course she is KGB. What else?' The letters produced the pause the utterance of them virtually guarantees. 'One thing puzzles me, though,' Henri said to Hamilton. 'She wants you to contact her. But I cannot imagine what it is she wants from you. The only possibility that occurs to me is that she wishes to use you to construct a model.'

There was a fresh outburst of obscene conjectures, but Henri held up his hand. 'It's true. The KGB like to study samples of various nationalities, and to build models from them. It is useful to them. Perhaps our Guy may be used as such a model: an Aussie journalist. Everything will be known about him—his tastes in music, after-shave lotions, and sex.' Amid a further wave of laughter and suggestions, he said to Hamilton, 'She will contact you, if you do not contact her, I think. Will you do so?'

Hamilton grinned. 'If the comrade wants to study my sexual habits, she's very welcome,' he said.

I noticed that Kwan had not joined in the laughter; and he spoke now for the first time, his flat voice unnaturally loud. 'If I were you, old man, I'd keep well away from her.' He stared at Hamilton as though no one else were present.

Pete Curtis, who seemed to bear Hamilton no ill-will over their recent clash, raised his glass. 'Take no notice of him, baby. Here's to jiggety-jig.'

Hamilton looked faintly embarrassed; and it was Kwan who answered. 'Ah, *that's* right, Curtis,' he said. 'Here's to jiggety-jig. It's our substitute for religion, isn't it, Curtis? Eh, Ham? We have our little sensations. We have our jiggety-jig.'

All of us, I think, began to wish him elsewhere. In his tired Hawaiian shirt, crouched at the edge of our group, he looked like a vagrant Indonesian wandered in off the highway. His outburst was embarrassing.

'I think you're pissed, Kwan,' Curtis said rudely.

Hamilton said, 'Time you went home to bed, Billy.'

Kwan's features relaxed suddenly into a broad, false smile, and he slapped Hamilton on the shoulder. '*All* right, *all* right—don't look so serious, old man. I got a bit carried away.' Trying to replace his empty glass on the bar, he dropped and smashed it, but did not appear to notice. 'Sorry, chaps, I shouldn't get excited, should I? I'll go to bed.'

And with a jerky, wheeling motion, he was away, shoulders hunched, head down, narrowly missing a Chinese screen, disappearing through the door into the arcade. There was a moment's silence.

'What was all *that* about?' I said.

'Ham,' Wally said, 'you must control your dwarf, you really must. Otherwise he's going to be barred from the Wayang Club. Hm?'

18 July
You have changed: you are capable of betrayal. I sense the invasion of Durga's darkness in you: she who turns time into sleep, and love into lust, and life into death: the Black One, the dancer in the burial ground.
(DOSSIER H 10: HAMILTON, Guy)

179

I'm not sure whether this entry on Hamilton's file—dated, I'm almost certain, a few days after Billy's outburst in the Wayang—refers to Hamilton's growing cynicism about the absent Jill, or to his interest in Vera Chostiakov, or to both.

But it shows an uncanny sort of insight, as well as an extraordinary interest in Hamilton's movements. Because in that week, Hamilton did something quite out of character for him: something that Billy had always seemed particularly anxious he should avoid. He made a nocturnal expedition with Pete Curtis to that territory on the city limits ruled by the lady of many names: the cemetery at Kebayoran.

'When we get there, baby, I want you to remember one thing,' Curtis said. 'Roll the windows up, and roll them up fast. And keep the door locked.'

Hamilton, driving the office Ford with one hand while his other arm rested on the frame of the open window, glanced at his companion with a questioning expression: the stream of air was all that made the night's heat bearable.

'If you don't, those hookers'll come right through the windows,' Curtis explained. 'They'll open the doors and be into the car in squadrons, before you can turn around.'

Speeding on New Jakarta's empty roads, they passed villas with ragged front lawns where 'night guards' squatted: shabby, dozing figures hired to protect the households of generals, bureaucrats and foreigners from the half-starved marauders in the city, who were growing increasingly numerous and desperate as the price of rice rocketed entirely beyond their means. The inflation was now dreamlike. One US dollar had bought us until recently 10,000 rupiahs from Pasar Baru's black-market money-changers: over the past two weeks, they and Mr Lal had begun paying 20,000. Any of the women at the cemetery could be had for the whole night, Curtis explained, for the equivalent of twelve cents. They waited there for the wealthy foreigners of Kebayoran.

Hamilton drove with a sombre expression; he did not appear like a man on pleasure bent. He had been drinking whisky with Curtis, and breathed heavily through his nose. They had found themselves alone in the Wayang tonight, and a common mood of truce had taken hold of them, generated perhaps by knowing that Curtis was being transferred in two days to Vietnam.

Pete had attempted an apology for his remarks about Jill; Hamilton had brushed it aside, and apologised for his violence. They had become almost sentimental over their whiskies, as frequently happens with rivals when their rivalry is ending. They had always respected each other professionally; now they could afford to reveal it.

'You made me run, baby, I have to admit it,' Curtis had said. 'But I guess I made you trot too, uh?'

'Right. I'm glad you're going, you horrible bastard. Don't get shot by the Viet Cong.'

'You'll be there too, damn soon.'

'No—I'll be here for the curtain. Something's going to happen here; I can feel it.'

Curtis had glanced at him curiously; it was then that he had proposed a visit to the cemetery. To his surprise, Hamilton had agreed.

Billy Kwan was right: Sir Guy had been invaded, since his trip to Tugu, by 'Durga's darkness', by a mysterious lust. Healthy and personable men, who never lacked for women in other circumstances, and would not normally have gone to prostitutes, were often visited by this formless lechery in Jakarta: but it had not happened to Hamilton until now. There must have been a breaking down of his usual scruples. Since his curious dream in the bungalow at Tugu, which continued to echo in him, he had been tantalised as ignominiously as Kevin Condon by the remote beauty of Javanese women: those serene figures in tight batik *kains* and *kebayas*, with their Attic shapes, who had cycled by on the road to Tugu; who had stood at the doorways in the kampongs. Some notion of purging himself of this longing, and also (I suspect) his anger at Jill, had led him, on impulse, to accept Curtis's invitation to the cemetery.

Jakarta's street lights were growing dimmer and fewer by the month, as the electric power shortage became acute; in the street they were now passing through, the lights had failed altogether, and Hamilton found himself navigating in an almost total darkness, in which only the meditating windows of bungalows glowed irregularly. There seemed to be no moon. He cursed as the car crashed over pot-holes deep enough to break an axle.

There was a sense of outskirts; and the darkness continued. They had come to the cemetery, and drove on the dry, rutted road beside a long wall overhung with frangipani-trees. 'Slow down,' Curtis said. Other cars jolted past them, searching; some of them were Indonesian Army jeeps, their headlights swinging alarmingly, like searchlights. A single dim street light illuminated a section of the wall; under it, Hamilton saw a group of women in elaborate national dress, their high-piled hair gleaming. One of them waved and smiled enticingly at the car; she wore heavier make-up than a respectable Javanese woman, and her high, swelling breasts were almost bare. 'Keep rolling,' Curtis said. 'You don't want *him*, do you dearie? It's a goddamn banshee.'

Under another street light, a crowd of some twenty women was gathered. All their faces turned: pale triangles in the sickly light, unnervingly intent. But none of them wore national dress; they wore shabby Western garb: cheap cotton frocks, or tight black skirts and blouses. Their hair hung on their shoulders; none of them wore the traditional buns, and Hamilton knew now that the stately, serene kampong women would for ever remain remote: figures in a bas-relief, and not for sale.

One of the crowd under the lamp detached herself from the others and ran directly towards the car, waving, picked out in the headlights. Just before the car reached her, she halted, and pulled her dress up to her chin; above the bunched material, the triangle of her face, the colour of old newspaper, stared at them with an expression like anguish; below, a second triangle, black, stared from her naked loins.

'She's showing you she's not a banshee,' Curtis said. He laughed briefly. 'Okay. Stop the car.'

The other women had been watching with that poised, uneasy intentness of a group of cattle debating movement; now, as the car stopped, they too began to run, with shrill cries, directly towards it. Beside Hamilton, his sweating guide was working on the handle of his window. 'Your window!' Curtis shouted. 'Get your window shut!' In the dim light his red hair was an unnatural colour; his freckles stood out like the markings of a disease. Hamilton rolled up the window, and the odour of their own sweat filled the oven-like cabin.

The women resembled those flying-foxes which flap against the evening sky in Java: they swarmed over every inch of the car except the roof, obscuring the windscreen and all the side windows. Their shrill cries came through the glass, their parchment-coloured hands moving on it in spidery eagerness. Wildly smiling faces peered in at the two men; some of them clawed and struck at each other to get better positions; others desperately drew up their clothes. Eyes shone; tongues protruded; many were young, but none of them was attractive. When PKI toughs had mobbed the car in the same way, Hamilton had found them less appalling.

Curtis was giggling hysterically. 'The trick is,' he shouted, 'to get the door open for a second, point to the one you want, get her inside, and shut the door fast. Okay? Go ahead, dollink—pick one.'

But Hamilton, one side of his mouth turned down in disgust, shook his head. He re-started the engine, and slowly moved the car off. Calling wildly, the women fell away.

'What the hell are you doing?' Curtis cried.

'It's not for me, matey—I'm sorry.'

The half-light made Curtis's face plaster-like. Staring at Hamilton in furious amazement, he looked like one of those masculine small boys who can only show rage, not tears, when their wishes are frustrated. 'Jesus, you fussy bastard,' he said. 'Well, I guess you always were like that. Here—let me out. I'll go after pussy on foot, if I have to.'

Hamilton drove off slowly into the darkness where the street lamps ended, back past the hopefully fluttering *bantji*. In his rear-vision mirror, the broad-shouldered, red-haired figure in its yellow sports shirt trudged grimly along the cemetery wall, under the fleshy white stars of the frangipani-trees.

It was the last time he would ever see Curtis, who went missing, presumed dead, eighteen months later, when the American patrol he was accompanying was ambushed by Viet Cong in Quang Tri Province. And that last sight of Curtis was always to trouble him. He had never seen anything less like a man advancing towards pleasure than Curtis patrolling the wall of the Kebayoran cemetery: he seemed rather to be furiously hunting some sort of destruction.

22 July

You are inconstant, when I had thought that constancy was your chief virtue. Hamilton, you betray our darling through the same sad lechery which keeps a man like Curtis tied to the wheel! Dear God, it's a matter for weeping.

But the spy is spied on. I am beginning a file on your KGB lady, here where all my images are made and stored!*

What scorn in that white Tartar face, as she looks at you! Can't you see? Fool, you fool, from a continent where ignorance is virtue, where bogies exist only in old, wicked countries overseas—or in your perverted Fleming thrillers! Can't you see?

It's a daughter of Durga! Every line of that body (corpse-white, as those of the red-haired always are) betrays a daughter of the Drinker of Blood.

Durga! Uma! Kali! You of many names: Time, and Sleep, and the Night of Doomsday! You who offer bliss, and dark disorder! You who soothe our fears, but put them back! You who doom us even with your play! Swollen world-nurse! Hag of death! Dance your fearsome lila!

23 July

Is it possible I was wrong about you, Hamilton? Is it possible you are not the Unmet Friend?

The reader is welcome to make what he can of these entries on Hamilton's file—dated, you'll notice, only a few days after the previous entry I've quoted, and also belonging to the period of Jill Bryant's absence in Singapore, when Hamilton had his Tugu encounter with Vera Chostiakov. But I can make little useful

---

*No such file exists. Possibly Kwan destroyed it.—R.J.C.

comment. The passage is highly generalised and overwrought; and although it hints at a relationship, it doesn't record any instance of meetings between them. Hamilton himself told me at the time that he had not taken up Vera's invitation to contact her in Jakarta. He had once found a message at the Hotel desk asking that he do so, but he ignored it. There were too many dangers in such a liaison, and he had no desire to find himself expelled from the country, or under suspicion at the Australian Embassy. And to enter into romantic competition with Kumar would have been rather ridiculous.

He may have been lying; he was reticent, as I've said, in sexual matters. But I don't think this is likely; he never lied to me, as far as I know.

And yet a doubt remains. No one tells us the whole truth, and the Chostiakov encounter ended by being very embarrassing to Hamilton. The doubt floats in the same area of my mind as the suspicion about that locked bathroom-darkroom of Kwan's, and his lyrical entries concerning Hamilton and Jill in Jill Bryant's file. His physical details concerning Vera—however inflated the rest of the entry may be—seem very exact; but then, his imagination was strong, and he would have met her at Soviet Cultural Mission functions. I'll never know the truth of this now—and perhaps I don't want to.

What is certain is the dawning of Kwan's bitter disappointment with Hamilton. I've no doubt he believed that sexual encounters were taking place with Kumar's Russian lady; and if they were, and if Hamilton was even taking Vera to the trysting-place Kwan had made available for him and Jill—then I have little difficulty in picturing Billy's feelings. To make clear how much he had wanted from Hamilton, and how much he now began to feel was lost, I can do no better than to quote from the opening section of Hamilton's dossier.

DOSSIER H 10: HAMILTON, Guy
NATIONALITY: Technically Australian; regards himself as British.
BORN: 1936, under the sign of Capricorn.
REMARKS: A hybrid Saxon-Celt, of attractive appearance . . . .

Moderate to conservative in politics. Somewhat 'correct' for a man of his generation: a 'gentleman'. The early colonial environment (and perhaps the widowed mother's nostalgia for it during his formative years—I am guessing here) has produced a distinct nostalgia for the vanished Empire . . . .

Fastidious to a fault. His danger is to shut himself off in a sterile orderliness, ruling neat lines around himself, making a fetish of his career, and making all his relationships temporary, lest they disturb that career. He must learn to give himself. He must learn to love . . . .

At the end of this summary, not typed, but scribbled by hand like an afterthought, is a strange exclamation and complaint:

He is myself! I should have been him. Why not, God? Why not?

There is only one other entry on Hamilton's file concerning Vera Chostiakov. This is far more specific, and far more hard-headed, proposing as it does the true reason for her interest in Hamilton: a reason the big man was remarkably slow to surmise.

28 July

You are apparently too stupid—or too vain—to have realised what the lady wants from you: the details and date of arrival of the Chinese arms shipment.

Little doubt of this. If the Russians calculate that the Chinese are going to back a PKI coup, and that the arrival of the shipment is the signal for that coup, they will do almost anything to find out the date. Chostiakov will have been given any freedom she needs, to associate with both you and Kumar—and no doubt a licence to offer you her body, money, or both.

But how did Kumar discover your knowledge of the cargo—told only to me? Eavesdropping, perhaps.

Fool! Guy—how can you be such a fool?

The question seems apt, since Hamilton, despite his decision to avoid her, did not deny being interested in Vera, who had a strong physical attraction for him. He admitted to me that had it not been for his commonsense reservations, he would have responded to that message of hers, and contacted her. He had kept me in complete ignorance of the matter of the Chinese shipment, of course; and I was therefore as much inclined as he was, in the absence of that knowledge, to see her interest in him as 'romantic' in some way. Perhaps she wanted to defect; or perhaps Henri was right, and at worst she wanted to use Hamilton as a 'model'.

'After all, Cookie, not many people get a chance for an affair with a beautiful Russki,' he said. 'It's like meeting someone from the moon.' He smiled in dismissal; picked up his drink.

But I saw that he stared after the receding lights of a fantasy in which he might have been caught up. Kwan was at least half right. Hamilton perhaps saw himself at the centre of some episode out of Ian Fleming: an episode with the double advantage (for him) of the risk to which he was addicted, and a relationship with someone not quite real—someone free of the tedious or difficult characteristics real women were apt to have. And he was half inclined to picture Vera as no agent at all, but simply as a romantically-inclined young woman from the Soviet Cultural Mission, locked inside that iron system of theirs and wanting to get out of it. This was the most seductive idea of all, of course; and I didn't find him altogether silly. Few of us consciously make contact with that sub-world of espionage which is the myth kingdom of our century. Intelligence agents from a foreign power are rather like hobgoblins in most people's minds: not consciously seen, they are irrationally thought not to exist outside the fables of the entertainment industry. I've known fellow-journalists with this attitude—even though some of their colleagues, unknown to them, were agents themselves, using the job as a cover. (Do you believe in fairies?)

Vera was a shadow, and would remain one. With the bogy mask of the Soviet Union looming behind her, she could never become a person for him.

16

It was now the beginning of August: hottest month of the year; last phase of the dry monsoon. Jill Bryant was due back on the third; and still Hamilton had no lead on the Chinese arms shipment.

He wasn't in immediate danger of following Curtis to Vietnam; his report to his news-editor had gained him a reprieve. But this was all it was. Despite the nation's rush towards absolute collapse, and the mounting violence in Jakarta, he knew that his broadcasts on this theme would not be enough to convince Biggins for long. What he needed, he said, was evidence that the PKI was truly poised for a takeover. And the Chinese cargo was that evidence.

In telling Billy Kwan about it, he had apparently managed to convince himself that he was not really breaking his promise to Jill, since he hadn't told Billy the information had come from her. And he had set out to trace the story himself; once another source had been found, he said, Jill wouldn't be seen as his informant. I doubt that he cared very much about her position, in the frame of mind he was in over her holiday with Henderson; but he did remain scrupulous enough not to break the story as a rumour.

The shipment must surely be landed at any time now—if it hadn't been already. The thought tantalised Hamilton constantly: he believed he was racing time, before some absolute showdown. To have held this key to what the future almost certainly held and not to have been able to produce it, must have been maddening. It was only when I was leaving the country that he told me of his efforts in that baking July-August to flush out evidence of the ghostly cargo.

He drove almost every day down to the port of Priok. He had deduced that the arms must almost certainly be landed there; and he reasoned that a consignment of such a size could not be landed without evidence: the Chinese ship would have to have a berth allocated, and there would have to be a bill of lading. The Indonesian Navy, which controlled the port, was pro-PKI: and he had no doubt, he said, that a false bill of lading would obligingly be issued. He had a contact: a corrupt naval officer who had done him favours for bribes in the past. Hamilton had paid him the equivalent of two hundred US dollars to alert him when any shipment arrived from the People's Republic.

Each day he visited the small, hot office near the docks; and his officer, a thin, slovenly man of middle age, in a cap with a broken peak and a khaki uniform with tarnished gold braid, would always lean back in his chair, drawing on a *kretek* cigarette, and repeat the same refrain: 'No news, my Aussie friend—no news.' He showed a mouth full of gold teeth in a smile Hamilton grew to dislike.

He began to fear that the man was secretly loyal to the PKI, and sometimes lay awake considering the idea that if the PKI were informed of what he knew he would be a marked man. To arrange a killing in Indonesia was simple enough, and even a Western journalist need not be immune at this stage, as the campaign of hatred against '*Nekolim* agents' mounted to hysteria. He was particularly concerned to keep the matter hidden from Kumar, although his assistant would have been far more likely than Billy Kwan to find evidence of the shipment for him—and perhaps already knew everything about it.

Occasionally, when they were working together in the office, Hamilton would glance up and find his assistant's hard black eyes secretly fixed on him; then Kumar would smile like the corrupt naval officer, and look away. It was sad, Hamilton thought; in other circumstances, in another country, there would have been liking between them. They never spoke of Vera.

One afternoon, he pushed an envelope across Kumar's desk

189

containing a large sum of money. 'I've been thinking about your uncle,' he said. 'This might help him to hold on to the shop.'

Kumar frowned. 'No, boss, I cannot take this. We are not beggars.'

'Take it. I make that much extra on the black market any month. Take it, or I'll be offended.'

Kumar sat with his head bowed, frowning at the desk. Then he looked up and smiled. 'That is good of you, boss. For my uncle, I will be a beggar.' And he added slyly, 'Perhaps it will be nice for your conscience, too. Is that right?'

'That's right,' Hamilton said.

Vera made her next approach to Hamilton on the day of Jill's return from Singapore. When the phone on his office desk rang, it was mid-morning. Kumar was out on an errand, but Billy Kwan was seated on top of his usual desk, reading a newspaper. In half an hour they were to drive out to the airport to meet Jill.

'I have been disappointed that you did not *contact* me,' the high voice said. It laid stress on certain words in a way that sounded oddly accusing. 'You promised to come to one of our film evenings, didn't you? Tomorrow night we have interesting films on the Soviet Asian provinces. I should be very pleased if you would come.'

Hamilton glanced at Kwan, who appeared to be sternly immersed in his newspaper, but who perhaps might not be. He cleared his throat, choosing his words carefully.

'I'm afraid that won't be possible,' he said. 'I'm leaving for Central Java early in the morning. I need to see what the PKI are doing in the countryside. On the way back I'll cover this Long March they're putting on.'

'How interesting.' The phone exaggerated an odd defect in her 's' sounds: she said 'intereshting'. 'I too am going to see the march, as it comes through Bandung. They say it should reach there next Tuesday. Shall we see each other in Bandung? It would be very nice if we could. I should be glad of an escort, Guy.'

Something in her insistence worried Hamilton. He said evasively, 'That's a possibility, yes.' He was sure now that Kwan was listening, behind his paper; and the high voice from the receiver seemed unnaturally penetrating.

'Good—so we can meet,' she said. 'I shall be booked at the Hotel Kellerman on Tuesday night. If you will book there too, we can be sure to find each other. Will you do that?'

'That should be all right,' Hamilton said. 'The Kellerman.'

When he hung up, he found Kwan looking at him severely, the newspaper laid aside.

'So you're going to Central Java,' Billy said. 'Why didn't you tell me?'

'I meant to—I forgot. This Long March ought to be covered. It's big.'

'You're not taking me? You don't want film?'

As far as it ever showed emotion, Billy's face looked hurt, and Hamilton spoke persuasively. 'I need you to hold the fort here— you've got to try and get something on that arms shipment story. I'll be away a week. I can't trust Kumar—I've told you that. You can get film of the march when it reaches Jakarta, Okay?' He stood up. 'We'd better get moving.'

In the car, as Hartono drove them towards Kemayoran airport, Hamilton tried to cheer Billy up by giving him the cue for their routine of happier days; they hoped to shoot film of a rally in Merdeka Square on the way back, and he said, 'How's old Bell and Howell? Loaded? Any hairs on the lens?'

But Kwan would not complete the dialogue. He shrugged sulkily, and said, 'Let me take care of that.'

Despite his recent mistrust of Kwan, Hamilton felt bereft. He suddenly saw how much the old, ebullient Billy had meant to him; he had a childish disappointment that Kwan would not say, 'You worry about the words, Hamilton'—as he used to do in the first months of success and happiness here. He wanted the old Billy back.

Suddenly Kwan burst out, 'You don't *have* to go to Central Java, just when Jillie's getting back. She'll be very upset, you know. And no one else is mad enough to go out there now—it's too bloody dangerous, with this skirmishing going on. What if the car breaks down? No spare parts, and no transport any more:

191

you'd be stranded. You've got a good chance of being killed, the way things are now. What are you being so bloody gung-ho for?'

'That's just it—no one else is going out there. It's time someone did. I want to know how strong the PKI really are. And the march is worth covering.'

Kwan turned to him. 'It's that Russian bitch, isn't it? That's who you're meeting in Bandung.'

'Look—stop poking your bloody nose into my affairs!'

Hamilton had almost shouted this; but Billy stared back at him fearlessly, with a Chinese poker face. It was the first time they had quarrelled outright. Half turned to each other in the back seat, they froze in this posture for some moments, like boys sparring, while old Hartono drove stiffly and silently; but it was doubtful if he understood what they were saying.

In his flattest voice, Billy said, 'If you don't mind old man, I'd like the key of my place back.'

Without a word, Hamilton handed it to him. There was silence for some minutes. Then Billy said, 'Are you really so stupid that you think she's interested in *you*? There's only one thing you've got that would make her compromise herself in the way she's doing—only one piece of information.'

Hamilton frowned at him in silence. Then he said, 'That's impossible. There's no one who could have told her that—except you. And even you aren't that bloody silly.'

'I don't know how she got it, old man, but she's got it. The simple explanation is that Kumar eavesdropped on us. Or maybe your original contact talked—you've never told me who that was. But that's the whole reason the lady wants you. Are you really going to be made a bloody fool of?'

'Knock it off, Billy.'

'Leave this sort of intrigue to the permanent adolescents, Ham. It doesn't suit you. Jillie needs you. She wants to marry you. But you care for nobody *enough*, do you?'

Hamilton now had too much to think about to be annoyed by this. He sat with compressed lips.

'Maybe you think she'll get over it;' Billy said. 'She won't.' He jerked forward. 'She's pregnant, Hamilton. She didn't want me to tell you—but it's time you knew.'

For this little shock, at least, Hamilton was ready. 'Really? She tells you more than she does me, then. Should I feel responsible?' He felt ashamed when he heard himself say this; but he was bitter enough to want to make Billy angry.

Kwan merely examined him gravely. 'Of course the child's yours,' he said. 'She was going to an abortionist, in Singapore, because she thinks you'll never marry her, Dr Chen. But I persuaded her not to. The rest's up to you.'

They were moving very slowly along Jalan Dr Sutomo, blocked by traffic. Billy looked at him now with an expression which seemed near to pleading. 'Take me with you on this trip, if you must go,' he said. 'And don't go to Bandung on the way back. Forget about Chostiakov. We'll do better together, on a stint like that: if there's any trouble, we'll have a better chance. We'll get terrific film.'

But Hamilton said slowly, 'I'm sorry—I can't do it. If the cargo story turns up, you should be here.'

Kwan's pause was infinitesimal; then he picked up his silent camera and swung open the door of the car, which had almost halted in the traffic jam.

'Then you'll have to do this job without me, old man. This and all the others. Go and see Chostiakov. But you'll be finished with Jillie. Good-bye.'

He jumped from the car, the heavy camera slung over his shoulder, and scurried among the jeeps and bicycles towards the kerb. Hamilton called out; but his cameraman was gone, swallowed by the crowds of the Old City.

Moonlight fell on Jill's dressing-table, illuminating a photograph of her parents: father firm-jawed, kindly, and sane-eyed, facing up to his firm's collapse; mother vague-eyed and patrician, with that illusory sadness of women in photographs. Unaware of the night's exotic furnace, they stared at Hamilton questioningly. Beside them sat an expensive electric shaver, a gift Jill had brought back for him from Singapore.

She slept, lying without covering. Moira was away at Bogor, which had allowed Hamilton to spend the night here; but he half-wished now that he hadn't. The heat of August was scarcely moved by the ceiling fan, and Hamilton, unable to sleep, had too many thoughts to trouble him since Billy's exit from the car this afternoon. He wished himself back in his clinical Hotel room, inside the air-conditioning. Easing himself carefully away from Jill, so that their bodies no longer touched, he propped himself on one elbow and stared at the objects on the dressing-table.

They added to the feeling of guilt he was trying to suppress: like the soft sigh she gave in her sleep, they tugged at him; they asked him to reconsider. The shaver was the latest in a series of gifts she had made him; and she not only took pleasure in giving, she was generous with herself—concerned about everything that concerned him. 'Mummy and Daddy', smiling at him with foolish kindliness from the photograph, asked him to believe that their daughter after all retained their virtues: those virtues of Hamilton's England. But this he would not believe: he remained inwardly obdurate, barring her from the country of his trust. He had not asked her about her pregnancy; and she had not hinted at it.

But remoteness had not been so easy for him earlier in the evening, when she had hurried towards him through the brown gloom of the customs shed, in the Kemayoran terminal. Her smile had radiated a delight impossible to manufacture; and in those first instants his body had surprised him by welcoming hers as it had welcomed no other in his life. Watched by the frowning soldiers who shepherded all foreign passengers in and out of the country, he had held the slight arc of her against him, lifted in a wave of gladness for which he had been totally unprepared. Startling him, it had made all his reservations and resolutions about her seem like the sterile chatter of a fool. But Hamilton was a man who listened to his head, and the fool would win.

'I missed you,' he said, and had meant it. He had forgotten how special her face was to him; both strange and familiar, as it searched his; no longer like his Rackham drawing: more like some distant relative in a photograph album; perhaps an ancestor. What creates such obsessions in us, so that we wait for the appearance of a particular face, strange and yet known before? What turns such defects as a recessed lower lip and a slight cast in one eye into haunting and precious attractions, which tantalise the mind? Perhaps we do seek our ancestors—or loves from another life.

When he spoke to me about Jill, I saw that much of Hamilton's obstinate, closed quality was based on pride. He was not totally closed to her, or he would not have been troubled enough to discuss her. But pride prevented him from accusing her of taking a holiday with Henderson; and his decision to withdraw from involvement with her stopped him from broaching Billy Kwan's story of her pregnancy. Perhaps he hoped that if he said nothing he need never take that story seriously. Or perhaps he even hoped that she had already done something about it in Singapore, with Dr Chen.

She tried now to nestle against him. She didn't look pregnant, he thought. But this was perhaps because he didn't want to think her so; he tried to ignore a possible enlargement of the raised areolas dominating her small breasts, standing out on the whiteness like ominous bruises.

He drew away from her. In the heat, they both sweated instantly they made contact, and it was easier here than in a cold climate to draw aloof, to resist the body's more humble appeals: for animal comfort; for affection. It's easier to be cruel in the tropics: perhaps this is why there's less charity there. She moaned, and said something in her sleep he could not understand. Before they had slept, she had begged him not to go to Central Java; her plaintive note now was the same.

She spoke again, in a pleading, childish voice, and this time the words were clear. '*I'm so cold*,' she said. '*Can't you love me at all?*'

He peered into her face, but her eyes were closed; she was certainly asleep, and there was a desperate loneliness in her voice that appalled him in spite of himself. He wondered if she actually spoke to him, in her dream, or to her ex-husband, or to someone else. He drew her against him, with empty pity.

But close though he held her, in the humid heat, Jill shivered as though on a winter's night in Europe, and moaned, and repeated without hope: '*I'm so cold. Can't you love me at all?*'

17

In that hottest month of the year, when Hamilton went out to Central Java alone, the *Wayang* of the Left were everywhere triumphant. They had planned their Chinese-inspired 'Long March' through the countryside as a show of strength, proceeding in relays from Jogjakarta to Jakarta.

No one in the Wayang Club other than Hamilton had any desire to cover its progress out there: certainly I didn't. Pete Curtis would have done; but Pete had gone to Saigon. So now only Hamilton had the youth, stamina, and foolishness to face the punishing journey, the risks, the inevitable attacks of gastritis, and the possibility of contracting dysentery—or worse. But he welcomed the Long March. He always saw risk as an answer to his other problems; and he hoped for a story to compensate for the elusive Chinese cargo. As well, he seems to have been drawn by the countryside itself. He simply wanted to be out there again, in those brilliant jade territories which were always a little unreal.

Hands drummed and thundered on the roof, more urgent than those of the prostitutes at the cemetery: louder, much louder than the monsoon rain had been when he and Jill had sat parked at Priok. Once too often, Hamilton said. His mind was stuck in a groove; he sat trapped in his halted car, waiting to be killed. There seemed to be nothing else to do.

It was late on Tuesday afternoon, and he was just outside

Tasikmalaya, a village about two hours' drive from Bandung, where he had joined a relay of the Long March. The engine was still running: he had the car in first gear, his foot jammed on the clutch pedal. But there was no way of moving; he was locked between walls of white shirts, singlets, old military jackets, gesticulating brown arms. To advance even a few feet would have meant running some of the marchers down, and this would certainly have sealed his fate. The big man poured with sweat in the metal capsule; all the windows were rolled up, and he felt himself suffocating. His heart pounded like a faulty machine.

'*Your window!*' Pete Curtis shouted, and Hamilton thought: How long did we think we could keep them all out?

He had an absurd desire to laugh; many of the wood-brown faces peering through the windows looked comically insane, and their shouting had become abandoned screaming, like that of spoiled children, or those rock-singers who specialised in vocal orgasm. Names in English came through the glass.

'*Bastard! Colonialist!*'

'*Nekolim pig!*'

But the desire to laugh soon passed, because they had begun to rock the car. A wave of intense cold passed through him, despite the heat. In Jakarta, he had never really been afraid in such situations: the game was played within limits, and no foreign pressmen had been killed; merely jostled or roughed up. But he was now alone in the countryside, in territory the PKI claimed to control, entirely beyond the reach of any sort of aid, and without witnesses.

No one would ever know what had happened; and Hamilton saw that they would turn the car over (as they so often did with empty cars in Jakarta), and then their excitement would carry them away. They would set this one on fire with a *Nekolim* inside it. He wondered, he said to me, why he was dying; and I smiled at this eleventh-hour realisation of the futility of his profession. A childish voice inside him protested: '*No. Not yet.*' And he heard as well, through the hate-crazed babble, the plaintive question Jill had asked in her sleep.

He tried smiling at the faces outside, which had often worked in the past, but there was no response; the car rocked more and more violently. He felt the wheels leave the ground, and began to brace himself to get out the door and take his chances on foot. But the Ford was heavy, the rocking would not seem to take it to the point of capsizing, and the motion began to slacken off. Hope flickered in him, and then returned: he saw that he might be spared. More and more of them were growing bored, and beginning to melt away.

Hamilton gingerly lifted his foot from the clutch, and began to inch his way forward. There was a parting drumming on the roof, spittle ran down the windscreen, but he was allowed to go. Drenched as though from swimming, he wove his way among the banners of the leading marchers, and was out on open road.

He whistled now as he drove, but a nerve jumped in his cheek; he found that he was trembling violently, and that his body was extraordinarily light. This was partly the result of fatigue, partly a reaction to his escape; and he was weakened as well by an inevitable gastric infection brought on by eating in the villages.

He had driven for six days through Central and West Java, talking to Muslim and PKI leaders in the kampongs and towns, and he had slept for about three hours out of the last forty-eight. In order to catch up with the Long March, on his way back to Jakarta, he had pushed on through most of last night and all through today, jolting over the ruined roads in the immense heat, worried always that the Ford would break an axle, slowed at times to ten miles an hour by slow-motion bullock carts, or by old Mercedes buses with bunched figures clinging to the sides and on the roofs, which still somehow ran without spare parts. He had joined the march two hours ago, and at first all had gone well.

There could not have been less than a thousand marchers on the road at any time, he told me, and later it built to perhaps five thousand, as groups joined it from villages it passed. PKI leaders led them in song through loud-hailers: they had, it seems, a particularly rousing 'Crush Malaysia' song to the tune of 'Michael Row the Boat Ashore'. 'I joined in the choruses,' Hamilton said. The late-model Ford, symbol of affluence, attracted jeering attention, but the countryside had made him carefree; he had laughed and waved as though taking part in a festival. When they brought him to a complete halt, as they occasionally did, he had a trick to deal with the situation: he would jump out of the car, smiling, and begin to shake hands. 'They didn't know whether to shake my hand or kick me in the crutch,' he told me. 'But most Javanese are so bloody friendly they couldn't help shaking my hand. Then they'd let me through.' But his system had broken down when the march was joined by a group of particularly aggressive People's Youth: the sight of his car had apparently enraged them.

He thought of Jill now, as he began to take in that his life had been spared. Her repeated question, sounding in his head, had assumed great importance for him. It had broken down his resistance: not just to her, but to that faceless baby he so much feared, which might imprison him in a suburb; and he realised, as he drove, that Jill was at the core of a remarkable new happiness.

He even thought with fondness of Billy Kwan, and determined to make up their quarrel when he got back to Jakarta. Chastened by his release, he decided to heed Billy's threat: he would not see Vera Chostiakov in Bandung. To break the arrangement was simple; he would not stay at the Hotel Kellerman.

As he neared Bandung, in its high valley, his feeling of lightness—almost of lightheadedness—continued: a giddy elation simply at finding himself alive. All the colours of the landscape—violet, marching volcanoes, jade paddy fields, orange flame-trees—seemed more vividly unlikely than usual: colours seen on a return to consciousness, after a blow. 'It was like a trip on grass,' he said.

But no 'trip on grass' could have brought him this vision without stimulants, this state of wonder at the world which is the greatest delight we ever find, and which has to be earned. Hamilton had earned it because death, with the blank casualness of all things in Asia, had brushed his big frame. Outside the huts with their white, palm-mat walls, in groves of palm- and banana-trees, classically shaped matrons were smiling him by again: cheerful, brown-faced nymphs from green pools. In a vast patchwork of lawn-green and gold rice-fields, like the parklands

199

of a *wayang* prince, girls clothed like butterflies swung crescent-shaped knives, harvesting; and they palmed these knives discreetly, so as not to offend Dewi Sri, the Goddess of Rice.

Covert violence, he knew, was stitched into every acre of this tapestry of peace. He would report in his radio piece how Muslim leaders had told him they would fight to the death against PKI blasphemers who spat on God—and whose mobs invaded their farms. 'They are like dogs,' one of these kampong heads had told him, with quiet certainty. 'They have no souls.' Tension hummed like a wire beside every mile of highway; yet despite his escape, despite what he knew was imminent here, it made no sense. The smiles of the kampong women said violence could never happen; they gave no hint that in four months' time perhaps half a million people would be hacked to death with cane knives, in the green on green of the paddies.

Twilight came, and the spaces between the palm-groves and kampong houses took on the smoke-blue of magic; little coconut-oil lamps trembled in open doorways. During the day, West Java is an Eden of images, but not of physical fact; it can never be that while sweat runs into the eyes and clothing is plastered to the body. But at nightfall this high, sly country becomes an Eden indeed, languid and mysterious inside warmth like a gentle oven. Perhaps this does something to explain Hamilton's experience on the road outside Bandung.

He had a sort of vision there apparently. I know of no other way of putting it, since I am reconstructing his experience in words that are not always his words. In trying to describe it to me, he spent much time on the physical circumstances: he was less articulate about his inward state. One has to see him driving into the descending night with the absolute alarm of the incident in the Long March still fresh. That drive through West Java, alone, with the giddy prospect of his own death retreating behind him, was obviously a peak in the graph of his life. It was his time: the time which says to us, 'You have arrived into the country of the secret; take it; it's yours.'

Full dark had come when he reached the outskirts of Bandung. He had a desire to get out of the car before going into the city, and pulled over, on a stretch of still-rural road, outside a row of little shops. 'The old Javanese night came crashing in,' he said, 'full of scents and queer smells—you know the way it does, Cookie.' I knew; and I have always remembered the way he put it, this usually hard-shelled, over-practical young man, leaning on our dark, confessional bar, his big chin suddenly tender: and I saw that he had actually been changed, and would always be a little different.

To say how, is difficult. He had decided to commit himself to Jill: that was simple enough. And he had come to be very fond of Java; but this says nothing, since such fondness was an illusion, for him and for me. The country was essentially unlovable for us, since we could not share its memories; our little staked-out claims to emotional attachment had no real meaning. But it had given Hamilton his time, his moment of vision, and in that sense he would carry Java with him all his life.

He stood looking about, easing his bush-shirt from his sweating back. The inevitable staring crowd collected around him: they would not go away, he knew, as long as he stood there. Little girls with streaming, blue-black hair stood giggling up at him, hand in hand; young men in shirts and sarongs, smoking *kreteks*, studied him and his car with care; and everyone smiled, with good-humoured curiosity: Jakarta's propaganda had not dispelled their natural friendliness. A voice said softly, from among the crowd, '*Slamat datang, tuan.*' He could not tell who had spoken, but Hamilton smiled and acknowledged the welcome in his bad Bahasa.

It was just a flat stretch of road beside a row of small Dutch-style commercial buildings, with galvanised-iron veranda awnings: beyond them were the houses of a kampong. Nothing unusual; he had seen a hundred similar scenes in the past four days; yet tonight the dark doorways of these little shops, where coconut-oil and kerosene lamps burned, were mysterious and novel to Hamilton. An old pedlar in a conical straw hat sat behind a tray of gleaming red peppers and beans, his slyly humorous, upturned face seeming to wait for applause, as though the trays contained gems; and Hamilton was enchanted by him, and by everything here; by the gentle evening heat, and the composite odour of Java: clove-smoke of the *kreteks*, and nutty tang of human flesh, innocent as that of the high-piled vegetables.

He saw a light, from the corner of his eye. Looking past the end of the line of shops, he found that it was the screen of a *wayang kulit* show, floating in the dark near the kampong.

He had seen these before, from the car, but had always passed them by: he knew that the *wayang* was in old Javanese, and thus completely incomprehensible. It had never occurred to him to look at one; they had not interested him, and anyway he had felt vaguely that they were out of bounds, an experience he could not enter. But tonight he had a sudden desire to approach the screen and watch with the village crowd: he was drawn towards the light.

The *wayang* had been set up in a clearing beyond the last shop, its lit screen hanging in the dark like that of a drive-in cinema. Approaching, Hamilton heard the gonging of *gamelan* instruments, and the guttural cries of the puppets. When he came to the edges of the crowd, brown faces turned and studied him briefly; then, grave and intent, they turned back to the screen, re-entering their ancient dream of the Kingdom of Dwarawati, Gate of the World, Kresna's kingdom, whose mountains are highest, women most beautiful, soil most fertile, men most noble. This had been their cinema since the time of Java's ancient Hindu kingdoms, and it seemed to Hamilton to have a weird modernity: a video-machine from an unknown civilisation. At the edges of the *wayang* show's arc of light were other small lights, where little stalls sold *saté* and cigarettes. People laughed together; came and went; children dodged among their legs. A line of flying-foxes glided overhead, like magic animals which had escaped from the screen into the air.

He had approached from the side of the screen where the priestly puppet-master worked, with his humble *gamelan* orchestra behind him. Three white-clad men played a wooden xylophone, a fiddle, and drums, while a thin woman with an infant at the breast and a cigarette slanting from her mouth worked with her free hand on a set of bronze gongs. The *dalang* was a small, stern man in spectacles and a ceremonial cap of midnight blue: above his head, a pressure-lamp, the source of the radiance, hung from a rope; rows of *wayang* puppets were stuck into yellow-green banana logs below the screen, waiting for their entrances, from the left and the right. Sheaves of rice (tribute for Dewi Sri) hung from each end of the screen. In the *dalang*'s upraised hands two of the flat, ornate figures in which Billy Kwan had tried vainly to interest Hamilton were moving now with uncanny life. With a chock held between his toes, the master of the shadows knocked constantly for attention on the side of his puppet-box: *tun-tun*; *tuk-tuk*.

People pressed close to watch the sacred theatre's mysteries; but Hamilton drifted away to the other side of the screen, to the magic side, where only the filigreed silhouettes could be seen, their insect profiles darting, looming into hugeness, or dwindling to vanishing-point. Their voices chattered things he could never understand, rising into the warm dark: but the schoolroom rapping on the puppet-box commanded his attention. Standing behind solemn elders from the kampong, for whom chairs had been placed on the grass, he seemed to be watching the deeply important activity of dreams.

The *dalang* was singing. His wailing, almost female voice climbed higher and higher, while the little drum pattered on underneath, and the gongs bubbled. On one wavering note, his voice was drawn out and out, until Hamilton, transfixed, seemed to see it like a bright thread against eternal sky; until it connected with Heaven. What was the *dalang* singing about? He would never know. Usually bored by things he could not understand, he could not now bring himself to return to the car; he lingered, locked in delight. The figures of this dream of Java's childhood tantalised him with the notion that he *ought* to know them, *ought* to recall them, from some other life. And they woke in him now a long-buried memory of his own.

At eight years old, he said, in hospital with appendicitis, he had been alarmed by the noises of the ward at night: agonised coughing, groans, distant crashes. And he had hidden behind comic books his elder brother had brought him, erecting them on his chest like screens between himself and the unthinkable landscape beyond his bed. He had not wanted to hear the coughing of the old man dying in the bed next to him; he had not wanted to smell his bedpan, or hear the bubbling of his bowels. And there came back to him now the peculiar affection he had felt for those little figures in the comic books which could make him forget what lay beyond their pages. He had followed Mickey Mouse and Tarzan and the Phantom from frame to frame (as he now followed the darting figures in the lit frame of the *wayang*) with mysterious pleasure, but without comprehension, whispering like runes the phrases they spoke. And it occurred to him now, Hamilton said, that the *wayang* frame was perhaps erected here for the same reason that he had propped his comic-book-screen on his chest: so that the people of the kampong could forget, for a whole night, the presences of hunger and pain and threat at the edges of their green world. He glanced about at the still brown faces with an affectionate compassion which was new to him. And he would ask me later: 'What can we *do* for them, Cookie?' The question was rhetorical, but it was genuinely felt.

A delicately built, Hindu-faced man of about thirty, with oiled, curly hair and a small moustache, was standing at Hamilton's elbow; suddenly he held out the rolled leaf of a *kretek*, speaking softly in Bahasa. Hamilton did not hear what he said; but he took the *kretek*, and thanked him. It tasted not unpleasant, he found, this clove-spiced cigarette of the poor. He had never smoked one before.

The moustached man spoke again, and Hamilton's limited Bahasa was sufficient for him to understand that he was being asked if he liked the *wayang*; he said that he did, and they watched for a time in intimate silence. Smiling at him from time to time with an appearance of remarkable fondness, the moustached man offered soft remarks about the story, some of which Hamilton understood. This was the first part, his companion said, which would run until midnight. (They were watching the court scenes, which correspond to the period of man's foolish youth.) At midnight, the hero Arjuna would enter, and the comical dwarf, Semar: you should wait for this, he told Hamilton.

The figures of India's great Pandava story, transformed into

204

weird cartoons, formally addressed each other, laughed and wept, prepared for battle in their chariots. Ogres who were coarse as Westerners ranted and broke wind, while the audience laughed derisively. Hamilton was introduced to the *Wayang* of the Right and the *Wayang* of the Left, who are in constant conflict. Kings with butterfly wings ascended into the air; evil spirits invaded the screen from the bottom, while the *dalang* narrated all in the deep tones of a father; growled; was shrill; sang.

But Hamilton would not be there when the Pandava brothers, led by Arjuna (a saturnine gnat, bow in hand), did battle with their cousins, the 99 evil Kaurawas; and he would never learn how Arjuna, through deep meditation, upsets the whole balance of nature—building up his *sakti*, the spirit-power which animates the universe—to bring on storms and earthquakes. Neither would he see Dwarf Semar, the god in mis-shapen form, whose breasts are female, sitting in tears: he would never understand Dwarf Semar's grief. All these things would come after midnight, at their appointed time; but Hamilton decided he must leave to book into a hotel in the city.

His two days without sleep, and perhaps his reaction to the incident in the Long March, had now begun to transform his lightheadedness into a fatigue which bemused him like a drug. He told the moustached man that he must go; but his new friend asked him earnestly to stay longer. Smiling indulgently, Hamilton lingered. A lacy, feminine shape with an elaborate head-dress flitted on the screen: when Hamilton asked who she was, the moustached man said that it was Dewi Sri; she brought the harvest, he said. I was puzzled to know what the Rice Goddess was doing in this sequence of the Pandava cycle; but strange things happen in the *wayang*, and Hamilton insisted that this was how she had been identified; she seems to have caught his imagination.

A light hand touched his shoulder, and a high, worrying voice said, 'You enjoy the *wayang*?'

He looked down from the bright square of the screen, and started: he had the impression, as his eyes adjusted, that he was looking at an extremely pretty white Javanese: a sort of half-caste.

Then he saw that it was Vera Chostiakov, her copper hair still drawn up in its bun, the Asiatic definiteness of her round cheekbones picked out in the mythic arc of light.

Inside his fatigue, it seemed to him for a moment that he had conjured her up; that she was no more real than one of the flitting silhouettes above their heads. He stared at her stupidly, while the changeless *gamelan* music gonged and ran on. 'How did you find me?' he asked.

She burst out laughing, her upper lip disappearing and distorting the regularity of her face. 'But I did not come *looking* for you, Guy. Out of so many millions in Bandung how could I hope to find you? I have expected to see you at Hotel Kellerman. I am so glad you are here.'

He continued to stare at her, with a regret that resembled dread. 'Surely you're not wandering about here on your own?' he asked.

'How funny you sound. Are you drunk? No, I have Peter my driver. He is waiting in the car. But he will not trouble us—once he drops me at Kellerman, he goes elsewhere. We were passing, and I saw the sticker of ABS on your windshield. It is very convenient, that sticker. I shall always be able to find you.'

She took his arm intimately, while Hamilton's forgotten guide stared at her in fascination: many dark eyes were turned, their whites gleaming in the light. In a beige sleeveless dress, still carrying the large handbag she had brought to Tugu, she looked freshly ironed, as though she had dressed in the last half-hour. 'When do you grow tired of these fairy tales? You look tired. Come back to Kellerman. Follow after my car.'

They moved away from the arc of light, and the *dalang*'s many voices. A black Zil limousine, with Soviet diplomatic plates, was parked behind Hamilton's dusty Ford by the line of shops. The driver was a heavy, stolid-looking man in an open-necked green sports shirt, with an American-style crew-cut; he was chewing something, and watched with a blank face as Hamilton and Vera approached.

After the Zil had lumbered off into the black and violet tunnel of the highway, Hamilton paused for a moment, his hand on the

206

door of his own car, his thoughts slow, considering the idea of driving in the opposite direction. But he knew he would not do it: he would follow. He opened the door, the little crowd of spectators watching his every movement. A soft voice behind him said, '*Slamat jalan, mas.*'—May your journey be blessed, brother.

It was the same voice which had welcomed him here; he turned and saw it was the little Hindu-faced man, his guide, reproachfully smiling as though he had been betrayed.

Hamilton raised his hand, with a feeling of guilt. '*Terimah kasih, mas,*' he said.

Biting on one of his small cigars, humming through his teeth and blinking to stay awake, he drove through warm, enigmatic blackness. Ahead of him, the red sparks of the Zil's tail-lights disappeared behind a bullock cart; then reappeared. He followed; his car seemed attached to these lights as though by a long cord. He talked to himself, and laughed.

Vera had been observant; his fatigue did resemble drunkenness; and this drunkenness was now shot through with euphoria. He supposed that their premature meeting had been accidental; but the lingering idea that it hadn't, that she had managed to find him out here, was awe-inspiring. Billy Kwan's last lecture had not been wasted: Hamilton now had little doubt what it was that Vera wanted from him, and the presence of the 'driver', whom he assumed to be also a KGB operative, made the whole situation more serious, he said.

So what did he think he was doing?

I was eventually to ask him this with some bluntness; but he was vague. He had the sensation, apparently, of being caught up in some pre-ordained sequence that had to be played out. 'I really wanted to know what they were after,' he said; but later, when he came to view that night as the beginning of all his troubles, he would call his action a 'bloody aberration', and try to convey the idea that he had drifted into it in a daze.

I suppose he did, in a way. And the field of risk surrounding Vera was probably more powerful in its effect on Hamilton than the sexual one had been. I don't doubt that he was sincere about his new feeling for Jill; and I believe that under other circumstances he would have avoided further contact with Vera. But he was moving now inside his own spy story, carried through a warm, wish-fulfilling dark alive with little lights: a place of speed, where boredom and the ordinary were banished.

The lacy shadow of Dewi Sri re-appeared, printed on his windscreen. He blinked; but he should not have been surprised. Paramount spirit of the countryside, she was more important out here than Communist or Muslim; and he was in one of the few places left where she smiles from the roadside as we pass.

They sat in Hamilton's bedroom in the aged Hotel Kellerman, drinking warm Bintang beer.

'I'm a bit claustrophobic,' Hamilton told me. 'And that bloody place would have given any claustrophobic hysterics.'

I understood; I had once stayed in the Kellerman myself, in just such a room. He dwelt on its fittings with obsessive intensity, as though the nature of the place did something to explain what had happened; and this too I found understandable, since the consequences of that evening were to prove very painful to Hamilton. He needed to explain it; perhaps to explain it away.

This second encounter with Vera, like the first, took place on a stage-set from the colonial past. The coincidence seemed to fascinate him, as though it were no coincidence at all, but had somehow been planned. The Kellerman, like Bandung itself, was locked in a box marked '1935'. Ghosts of lowland Europe in that decade moved in the wide Dutch streets with their solid commercial buildings; and these ghosts were thick in the Kellerman, whose corridors contained the *ennui* and dread of lost time. A whole detachment of tiny porters in starched white jackets had carried Hamilton's bags up a once-grand staircase, past semi-nude matrons in wrought-iron draperies, whose faces wore expressions of erotic torment. On the walls of the stuffy corridors hung sun-faded photographs of luxury ships from another age: the *Empress of Britain*; the *Strathnaver*.

Now they drank their beer (delivered with enormous ceremony

by the tiny porters) in this room which caused Hamilton such unease. Tall, entirely without windows, with blotched pink walls and high, sombre furniture, it resembled an upended coffin. A big, frightening fan turned in the ceiling overhead, doing little to alter the heat which enveloped even high Bandung at this time of year. He had taken his own room; Vera's was on another floor: he was careful in making me realise that. The driver seemed to have vanished, and he had felt it reasonable to ask her to join him for a drink; the alternative was to take her to a bar, and his two days without proper sleep made him more than reluctant to face that. He was still lightheaded, and grew more so as he sipped his Bintang. Then he realised, he said, that she had managed to put something in his beer: some drug.

I laughed at this. Too much James Bond, I suggested. After all, he hadn't slept; he was exhausted by the drive from Central Java; he had just had a narrow escape, and was possibly suffering from delayed shock. I couldn't believe that Vera would use methods so crude. (I had an exaggerated respect for the KGB's subtlety, then.) But perhaps subtle methods hardly seemed necessary, with a simple Australian news-man; and time was running out. I imagine Vera was under considerable pressure to produce results.

Hamilton was insistent: he had been drugged. I think he would have wanted to believe this, even if it had not been so. 'And the funny thing was,' he said, 'that it was all for nothing: I still didn't know the date of the cargo's arrival.'

Everything took on unnatural distinctness, without being truly distinct. He was sitting on the edge of the bed, in the centre of which lay a long, tubular form which suggested squalid, onanistic nights from a long-gone decade: the inevitable Dutch Wife. Above him rose a canopy of mosquito-netting the colour of mummy-cloths. Vera sat opposite, in a dusty velvet arm-chair. The dense heat grew unbearable, and seemed literally to threaten them with suffocation. She raised her arm to drink: worrying luxuriance of damp under-arm hair.

'This climate is terrible,' she said, and sighed. 'I think I cannot bear it much longer. I am so missing Moscow. I love to go ice-skating, and I cannot stop thinking about it.' She smiled with a hint of fatigue. Her eyes, watching him, were as interested and impersonal as those of a technician examining a mechanism.

When he answered her, he did not know quite what he had said; but he did still manage to converse, at this stage.

What did they talk about?

'The Muslims,' Hamilton said. 'Of all things, the Muslims. She wanted to know about my trip, and what I thought of relative Muslim and PKI strengths in Central Java. I had to disappoint her—the Muslims were stronger, they'd given me safe passage everywhere. Then she got very contemptuous about the Indonesians—said their revolution was a farce. But I wasn't really concentrating, Cookie. That room was horrible: you couldn't breathe. And things began to get more and more queer.'

He found now that there were gaps; periods when he was not aware of what was happening; but then her voice and her face, with the analytical grey eyes he still found attractive, would return into his field of vision. She had come over now to sit next to him on the bed, and looked at him sideways: but her face grew smaller and smaller, until it was the size of a tennis ball. Then it grew immensely large. And all the time, at the back of his mind, he was concerned that Peter the 'driver' would appear: he grew annoyed at the thought that the man was still in the building, perhaps in a room near by, and would try to use strong-arm tactics.

He was aware that Vera was talking, but did not know what she said. He also had the notion that he was making some fatal error, but was powerless to avoid it. The dim orange light, in this airless chamber of thirty years ago, seemed to be fading out altogether. Time itself seemed to be fading out; it was being drained off, perhaps, somewhere in the bowels of the Kellerman.

'Guy! Guy! Can you not listen?'

She was talking, but he did not know what she said; and her face, peering into his, had grown angry.

'I know it sounds silly,' he said to me, 'but all of a sudden she seemed to be an aunt of mine—an aunt who died young. She used to live with us in Singapore: I must have been five years old. I have a very good memory for that time. She was quite pretty; she had red hair like Vera, but I don't think the resemblance was very strong otherwise. She got angry with me when she found me in her bedroom one afternoon, playing with a humming top—and it all seemed to be happening again. Ridiculous. I could even hear the top humming. My aunt stood there in her underwear, I remember, ticking me off, and I didn't understand why she was angry. And the Kellerman was like Singapore in those days too. Yes, Vera doped me, no doubt about it.'

I found this interesting: I could see now how the whole situation must have worked on his mind—already turned back towards childhood by the *wayang* show and the Kellerman. Vera (who must always be a shadow, and who might have stepped out of the nineteen-thirties herself) somehow belonged here in the Kellerman, with the wrought-iron matrons and the Genoa-velvet arm-chairs; and she had now actually become a shadow from that colonial childhood of his! It was like a form of brainwashing; but the Russians could hardly have arranged it.

He knew she was asking him something with annoying insistence; but it made no sense. His head buzzed; his tongue was thick; the top hummed louder, and he thought cunningly of Peter. Where was he?

'What?' he said. 'I don't know, Vera, that's the point. I've never found out the date. Now get that bloody driver of yours out of my room.'

His aunt's eyes, so unaccountably angry, grew narrower. 'You don't know?'

'I don't know.'

He closed his eyes, and this time there was silence, except for a decisive sigh from the aunt who had died; then there was a faint rustling, over the long, smooth whirring of the humming top. She did not speak again, and before he sank into unconsciousness, he was aware, with relief and regret, that she had gone.

He woke next morning with a headache, and an irrational fear that he would never see Jill again. The room was still so dim that he had no way of knowing the time. Near him lay the Dutch Wife. He kicked it away with disgust, as though it were the cause of his ridiculous misadventure, and urgently pushed free of the fusty tangle of netting.

211

18

The Chinese shipment has passed into the realm of myth. It did enter the country that August, and in the way Hamilton had guessed it would. But he was not to run it to earth; and neither were the Russians, nor the Indonesian Army, nor anyone else who was not intended to know of it.

It seems it came in at Priok disguised as building materials; some cases were taken out to the Senayan Sports Complex, where the Chinese were helping Indonesia to prepare for GANEFO: the Games of the New Emerging Forces, to replace the decadent Olympics. Other cases are said to have been taken into the care of the pro-PKI Air Force, and hidden out at Halim Air Force Base—headquarters of the conspiracy of September the thirtieth. But the shipment was never to be used. After that night of the thirtieth—now only weeks away—everything would be changed for the PKI, and Bung Karno, and Indonesia.

No doubt much of the shipment was scattered, as the September thirtieth conspirators fled from Halim. Perhaps, like so many gifts in Java, it ended in all sorts of hands. Or perhaps it lies in some cave in the jungle, waiting, like the ghost of Barbarossa, to be called on again. But however ineffective it turned out to be in Indonesian affairs, the cargo was to have a continuing effect on Hamilton.

He got back to Jakarta a few days before Merdeka Day: the end of the Sukarno year. When he came into the Wayang Bar that afternoon I was drinking at one of the tables with Henri Bouchard and Harold Sloane.

Answering our questions about his trip, Hamilton was brief and distracted. 'Have any of you seen Billy Kwan?' he asked abruptly. 'I'm looking for him. He hasn't been into the office the whole time I've been away. I checked his bungalow, but he's not there.'

There was an awkward silence; then Sloane said, 'Lost your dwarf? I thought he was in your keeping.' He smiled at Hamilton with a provocative air, his sharp nose unfriendly; then he looked at Henri and me. 'Doesn't he know?' he asked.

I realised that Sloane was going to make his announcement as unpleasant as possible, and decided to take the initiative. 'Billy's been expelled from the Wayang,' I told Hamilton. I had hoped to make it sound light, but it didn't come out that way.

Hamilton frowned and turned to Henri, who pushed out his lips regretfully. 'It is true,' Henri said. 'Quite serious, I am afraid, Guy. He is banished.' He shrugged, and raised his eyebrows with regretful finality.

'You're joking,' Hamilton said.

'We're not joking,' Sloane said. His unfriendly air was increasing; he had obviously decided to hold Hamilton responsible for Billy. 'Why don't you ask us where Wally O'Sullivan is?' he said.

'Wally?' Hamilton turned to me. 'What is all this, Cookie?'

Sloane stood up, his face pinched, and I saw that he had decided to give way to righteous rage. Staring at Hamilton, he said, 'Yes, tell him, Cookie. Tell him how the best journalist who ever filed from this mad-house has been forced out of the country—all through that bloody vicious midget. But I don't think I'll stay and listen. Come on, Henri, let's cool off in the pool.'

Henri stood up, waved apologetically, and followed Sloane through the darkness towards the exit.

I fumbled in my shirt pocket, and drew out a folded, two-day-old sheet from the English-language version of *Antara*, the Indonesian news agency report, and pushed it across the black formica table-top to Hamilton. 'You'd better read this,' I said.

I watched him as he read. He held the scrap of paper in his big hands as though dubiously scanning some offered pornography —which in a sense it was.

The well-known Australian journalist, Mr Walter O'Sullivan, of the Sydney Courier, is to leave Indonesia at the request of the Foreign Office. Mr O'Sullivan's reports on Indonesian affairs, which are widely syndicated, have exhibited a reactionary bias, and outright distortion of the progressive policies of the Indonesian Government. He has been informed that this is no longer acceptable to the Government, and that he is persona non grata here. We understand that his private life in Jakarta has also been of a scandalous nature, and this has contributed to the Foreign Office decision, which may well be a warning to other representatives of the imperialist press.

Hamilton looked up. 'Jesus,' he said. 'What did he *do*?'

'They were gunning for him for a long time over his articles,' I said. 'But I don't think they would have been enough to force him out. The sting's in the tail of that thing: Wally was framed. He told us about it the other night. He was called in to the Foreign Office —obviously on Subandrio's instructions. Some BPI types were there—security spooks. They apparently accused him of taking boy prostitutes to his bungalow. And they let him know in a nice Javanese way that unless he agreed to leave the country on the basis of biased reporting, they'd blow the whole thing about the boys, and disgrace him. As you see, *Antara* seem to have got hold of that. Fortunately, they haven't been too specific. Wally flew back to Sydney last night.'

'But that's crazy,' Hamilton said. 'Wally rented boys? I don't believe it.'

'Nor do I,' I said. 'But apparently he thought some of the mud might stick, and he wasn't prepared to risk it. So they got what they wanted.'

Hamilton was frowning into the candle that flickered between us. 'But where the hell does Billy fit into this?'

214

'Sloane's a stupid prick,' I said. 'I don't believe there's anything in it—but Billy passed a remark, last Monday night, about Wally's being interested in boys. It was offensive, and it caused a bad scene, but I don't believe it means that Billy went running off to Subandrio's spies and gave them something to frame Wally with. I don't think Billy's got that in him, and I don't see any motive. But it's a nasty coincidence—and, of course, if Billy showed his nose in the Wayang now he'd have it knocked off. Fortunately he hasn't tried.'

I did my best to describe for Hamilton the scene that caused Kwan's expulsion, and—as I see it now—marked the end of the Wayang Club. Because it had been Great Wally's club; one saw that as soon as he left: without his monumental shape seated with reassuring permanance on its stool at the round bar, the club ceased to have form. It drifted into dissolution that August, as Merdeka Day approached and the Sukarno year drew to its end.

It had been an evening like any other, until Billy came in. Wally, Kevin Condon, Harold Sloane, Henri Bouchard, and I had been drinking with two Japanese journalists who had addressed us in jovially mangled English, and who left just before Billy arrived. The talk had then turned to Sukarno, as it always did; and Kwan had launched without warning into a diatribe against his former hero.

Accustomed to hearing him defend the President, we had all reacted with startled amusement. In order to urge him on, we had offered a broadly sarcastic defence of the Bung. It became a communal joke; but since Billy was unamused it also became a baiting.

'Ah, he's lost all touch with the people,' Billy said. He shook his square left hand repeatedly in front of his chest, seemingly without reason: a new nervous tic. He looked drawn and sickly, I thought: but this could have been a trick of the light.

'But, Billy,' Wally said, 'surely you've told us that only the Bung understands the people—only he holds them together. He was born with the *betjak* boys in the flames of revolution—you did *say* that, you know. He's doing it all for the Marhaen.'

Kwan stared blank-faced into Wally's ridicule. 'He's forgotten the Marhaen,' he said. 'He's forgotten them, as people. They're nothing but an extension of himself, to make speeches to. He said it himself: when he speaks to the people, it's a dialogue with his alter-ego.' His voice rose above the drunken conversation. 'What a disgusting admission, while the people starve,' he said. 'The Bung's a Marie Antoinette; but *he* says, "Let them eat rats." ' He broke into cracked laughter; but the laughter around him was mocking rather than concurring. No idealist can publicly change his mind without being mocked, I suppose.

'They have no rice,' Kwan said, 'and Sukarno won't give them rice. Instead, he and Subandrio tell them to plunder. You've heard the new speeches, the new advice to the people. "Plunder the capitalist bureaucrats!" Christ! What does that mean?'

'What *does* it mean, Billy?' Wally's slow burr mocked Kwan's passion; we all grinned at it—myself included, I'm afraid—as though he were performing a juggling act for our amusement. We were scarcely listening to his words: we had no wish to be serious that night, and it made us cruel.

'It means they plunder one *another*,' Kwan said. 'Who's a "capitalist bureaucrat"? The owner of a kerbside stall; or the smallest peasant. Plunder the small farmer! It's the green light for the PKI, and a class struggle invented for the cities of nineteenth century Europe. The nation to eat its own entrails! Marhaen to lose his plot of earth, while bully-boys and thieves operate on the highest moral principles!' He laughed again, with an unpleasant, staccato sound. 'Criminals and tyrants join hands! It's the unholy alliance of our century.'

Wally took a mouthful of peanuts, and munched thoughtfully. 'And you really feel your beloved leader is responsible for all this?'

I wondered when Kwan would see he was being mocked: but he was too possessed with his theme to notice. And we watched this small, electrically crouched figure as men without mental passions will always watch one in whom such passions are excessive: with indulgent grins. One could almost hear him humming like a wire.

'Sukarno's one of the great betrayers of history, just because he *was* great,' he said. His stare remained fixed on Wally with a sort of despairing intensity, as though the fat man were an obstacle he must climb. The hand shook in front of Kwan's chest. 'What a pity that bloody kidney doesn't fail,' he said. 'He should die, before he sells out completely, and the people are made slaves. He should die *now*.'

These words checked our laughter, even though we failed to take them seriously. Uttered at that time in public, they were more than dangerous, and Kevin Condon shifted uneasily, glancing into the dark to see if Ali the barman was near, and murmuring guiltily, 'Steady on, Billy.'

Wally munched, his hands motionless on his knees, contemplating Billy with a frown of genteel surprise. 'Are you offering yourself as the assassin?' he asked, softly.

Billy looked past Wally's shoulder into the dark, his face expressionless. He said nothing.

'You see Billy,' Wally said, 'I've never really agreed with you that Marhaen meant much to the Bung. I've always felt his basic philosophy was Sarinahism. You must know the story of Sarinah. The big department store he had built is named after her. She was the servant in his father's house when he was a little boy; he used to share her bed. It must have started him on his great career as a cocksman. He reckons Sarinah is the representative of the little people, too. And after all, what he most wants to do with the little people is to get into bed with them—the female ones, that is. I think he'd rather plough Sarinah than plough a field with Marhaen.' He raised his gin-tonic. 'Sarinahism. Hm?'

Since it broke the tension Billy had created, our laughter was probably more extravagant that it would otherwise have been. Kwan did not join in; he glared from face to face, his gaze finally returning to Wally.

'Ah yes, I know, it's all a joke,' he rattled. 'It's a joke that the Indonesian people will be handed over to Aidit—that they died for *Merdeka* for nothing. Sarinahism—that's a good coinage, Wally. I agree, Sukarno's guilty of it—he uses the people as objects for his pleasure.' He had adopted his 'light' tone, and he suddenly sounded almost carefree. 'But so do *you*, don't you? Only in your case they happen to be boys.'

There were angry exclamations. Harold Sloane seized Kwan by the shoulders and slammed him up against the bar, holding him with both feet suspended from the floor, like a doll. I was moving to intervene, and Sloane had begun on some righteous exclamation of disgust, when Wally's throaty voice, with its actorish power of projection, cut through.

'Put him down, Harold.' He had not moved since Billy had spoken. His great back was curved as though under a burden, his hands were still on his knees, and I was appalled to see now that the round hazel eyes were full of tears. 'Put him down,' he said, looking at no one.

Reluctantly, Sloane lowered Billy to the floor. Immediately his feet found the carpet, Kwan moved away sideways, not looking back. As he disappeared through the entrance to the arcade, I stared after him, to where the butterfly king on the wall pointed a scornful nose. I was seized with an impulse to follow and take him to task. I was angry with him; but I also feared for him.

I went swiftly across the room, leaving the outraged voices of the others behind me, and out into the heavy heat of the arcade. But through all its long, tiled perspectives, there was no sign of Kwan. I was beginning to have a headache, and lingered.

There was a smell of cloves from somewhere; faintly, the bonking of the *betjak* bells sounded from the Car Park. I didn't want to return to the bar: I was depressed at the thought of Wally's eyes meeting mine in mute protest at the betrayal of his secret. I hadn't betrayed it, and I didn't know who had.

Billy, for all his eccentricities, had been one of us in our beleaguered club, even though he had never felt sure of this. Now, irrevocably, he was one of us no more. I wondered where he would go.

Part Three
Patet Manjura: Amok

19

There is a definite point where a city, like a man, can be seen to have become insane. This had finally happened to Jakarta when we reached the seventeenth of August: Merdeka Day, and the end of Sukarno's year. *Amok* is an old Malay word; and Jakarta had now run *amok* with classical completeness.

For a long time, a man may be unbalanced, given to irrational hopes and irrational rages; and though these signs are disconcerting we continue to think of him as eccentric but sane. It's always difficult to believe that someone we know well has crossed into that other territory where no one from our side can reach him, and from which messages crackle back that no longer make any sense. But finally something happens to jar us into seeing this. That's how it was with Sukarno's Jakarta, in the middle of that weird August, the end of the dry monsoon.

The government's printing works could no longer churn out their worthless rupiahs in sufficient quantities to meet the demand; and the supplies of rice, which so many of the people received as a substitute for wages, were dwindling by the week. Yet Bung Karno still spent without stint: on his monuments, his arms, and his toys. And now, for the Merdeka Day celebrations, he appeared as usual to the crowds on Merdeka Field, still the god-man, the magic ruler, his beautiful, dove-grey uniform donned like armour against the ills that nagged his body, to announce a new year: the Year of Self Reliance, whose sub-title was 'Reach to the Star'. (Why only one star? I wondered, and compared transcripts with Henri Bouchard, who was sweating beside me in the crowd under the morning sun. Yes, it was only one star.)

In this year, Sukarno cried, the economic textbooks from Harvard and Leyden must be thrown away. We grinned wearily; they already had been, and the brown-faced sea brimming to the edge of the road by the palace did not cheer with its usual enthusiasm, but with a sound like helpless rage. But Sukarno, seemingly indestructible, almost inhuman in his sun-glasses and *pitji* (his 'mask-like props' as Billy Kwan calls them), had found an answer, a new phrase in response to their desperate demands for rice. He gloried, he cried, in their 'exploding demands'— demands which meant that 'a new stage in the revolution' had been reached.

There was a certain mad logic in it. Confrontation of the outside world had come to a stalemate: now there was only one struggle left to kindle his aged blood, to answer his boy's need for tumultuous events: Confrontation within the nation.

They cheered. They had already taken him at his word, and had begun to raid the shops. Their prime target was the *baba*, the Chinese merchant: sad myths that he hoarded vast stores of food and goods had begun to circulate, and the terrible fate of the scapegoat loomed ahead of him. Meanwhile, high on his daís in front of the palace gates, Sukarno called jauntily to the world: 'Hey, you imperialists, we will win!' Bankrupt Indonesia was to rule the waves; the Indian Ocean had recently been re-named the Indonesian Ocean, and a vast ship-building programme launched on paper. The zero meridian had been transferred from Greenwich to Jakarta. And Indonesia, aided by China, was to produce its own nuclear bomb: known as a 'garbage bomb', it would scatter radio-active pellets.

Henri and I laughed helplessly at all this, surveying the stands laden with solemnly listening dignitaries from all nations, under the glaring sun. But there was an appalled quality in our laughter. Sukarno had now driven his runaway bus into that territory where reality is finally left behind; yet he never doubted that he alone must remain at the wheel, nor did the people.

And he had yet another phrase for us. A time had come, he said to 'swing the steering wheel over': a time of *banting-stir*, which means 'absolute change'.

That at least was true: we felt it, we survivors of the Wayang Club, in every hot, decaying byway; we knew it in the humming of our blood. We had begun to see our enforced departure in terms of weeks rather than months. We were now jeered at even by the swimming-pool attendants at the Oasis: the ship of privilege had begun to spring leaks. Kevin Condon had an ugly ten minutes at the hands of a mob near Pasar Baru, and came into the Wayang shaken and displaying bruises. I found it increasingly unnerving to be glowered at by so many conditioned brown eyes, and to contemplate the posters showing wailing, abject white men being slaughtered by noble-faced Indonesians wielding the *kris*, or the long-bladed *golok*. I never again want to be a thing of paper: a living cartoon.

On the day after Merdeka Day, late in the afternoon, Hamilton called to me as I passed him in the Hotel's arcade.

'I can't find Jill,' he said. He loomed over me, staring urgently as though I were somehow responsible. I had to suppress an unworthy smile; there's something irresistibly comic about a large, confident man made anxious by love.

'It isn't funny,' he said. 'Ever since I came back from Bandung, things have gone crazy. I've been phoning her at home and at the Embassy for the past five days. She's never available. They tell me she's busy and she'll call me back, but she never does. I've just been over to the apartment, and all Moira would say was that Jill was out—she didn't know where. Out!' His usual calm was broken by a tendency to shift and fidget. Something was wrong, badly wrong; this was what he wanted to convey to me, but he could not substantiate it, except to dwell on the coincidence of Billy Kwan's disappearance.

'You mean Billy still hasn't come in to the office?'

'No—so I've got no bloody cameraman. And he's never at home, either. I've called, and sent Kumar across there a dozen times. I'm going over again now. Come with me, Cookie. If he's there, you might get some sense out of him.'

We took my battered Volkswagen from the Car Park, and drove the short distance down Jalan Thamrin to Jalan Kebon Sirih, and to the little byway where Kwan's bungalow stood, in the garden of the rich man's villa. As we made our way through the long grass to his door, swift sunset was in progress. Small birds and evening bats flickered like nerves against green sky; the upper branches of the banyan-tree made a tracery there like veins. Far off, across the garden's stucco wall, pink clouds rose in many domes, touched with a burning gold lava at the edges. The huge false-alarm of the tropics had begun, warning us of some fatal event beyond the horizon. I wondered if Sukarno watched it as he wrote his speeches.

I disliked these tropical sunsets, and the spurious emotions they excited; but I was still susceptible; and as Hamilton knocked on Kwan's door, and purple leaked into the silently roaring pink, I found myself conjuring with the possibility of disaster. I even wondered whether we might find Kwan dead inside the bungalow. He was a great pill-taker, and who knew what region of depression he might have entered when Wally's fall was made known to him? Beo sulked in his bamboo cage, looking maliciously sideways.

There was no sound. 'It's always the same,' Hamilton said, and the motionless palm leaves hanging above the tiled roof put me in mind of ragged, unpaid bills, jammed on spikes in a derelict office. He knocked again, ready to turn away. But this time there was faint movement inside; bare feet thumped to the door, and it opened.

Kwan looked ill. I had never thought of him as having purely Chinese colouring, since he always had the appearance of a European with a healthy tan, but now his face had the old ivory hue of the northern Chinese. He was thinner, the hollows under his cheek-bones were more pronounced, and he stood blinking up at us, clad in an old pair of khaki shorts and a wrinkled white shirt. There was a silence of perhaps five seconds; then he said flatly, 'Hah.'

Hamilton said nothing. I said something ineffectual about having been worried. I asked Kwan if he was all right.

His eyes went quickly from one to the other of us. 'I had nothing to do with what happened to Wally, if that's what you've come about,' he said.

Hamilton cleared his throat. 'You'd better not have,' he said. 'Where the hell have you been hiding?'

The *membeo* made a drawling sound, like an old woman protesting at something, and Billy looked at Hamilton with an expression that was distinctly unfriendly. 'I've had my usual bout of dysentery, but that's something I live with,' he said. And then, abruptly: 'I don't want to work for you any more, Hamilton. I thought I made that clear.' His hands were crossed over his stomach, as though to hold something in.

His mouth gone thin, Hamilton stared down in silence at the dwarfish figure in the doorway. Their near-identical pairs of pea-green eyes locked: Kwan's implacably hard, Hamilton's having a sort of sleepy stupefaction. In the pause, I could distinctly hear the steady in and out of breath through the big man's sun-burned nose. Then, visibly, he tried to banish his annoyance.

'Come on, Billy, I don't take that nonsense seriously,' he said. 'What's all the drama about? Nothing important's happened. What are you *doing* to me, matey?' He extended one hand in a mock-Italian gesture, looking more absurd than he intended as he stooped big and pleading over his motionless little associate. But I wasn't amused; they had been fond of each other, and I sensed that the need had not been solely on Kwan's side.

'Come back to work, for Christ's sake,' Hamilton said, 'and stop all this bullshit. You still take the best pictures.'

But Billy began to close the door. 'I'm sorry, old man, there's no question of reconsidering. There's no longer any point. I think you know that.'

Hamilton put his foot in the door, and the *membeo* screeched. I felt it was time for me to intervene, although I had no idea then what their disagreement was about.

'Why don't you let us in,' I said to Kwan, 'so we can talk things over sensibly? We don't believe you shopped Wally. And I hate to see you chaps quarrel--you were a great team.'

Billy looked at me. 'What's the matter, Cookie? Can't Hamilton function without me?'

Hamilton took his foot from the door. 'I can function very well without you, if that's the way you want it,' he said.

The sunset was almost over, and Billy's large ivory face became unnatural in the terminal illness of the light. I could think of nothing to say now to heal the rift between these two—who were, it seemed, linked so strongly that Kwan couldn't shut the door, nor Hamilton bring himself to turn away.

'You see, Cookie,' Kwan said suddenly, as though we had been conversing for some time, 'I can't work for a man who's treacherous. He's just wrecked Jillie's career for his own bloody advantage.' He turned back to Hamilton. 'Well, I've told her, Ham.'

'You've *what*?' Hamilton said. His face had flushed; as he stepped forward again, Kwan quickly slammed the door; and Hamilton stood staring at it with an expression of disbelief. Then he raised his voice in a shout. 'What have you *said*, Billy?'

From inside the bungalow, Kwan's muffled voice called back: 'You won't marry her, Hamilton—I've seen to that.'

Hamilton made a move towards the door, but I grasped his arm. 'Enough's enough. Ham,' I said. 'The poor bugger's sick. Leave him for now.'

But as he walked with me up the grass-grown path he kept staring back at the garden house, like a pilgrim retreating from the shrine of a spiteful and inaccessible oracle. And he was fated to return and stand there many more times, in front of that untelling brown door.

The next day there was a note from Jill at the Hotel desk, on the familiar blue paper. Hamilton was distracted enough to show it to me.

I suppose you never considered that I had a career too? I'm grateful to Billy for opening my eyes. I've resigned, of course. Don't worry about the other matter Billy told you about. In a few weeks, I'll be seeing Dr Chen in Singapore. After that, I'm going back to

England. The funny thing is, I've never been pregnant before. My husband thought I couldn't have a baby.
Good luck with your future, Guy.

Jakarta's nerves, like those of a dying animal, were now blinking out. Trains rarely ran any more; to see one of the city's long-suffering buses on the road was a novelty, and now the telephone service was failing. It became more and more of an adventure simply to get through, even with local calls.

The girl on the switchboard of the Hotel announced to Hamilton that Jill's number could not be raised.

'Please try again,' he said.

'Many numbers are difficult to obtain now.' The girl's voice was flat, drawling and patronising: there was little attempt, even in the Hotel, to be courteous any more.

'Please try again.' He stood rigid, gripping the receiver, listening to far rushing and hissing noises like those on his radio circuit with Sydney, while through the sealed windows the hungry bells of the evening *betjaks* came up to him, mocking his silly anxiety, his European game of romantic love.

This time the number rang; but it was answered by Moira, who told him coldly that Jill was not there. 'You know she's resigned, I suppose. She's taken two more weeks leave, and gone up to the hills.'

'*Where* in the hills?'

'I'm afraid I can't tell you that.'

Moira's voice seemed to Hamilton to have a smug sound. Loud and definite, it had something of the quality of a hospital matron's. He had only met her once. She was a study in many shades of brown, he said: flat brown hair, amber eyes, brown gums. I quote this caricature description as an indication of his distraught state: he really seems to have felt himself locked in a continuing nightmare, which had begun in that bedroom of the Hotel Kellerman.

Quelling a rush of rage, he said carefully, 'I don't understand, Moira. Why can't you tell me?'

'For the very good reason that Jill's asked me not to, dear. She's very upset. I feel very sorry for her.'

'Where is she in the hills, Moira?' He was shouting. But there was a click. The connection had been broken—either by Moira, or by the goblins who now inhabited Jakarta's dying telephone system.

'You'll get her back,' I said. Wanting it to be true, I had decided that it must be.

But he shook his head, swaying hugely on his stool in the Wayang Bar. He had insulated himself successfully all his life; now the insulation had cracked, and the tailored safari suit and Bally shoes were powerless to protect him. He had learnt to care rather late in life, and here was the result.

'Do you know what's really wrong, Cookie?' he said. 'She's not running away because I let her down. She's running away from having a baby. How can a child have a child?' He nodded profoundly, waved once, and made off towards the door.

I was struck by what he had said, but I decided that he was wrong. All promiscuity is a search; and what Jill had been searching for, I decided, was her baby. So she would not leave Hamilton. I nodded my head sagely; but I had not really convinced myself.

I pictured him going up to his air-conditioned room, to the sterile order created each day by the Hotel's room-boys. His row of books and Japanese print and silver-backed hair-brushes—the odds and ends with which he lined his transient's nest—would no longer be enough; I was certain of that. I didn't often feel sorry for younger men; but Hamilton, I saw, had come to that last suburb on the road of youth, where we drift down deceptive byways, imagining there is still plenty of time, still plenty more choices—only to find that each little street was important after all, and that there are few more choices left, before the final outskirts wanly face us; and after that, a vacancy. The vacancy is not at first appalling; it is just that: a vacancy.

He tried driving up to Bogor and Puntjak and making inquiries; but he could not find her. His uncharacteristic tension and moroseness seemed to increase daily. And tracking down Billy Kwan, whenever he had spare time, became an obsession with him. He now had to work with an Indonesian cameraman; but he refused to accept Billy's withdrawal. He also refused to talk any further about what he planned to do when they met. He had told me the whole story; and he seemed to have become slightly deranged about Billy's 'treachery' in betraying him to Jill.

I had seen others get into this state, in Jakarta, for other reasons. Underlying it, for everyone, was a sense of lost connections in the city: an increasing, insane absence, which played on the nerves. And for Hamilton all connections were snapping now with sly completeness. Even his radio circuit link with Sydney could no longer be counted on: he had failed to get through with some vital pieces.

He had come, I think, to see Billy as the cause of all his troubles. Perhaps he thought that by finding him he would find Jill, at the same time forcing Kwan to retract whatever charges he had made.

In this last week of burning August, there was not a day when he did not make the pilgrimage to Billy's little bungalow in the garden: always to find the hot brown door locked, the window shutters closed, the place silent and apparently empty. He suspected at times that Billy was inside, lying low. But the Indonesian businessman up at the house had told Hamilton that although Kwan still paid rent he did not often come there now.

I see Hamilton, grimly calm, moving like a hunter in that garden under the great banyan-tree, whose trunk is intertwined with a forest of creepers, and near which, if Billy is right, the mischievous spirit lurks. He hammers on the brown door, perhaps calling out to the malicious presence inside which was once his cheerful attendant, while the wretched *membeo* shifts in its bamboo cage and mocks him with a guttural imitation of Billy's accent: 'Gooday, sport.'

'I left a note for him,' Hamilton would say grimly. 'It said: "*I called, and I'll call again.*" His nerves have got to go eventually.'

'Or yours have,' I said.

Having gone to earth, Billy Kwan preoccupied us in the Wayang more than he had done when he was visible. Perhaps it was a symptom of our own general exhaustion and malaise. Even Henri Bouchard and Kevin Condon discussed him to an extent they would not normally have done. Wally's expulsion, and Kwan's suspected part in it, made some post-mortems inevitable, but they continued to a morbid extent: we were like voyagers on a cruise that had gone on too long. And outrage became replaced by a black amusement.

'Poor Wally,' Henri said. 'He has been swept away by the last breath of the dying typhoon.' We laughed excessively, guilty for being amused. From then on Billy was often referred to as 'the Dying Typhoon'.

He was still in Jakarta; this was what fascinated us. He was seen in the city from time to time. No one could imagine why he stayed, or what he was doing.

'One thing's for sure: he's not working.' Hamilton said. 'Only the Japanese can give him any film work if I don't, but I've talked to the NHK guy and Billy hasn't come near them. What the hell does he think he's doing? And how long can his money last?' He looked vicious; but the others began to refer to Billy with a reluctant amusement that was becoming a sort of perverse fondness.

By exiling himself, he had moved outside normal standards. His good qualities, the qualities of that gay and swaggering little Billy of earlier in the year, were vividly recalled; his defection and supposed treachery to Wally came to be seen as tragic. And the comic side of his outrageousness provided the Wayang with amusement: swapping Billy stories came to replace swapping Bung Karno stories.

Kevin Condon became quite sentimental. 'The old Typhoon really cared about us, you know. That was the trouble—he thought about us all too much—especially you, Hamilton.' He nodded his head unctuously. 'Billy had these standards he wanted everyone to live up to. They were impossible, of course, and then he got angry.'

Billy-sighting became almost a sport, in those weeks.

'Anyone seen the Dying Typhoon lately?'

'He was at the Sukarno rally out at the Stadium—I sighted him in the crowd.'

'Flashed by me yesterday on his motor scooter, near Merdeka Square.'

And Condon, in one of his boob-spotting cruises along the canal banks, had sighted Billy wandering on foot into the Krekot Kampong area. Kwan had nodded significantly at Condon, but had quickly vanished round a corner, and I wondered vaguely whether Billy had been imitating those hobgoblins who are supposed to have nodded at men from thickets, as though trying to tell them something.

'He'll get himself killed,' Condon said virtuously, 'if he's going in there at night. Do you think he's shacked up with an Indonesian woman?'

He had become a rumour in the city, and no longer quite real: a figure one might hope to see only in the middle distance, in the hazes of heat, moving on his little green chariot, or wandering on foot by the canals. Why did he stay? Sometimes I thought I knew, and that Wally had guessed it on Billy's last night in the Wayang; but I dismissed this as fantastic. One should never do that: the fantastic breathes always at one's elbow, as other people's anguish does.

Lost connections, as we entered September: the month whose final night would see the smash of the runaway bus, and the unimaginable downfall of Bung Karno. Few people sensed it: everything was drifting, drifting. So unsuspecting was my news-agency, in fact, that on Tuesday the seventh my masters informed me that I was to be posted to India within a week—that country having just invaded Pakistan.

Hamilton seemed genuinely upset when I told him of this. Another lost connection. I found I was sad myself, although I had longed for over a year to escape from Indonesia. I would not, after all, see the end of Bung Karno's ride, I said; nor would I find out what it was that kept Billy Kwan lurking about Jakarta.

But I was wrong, on that last count. In forty-eight hours Billy would arrive at his destination.

20

Hamilton sighted his quarry quite unexpectedly, in Pasar Baru.

It was about eight-thirty, well after dark, on the evening of September the eighth. He had taken to moving at night about some sections of the city on foot, partly to watch the mob lootings of shops, partly because of his restlessness. Down the narrow hallway between the leaning, tile-roofed commercial buildings, under the tattered sails of the awnings, he was carried in the human river that filled the bazaar from one side to the other, in the threadbare light from strings of electric bulbs. A heavily built Sundanese prostitute with oiled, curling hair, in a short cotton dress, was borne near him on one of the eddies and drifted at his side, smiling into his face like a dull schoolgirl on her first date, and muttering her ritual question with maddening frequency, although he shook his head: '*Oom, mau perempuan?*'—Uncle, want a woman?

He lost her eventually, about half-way along the bazaar's alley. Breathing in the Javanese compound of smells, he half forgot Jill, and his anger at Kwan, which was quite impossible to do in the Nordic coolness of his room. He liked Pasar Baru, even in this time of increasing violence. From the cave-entrance of shops, shopkeepers smiled and muttered invitations, like emissaries of damnation.

He stopped to watch a *dukun*—one of that race of magicians who charted the future, and sold potions against all ills—making his sing-song address to the small crowd. Sukarno himself relied on a *dukun*; and this one, Hamilton thought, looked not unlike the Bung, being stocky and middle aged, and wearing a *pitji* cap. He could understand now why Sukarno would come to Pasar Baru—why the warm wave of spurious love with which this humble swarm filled him would make him forget his political nightmares for a time; and he was briefly sad for the dying, half-mad, jaunty little *dukun* who had wanted his people to have everything, and would leave them instead with monuments, cheap sun-glasses, sickly coloured drinks, a little rice and *saté*. He pushed on, under the flaring lights, and suddenly caught sight of Billy Kwan.

His ex-cameraman was moving towards him along a row of stalls, examining the goods—square shoulders slightly hunched, black crew-cut head thrust forward, clad in his usual Hawaiian shirt and wrinkled slacks, and carrying a paper shopping-bag. He looked native to the place: not merely because of his features, but because he appeared at home here, among the cheap shirts and combs, the shoddy arrays of household utensils. Their eyes met, and Kwan came to an instant halt, some ten yards away.

Although he was the hunter and Billy the quarry, Hamilton's heart jolted as though from fear. But it was with a sort of base elation that he saw the usually static Chinese face take on a frozen tautness more dramatic than any European dismay. Then Kwan turned and made a frank attempt at flight, plunging into the crowd and heading back up the bazaar in the direction from which he had come.

'*Oom, mau perempuan?*' There was a smell of coconut oil; she had come back again. Hamilton shouldered her aside and set out after Kwan, teeth clenched, unable to run outright because of the press of bodies, but skidding forward over decaying vegetables and papers in a sort of parody of old-fashioned ballroom dancing —a fox-trot, perhaps. His height gave him the advantage of being able to keep Kwan's spiky head in view; and when Billy shot out of the bazaar's alley into a narrower lane between old Chinese buildings, Hamilton was still behind him.

A group of half-naked small boys played at the entrance of this secondary alley; but inside it was deserted, being little more than a fissure, its only illumination coming dully from shuttered windows two and three storeys up. The place was filled with a stench remarkable even for Jakarta: overflowing drains perhaps, and it caused Hamilton's fury with Kwan to increase. The hammering of their feet echoed off the walls. Kwan was no runner; the abbreviated legs worked ridiculously, like a kindergarten child's, and Hamilton overtook him, passed him, and massively blocked his way.

Billy, his back to the oozing wall, dropped his shopping-bag and put up his fists in the stiff, mechanical pose of a nineteenth-century pugilist. Hamilton wanted to laugh, but did not, staring down at the waxen, fixed face whose discordant green eyes were fixed on him without fear. There was no doubt in his mind that Kwan would have fought him—without explanations, without hope—and his anger struggled against some sort of shame.

Reaching out, he took the surprisingly strong wrists and pulled Kwan's arms down. 'Oh, for God's sake, Billy,' he said. 'I'm not going to beat you up.' The intense, completely unknown stench filled his nose; its majestic foulness distracted him.

Kwan spoke for the first time. His voice was more cracked and harsh than Hamilton remembered it. 'You're not? What *are* you going to do then, Hamilton? Get me to take back what Jillie knows about you?'

Hamilton panted, trying to catch his breath. 'Do you know what you've done, you mad bugger? Look—I know about the baby. I want her to have it. I'm going to marry her.'

Kwan laughed contemptuously; Hamilton continued to hold his wrists. So they stood, chests heaving, sweat oily on their faces, the whites of their eyes catching the dull light. Down the tunnel, Pasar Baru squeaked and cried. 'People like you,' Kwan said, 'seem to imagine that life's a game of Snakes and Ladders—that you can go back and start again. Do you really think that Jill will ever marry you now? You're old enough to know better, Hamilton. There are actions you can't take back.'

'Just tell me one thing. What exactly did you tell Jill, and why?'

'Let go my wrists.'

'When you answer me. Why?'

'I gave her to you. I took her back. I decided you weren't worthy of her. That's all.'

Hamilton dropped the small man's wrists, and stood staring down at him incredulously, as though to assure himself that the other was real. Finally, he said, 'We were friends, Billy, weren't we? I don't recall ever doing anything to hurt you.'

But Kwan interrupted, words coming from him at great speed, as though rehearsed. Perhaps they had been. 'Friends? We were a good deal more than friends, old man. You don't seem to understand. You did nothing to *me*—the harm you did was to yourself. When you came here to Jakarta, I saw what you could be. I helped you to become it.'

This time Hamilton interrupted. 'Look, that's history, for God's sake. Why am I listening to your ridiculous preaching?'

Billy pulled a face, and the old, hectoring tone of more normal occasions returned. 'I'm not talking about *business*, old man, surely you know that. Our link was more than a business one.'

'Yes, it was.' Hamilton was surprised to hear himself say this; words were now wrenched painfully from him. 'I trusted you,' he said. 'I *liked* you, damn it. But if anyone gets too concerned about you, you have to hurt them—you have to punish them for liking you. Then when they chop you off you can make yourself into a martyr. Right?'

Kwan blinked, and said nothing. And what am I doing, Hamilton thought, with this deranged little creature, in this disgusting alley? He had not expected to speak with such passion; it didn't fit with his conception of himself, and he felt an overwhelming disgust for the sourceless stench. There was nothing to be done with Kwan. Aloud he said irrelevantly: 'This is a filthy place we're in. What's that damned stink?'

'Just a stink, old man. Look, perhaps I should explain, although I'm sure it's hopeless. There are only two sorts of men, Hamilton—men of light and men of darkness. You were incomplete—I knew that. You were mainly concerned with yourself. But you *were* a man of light, and that's why I chose you.'

'*Chose* me?'

'I thought you *knew* that, Hamilton. All that matters now is to know what light is, and what darkness is. And you knew. If we lose the capability of sensing that, we lose everything. We worship shadows, we worship foulness. And there's nothing so *tedious* as foulness. How tedious, those trips to the cemetery of Curtis's!'

'Jesus. Why am I listening to this nonsense?'

'Desire, lust, then anger: that's the sequence for the sensual man, and for our whole society. You're angry *now*, aren't you? You think that jokes can break the sequence you're locked in— just like Curtis. Only boyish capers, those trips to the cemetery, to use the bodies of those wretches fighting starvation! Well, the Black One must have laughed to see you there. She's the patron saint of all world capitals now, Hamilton. We're sliding into the pit. It'll take a few years yet—perhaps a decade. But we're on the way.'

'You're a nut. Do you think if you keep on with this garbage you won't have to explain about Jill?'

'Have you seen the new pornography from London and New York?' Kwan smiled cordially, his tone conversational. 'Something bloody unique's happened in our time, old man—we've begun to give de Sade to the masses, along with their corn-flakes. The torment of a degenerate psyche for whole populations! Copulation no longer amuses them: love's an enema at some mad health clinic—they look up each other's anuses, old man, like sad monkeys. The clinic's a waiting-room of Hell. And you know what's next. The bodies they use will become more and more tedious, the anger of tedious lust will grow, and then they'll want a little mutilation—a little actual butchery. We'll watch it on our films, at first.'

'Sex is an old problem, isn't it, for ascetics like you? That's why you keep raving on about it.'

'Ah—one of the great lies, old man, is that little cliché: that to be concerned with the death of love, with the abuse of the body, is just frustration speaking. But it's not for nothing that evil's so much tied up with losing our sexual integrity. It's through our bodies that we most easily enter Hell. How else? When we abuse each other's bodies, then we become demons. Poor sick monkeys! But the spirit doesn't die of course; it just becomes a monster.'

Hamilton attempted to laugh. 'All this because I went out to the cemetery with Pete? Or because I saw Vera?'

236

'All this because I banked everything on you. You seem to think I just got you leads for stories.' He picked up the shopping-bag, and tilted his face up to Hamilton's again. 'Stories! Is that what life's about? What's a bloody journalist, really? Nothing but a Peeping Tom. You slow idiot: I put you on course; I made you see things; I gave you the woman I loved, who loved you, who's carrying your child: she needed all your understanding, all your constancy.' His voice rose to a flat shout. '*I created you!*'

The three words rang from the walls of the towering alley; and Kwan wheeled and ran, as though chasing their echo, making for the long, narrow rectangle at the fissure's end.

Hamilton did not give chase.

I created you! These words, when Hamilton reported them to me, told me more about Kwan's 'secret system' than anything else had done, or would do, before I came into possession of the files. He had gone into a region where we could no longer follow him. But *I created you!*—yes, I understood that, I thought.

I had given up my bungalow and moved into the Hotel Indonesia, for my last week in Jakarta. And I now shared, in a mild way, in Hamilton's sense of disorientation. I should have grown used to changing countries at short notice; but I had been a long time in Indonesia, and I could not grow used to the idea of release now that it had come: like a soldier suddenly discharged, I wondered if this was what I wanted after all. On that night of his encounter with Kwan, I lay in a room identical to Hamilton's and listened, as he was no doubt doing, to the piped music system playing from the receiver under the window.

Why does the ballad 'Sukiyaki' bring Billy Kwan back to me now, like a shirt he wore? The truths of sentiment are rarely accurate; he may scarcely have been aware of it. True, I once heard him whistling it; and on a happy, inconsequential evening when all four of us dined out together, he and Hamilton and Jill hummed it in unison. Anyone who frequented the Hotel had to be aware of that wistful little hit tune which always seemed to me to contain the sweet distances of *Ukiyo-e*: the Floating World of the Japanese woodblock prints. 'Sukiyaki', which had trickled in the corridors, lifts, and bars all through the year, was like a thin secretion the place harboured always; like the dissolving shallows of sun lying in the arcade. It had moved through all our minds, and now it brings that whole time back, instant as the smell of heat and sun-bleached clothing. But most of all it brings back Billy, whose rocking figure and large, spiky head for ever recede as I watch: so perhaps the tune's mystery does belong to him, together with my middle-aged grief. Billy! No grief is pure: I miss the Wayang Club, I suppose, and Java's play of shadows, in that decade which already begins to be quite long ago.

'He's mad.' Hamilton said this after the encounter in Pasar Baru: most of us had said it at one time or another. But I hesitated to agree or to use the word myself; and even now, turning over Kwan's files for this period—the weeks leading up to Wednesday, the eighth of September, after which all entries close for ever—I still hesitate to use it.

Yet, on the evidence of the files (particularly those on Ibu and Sukarno), Kwan had set himself on the sort of path that can isolate a man utterly. If such isolation is a sort of madness, then in that sense I suppose Billy was mad. Perhaps, too, he was affected by Jakarta's general derangement of September, when the final collision of the thirtieth loomed ahead, and Lieutenant-Colonel Untung waited in the wings.

When the entries in the dossiers of Hamilton and Jill Bryant cease, those in Sukarno's and Ibu's files mount in frequency and intensity, as though in compensation. And the files reveal that ever since May Kwan had been visiting Ibu's kampong house regularly, with his gifts of money and food. They explain how it was that he had been able to disappear from his bungalow for such long periods in August, when Hamilton was hunting him: Ibu obviously permitted him to stay in her shanty. It's a testimony to Kwan's Spartan (or perhaps Chinese) indifference to normal comforts that he was able to do this for long periods—enduring the heat, the dirt, the complete absence of sanitation. Whether he was intimate with Ibu remains unclear; I must say again that I think this unlikely.

What is clear, however, is that she and her small girl and sickly infant boy become of more and more concern to him; that he comes to regard them in some way as his 'family'.

25 August
Today at Ibu's we ate a rice and saté meal together. She has bought clothes for the children: new furniture. But I can't make her understand that the canal in which she and the girl bathe is infected.

The little girl and I played a dice game on the floor, while Ibu watched. Trust. Happiness. This is my family. But I worry about little Udin, the baby boy. He is not well, and although Ibu says she consulted a doctor as I asked, he does not seem to improve.

A crucial entry occurs on Saturday, 28 August. Kwan visited Ibu that night; he must have returned to his bungalow later and made the entry in her dossier. It begins: *Little Udin is dead.*

I see Billy, in the kampong near Pasar Baru, with its humped shapes of bamboo huts and packing-case shanties; there would have been a small, humid wind, at that time of the year. Carrying a set of parcels, he moves along the plank walkway through the mud to Ibu's hut, from which a light glows, sluggish as the refuse drifting on the canal.

Billy records that for some time after his arrival Ibu would neither speak to him nor move from the bamboo bed, where she sat rocking herself to and fro monotonously, hugging herself.

I am given few more clues from which to reconstruct this encounter; and whether Ibu, even in her grief, became more than a shadow or an idea to him is difficult to surmise; but he does record their conversation, in that dialect with which he obviously struggled, and which hung between them like the thick blanket of the heat. I translate as best I can.

'*Meninggal?*'—Dead?
'*Ya, meninggal.*'
'*Apakah dokter datang?*'—And you had a doctor?
'*Dokter 'nggak ada. Dokter tidak mau datang kesini.*'—I could find no doctor. They don't like to come here.
I have said that these entries are often disjointed. His next

239

and final sentence reads: *Rain began, blown in from the bay at Priok.*

I hear it pattering on the palm-mat walls; I see Ibu rocking in the light from the kerosene lamp, beyond his charity or concern, her long, equine face no longer a comedienne's.

A coherent entry follows for the next day: 29 August.

Little Udin was buried today. There is great respect for the dead among the kampong people, and Ibu's friends arranged a funeral procession of betjaks. I walked beside it with the other mourners. A special sarong had been bought to wrap Udin's small body in. Ibu, holding him, rode in the leading betjak, on which a yellow cloth had been tied: the colour of death, indicating to other traffic that this was a funeral of the poor.

And traffic gave way to it, even on the Gunung Sahari highway, along which the procession moved to a pauper's burial area, beyond the city limits.

Ibu wept now, riding in her betjak. Did her wails reach your ears, Bung Karno, in the Merdeka Palace? Udin died of a simple complaint, from which no child in the city need die, were it not for your folly: gastro-enteritis.

The infant Udin is dead. I mourn him as though he had been my own. I say Sukarno killed him, as surely as though he were a Herod. He builds his futile monuments, instead of drains which would rid the city of disease! He starves and kills, with his egomaniac foolishness, the children of his people.

This is enough. Ibu and Udin will be revenged. There must always be an instrument to end tyranny's folly.

So Wally O'Sullivan had guessed correctly. In this obviously distraught entry on Ibu's dossier, Kwan's unlikely resolve to assassinate Sukarno appears for the first time. The rest of his progress towards his attempt to carry out that intention appears in the dossier of Sukarno himself. Had Billy succeeded, this account of mine would of course be the record of a famous assassination—or else, more likely, the files would be in other hands than mine.

The entries in Sukarno's dossier for July and August, after Kwan has moved away from his qualified hero-worship earlier in the year, vilify the President with greater and greater intensity. The intensity begins to peak, it seems to me, after Kwan's expulsion from the Wayang Club. I suppose he had too much time to think, then, in his garden house. He was a man who needed other people; and had he not been deprived of our company perhaps he would have been content to assault Bung Karno with his tongue. But he was alone, except for Ibu; and after his final break with Hamilton, and the death of little Udin, he would find himself alone completely.

I must stress that, until the very late stages, there is nothing really irrational or deranged about this process. If there were, I would feel little involvement with Billy; he would become a human unknown: one of those sad, deluded monstrosities like Lee Harvey Oswald or Sirhan Sirhan. No; Billy was not one of those; and this is why he haunts me. When Hamilton disappointed him, when Billy ran off down Pasar Baru (a little over a week after Udin's death), he did finally cross some sort of boundary; but the process that led him to this boundary might have led anyone else there too.

Surprisingly, Kwan nowhere asks himself whether he was morally justified in his resolve to take life. It makes me wonder whether he seriously intended to go through with it; or whether, like a would-be suicide, he played with the idea. I can't imagine how he squared it with his Christianity; but then, Christianity had never quite 'taken' with Billy, any more than humanism had. Perhaps he was inspired by Krishna the charioteer (Dwarf Semar's mighty counterpart in the *Bhagavad Gita*), steeling Arjuna for spiritual battle: *'There is a war that opens the doors of heaven, Arjuna! Happy the warrior whose fate is to fight such a war.'*

31 August
Ibu is gone. Went to the kampong today and found another family occupying her hut. She gave me no warning, and I can't discover

241

where she is. Kampong people would only tell me that she had gone with a man. Sniggering. All her effects have disappeared from the hut: it must have been done yesterday. Good-bye, Ibu. Good-bye, my little family.

1 September

The poor die every day along the poisonous canals: yet more and still more drift in to the strangling city, from a countryside which no longer sustains them.

Little Udin died, but Sukarno continues to strut, in his mask-like props—the sun-glasses, the pitji—*a rotting kernel inside the clean husk of his uniform. It is while you live, Sukarno, that Aidit will take over. Then you will rule as a puppet from Merdeka Palace: Aidit will be the* dalang *then!*

I see all this: and I see that someone must do the job to free the Muslims' hands. The Muslims can do nothing against you themselves, Sukarno, since the people are still deluded by their god-king, their Ratu Adil.* Yes: the Muslims need an instrument.*

You talk now of 'swinging the steering wheel over', to a new stage of revolution. I must swing the wheel over instead: this will be my destiny! It will mean struggle, before you die: but it is a struggle the Muslims can still win. And for all their shortcomings, they will prevail over a country where love of God and freedom of the spirit can survive—all those things you have betrayed, Bung Karno.

You do, after all, bear the mark of the Beast, I believe. The Satanists say their new age begins next year, in 1966: the double six again! Is it possible that you were marked to precipitate this new era, whipping the people to frenzy with your lies of glory—yourself in a secret frenzy fed by violence and by lust? Terrible violence is simmering, simmering. Your country is sick with the fever of evil: is it possible that the Beast has chosen Java as a crucible? Is it possible that here is where those marked by the Beast and those still struggling for the light must confront each other? Is this *your* Konfrontasi?

*Kwan refers here to the Javanese concept of the Just Ruler, who was quasi-divine.—R.J.C.

'*And they worshipped the dragon which gave power unto the beast; and they worshipped the beast, saying, Who is like unto the beast? who is able to make war with him?*'*

7 September

An unexpected opportunity. You are to go to a reception being held at the Hotel Indonesia the day after tomorrow. Thursday 9th: a celebration of Bulgaria's National Day. The absurdity is entirely suitable. You must, of course, be driven up to the main entrance as usual. My press badge will give me freedom of movement.

Have I the strength? Oh, Bung Karno, almost I feel fond of you again! Why did you cease to come to Pasar Baru?

---

* *Revelation*, xiii, 4. — R.J.C.

21

By seven thirty on the evening of Thursday—Bulgaria's National Day—most of the surviving members of the foreign press corps in Jakarta were present and comparatively sober on their stools in the Wayang Bar. Kevin Condon had recently been withdrawn, but Henri Bouchard was there, and Guy Hamilton, as well as a tacturn Japanese, a cheerful Lebanese working for one of the wire services, and a number of others who have faded from my mind. Red press badges were fixed to the lapels of lightweight suits, obligatory collars and cuffs gleamed, as we waited without enthusiasm to cover the formal reception Sukarno was scheduled to attend at eight o'clock in the Hotel's banqueting room, next door to the Wayang.

We didn't expect to get much of a story, but it was always possible that Sukarno would launch into a newsworthy anti-Western diatribe, or publicly humiliate one of the ambassadors. As we waited, Hamilton, Henri, and I invented possible *tableaux* which grew more and more fantastic. Our humour was somehow sickly: some sort of unexplained tension enclosed us. Perhaps, though, I'm investing the scene through hindsight with a foreboding that didn't exist. Everything was as usual in the changeless dark of the Wayang: high on the gold walls, the *alus* princes and heroes bowed above our noise.

When I had left my room on the ninth floor to come down to the bar, an Indonesian in a well-tailored tan suit had passed me in the empty corridor; he had put me in mind of one of these figures. Thirty-ish, fit-looking, saturnine, with a thin moustache and finely cut features which hinted at Hindu ancestry, he had distinctly been an *alus* type: refined. He had passed me at a jog-trot run, closely followed by a companion in an expensive blue suit, a man of heavier build, with blank, stolid Malay features and a brutal crew-cut: undoubtedly *kasar*. They were, I had realised, members of the BPI, Indonesia's intelligence service, sent to check the Hotel from top to bottom before Sukarno's arrival.

Looking up from my drink, I now saw the *kasar* type in the blue suit moving round the bar, examining the drinkers with insolent intentness: we all received the benefit of his flat Malay stare before he moved on. Hamilton glanced at his watch. 'If the Goon Squad's getting nervous,' he said to me, 'it could mean the Bung's arriving early. Feel like strolling along to the steps and watching the caravan appear?'

I followed him out into the arcade, our claustrophobic boulevard. We moved along its sand-gold tiles towards the section by the main doors, where the ceaseless flow of black official cars purred up to the steps, discharged their dignitaries, and then moved on around the arc of asphalt driveway, back into Friendship Square. The floodlit asphalt beyond that semicircular procession, looked down on by the Hotel's two cliffs of windows, was empty as a stage. We passed the arcade's news-stand, where some Western papers were still permitted to go on sale, although heavily censored. Huge black bars of ink blotted out passages considered offensive to Indonesia: on magazine photographs where men and women kissed, a black bar neatly obscured the meeting lips. I stopped and bought the *New York Times*, indulging the illusion that I was in a normal country, at a normal paper-stall. I decided it was good to be leaving, and had a sudden premonition that I was doing so just in time. 'You ought to get that outfit of yours to pull you out,' I said to Hamilton. 'Enough's enough.'

'They are, soon,' he said. 'I got a letter today telling me I'll take over the London office in a month.'

'But that's marvellous,' I said. 'Isn't it what you wanted?'

'Yes, I suppose it is,' he said flatly; and I knew he was thinking of Jill.

A red carpet had been laid down the arcade's steps. The ubiquitous little green-clad soldiers with sten-guns were already stationed by the potted palms, and a small crowd had gathered, watching for the Bung's arrival. Here Hamilton suddenly halted, and I saw that he was staring fixedly through the glass doors leading to the bright, air-conditioned zone of the foyer.

Following his gaze, I caught sight of a group consisting of Jill Bryant, Colonel Henderson, an unknown young man with long, fair hair who was almost certainly a British Embassy attaché, and Billy Kwan. Jill was in a full-length evening dress of pale blue silk, and looked pretty, but artificially so: the intervening plate glass and the foyer's bright lights combined to make her slightly unreal: a model in a department store window. Kwan wore a particularly loud Hawaiian shirt, predominantly yellow and green, which was in disreputable contrast with Henderson's white mess jacket, the unknown young man's tuxedo, and all the other formal suits and evening dresses. Only a cameraman could have got away with it. The red disc of his press badge was prominently displayed, and 'old Bell and Howell' hung from his shoulder. The group was laughing and animated, but I wondered whether Billy was amusing or embarrassing them.

'So she's back,' I said. 'What are you going to do?'

'Nothing,' Hamilton said softly, watching her. She hadn't seen us, none of them had.

'Go and talk to her,' I said.

'And make an idiot of myself in front of Henderson? No thanks, Cookie. I'll catch up with her later.' His tone warned me not to pursue the subject. Without taking his eyes from Jill, he asked, 'Who the hell do you suppose Kwan's filming for?'

I ignored this. 'There can't be much time left before she leaves the country,' I said. 'Don't let this go by, Ham—barge in.'

'Later,' he said and, turning abruptly, walked out of the arcade and down the steps, close to Sukarno's red carpet. Dodging in front of an arriving black Chrysler, he strode off across the empty island of asphalt. I followed, and he led me to that invisible perimeter separating the Hotel driveway from the stony ground of the Car Park, where the *betjaks* and jeep-taxis waited, and the vagrants and the *bantji* kept their watch on the theatre of the glowing arcade.

At the sight of us straying here, the *betjaks* stirred restlessly, as they always did when Europeans appeared on foot. But Hamilton, with an outward sweep of his right hand, dismissed their hopes and stood motionless, staring past them into the dark spaces of Friendship Square.

The great wheel of lights revolved there as usual; in the centre of the artificial pool the twin, towering pylons of the Welcome Monument and the ecstatically arched couple they supported in the air were illuminated by floodlights. A single *betjak* man had separated himself from the rest, and pedalled with weary deliberateness across the stony ground towards us. He was all in black: loose black shirt, open to reveal his prominent rib cage, and black shorts. He wore a limp, wide-brimmed straw hat. The side of his *betjak* bore the yellow legend: *Tengah Malam*. He was not young, as most of the other *betjak* boys were; he would never again wear a cheeky grin as they did; his gaunt face had the dull and stricken calm of the immemorial Asian coolie. He seemed to look at us from a zone of weariness where not even despair is felt, because that is feeling, and such weariness is fathoms deeper than feeling.

Hamilton shook his head at him. The dark eyes in the skull-like, cardboard-coloured face, with its knobbed cheek-bones, looked back without resentment. He sat, one foot on the pedal and the other on the ground, staring at us quietly for a moment longer; then he turned his ponderous machine and rode creaking away, in his flimsy, crow-black clothes, not back to the squadron of other *betjaks*, but out onto Jalan Thamrin, and so into the night. It was as though he had despaired permanently of our ever paying for his hire.

'Go in and see her,' I said. I knew that I was soon going to irritate him with my insistence, but I felt a sense of urgency. 'For all you know, she could be leaving for the UK within days. You won't get many more chances.'

But he simply made no answer; and I sounded to myself what I probably was: an ageing, isolated man—a casualty, like so many journalists, of a broken marriage—continuing fatuously to nurture the myth of romantic love on which I had been brought up. Marooned in these circumstances with a younger man, I had no doubt grown sentimental about him and his Jill; perhaps something of Billy Kwan's intensity about them had rubbed off on me. But sometimes two people seem to live that myth and fill it full of sap again, as though it has never been debauched; and that Hamilton and Jill should be separated seemed to me a perversity I could not accept. I turned to Hamilton to speak again, formulating my thoughts; but I was never to utter them. An extraordinary sound from the Hotel behind us made us both swing around. It was a sound I'll never forget, and yet it is almost impossible to describe.

The front of the Hotel and the wing that ran out from it—to a point just opposite where Hamilton and I now stood—enclosed the asphalt desert like a great inverted L; and from those floodlit cliffs, from the Hotel's parallel trains of windows, the sound bounced and echoed. It came from only a few throats; and at that distance it was like a cry made in dreams by some faceless chorus. I saw him fall: saw, from the corner of my eye, for a suspended pulse-beat, the yellow and green Hawaiian shirt swoop with deadly finality past level after level, picked out by the floodlights and lit windows. It might have been a bright rag, some laundry pushed off a sill, except that it fell much too fast. I had the impression—although this could have been fancy—that his body was tremendously arched, facing outwards into the warm, upper air like one of the people on the Welcome Monument; as though some ecstasy had removed it from natural laws, and powered it with flight.

I didn't see him hit the asphalt, even though nothing stood between us and that spot, some twenty yards away. I heard him strike, and would like to forget that sound; but I didn't see it: either because I didn't choose to, and closed my eyes on the instant, or because I was looking at the one open window from which he must have fallen: a window on the seventh floor of the wing opposite where we were standing. From its sill an extraordinary banner now hung, large enough to cover the window of the floor below almost to the bottom. It appeared to be fashioned from bed-sheets, and on it, in English, painted in black letters, appeared the legend: SUKARNO, FEED YOUR PEOPLE.

A figure had appeared in the silver-framed window, and I recognised the *alus* BPI man, the Hindu type in the tan suit. He leant out to contemplate the quiet patch of colour on the asphalt, then abruptly hauled the banner in and disappeared, and SUKARNO, FEED YOUR PEOPLE no longer frowned on the Hotel's bright cliff. It had all been very quick. It was still not quite eight o'clock.

A small crowd, peering and pointing, had gathered about the steps by the distant main entrance, trespassing on Sukarno's carpet, holding up the line of arriving cars, their feminine cries continuing. There had been very few people walking on the section of arcade in the wing from which he had fallen. A few figures stood there motionless, staring at the bundle on the asphalt, but making no move to approach it. Soldiers were barking angrily. I now saw that three of them, their sten-guns raised, were preventing the increasing crowd over by the entrance from advancing any nearer, and two more, in their white helmets, came running across the asphalt in our direction, to point their guns warningly at the people in the arcade, standing with their backs to the body and to us. Hamilton and I, alone in shadow by the Car Park, apparently went unnoticed.

I recall his long white face looking questioningly into mine, as though I might offer some explanation; then, without speaking, we moved towards the body. We halted within ten feet, and the soldiers still didn't see us; they were gesturing up at the window and chattering.

He was lying on his face, and I was glad of that. I had expected him to look small, on the asphalt desert: instead he looked surprisingly big. Perhaps it had something to do with the shirt's bright yellows and greens. I had also been afraid, in my ignorance of such things, that he would be mangled beyond recognition, or

249

exploded like a fruit; but he was not. All that told of his fall was the dark red pool spreading from beneath him, and the weary limpness of the body, which recalled a fallen puppet: a puppet of leather. As Henri Bouchard was later to explain, with Gallic detachment, it's the bones that are smashed; the damage is mostly internal.

The few faces in the nearby arcade—mostly European, but some Indonesian—looked down with conventional frowns of horror; but some, I saw, wore inexplicable smiles. So there really are devils in human form, I thought. We all seemed to be waiting for that superior officer to whom all problems of life and death are simply matters to be dealt with, like garbage disposal. And he came, at a measured pace across the asphalt: a tall, stony-faced Tjakrabirawa officer in peaked cap and tailored uniform. Behind him came the BPI men: the crew-cut *kasar* type in the blue suit, with his imperturbable Malay face, and the *alus* type whom I had seen at the window, with his old-fashioned matinée idol's good looks. Watching them approach, I had not noticed Hamilton, who had dropped to one knee beside the body.

The soldiers swung on him, shouting in Bahasa: I heard a click as one of the sten-guns was cocked. Hamilton glanced up once, and then ignored them. His face was absolutely drained of blood, and seemed to make them hesitate. He ignored, too, the officer and the two security men, who now stood over him, giving him a careful examination: dark eyes studied the press badge on the tan lapel of his formal suit—a suit, I noticed irrelevantly, like the *alus* security man's. The officer gave a brief order to the two soldiers, who backed off a few paces, but kept their guns on Hamilton and me.

Hamilton, having finished his examination, looked up at the *alus* type. 'You shot him,' he said. The BPI man said nothing. 'He didn't jump, you bastard,' Hamilton said. 'You shot him. Why?' His voice was full of stretched wires. I thought I had seen what looked like a wound in the side of the neck, but I did not want to look again. I looked at Hamilton, whose swimming eyes flared unnaturally pale green, like Billy Kwan's.

The *alus* type still didn't answer, but spoke in Bahasa to the Tjakrabirawa officer. I understood enough to realise that he was

250

suggesting the body should be moved before the President's arrival, and one of the soldiers departed at a run. The officer then took Hamilton by the arm and attempted to jerk him to his feet; but he might have been jerking at a cask. Remaining on one knee, Hamilton glared at him; then he got up slowly of his own accord. 'Take your bloody paws off,' he said.

At this juncture the *kasar* BPI man moved close to me, while his *alus* companion spoke softly to Hamilton in English. 'This man has jumped. He is a lunatic, and might have killed the President. If you are knowing him, it is my duty to ask you to come for questioning. Please do not move. I see you are a press man. I should like to see your documents and accreditation.'

Our passports and press-cards were examined. It occurred to me to wonder, in the pause, whether Colonel Henderson's party had seen what had happened. Peering across the asphalt to the crowd still detained at the steps by the main entrance, I recognised his uniform and Jill's blond hair; they were staring intently, and she had one hand raised to her mouth. I saw no news-men: the Wayang Bar must still be unaware of the incident.

'The man is Chinese,' I heard the *alus* BPI man say to Hamilton. His voice was pleasantly low, and his manner unaggressive. 'What do you know about him?'

'His name was Kwan. He was an Australian—and a member of the press,' Hamilton said. 'I insist you inform the Australian Ambassador immediately.'

'We shall speak to the Ambassador. I can understand that you are upset,' the *alus* type said. 'But this man was in possession of a pistol. On our entering the room, he jumped. That is all. You would be better to believe that—however, we shall discuss further. You will come with me, please.' He took Hamilton's arm again.

Nobody took my arm. 'You go,' the *kasar* type said to me abruptly. So I was able to drift off into the arcade. I could hear a distant wailing, growing steadily nearer: sirens—the Bung's mating call. Sukarno was arriving, late as usual.

I then did one of the rashest things I'd ever done. Instead of going

251

back along the arcade to join the crowd at the main entrance, I hurried in the other direction, down to the Hotel's garage, where my car was parked; and I drove off down Jalan Thamrin towards Jalan Kebon Sirih, and Billy Kwan's bungalow.

I wanted the files: that was all I could think about. I didn't want them to fall into the hands of the BPI. I told myself confusedly that the dossiers could be made into some sort of sensational case against the remaining Western press corps in Jakarta. If the BPI got its way, it seemed likely that Billy's death would be hushed up as a suicide; but I couldn't be sure, and if Indonesian Intelligence examined the files their conclusions could be dangerous, or at least embarrassing. It seemed probable that dossiers like the one on Jill existed on others of us, and I did not want them used; I wanted to save embarrassment—and perhaps to protect Billy's memory too.

He was an impossible, tormented creature; have I said that I was fond of him? I was fond of him, as far as one can ever be of someone who can't quite be reached. He had always made me feel grossly self-indulgent, as though I were living life half asleep instead of fully awake. Perhaps Billy's refusal to do the same had been his undoing. It just isn't bearable to be fully awake.

I was compelled by grief, and a sort of rage. I drove my long-suffering Beetle at its modest top speed down the pot-holed super-highway, through a townscape the colour and consistency of brown paper. I swerved wildly to miss cyclists and trundling *betjaks*. My grief surprised me; it was like an unbearable balloon in my throat, swelling to bursting. We were all Billy's murderers, I said. And in a way I suppose we were. We should not have barred him from the Wayang; we should have borne with him.

I knew almost nothing then of what awaited me in the files. But whatever had happened to Billy, I said, had happened because he had been made an outcast from the Wayang Club—the only community to which he had ever really belonged. I knew, as one always knows too late, what it was he had really wanted, and I said that it all could have been given to him quite simply. He could have continued in Hamilton's service, faithful as Hamilton's other self; the auditor of his conscience, and the best cameraman

252

in the business. He could have lived through big Ham. Was it so much to ask? I remembered how they had amused each other in the early days. ('You write the words, Hamilton.') And I could not stop thinking of the night of Wally's party, when Billy had ridden on popularity's peak, on a tide of affection: our mascot, our outlandish spokesman. What was it he had said? 'Anglo-Saxons are better in the tropics.' He had wanted to love us all. Why had love not been possible?

There were no cars parked outside the villa whose garden harboured Billy's bungalow. There were lights on in the steep-gabled house, but I knew from experience that no one would notice a visitor to the garden. I parked my car a little way up the street, and walked back. The risk I took of course was that the BPI people would by now have Billy's address, and would come to search the place while I was here. Or perhaps they were already inside. I thought of the charges that could be made against me: breaking and entering, the seizing of evidence concerning the would-be assassin of a head of state . . . I still get chills when I think about it; but it's one of the few silly acts in my life I don't regret. I took a deep breath and made my way down the little lane at the side, to find myself in the dark garden under the big banyan-tree.

It was extraordinarily dark there, in the long grass, and somehow frightening: I don't think this was purely because of my state of nerves. A lethargic breeze had come up; the sky was overcast, and I could see no moon. The palm leaves drily rustled above the humped roof of the bungalow, and I remembered the spirit which, Billy had once said, 'bumped around' in the garden and in his dark-room. I thought I heard something move, and stood stock still. But there was nothing. I moved cautiously forward again, the heat and my stretched nerves causing sweat to stream down my face and drip from my chin. I pulled off the tie I had worn for the Bulgarian reception.

The bungalow was in darkness. The bamboo cage still hung from the eaves, but it was empty, its little door standing open. Had he freed Beo before he left, knowing he would not come back?

I'm no burglar; I had to use crude methods to get in. With an

253

old tyre-lever I had brought from the boot of the car, I forced open the locked window shutters. The screws of the metal fastenings securing the bolt inside came away fairly easily; the wood was rotten.

The room smelled of medicine; a half-drunk cup of coffee stood on the table. I had brought a torch from the glove-box, and moved its beam around. Nothing seemed to be disturbed. I saw him here, night after night, jerking, muttering to himself, working on his papers, taking his pills. I made for the filing cabinet, taking off my glasses to wipe away sweat and ridiculous tears.

My fear, of course, was that the drawers would be locked. I hoped that this was a precaution he had taken only when he lent the place to Hamilton. But had he expected to die? And, if so, would he have left the dossiers to be discovered?

The grey cabinet wasn't locked. In the two top drawers I found many files; in the next, a set of notebooks, handwritten, which seemed to be journals. I took them all, an armful about three feet high.

There was no note that I could see, on the desk or on the table. But next to the film cans on the table, a Bible lay open at *The Revelation*, and a passage was heavily marked in black pencil. I read it by the light of the torch. *If any man have an ear, let him hear ... He that leadeth into captivity shall go into captivity: he that killeth with the sword must be killed with the sword. Here is the patience and the faith of the saints.*

One change in the room shocked me: three of his *wayang* puppets —King Kresna, Arjuna and Princess Srikandi—lay broken on the floor, as though they had been flung down in a rage. By now I was getting more than nervous about the arrival of the BPI, and I did not linger to look further.

As I went back through the garden with my burden, I thought I saw a figure out of the corner of my eye, in the pool of dark by the great trunk of the banyan—an Indonesian or Chinese child, watching me with a stricken expression. Electric terror shot through me; but when I peered closely there was nothing there. I wasn't made for intrigue: soon I'd be hallucinating.

I was back in the Hotel garage some twenty minutes later.

Carrying the files, I made my way to my room by the back stairs, thus avoiding the foyer, and passing no one but a harmless laundry-boy, pushing his trolley. I lay on my bed in the dark, trembling: I had no desire to begin answering the questions of the rest of the press corps, and I had decided to miss the Bulgarian reception. I would not look for Hamilton yet; the BPI people were probably still questioning him. It was still only nine o'clock.

But Hamilton was already back in the Hotel, sitting inside the Java Coffee Shop. This little quick-service restaurant was in the arcade close to where his one-time cameraman had fallen. Nobody sat at the wrought-iron tables outside now: the promenade here was deserted. Cleaning-boys had already removed all traces of Billy's impact, and rain had recently fallen so that the asphalt steamed.

An Indonesian waiter, moving with the required American briskness, set down a cup of coffee in front of Hamilton, who ignored it, reading senselessly through the menu on the paper place-mat in front of him, from which he chose his breakfast each morning. The place was empty except for a group of silent Yugoslavs at a far table, who had escaped the Bulgarian reception —which Hamilton, like me, had decided not to cover. And, like me, he couldn't face the Wayang Bar, to answer the questions of the press corps; nor did he want to face his room upstairs.

He noticed the Yugoslavs staring at him, and realised his expression must have been strange. Fumbling in the pocket of his jacket for cigars, he came across a piece of paper, which he slowly spread on the table. He had not worn this suit for some time, and the paper had somehow survived in the pocket for many months. He sat reading carefully.

They brought us to the wastes beyond the town,
Where river mists fall heavier than rain,
And the fires on the hill leap higher than the stars.
Suddenly I remembered the early levees at court
When you and I galloped to the Purple Yard.
As we walked our horses up Dragon Tail Street

We turned and gazed at the green of the Southern Hills.
Since we parted, both of us have been growing old;
And our minds have been vexed with many anxious cares;
Yet even now I fancy that my ears are full
Of the sound of jade tinkling on your bridle straps.

Since Billy had used a typewriter to transcribe the poem, there was nothing very personal about this ragged memento, except the legend 'by Po Chü-I' written on the top with a blue ball-point. Raising his head from it blindly, Hamilton found himself staring at Jill, who stood inside the coffee shop's entrance, looking back at him. She was alone.

She attempted a smile, but it was unsuccessful; it became instead a wincing twist of the mouth. Her high-bridged nose was pinched, giving her face its most Gothic severity; making it look older. She moved quickly across to his table, the pale blue evening gown rustling. 'I've searched for you in every bar in the place,' she said. 'I didn't imagine you'd be drinking coffee.' It was perhaps intended as a feeble joke. Fidgeting with a little silver evening bag she held tight against her stomach, she glanced inquiringly to one side, as though she had mislaid something. This, Hamilton knew, meant she was trying not to weep.

He had stood up, and now began to draw out a chair for her, without speaking. Two Indonesian waiters watched them with cheerful smiles; the Yugoslavs also studied them.

'No,' she muttered. She shook her head, the blond curtain of hair swinging. 'I don't want to stay here. Let's go somewhere we're not on show.'

'Is there such a place?'

'We can walk in the arcade—anything. Please, Guy.'

The arcade still had no occupants. At the corner where it turned into the main block, a small soldier stood guard. In the other direction, the ceramic-tiled hallway receded in absolute emptiness, and they walked it to the end, where they halted in shadow, looking across to the Hotel gates.

I see them inside night which had become a territory of paper—as it had for me when I drove down Jalan Thamrin towards Billy's bungalow. Lights the colour of brown paper were reflected off the

256

dense wall of tropical dark; paper-coloured, too, the couple riding high on the Welcome Monument. Jill's face was a paper cut-out, which Hamilton might never see again. He needed all his strength to snatch her back, but his strength was sapped by his grief for Billy: a grief he would not have anticipated, and whose power he found bewildering.

'*Why*?' she asked. 'Why did he do it?' Her fast mutter was as low as usual, but with an edge of hysteria.

'It depends on what you think he did,' Hamilton said.

'For God's sake, you were *out* there, I know you were talking to the military. Ralph Henderson's been questioning some of them, too, but he can't find out a thing. They only say he jumped.'

'Yes, that's going to be the story. I've just spent some time with one of the BPI. He was quite a polite fellow: very good manners. He's the one who shot Billy.'

The crooked gaze fixed on his face had an intensity he found hypnotic: the dark blue irises seemed to be dissolving, like spots of colour dropped in water.

'When he let that banner out of the window, he was standing on the ledge,' Hamilton said. 'They came into the room and surprised him, and they claim he had a pistol. So they shot him without asking questions. Real men of action.'

'What are you going to *do*?' She was weeping now, without attempting to wipe away the tears, her mouth misshapen.

'Nothing,' Hamilton said. 'There's nothing we can do. I believe he only went there to hang out that stupid bloody banner, not to shoot the Bung. Not very likely, is it, with a pistol? But if they want to hush it up as suicide, let them. That's right, *let* them, Jillie. How do you want Billy remembered? As a mad gunman? His family won't. I don't. And he matters.' He looked away to the wasteland beyond the gates, where little flares on the stalls of the poor burned like forlorn hopes. 'He matters,' he said again.

She had bent her head, fumbling in her handbag for a handkerchief. Hamilton searched her down-turned face with intense concentration, as though to memorise it. Then he put his hands on her shoulders, touching her for the first time. 'I'd forgotten your face.' He only knew he had spoken aloud when her head lifted; the handbag fell to the tiles, and they clung to each other, murmuring, while vagrants by the gates grinned and pointed at them, and the small soldier watched from down the arcade.

'You'd have let me go, wouldn't you? You were ready to do that anyway.'

'No. I used to walk away from things I thought I might lose. Not any more. Not from you.'

Happiness, whose returning tide could be sensed at a distance, was nevertheless in check; and Jill, in his arms, had an unfamiliar weight—as though grief were an actual substance, loading her body.

'He wanted us to be a perfect pair of lovers,' she said. 'He picked the wrong pair, didn't he?'

'No. No he didn't. But he thought he and I would be perfect friends—that's where he made a bad choice.' Hamilton's mouth twisted in self-disgust, and he gripped her bare shoulders so that she winced. 'Don't go to Singapore,' he said.

'I'm booked. I must. It's only a few weeks, and you'll be with me in the UK.'

'Promise not to go to Dr Chen.'

'If you say not. I don't have babies very easily, apparently. A pity to waste this one.'

'Of course you'll have it. Even if it isn't mine, I want you to have it,' he said. He had meant this well, but instantly regretted saying it. Too late; she stared up at him as though to make sure of what she had heard.

'Christ,' she said, 'do you think I'd lie about it? Whose do you *think* it is?' She looked ashamed; but Hamilton saw that the shame was for him, not herself. She turned her head away, ignoring his apology.

'Wait with me here in Jakarta,' he said. He had never pleaded with a woman before, and his tone was peremptory. 'You don't have to go to Singapore.'

She shook her head. 'I'd be embarrassed to stay,' she said. 'I've said all my good-byes at the Embassy. And I'm staying with the

258

Palmers in Singapore—it's all arranged. Now that you've got this London posting, it's all right, isn't it?' She was suddenly polite, attempting cheerfulness, her voice at its most clipped and English. 'We can fly to London together, when the time comes—from Singapore. It'll give you time to think. You probably need to think twice.' She would no longer look at him. 'I really need to think again about us myself. Maybe you do best living in a hotel, Guy—there's always someone to clean up the messes. And you don't like messes, do you?'

He wanted to tell her he was different now, but couldn't find the words. When he held her again, talking to try to change her mind, she merely shook her head, beginning to cry again, and clinging to him with passionate sadness. He heard her murmur Billy's name, against his chest.

22

Five days later, on September fourteenth, I was to fly out of
Jakarta for New Delhi, taking my secret hoard of files with
me unchallenged. I had not had time to read them thoroughly;
but, having dipped into them, I had decided to keep them secret—
even from Hamilton. I had not told him of my visit to the
bungalow.

Despite the final entries on the Sukarno file, I don't believe
Kwan would have assassinated the man who had once been his
hero. I believe he had already changed his mind when he booked
into that room on the seventh floor. God knows what he was
doing with a pistol—if he had one: the BPI men may have lied. His
rage against Sukarno was genuine, and it honours him; but it was
not in his nature to kill. Perhaps he realised this in the last twenty-
four hours when he must have prepared his huge, sad banner.
Words, in the end, would remain his only weapons: those four
hopeless words the *alus* BPI man's prompt action had ensured
that Sukarno would never read.

The BPI had its way, and Kwan's death was passed off as
suicide. Under the questioning of the other members of the press
corps, Hamilton and I professed ignorance. There was so little to
go on that nothing much could be made of the incident; it never
became a story of any consequence. One Sydney newspaper, I
remember, gave it some play when they picked up my brief wire-

service item; but the interest lay mainly in the fact that he was a local man. The item died, like Billy, very quickly.

Hamilton took charge of all the arrangements concerning his body, which was flown home to Sydney for burial, at the request of Billy's father.

Hamilton saw me off at Kemayoran airport. As we sat waiting for my plane to be called, on the terrace of the shabby terminal building, we told each other we would soon meet in London. I was to be moved there myself, when the Indo-Pakistan war had run its course.

Out in the orange spaces of sundown, immaculate silver visitors from a more ordered world taxied on the cracked runways, past moping palms and the anti-aircraft guns that still waited against the sky for a British invasion. Hamilton, although he spoke cheerfully, seemed wistful; for those who were staying, farewells at Kemayoran were always unsettling. He was sad at my leaving, I knew, but I sensed that there was something else.

'Cheer up,' I said. 'You'll soon be seeing Jill again.' He had told me of their plans to marry, and also of their arrangement to fly to London from Singapore. When Hamilton's flight came through there on October the ninth Jill would join it.

'I just hope she's on it,' he said suddenly.

'On the flight? Come *on*,' I said, 'why shouldn't she be?'

Then he told me about the tactless remark he had made to her on the night of Billy's death. It was her expression that had worried him, I gathered, rather than anything she had said.

My plane waited on the tarmac, and I said, 'An expression wouldn't have worried you once, Ham. Write to her and apologise. She won't hold it against you. I'm sure of that.' This was a white lie. I was already uneasy that she hadn't stayed with him, even if Jakarta was now no place to be.

We shook hands by the wire-mesh barrier of the Customs section, where the armed soldiers watched departing passengers broodingly, as though considering last-minute detentions.

'Good-bye, Cookie,' he said. 'It looks as though neither of us will see the Bung's final curtain. Who cares? I'll be glad to get out of here.' Then, in a low voice whose feeling surprised me, 'Jesus, I miss Billy—I never would have believed it. I'll miss you, too. Take care.'

He was now one of the last English-speaking news-men left in the country. I told myself he could surely survive another month, and I was not over-concerned for his safety. I looked back at him as I headed for the doors. Towering above the throng, perfectly turned out as usual in his tan safari suit, Hamilton grinned and raised one hand. He looked self-sufficient yet somehow forlorn behind the wire: a beautifully dressed prisoner.

23

May silence prevail. May the strength of wind and storm be mine. The shadows are closing around Bung Karno: the shadows of September's last night.

Good-bye, Sukarno.

'*Oh Bung Karno, almost I feel fond of you again. Why did you cease to come to Pasar Baru?*' Billy Kwan was right: you were all things to your people; they lived through you in the great years. But you ceased to go to Pasar Baru.

Dead dictators, such as Hitler and Stalin, have a dwindled, sub-human quality, viewed through our reversed telescopes. They depress; they are like insects. You don't have that quality, Bung Karno, and it makes me judge your sins as venial rather than mortal. You smile up at me now from the photograph in Billy Kwan's file, *pitji* jauntily cocked, and I smile back wryly, as one does at a con-man one cannot help liking. *Hey, Sukarno!* The ghostly charm and the ghostly life-force are so strong they rise from Billy's 'glazed card' and fill the room, as they once filled the Jakarta stadium. And it is a young man's charm, although you are in your sixties in this picture: a wilful boy's.

You remained an adolescent, Sukarno, shamelessly in love with yourself; and it's easy to despise this. But your young man's hunger for the world was giant-size, and only the mean and impotent can easily despise that hunger.

You didn't understand economics; you were a boy who could

not do sums. What you wanted, for yourself and your people, was glory; and everyone was supposed to love you, as your 'angel mother' had loved you, as Sarinah the servant girl had loved you. Almost everyone did. But this love had to be one-way; it had to come up to you in waves, while you stood high on your dais, and bathed in it. The *Wayang* of the Right and the *Wayang* of the Left had to love you, although they could never love each other! This was the due of the Just Ruler, who united all opposites in himself, and united the three thousand islands. You were not simply Muslim or Socialist; you were both; and you were also Hindu and Christian: a man of dualities, as Billy Kwan said.

But when all the opposites cancelled each other out, Aidit and the *Wayang* of the Left began to move in. Now that the huge toys necessary to the nation's self-respect could not be paid for, and the absurd account books the West insisted on would not balance, and the glory fluttered from the air around your monuments, there was nothing left but anger for Aidit and his men to feed on.

Real deaths, real tortures would now take place. But it had all begun over toys.

I am glad I didn't see you at the end, Bung Karno, confined to your private house at Bogor (the Dream Palace of the Holy Bima), stripped of the Presidency, stripped of the uniforms, shuffling about in a singlet and crumpled trousers, your face bloated and aged, divorced by all your wives except the faithful Hartini— 'silent,' you said, 'in a thousand tongues.'

I see you now as a little boy—one of the many little boys with eyes shining like glass, who squat on the fringe of night to watch the glowing screen and darting, magic shadows of the *wayang*. You will be Bima, you say: Bima the *kasar* one, whose boldness makes up for all his coarseness.

Hey, Sukarno ... I see you, in the time of struggle against the Dutch, a lone political prisoner on the island of Flores, sitting like Arjuna in contemplation under the *sukun*-tree; building up your spirit-power, your *sakti*. In the *sukun*-tree's buds, you see Brahma the Creator; in its oval fruit, Vishnu the Preserver; in its dead branches, Shiva the Destroyer. And you watch the ocean, and call it as irresistible as your Revolution. But is it just endless revolution you want? Or does your soul hunger for a soaring, nameless event for which 'revolution' is just a poor label, the only one you can find? The ocean surges like the force within you, which must have its outlet, but for which no outlet will ever be enough. For you are a man in whom the senses and the spirit struggle against each other with equal force; and they will give you no rest, Bung Karno. Like Arjuna, you combine grandeur with fickleness and a selfish coldness; and such a man's soul will never be refined.

I see you talking to little Marhaen, outside Bandung.

'Do you ever sell your labour?'

'No sir. I must work very hard, but my labours are all for myself.'

'What is your name?'

'Marhaen.'

'But brother, you live in poverty.'

'That's right, I live poorly.'

I see you in the Year of Living Dangerously, old and tired and full of sins, asking that when you die you should be buried outside high, cool Bandung, the land of your youth, where you first met Farmer Marhaen, riding on your bicycle. (Your wish is not to be granted: when you die, you will be buried quietly at Blitar, next to your mother, whom you said you had sought in all women.)

There is an unspoilt, selfless moment in every man's life—even in the life of an egotist. Marhaen gave you your moment. Billy Kwan knew this. You would have liked Billy, who never met you personally; he could only watch you at receptions and press conferences. Once, at a conference Kwan got in to at the Palace, he put a question to you—which a cameraman had no right to do. I've forgotten, now, what the question was.

The West asks for clear conclusions, final judgments. A philosophy must be correct or incorrect, a man good or bad. But in the *wayang* no such final conclusions are ever drawn. The struggle of the Right and the Left never ends, because neither side is wholly good or bad. The *kasar* can have noble qualities; the *alus*, mean ones. So it was with you, Bung Karno. Unlike Arjuna, you failed to heed the advice of Krishna—that advice which Billy was so insistent about. *All is clouded by desire: as fire by smoke, as a mirror by dust ... Through these it blinds the soul.*

On the night of Thursday, September the thirtieth, Sukarno was scheduled to speak in the indoor stadium out at Senayan. Hamilton did not often cover these meetings now; Sukarno would say nothing he had not said before. But on this particular evening he decided to go.

There was a full moon. Whether this affected him, I can only guess; but when he and I reconstructed the events of that night, in London two months later, I gathered that he had been driven by an electric restlessness which had possessed him ever since Billy Kwan's death and which made it difficult for him to sleep.

In the covered stadium, with its steep banks of seats holding a crowd of many thousands, its coloured banners and glaring, bone-white floodlights, there was the usual big hum, the usual spicy reek of *kretek* cigarettes, and the collective odour of perspiration which always reminded Hamilton of rice being cooked. There had been slogan-shouting; cheerful laughter; singing. Now the crowd was quiet, all eyes fixed on the stocky little figure in the white uniform and black *pitji* which had come down the petal-strewn stairs to a dais on the floor of the arena.

The President stood impassively, looking about the banks of brown faces, white shirts and butterfly-bright *kebayas* and *kains*. He had put on flesh, Hamilton thought: his face was puffy. On the table in front of him, as always, stood three glasses with silver lids, one of which was said to contain medicine. Microphones sprouted like magic black flowers; Sukarno flicked one of these inquiringly with his index finger, as he always did, appearing to balance on the balls of his feet: a faintly erotic stance that suggested a pop singer rather than a dictator. When he began, his throaty voice had its usual deceptive quietness; it was almost a whisper, approaching the audience with true Javanese diffidence. Nor were his gestures emphatic; he stabbed at the heavy air with a languid finger.

'Sisters and brothers . . . .' He did not command them to attend, as a Western rabble-rouser would have done; his voice caressed and coaxed them, and they listened in silence. But later, Hamilton knew, the great *dalang*'s voice would rise a little, and quicken, and they would all begin to roar, their light-hearted mood utterly replaced. They were still entirely his, as they listened.

Since Sukarno spoke in Bahasa, Hamilton found it a strain to follow. He stood holding a light run from a battery pack, illuminating the immediate area for the benefit of the stolid Indonesian cameraman he had now hired to replace Billy Kwan. He had also brought Kumar, who stood on the other side of him in silence, studying the President with absolute attention.

When Sukarno suddenly broke off from his speech, it was a few moments before Hamilton realised what had happened.

He had been directing Sutopo the cameraman to get a shot of a section of the crowd, and he looked back to the dais to see that the figure in the gleaming operetta uniform was shuffling away from the microphones. A few moments later, steps faltering, flanked by his palace guards, Sukarno had disappeared. There was a tidal sighing in the crowd; the deserted microphone-flowers waited. Hamilton turned to Kumar.

'What's happened?' he demanded. 'Is he ill?'

'He did not say.' Kumar was frowning at the platform, and the skin of his face appeared taut. His hands were in his pockets, and Hamilton had the impression that he held them there to conceal his tension. 'I think it must be serious, or he would not leave,' Kumar said. 'Perhaps his illness has grown worse. You know what this will mean, boss.' He looked directly at Hamilton. 'I will go and find out,' he said. It was a statement, not a request; but Hamilton nodded.

Kumar turned away; then he turned back, as though remembering something. 'There is something I want to say to you, boss. If the President dies, you should go back to Australia. Do not waste time, but leave this country immediately. If you do not, you will certainly be killed. You are on our death list.' The usual sardonic glint was absent from his wide-set eyes. He was gone before Hamilton could reply, moving lithely down the stairs between the tiers of seats.

Five minutes later Sukarno reappeared on the dais, and continued his speech as though nothing had happened. But Kumar did not come back. At the end of the meeting Sutopo and Hamilton searched for him; but he was not to be found.

This took place at around 10 p.m. Hamilton, when we held our post-mortem in London, was uncertain about the time; but other sources confirm it. The twenty-four hours that followed are very well documented, even if their mysteries still remain unsolved.

One of these mysteries is the real reason for Sukarno's disappearance from the dais. Some say that he had a serious attack of some kind, and went out to receive treatment from his Chinese doctor. And they say that the *Wayang* of the Left, realising what had happened, decided to set in motion the events which would take place before dawn. This I don't believe; nor did Hamilton. Those events had to be plotted well in advance, and I'm inclined to the theory that Sukarno had finally decided to back the *Wayang* of the Left against the *Wayang* of the Right, and had been called from the dais to be given a last-minute briefing on what would take place after midnight.

My opinion is no more informed than any other, and whether he really released the Left at last is the greatest mystery of all; but it's a fact that the men of the Left had gained his ear more and more in the past months. Muslim Army men of the Right, they said, were giving aid to *Nekolim* agents and plotting the President's death; a 'Council of Generals', they said, was planning a takeover.

Even as the Bung disappeared from the platform the *Wayang* of the Left were gathering their forces in secret out at Halim, the Air Force base on Jakarta's southern outskirts. Truckloads of troops were now moving out there; the People's Youth were there, as well as *Gerwani*, the PKI women's organisation. The Chinese cargo had arrived, and D. N. Aidit had his Fifth Force at last. Aidit himself would soon be there; so would dandily handsome Omar Dhani, commander of the defecting Air Force, together with the apparent leader of the coup, Lieutenant-Colonel Untung, commander of the Tjakrabirawa, the President's own palace guard. Their combined fighting force was divided into three sections, and code-named after characters in the *wayang kulit*. One of these, the Pasaputi force, would leave Halim in trucks soon after midnight and enter Jakarta's sleeping suburbs. Its mission was to kidnap and murder the most important *Wayang* of the Right: Indonesia's top Army generals.

I have been out to Halim at night. Today, it has been transformed into an international airport; then, its runways were often silent, their vacancies lined with mysterious blue landing-lights, like evil spirits. Far beyond these lights, in the moist heat, there brooded a swampy region where there was a well known as Lubang Buaja: Crocodile Hole.

The electric tension which had sent Hamilton out to the stadium at Senayan had not been purged; it had increased, if anything, and he knew that sleep would be impossible. It was nearly midnight, and he stood by the window of his darkened room, staring at the city's lights. He was not angry with Kumar: his assistant's last remark had taken the situation between them beyond anger. Hamilton didn't doubt for a moment that Kumar's warning was based on simple truth; and he was almost touched. He had not thought that Kumar liked him enough to tip him off. But he had the weary suspicion that he had now lost his assistant, and would probably never see him again. '*On our death list!*' he muttered, and breathed a rueful laugh. Kumar could hardly appear in the office as usual after that 'our'.

Hamilton wondered if he should be making plans for escape; whether he should now contact the Australian Embassy. But he wasn't really alarmed enough, he said: Sukarno's reappearance in the stadium had convinced him that the President's death would not come yet to free the *Wayang* of the Left. Half an hour before, when he had driven into the driveway of the Hotel, he had seen the tail-end of Sukarno's wailing motorcade leaving by the other gates; the President had been collecting Madame Dewi, the beautiful Japanese bar-girl who had become his latest wife, from the night-club on the Hotel's top floor. It seemed to Hamilton now that he could still hear the wailing of Sukarno's sirens.

He sat down in an arm-chair, in the dark. The real reason he couldn't sleep, he decided, was that there had been no letter from Jill since she had gone to Singapore. He knew he should not expect this; letters to Indonesia hardly ever got through now, or if they did they were many weeks old; it was rather like putting a message in a bottle. Jill and he had agreed that they should not expect to make contact before meeting on their flight to Europe. But they had agreed to write just the same; and Hamilton, already afraid of losing her, grew irrationally more so each day when no letter came.

He flicked on his standard lamp, and drew one of his books from the shelf. He wanted to keep his thoughts from Jill, and also from Billy Kwan, whose flat, nasal voice had a habit of sounding in his ears when he was alone at night.

He was probably still awake in his chair when the killer squads from Halim reached the sleeping villas in the nearby southern suburbs; when General Yani, head of the Army, was shot in his living-room in front of his young children; and when General Nasution fled his would-be murderers, who shot his five-year-old daughter.

But Hamilton had certainly fallen asleep in the hour before dawn, when three men in pyjamas, bound with ropes, were led into an open place in the swampy area out by Halim known as Crocodile Hole, to find themselves surrounded by a frenzied mob in pseudo-military uniforms, most of whom were women: the *Gerwani*. I see the surviving generals there, under the full moon, beyond the pitiless blue landing-lights, listening to the *Pemuda Rakjat* songs and the wild hatred of the women's screaming, knowing there is now no hope.

'Kill the capitalist bureaucrats!' Rifle butts and knives rise and fall; blood finally flows; the generals cry out. And the women, fiercer than the men, struggle to get closer, in the ecstasy of this unique night: they will torment the generals sexually, and then castrate them; they will cut out their eyes with razor blades. The blue lights watch, like evil spirits.

24

Move the needle of your radio receiver along the short-wave band. Between the foreign voices and alien anthems crowding the invisible frequencies, there stretches a deep gulf. The gulf is filled with an enormous hissing, and sometimes with a prolonged, humming blare, like wires stretched between the stars. You are listening then to the size of the world, and its false, electronic intimacy. You are listening perhaps to what the Hindus call *ākāśa*: the dark which has no end.

Every time I had the chance, in New Delhi, I would switch on my big Japanese transistor and search for Hamilton's voice, in the gulf. Occasionally I would succeed: ABS or the BBC would carry one of his pieces. The position during my first two weeks in India seemed more or less unchanged, but I continued to listen; I was still in Jakarta, emotionally, and could not break the thread.

I picked up Hamilton's October first broadcast at a little after four in the afternoon, while I was sitting on the balcony of my hotel room drinking tea. ABS led with Indonesia, that day, and the announcer's voice was charged with the solemnity reserved for big stories. He stated baldly that President Sukarno appeared to have been overthrown by a left-wing military coup, and had disappeared: then Guy Hamilton's voice came on. I fumbled wildly with the volume control.

How electrically important it seemed that hot afternoon, and how hard it is now to recapture—the unique, present importance of news, whose full flavour can be tasted only once! I remember nothing now of what Hamilton said, although his piece was to be repeated by every English-speaking news service in the world, and would make him briefly famous. The familiar voice, with its fugitive Australian vowels, pitched up as though he called from a hilltop, fluctuated in the hissing gulf, and has now been swallowed by it for ever. 'This is Guy Hamilton, reporting from Jakarta.' He was gone. I wondered how safe he was.

And I remember smiling, with a mixture of affection and bitterness. 'So it's happened,' I said. 'And I wasn't there.' To a news-man, the statement is never less poignant for being silly.

He drove down Jalan Thamrin in the Ford, the early sun making him blink wearily behind his sun-glasses after his sleepless night. It was just on seven fifteen as he drove past the high, Babylonian terraces and steps of Sarinah, the Bung's great department store. Hamilton remembered the time clearly, when we held our post-mortem: he was on his way to his office, and had no notion that anything was wrong, he said; nor, at that hour on Friday, did the rest of Jakarta's population.

But in five more minutes, the first broadcast by the 'September Thirtieth Movement' would come over Radio Republic Indonesia, announcing Lieutenant-Colonel Untung's takeover. Hamilton was not to hear it, his car radio being off; and with his weak Bahasa it's doubtful if he would have understood much of it, anyway. He remembers sensing something—an absence, a void in the city; but this could have been caused by his own state of mind. He wondered, without much hope, whether Kumar would appear in the office after all; and the crude black signs daubed on bamboo fences passed by like the aftermath of a hooligan orgy, which someone must soon clean up: GANJANG MALAYSIA; CRUSH EVERY FORM OF IMPERIALISM.

He became aware of a black Austin flying a small Union Jack running level with his own car; its horn sounded twice, and he recognised Colonel Henderson, who signalled to him to pull over, and halted some distance ahead. Hamilton stopped behind the Austin, and got out.

The Colonel walked back to him at the roadside, his tanned head gleaming as though he had polished it for the day. He was in civilian dress: white shirt and regimental tie, tan slacks, and the 'eternal' suede shoes. Above the buzz of the traffic, he called out a greeting that sounded more affable than Hamilton had expected, and smiled.

It had been some time since they had spoken together. They had never referred to their rivalry over Jill, but the mutual knowledge of it had made them uncomfortable: the Colonel's manner had hardened, and their meetings to exchange information in the Hotel's cocktail bar had lapsed, by unspoken consent.

'Sorry to hold you up, but I think you may be interested in something.' Henderson stood with his head tilted slightly back, hands on his hips, in a pose which somehow made the difference in their heights not a disadvantage to himself but a physical deformity in Hamilton. 'There's something wrong,' he said briefly.

'Wrong?' Hamilton thought instantly of Jill's pregnancy.

'I thought you might like the tip,' Henderson said. 'There are troops in Merdeka Square. I've just been there.' He waited, as though for a response from a backward schoolboy.

'So?' Hamilton said. 'There are quite a few battalions in town at the moment. They're here from all over Java, for the Armed Forces Day parade on the fifth. But you must know that, Colonel.'

Henderson's mouth became thinner. 'Yes, that *is* my business,' he said. 'And they're supposed to be stationed on the city outskirts, old boy: they're specifically forbidden to come into the city. But that's just what they've done, it seems. The troops I saw had green berets: and that means they were an East Java battalion.' He paused. 'Now what do you suppose East Java troops are doing in front of the palace at seven in the morning, setting up road-blocks?'

Hamilton stared into the bright, triangular grey eyes. 'They're blocking off the palace?'

'Exactly. I think we have a coup on our hands, or something

273

very like it. You'd better get in there pretty damn quickly, if you want a story. It may be the last you'll get. Of course, you may prefer to sit it out in the Hotel—I understand that's what most news-hounds do when the going gets rough.' His moustache twitched, and his smile was contemptuous. He was challenging Hamilton again.

'I'll go to the square,' Hamilton said.

Henderson raised his eyebrows. 'You'd better think twice,' he said. 'If the PKI win, it may be very sticky to have a white face. Come to the Embassy, if that happens. We might be able to evacuate you to Singapore, along with our staff.'

'Thanks, Colonel. You'll make me an honorary Brit., will you?'

But the Colonel, who had turned on his heel and was walking back to his car, did not answer. As he opened the door of the Austin, he called back, 'I've already alerted the Embassy. I'm going to the square again to have another look. Keep your head down.' The car door slammed.

Hamilton drove first to the office. Rosini was there, and Sutopo the cameraman; they had apparently not heard the 7.20 broadcast either, and were chatting calmly, unaware that this was not a day like any other.

Kumar was not there, and Hamilton stared wryly at his assistant's empty desk. He understood everything now; this was Kumar's day. By nightfall he might well be one of the country's new leaders. Hamilton wondered briefly whether his assistant would plead for him if the PKI arrested him. But there was no time for conjectures of this kind. He began hurriedly to give orders to Sutopo, explaining that they were going over to Merdeka Field.

And in a curious way he was happy, for the first time since Jill's departure. His yearning was for more than news, I think: it was a metaphysical one, for that vast, ultimate event which would change everything.

May silence prevail. Sir Guy is the only Western 'news-hound' (to use the Colonel's archaic term) who will go to Merdeka Field this morning—and the only one who knows, at this hour of the day,

274

that anything is happening. But what is it that is happening? Hamilton has no idea. Trespassing on the main arena of events, he remains quite ignorant of their nature and, like all of us, will remain so until long after they are over.

He and Sutopo the cameraman have been driven by old Hartono to Jalan Merdeka Timur, the road which skirts the eastern side of the vast field; and they have found that Colonel Henderson was right: there are barbed-wire entanglements up where Merdeka Timur joins Jalan Merdeka Utara, the road in front of the palace. Numbers of armed troops in green berets are gathered there, beside the prehistoric shapes of armoured cars. Merdeka Timur, usually busy with cars and *betjaks*, is unnaturally empty; so are the vast, threadbare levels of the field itself, and Hamilton has decided to go the rest of the way on foot, leaving Hartono parked under a tree. He and Sutopo walk up Merdeka Timur, keeping in the shade of the banyan-trees. It is now 7.45.

They pause at some distance from the first road-block, and Hamilton directs Sutopo to shoot film of the scene, which the cameraman does reluctantly. The soldiers have begun to look in their direction, through the glare.

'Better go back now, boss. Bad trouble here,' Sutopo says. He is a stolid, balding man with a small moustache, and deep furrows in his forehead, which now grow profound. He is sweating, and obviously afraid. Hamilton, suddenly sorry for him, tells him to go back to the car. He then moves on up the road alone.

It is very quiet. The climbing sun beats down, glinting on the gold flame of Sukarno's great *tugu*, far out in the vacancies of the field. Hamilton is not particularly apprehensive at this point; there is nothing to make him so. The burning distances of dry grass are too meaningless; the white sky too stultifying. Nothing seems likely to happen, because nothing can be brought into focus: unless it is the grave, nineteenth-century palace with its white columns, frowning far off with the cool solemnity of another hemisphere. Sir Guy's foolhardy intention is to try and enter the palace, using his press pass.

I find his action ridiculous and unnecessary. His career is now assured; he might just as easily go back to the office or the Oasis pool and await events there—and still turn in an adequate story at the end of the day, if circumstances allow it. Instead, he walks towards the road-block and the figures in green berets: not for money, not for advancement, not even for an ideal, but because of the Colonel's smile; and also because of his lust for that final event, intense as an ascetic's lust for visions. And he walks an invisible grid, inside a story where things are not what they should be. They seldom are, in Java.

The coup has already been botched. The actors on Merdeka Field are not even certain of their rôles; and the drama set in motion during the night by Lieutenant-Colonel Untung and his friends, which should have been brutally simple, is turning today into something else; is losing itself in the yellow, dry-grassed spaces like a tedious dream. The paracommandos Hamilton sees in front of him—rebel battalions from East and Central Java— hold three sides of Merdeka Field, together with the nearby radio station and the telecommunications building from which we sent our stories; but they don't hold the fourth side, along which Hamilton is walking. Here the KOSTRAD building—the head-quarters of the Army's Strategic Reserve—is already under the invisible control of one of the *Wayang* of the Right: the quiet, uncon-sidered Major-General Suharto, who will emerge at the eleventh hour as the drama's *alus* hero, and his country's new prince. The king at this stage is absent: Sukarno has spent the night in Dewi's bed, in the Hollywood house he has built for her at Slipi.

The men of the rebel battalions are supposedly 'guarding' the palace and its absent king, whom their leaders claim to be protecting; but Suharto has already discovered them to be so uncertain of their function that they salute the envoys he sends across there. Soon, with a mixture of toughness and *priyayi* delicacy, the prince will begin to suggest that they acknowledge their mistake and surrender, or be blasted from the field.

But Hamilton is as ignorant of all this as the city and the world are: as even the coup leaders out at Halim are. He has now reached a barbed-wire barricade, by the spangled lake of shade laid down by a banyan-tree. Half a dozen men in green berets stare at him: they look extremely fit, and their faces, he notices irrelevantly, are much darker than those of the Jakartanese, presumably from the suns of East Java. Two of them cock their rifles and shout at him in Bahasa to halt.

Hamilton does so, smiling pleasantly, and holding up his press card. He removes his sun-glasses, remembering the desire of the Indonesian military to see a man's eyes: they claim to be able to tell an assassin by his eyes. 'What's the road-block for?' he asks.

But no one understands English. He tries it in halting Bahasa, but there is silence, and not a face smiles. Eyes like nocturnal pools examine him coldly; he is a freakish creature, these eyes say: so outrageous that they are beyond being amused. A middle-aged sergeant, tall for a Javanese, with muscular fore-arms, a broad chest, and green beret pulled low to meet a large pair of sun-glasses, moves forward and shouts some commands which Hamilton doesn't understand.

He decides to bluff, hoping that some of them understand, and are affecting not to. 'I'm going to the palace,' he says. 'I have a pass for the palace—okay?' He repeats it in Bahasa. They are all looking at him, saying nothing. Hamilton, holding up his press card once more, salutes them vaguely, and walks off the road onto the worn grass of the field, with the intention of circumnavigating the barbed-wire.

He hears thudding feet, and turns to see the sergeant behind him, the cap and sun-glasses masking all human qualities in his face. His rifle is raised, butt-first. He doesn't swing it, but pushes it like a javelin. It is too late to avoid it; Hamilton has turned just in time to receive the butt directly in his left eye, instead of in the back of the head.

He hears a howling cry he can't acknowledge as his own. It floats out onto the field, to be dispassionately swallowed in the heat. He doesn't fall, but stands stock-still, his hand cupped over his eye. Fingers grip his upper arm; he can smell the sergeant's body-odour; phrases in unknown dialect come through a yellow fog; somewhere, a voice shouts in English. Hamilton begins to walk back towards the barbed-wire barrier, finding that the numbing fingers on his arm permit this.

Crookedly, he sees the other soldiers and, pushing through them, Colonel Henderson. The clipped, arrogant voice, raised in what sounds like a parody of itself, pierces all other sounds. 'Now look here. Military Attaché here . . . witnessed this attack . . . . Demand that this man be surrendered to me immediately . . . . Responsible . . . . British subject. You what? What? Don't be bloody silly.' The voice, just as peremptory, changes to fluent Bahasa.

Henderson's face appears, filling the vision of Hamilton's remaining eye, and the hard gaze appraises him for the second time this morning. 'Your eye, is it?' There is no sympathy in his voice. 'Get the hand away, will you—let's see.' Hamilton lowers his hand. 'My God.' The tone is now one of quiet distaste, as though at some regrettable mess. 'I'll have to take you to the Embassy. We've a doctor there. Can you make it to my car? Down the road a bit.'

Hamilton's hand cups his eye again; it is very important to him to do this. He feels no pain, but his body rings like a struck bell; and it seems that every few seconds the rifle-butt is mightily thrust in: again; again. He senses that it has barely touched the bone around the eye; its corner, with great accuracy, had gone directly into the eye itself.

'Put your arm over my shoulder,' the Colonel says. Hamilton is embarrassed by this suggestion, and says that he can walk unaided.

Sitting in the front seat of Henderson's Austin, he removes the hand, to find himself at the source of the yellow fog: it lies in a thick screen across his eye: light comes through it, but no images. He replaces the hand.

They speed up Jalan Thamrin, which now has many jeeps and trucks in it filled with men and youths carrying rifles and sten-guns: a sprinkling of the three thousand or so armed Communist civilians now moving into the city, although Hamilton and the Colonel are unaware of this.

'How is it?' Henderson asks tersely.

'Blind,' Hamilton says. Speech grows more difficult, and nausea advances on him like a wave.

278

'I wouldn't jump to that conclusion yet,' he hears Henderson say cheerfully. 'That's the trouble with you Australians—you panic.'

Hamilton briefly hates him, but his thoughts are unclear. He concentrates on holding his hand over the ruined eye: he feels ridiculously sorry for it, and at the same time guilty about it, as though it is not his own, but an exquisite, ruined object which has merely been lent to him.

Henderson took him to the big villa on Jalan Diponogoro where Jill Bryant had lived. The Embassy leased this whole well-appointed house for its staff, and an apartment on the ground floor had just been vacated. The Colonel left Hamilton in the bedroom to wait for the doctor.

When he came, the Embassy's doctor studied the injured eye with a small light, his face brought ridiculously close to Hamilton's. Stocky and neat in the huge white shorts some of the British still wore, he had a long frown-mark between his brows, and did not at first speak or smile. But he had brought with him the normality of another life: or so it seemed to Hamilton. Outside, all constraints holding back the *Pemuda Rakjat* would by now have ceased to exist, and a mob could reasonably be expected to burst in at any moment; yet such notions became unlikely with Dr Ross here, breathing seriously through his nose. What was outside was surely a grey, decent street in an English provincial town.

He made Hamilton take two tablets to forestall the pain he assured him was imminent; then he said: 'I want you to keep your head down and lie flat on your back, with as little movement as possible. You should stay that way for ten days—maybe a fortnight.' He smiled dubiously. 'Whether you can do that under the present circumstances remains to be seen: but we must hope so.'

Hamilton sat up. 'Come on, doctor, I can't even afford a couple of hours here, you must know that. And I'm flying to Europe in a week.' The idea of missing the flight with Jill was suddenly more appalling than the coup.

Dr Ross put his hand on Hamilton's shoulder, and pushed him angrily back on the bed. 'You don't seem to understand, Mr Hamilton. You must lie *flat*. To tell you the truth, the odds are that the eye will be totally blind. Do you want that?'

Hamilton subsided, and stared at Ross mutely, his good eye asking to be told a mistake had been made.

'The iris is filled with blood,' Ross said. 'I can't get behind to see the retina. We must wait until it clears. I think the retina is probably smashed—in which case, you'll lose the sight. However, it could be merely detached.' He paused. 'If it is, then it may right itself—but only if you remain flat on your back for the period I've told you to, and only if eye movements are reduced to a minimum. That's why I'm going to bandage both eyes. I'm trying to give you a sporting chance. It's not a very good chance, but it does exist.'

'For Jesus' sake, I won't even be able to feed myself. And I can't stay here. No—it's not on.'

'Fortunately you can stay here. Colonel Henderson tells me this apartment is vacant. What we all have to hope is that we won't be forced to evacuate to Singapore. No sense in thinking about that yet, though. We'll arrange an *amah* to feed you and so on. Now stop fighting it, will you?'

Saturday, now, and mid-morning. Sir Guy lies bandaged in permanent night; but knows that another day has come because the *amah* recently brought him breakfast, feeding him with a spoon. The pain-killing drugs he must take cause him constantly to doze; how much of the morning has gone, he has no idea. He is now intensely conscious of sounds: the occasional rumble of a heavy truck in Jalan Diponogoro; the harsh cries of Javanese birds, coming through the shuttered windows; the broken breathing of the ceiling fan.

The heat makes the bandage hard to tolerate; sweat accumulates under it constantly, and it prickles. He lies thinking about the prospect of losing an eye; of being a one-eyed man. He will not believe it. When the blood clears, his sight will still be there. It may be there now.

He decides to defy Ross, and to lift the bandage. He struggles through an unaccustomed prayer, offering the predictable, ignominous bargain: give me back the eye, and I'll pay more heed to You than I've done; I'll try to live as You want. And he tells himself that if he can see the dial of his watch with the injured eye, it will be a sign that the sight is coming back. Gingerly, he lifts the bandage, looks at his wrist-watch with his good eye, and then closes it to test the other.

The shattered eye can see nothing: the yellow fog has darkened and become the colour of brown paper. God, it seems, is not available for bargains.

While Hamilton had lain in his darkness during the past twenty-four hours, drifting in and out of sleep, the forces of *banting-stir*, which nobody understood, had wrestled outside in the stunning heat, with their curious Javanese quietness. The foreign community, and most Indonesians, had remained indoors by their radios, listening to the broadcasts from the occupied studios of Radio Indonesia.

And the conspiracy of September the thirtieth had been beaten at the outset, it seemed. No pitched battles had been fought; few shots had been fired; but the *Wayang* of the Right had already triumphed over the *Wayang* of the Left when today dawned. The country, having briefly changed hands, had now changed hands again, through a mixture of bluff and threat: through the *priyayi* conversation on Merdeka Field. It would be weeks before the world understood what had happened.

Yesterday, throughout the day, Lieutenant-Colonel Untung's September Thirtieth Movement had made its proud pro-clamations at frequent intervals on the radio. It had moved, it said, against the mysterious 'Council of power-mad Generals' to stop their plotting with CIA and *Nekolim* agents to overthrow the President. It had set up a Revolution Council to run Indonesia, and had taken President Sukarno under its protection. It did not say where the President was; but at the time when Hamilton was walking onto Merdeka Field, Sukarno had allowed himself to be driven in a humble Volkswagen out to the rebel command post at Halim, to join the conspirators there. He would later deny his involvement with them, but in vain; and it would lead to his ruin, since all positions in the *wayang* are clear and unchanging. No one can inhabit the left side and pretend he has been a figure of the right, or of the centre: and no one can pretend any more to be the *dalang* when he has become merely one of the puppets.

By eight o'clock that night, when General Suharto had induced the troops on Merdeka Field to surrender, the *Wayang* of the Left, who had attempted all day to direct events from Halim, were in despair. The *alus* prince had gained control of the radio station, and at dawn today, he had moved on Halim. There was no fighting: the *Wayang* of the Left had all fled during the night. D. N. Aidit had flown to Jogjakarta, in Central Java, where he would soon be hunted down like an animal, and killed. Sukarno had withdrawn to his palace of dreams at Bogor, hoping to be above the fray.

And just for now, he was. Even at this stage, everything must be done in the raffish god's name: the *Wayang* of the Left and the *Wayang* of the Right had both claimed him in their broadcasts, both saying that they had acted on his behalf. But all would emerge in the end—like the bodies of the mutilated generals from Crocodile Hole.

In the months to come, Bung Karno would continue to wear his *pitji* and his uniforms; would continue to be President, and address his crowds. But it would be like speaking to faces in a dream, faces that paid no heed.

His *sakti*, his magic power, would drain away, and in the end his *marhaen* and the city's student demonstrators would shout insults at their *dalang*, while the *Wayang* of the Right, with slow *priyayi* courtesy, would remove all the trappings of his power.

Colonel Henderson brought Hamilton news of these sequences, and passed on to him whatever clues to the puzzle he and his intelligence staff had been able to put together. And the Colonel had helped him to record the radio piece I had heard on the day of the coup—holding the microphone of a portable tape-recorder while Hamilton lay bandaged on the bed. Since the telecommunications building was occupied, one of Henderson's staff got the tape into the hands of an obliging passenger on the last Singapore-bound KLM flight allowed through Jakarta. All communications with the outside world were then cut completely.

Hamilton waited impatiently for Henderson's visits. The Colonel was now his only reliable link with events; a sound rope connecting him with the sly, twittering life outside. More importantly, he was a human voice in the darkness; the only one Hamilton heard besides Dr Ross's and the *amah*'s.

Sir Guy's position was hard for him to bear. Deprived of the drug of action, he was trapped in the blind room of his mind; and his worst torment was the thought of Jill. There was now no way he could get through to her, and he had now come to believe that unless he was on the flight through Singapore as they had arranged—only a week away now—he would lose her for ever; and also that, in her bitterness, she would have the threatened abortion. Her last reproach to him on the night of Billy's death now took on a tormenting significance; he said that she needed only one more disappointment to decide against him.

Hour after hour, his thoughts revolved around the two factors that could prevent his catching the flight: Dr Ross's insistence on two weeks in this bed; and the likelihood of there being no flights through Jakarta next week. He began to wonder if he could send a message to Jill in Singapore through the Embassy's radio link. But he would have to ask the Colonel; and this would be embarrassing.

'Hullo there—how are we getting on?'

It was the Colonel's voice: his usual greeting. His boots creaked as he lowered himself into the chair by the bed. He was affable but entirely impersonal, as always; he would never abandon his maddening, upper-middle-class formality.

'We still don't know much,' the Colonel was saying, as though addressing a meeting, 'and Sukarno's still out of sight—but there's no immediate panic now, where we're concerned. Suharto's got the city under control. Good chap, Suharto—I've met him once or twice, and he's a cool customer. Turned the tables on them beautifully, it seems. The coup leaders must have under-estimated him. So did you chaps, eh? You always saw General Nasution as the saviour, I think—but he seems to be lying low. Didn't have what it took, in the end. Of course, there may be civil war in the countryside—but meanwhile we sit tight and hope for the best. And you can stay on your back for a while longer; that's something.'

'I'm very grateful to you, Colonel, for all this.'

'Nonsense—I feel responsible.' The voice was embarrassed now.

'I want to tell you something,' Hamilton said abruptly. 'Jill Bryant and I are going to be married.'

'Really? Congratulations.' It was the British 'really' at its most coldly devastating; it forbade any attempt at intimacy, and Hamilton felt as though he had been slapped in the face. He was glad he could not see the Colonel's expression, nor the Colonel his. He had been stupid enough to want Henderson's blessing.

'I want to get out of here next Saturday,' Hamilton said. 'We're flying to Athens together. I thought you might book the flight for me, and help me wind things up.'

'Impossible,' Henderson said. 'You know that. Unless you want to lose that eye.'

Hamilton flushed under his bandage. 'I see. I'll have to handle it myself, then.'

'I shouldn't advise it. Of course, we can't prevent you.' The chair creaked as he stood up; his feet moved to the door. 'Keep your head down,' he said. 'Cheerio.' The door closed.

Hamilton resolved to ask the Colonel for no further favours. But he still waited for him to pay another visit. He remembered as a small boy waiting in bed for his father to come and say good night, dreading, on occasions when he had committed some offence, that his father might not do so. It was like that now. Resentful though he was, he still waited for the creaking boots, the sound of the coldly cheerful voice.

But the Colonel never came again.

The *amah*'s voice told him she was youthful: and he imagined her as small and slim. In disobedience of Dr Ross, he finally peeped at her from under the bandage; he had been right in his guess: very small, she had a plain, Chinese face, her hair tightly drawn back in the traditional bun. The brown screen was still across his eye; if anything, it had thickened. This was the evening of Tuesday.

'Doctor says no peeping,' she said, and they laughed.

After that, she remained a small, piping voice; she spoke very little English. A delicate, boneless-seeming Javanese hand rested for a moment on his shoulder as she nudged at his mouth with a spoonful of *saté* and rice: the evening meal.

'Your eye—will be better?' the piping voice inquired.

'I hope so.'

'Lucky not two gone. Open mouth please.'

He laughed; it was a very Javanese answer.

After the *amah* had gone, Billy Kwan's voice sounded in his head, as it often did. 'You care for nobody *enough*,' Billy said, and a dream began. He and Billy were in a huge new building: the headquarters of a strange religion. They were shown into a small room, and the door was closed. The room startled Hamilton: it was windowless, sealed, and had a smell of newness, but its walls were painted with incredible crudity—the paint had been slapped on as though by children, so hurriedly that in places the cheap, fibro material was not covered at all.

On one wall was a mirror. Hamilton pulled the mirror aside and found himself looking through a panel into darkness; in the darkness, the face of a bald, heavy, middle-aged man appeared, a face of great cruelty and power. 'You can't come through here,' the man said, and began to laugh triumphantly. His laughter was enormously loud and alarming, and as he laughed his face became a mask of brass, wrought into features of blank mercilessness.

Recoiling from the panel, Hamilton found Billy also transformed. He too wore a mask: the features were primitive, and he was half-naked, in a costume of feathers and beads. He advanced on Hamilton, and stretched up his hands to throttle him, and Hamilton now became aware that he himself wore a mask. 'Wait!' he said. 'I know what kind of mask *I'm* wearing: it has a white face and yellow hair—am I right?'

'Yes.' Billy's muffled voice.

'Well, don't you see?' Hamilton said. 'This is what they want— they *want* us to fight each other. And we'll miss the flight.' They had only half an hour to catch the last international flight that would ever touch down at Jakarta.

But Billy reached for him again, ignoring his words, and they wrestled, and would do so for hours. And he knew that Jill was wandering near by, going off to sad reaches where he would never find her. The plane took off from Kemayoran.

Groaning aloud, he woke to his changeless darkness, and found the bandage damp not only with sweat but with tears. He was in the grip of an extraordinary grief over Billy, whom he had believed in the dream to be alive again. The grief was greater through this dream than it had been on the night of Billy's death, and was made more intolerable by his now seeing that he had done nothing to help Billy or to save him. A part of himself now seemed damaged by this death; and yet Billy alive had scarcely been more than a joke to him. Fumbling on the bedside table, he switched on his transistor: it was tuned to the BBC overseas service, which was playing something by Vaughan Williams. He pressed both hands over his itching bandage, rubbing at the sweat inside.

And Jill's cheerfulness reproached him now, too. He had taken her for granted, as he had Billy, and he would almost certainly pay for this. She began to become ominously unlikely in his mind, as though she already belonged to an irretrievable past. Her face more than ever hinted at some elusive ancestor; and to try and recall the way she set her lower lip was an exercise in pain. He gave it up, and as he drifted into sleep she walked towards him sadly, the flat coast of Norfolk behind her. Incongruously, she carried a brief-case. She didn't see him; her hair blew in the wind from the North Sea.

He was woken by a rattling somewhere. Clenching his teeth, still propelled on the empty gale of his longing, he came to a passionate decision. Nothing would prevent him from being on the flight next Saturday; if it cost him the sight of the eye, that would be the price he would pay. It was the door-handle rattling, and there was a tapping on the door.

'Come in,' he said. The Vaughan Williams was still playing, and he switched it off.

'Someone for see you.' It was the *amah*'s voice. The door closed.

Hamilton, propped on one elbow and, raising his head against orders, faced the door. Evidently the *amah* had gone, since only one pair of feet advanced across the room. Someone lowered himself into the bedside chair, but did not speak. Hamilton assumed it was the Colonel, and spoke his name, but there was no answer; the silence was odd.

'Who *is* that?' Hamilton demanded.

'It's me, boss.' The quiet voice was Kumar's.

Hamilton broke the second rule, and pushed up the bandage from his good eye. Kumar, whom he had not expected to see again, sat erect and still in his usual well-pressed sports shirt and slacks, wide-set black eyes alive as ever with secret thought. And Hamilton had an entirely disconcerting rush of gladness, as though he had been missing Kumar and had not realised it.

'You should not lift the bandage,' Kumar said. '*Amah* says to give you this.' He handed Hamilton a cup of tea, and smiled.

Hamilton replaced the bandage, and sipped the tea. He was still hauling himself from the vast shallows of his dreams, which had made his body ring and echo; the taste of the tea was intense, as though he had not drunk tea before.

'Your eye is very bad.'

'Yes—the sergeant did a good job. You should have been there. Maybe you could have stopped him.'

'I am sorry I was not there, boss.' It seemed to Hamilton that the hushed voice, although almost neutral, had a sympathetic tinge. 'I could not come,' Kumar said.

'I'll bet you couldn't.' Hamilton decided to broach what had never been broached before. 'It surprises me you're still in town,' he said. 'The PKI are pretty unpopular today, I believe; and it's going to get worse. You heard Suharto's broadcast last night?'

'I heard.' Kumar's voice was just audible; then he fell silent, and Hamilton, in his darkness, allowed the silence to extend.

In a broadcast on the previous evening, the *alus* prince had created an anger in Java which would lead to a blood-bath: he had told of the discovery, on Sunday night, of the corpses in Crocodile

287

Hole. Today, the bodies of all the murdered generals had lain in state at army headquarters in Merdeka Square, while thousands shuffled past the coffins; afterwards, followed by sobbing women, they had been given a hero's burial at Kalibata Cemetery. And the *marhaen* grieved: flags flew at half mast in the gardens of Jakarta's small houses, and in the kampongs. In the weeks that followed, the anger would grow.

Kumar broke the silence. 'In a struggle, such things happen,' he said. 'It is a pity.'

'It's more than a pity,' Hamilton said. 'I never thought Javanese would do things like this.' He found his heart was hammering with some sort of vicarious anger, and checked himself. I wasn't there, he said, at Crocodile Hole; they're not my people. Why am I angry? Or am I angry at what they did to me?

As though hearing his thoughts, the quiet voice went on: 'Their deaths may shock you, but of course you are very concerned about the taking of life. To me there are worse things. Continuing misery is worse. The misuse of this country's wealth has caused misery of which you really know nothing. But you don't have to care. You can go to another country, and write other stories there.'

To this Hamilton said nothing, and as though regretting his words Kumar said, 'I am sorry about your eye. Is there much hope it will be saved?'

'Not much.' Saying this, he suddenly knew it was true.

When Kumar spoke again his voice expressed the naïve hunger Hamilton remembered. 'If I could come with you to Europe, boss, and be what you are, I would give an eye. I think if I had been born in Europe, I would be as good as you.'

Perhaps people reveal themselves to you when they know you can't read their faces, Hamilton thought: blind, you are harmless. 'Yes, Kumar,' he said, 'you could have been as good as me—or better.'

'Tell me something, boss. Am I a stupid man?'

'No, Kumar, you're damn good. I'm glad I had you working for me.'

'Thank you. Then why should I live like a poor man all my life, while stupid people in your country live well?' The low voice came as close to being passionate as Javanese restraint allowed. Hamilton knew what the narrow, wide-set eyes would look like; he felt them through his bandage.

'There's a packet of Yank cigarettes on the table, Kumar. Light two of them, will you, and give one to me?'

A match was struck; a cigarette placed against his lips.

'Still the good cigarettes, boss.'

'Water from the moon, Kumar.'

'Water from the moon, boss.'

Hamilton chuckled, but he did not hear an answering chuckle. Kumar's tone had been that of a man who watches something infinitely precious recede. The voice said now, 'You have not answered my question.'

'I didn't because I can't.'

'You are honest. At least one can say that. Perhaps that is why I like you, although you are so reactionary. And if you cannot answer, why do you condemn those in my country who have the will to do something about that question?'

Hamilton raised himself on one elbow, and turned his bandaged face towards the interrogating voice. 'Maybe your people tell you that a little killing isn't too high a price to pay,' he said. 'I think it is too high a price—that's all.'

'Of course—you Westerners worry about "conscience". I tell you something, boss—we do not understand what you mean by this conscience. I do something wrong, and I am caught, I lose face. That is all. But conscience, what is that? If we worry about it, how do we change things?' The voice was angry.

Hamilton sank back, feeling suddenly tired. He was a watcher, a watcher merely: a Peeping Tom, as Billy had said. And Peeping Tom had lost an eye. 'I can't give you an answer to that either,' he said.

He could hear Kumar blowing out smoke, and tapping with his nails on the arm of the rattan chair. 'Mr Billy Kwan was right,' Kumar said suddenly. 'Westerners have not many answers any more.'

'Yes; he was right about a lot of things.'

Silence followed; then Hamilton said, 'It was nice of you to come in. I'll be leaving on Saturday—there's a new man coming to replace me the following Monday. Some Australian Embassy people have been helping me wind up my affairs at the office—but I'd be glad if you'd be there to hand over next week. By the way, you're owed some pay.'

'No; I came in to say good-bye. You are right; Jakarta will not be safe for me now, and I am going to Jogjakarta tonight. We shall reorganise, you see, boss, in Central Java. They may try to crush us, but we will come back.' The low voice had become gay, almost affectionate. Hamilton did not answer: it was no longer Kumar speaking, but an abstraction: a voice. 'We will win,' Kumar said, 'because we know what we believe—and you believe in nothing but your pleasures. Don't worry, though, it will take time. I think I must leave you now. It was good to work with you.'

'Those cigarettes—take the pack. I'm definitely giving them up.'

'Thank you. Westerners give up their vices, and we take them over, isn't it so?'

'Give me your hand, Kumar.'

The hand was larger and stronger than that of the *amah*, but it had the delicate elusiveness of all Javanese hands; it was like holding a leaf. Hamilton said into his darkness, knowing it was useless, 'Don't follow that bastard Aidit: they'll kill you out there along with him. I've already told ABS you're the best man we could possibly have, You deserve—' He broke off. It was stupid, trying to tell Kumar what he deserved.

'Thank you—but I will follow Comrade Aidit. His day will come. Think of me when you are sitting in some nice café in Europe.' The voice became softer again. 'In my dreams, I am always sitting at a table by the footpath, drinking coffee, with flowers growing in tubs.' The hand was withdrawn, and the voice, with perhaps a note of irony, used Hamilton's name for the first and last time. 'Good-bye, Guy.'

His footsteps went quickly to the door, which opened and closed with discreet quietness.

25

The British Embassy's Austin, with its silent Indonesian driver, carried him for the last time along Jalan Thamrin. He wore, with some self-consciousness, a black eye-patch the doctor had given him.

'It's hopeless,' Ross had said angrily. 'There's still so much blood there I can't make a proper examination; there's nothing more to be done until you see a specialist in London. You needed another week, if that retina was to have any chance at all. Whatever it is that won't wait, I hope it's worth an eye.'

His good-bye had been barely civil; and there had been no sign of the Colonel.

Craning his neck, Hamilton saw now that fresh, angry black signs were daubed on bamboo fences and the walls of buildings, shouting messages no one would have believed possible in the year that had gone: GANJANG PKI (*Crush PKI*). AIDIT GANTUNG (*Hang Aidit*). AIDIT SETEN (*Aidit is Satan*). GERWANI TJABOL (*The Gerwani are whores*).

Jakarta's violent children had been unleashed against their heroes: and the vehemence was the same and the terms were the same as those they had used against their former bogies. It was like a dream in which things became their opposites, and the city no longer seemed real.

He leant forward and asked the driver to go faster; he was afraid of missing his six o'clock flight. The man showed no sign of having heard, and Hamilton tapped him on the shoulder, searching for the word for 'fast'.

'*Lekas*,' he said. '*Lekas*.' The car moved with maddening slowness, blocked by bicycles and *betjaks*.

Jill had not caught the flight.

In the dim blue tunnel of the 707's cabin, where rows of lamps had come on for evening, Hamilton sat absolutely still, holding his hand over his good eye. He had always known this would happen, he said. The plane hissed, ready for its take-off from Singapore.

He had searched the multi-racial flow of faces in the transit lounge outside, until doom-hollow loudspeakers made their final calls: *New Delhi*, *Karachi*, *Athens*. Moving in his bisected world, he had lurched drunkenly against vinyl furniture; had grown giddy and disoriented with the unaccustomed movement, after his week in darkness. She was not to be found, and he had come back out onto the humid tarmac carrying in his belly what felt like a mass of lead.

The motors had not yet started. From rows of blue chairs, waiting voices drawled, intimate and maddening as those of domestic hens. Piped music tinkled in the lulling twilight: he detested it unreasonably.

Somebody touched his shoulder. He opened his single eye joyfully, expecting Jill, but found instead a young Dutch steward with a schoolmasterly face, who frowned suspiciously, examining his melodramatic eye-patch. 'You are not looking well, sir. Is there something I can get you?'

Hamilton shook his head, and closed the eye again. There was a banging and roaring somewhere. From a distance, he thought he heard Jill's indistinct voice.

Let silence prevail. I farewell now not just Guy Hamilton and his Jill, but the night of *ākāśa*: the dark which has no end.

Bound for Athens, journeying out of Asia into Europe, the KLM 707 drones on and on, through a dark of some sixteen hours, following night's shadow on the globe. Blue lamps burn, like those in a late-night hospital ward; faint voices murmur nonsense out of dreams. Jill sleeps wanly, almost invisible under a tartan rug. Hamilton sprawls happy but sleepless beside her, longing for the dawn.

But dawn and Europe will not seem to come: Asia is a tunnel without end. The jet slows almost to a halt, and hangs in the gulf of night. It's time to touch down at Karachi.

Beyond the silver hulls of other refuelling jets, whose printed tails proclaim new nations, blue and orange lights burn, on strange, distant levels of the field. Out there, at this deepest hour of night, Maha-Kali dances: she of many names, all of which mean Time.

In a few weeks more she will caper in the paddy fields of Java: that curious island to the south where India's gods have turned into shadows. She will have blood enough then to suit her, as the *marhaen* take their revenge for Crocodile Hole, and for all their stifled hopes. First, the PKI will be hunted down; then, as the lust of Durga takes hold, the Indonesian Chinese; then, anyone with whom one has a score to pay—man, woman or child.

No clear tally will be kept, as the killing goes on; tallies are never certain, in Java; and those who kill will say they often lose count. But as the year ends, it will be said that half a million have died, perhaps more. Who will ever know? In circles of lanterns in the paddy fields at night, the cane-knives will chop and chop at figures tied to trees; and trucks will carry loads of human heads—all pleasing to the dancer at the cemetery.

The jet drones on again: the vents in the cabin ceiling blow hot air instead of cold, and Hamilton fights to breathe. But quite suddenly he falls into sleep, with no dreams.

Light waved in the cabin, like bright gauze. He opened his good eye to discover a dawn of salmon and gold towers, above a dark green sea. Feet thudded by in the aisle; heads came from under rugs.

He turned to Jill. Her head half out of the tartan rug, her heavy blond mane tangled, she slept profoundly, a short-sighted young woman of twenty-seven whose youth was already threatened;

293

who had, in the clear light, deep lines beside her mouth and at the corners of her eyes, and whose lower lip had relaxed in sleep to reveal her two top teeth. The face under the yellow mane was not as beautiful as it had seemed in his prisoner's dreams in the villa on Jalan Diponogoro: and her character, he saw, would always sway between the sweetness and unreliability of the weak. But she was the woman with whom he would spend his life; and his joy did not recede, as it once would have done, in the face of this day-flat clarity.

And he had never felt such joy as this dawn brought him. Night's egg had cracked; outside the porthole was the sweet, crystal ether of the north. He bent over Jill, and kissed her. She smiled sleepily, her arms going around his neck.

'How's the baby?' he asked.

'Getting obvious. I'm getting bigger at last. See?' She drew his hand against her belly, which perhaps had grown a little fuller. Her expression changed to concern. 'Darling—what about your eye? You didn't make much sense last night. It will be all right, won't it?'

He lied, as he had lied to Dr Ross, not wanting joy to be put off its course. 'The vision's coming back,' he said. 'It'll be fine.' Then, in a Javanese accent, he said, 'Lucky not two gone.'

She laughed. 'You fool. If it's getting better, why the patch? You probably know it makes you look sexy, like General Dayan. Lift it just for a moment. See how it is today.'

To oblige her, he lifted the patch; the brown screen was still there.

'It's fine,' he said. 'I can see a lot more than I did yesterday.'

'I'm so glad. Not that I would have objected to a one-eyed man.' She hugged him in a quick spasm of pleasure: she had always been generously excited by any good fortune he had. Then she pointed to the sea below, under the fire-coloured domes.

'Look—the Aegean.'

'So it is—I hadn't realised. I've never been to Greece.'

In the seats across the aisle, a trio of Greeks had woken to watch the sunrise: a tortoise-faced old man, and two dark-jowled younger men in pastel business suits, obviously his sons. They murmured quietly, as though reciting litanies, and pointed at the ocean, their money-wearied eyes alight with pleasure.

'*They* seem terribly pleased to see it,' Jill said.

'Well, it's their sea.'

'Is it true about London?' Jill asked. 'Will we really be able to stay there?'

'For a year, at least. Then maybe it's Saigon.'

'No more of Asia, sweetie, for God's sake. Remember all our talks? You do want to stay in Europe, don't you?'

'If I can belong there.'

'Can't you? You always said you could.'

'Billy didn't seem to think so,' he said.

The fair Dutch hostesses and stewards, formidably clean and revitalised, hurried by in the aisle: ahead lay Europe, and the hard, bright business of day; Asia's burning dark lay forgotten in their wake. Children of the north, the cabin crew were now nearly home: mentally already in Athens, Amsterdam, Paris, as the north's autumn clarity surrounded their capsule. And Hamilton watched them with calm wistfulness: their Europe would never be his. He would always be a temporary resident; in the end, the other hemisphere would claim him.

'I never told you this until now,' Jill said suddenly, 'but that night in the lobby of the Hotel—before he went up to that bloody window—Billy was talking to me.'

'Yes. What did he say?'

'He talked about *you*, at one stage. He wasn't hostile. He was in one of his frantic states, laughing too much and being loud. He said he'd be leaving Jakarta in a few days to go back to Sydney. He asked me to say good-bye to you.'

She glanced at Hamilton, who turned away; he was forced more and more often lately to mask his distress. Her hand covered the back of his, and he was grateful; they sat in silence.

Sunrise was over: he stared out the porthole into hard, sane light whose edges did not blur. He was trying to recall where friendship had begun, and where he had ignorantly turned from it; but all that came back now, with grief's mechanical repetition, was Billy saying something about riding up Dragon Tail Street.

The plane had begun to lose height, making its run into Athens. His good eye burned, and he closed it for a moment. As soon as he did so, a dark shape pedalled and creaked across his middle distance: a *betjak*, whose rider wore a black shirt, black shorts, and a limp straw hat, and the name of whose machine was *Tengah Malam*: midnight.